HMS LEVIATHAN

HMS

John Winton

LEVIATHAN

Coward-McCann, Inc.
New York

HMS LEVIATHAN

1

The new Commander of HMS *Leviathan* stood by the quarterdeck guard-rail, watching the tail-lights of the taxi carrying his predecessor to the railway station receding into the darkness of the dockyard. It had been a melancholy and an embarrassing leave-taking. The new Commander had tried to be tactful, to conceal his own eagerness to take over the appointment, but while his predecessor had been showing him round the ship he had had the poignant sensation that he was being paraded past another man's dreams. He had relieved many officers, in many appointments, but he had never before experienced this present feeling that he had just conducted the funeral rites over a fellow officer's career. Tony Dempster, sitting in that taxi, had had such high hopes for *Leviathan* and had seemed to be the very man to carry them out; his appointment as *Leviathan*'s Commander had been a logical and natural step in his progress towards the rank of Captain and, eventually, to his flag. Now, Tony Dempster would be fortunate if he ever went to sea again.

The story of *Leviathan*'s first year in commission was now gloomy Service history. She was the largest aircraft carrier ever built for the Royal Navy. Her design incorporated much of the experience learned from the wartime carrier actions in the Mediterranean and the Pacific. The Admiralty Departments who dealt with officers' appointments under the Second Sea Lord had exerted themselves to hand-pick her first wardroom. Some of the most able and ambitious officers in the Service had competed to commission her, calculating that a successful tour in such a ship would be a giant stride towards promotion. Five of the best squadrons in the Fleet Air Arm had been chosen to form her Air Group. The Drafting Commander at her home manning port had scoured his lists, and robbed other ships, to start *Leviathan* off with the best possible ship's company. In theory, *Leviathan* should have been the most successful aircraft carrier ever brought into service, a show-piece for the Fleet Air Arm and for the Navy.

In practice, *Leviathan* had limped from one crisis to another, until she was recalled to Portsmouth halfway through her first commission. Her squadrons had been disembarked and her ship's company paid off. An Admiralty statement explained that *Leviathan* was to be placed in dockyard hands while important modifications were made to her catapults.

The new Commander had been serving in the Far East on the staff of the Commander-in-Chief when *Leviathan* commissioned but even in Singapore the stories about her had reached him, with all that wealth of circumstantial detail which gave naval gossip its special relish. *Leviathan*'s first year at sea had followed the classic pattern of an unhappy commission. No stigma of a bad ship had been spared her. Hers had been a history of absentees at every port, of a dozen punishment warrants read out every week, of boats which never ran to time, of unsupported ship's sporting fixtures and of boycotted ship's activities.

The Commander had been on his way home to the United Kingdom when the final incidents occurred which led to *Leviathan*'s premature paying-off. He was present now for the aftermath. The truth about *Leviathan* was an open secret throughout the Navy. *Leviathan* had been purged. In any circumstances which even approached mutiny, the Service exacted a traditional and terrible vengeance. The affected parts in *Leviathan* were brutally cauterised. The former Captain, the Commander, the Commander (Air) and a string of junior ship's and squadron officers were relieved of their appointments. They were not dismissed their ship: that would have been punishment, and the processes of retribution were too deep and too complex to be simplified under such a name. There had been no courts martial, not even a board of enquiry. The officers concerned were merely removed and given other appointments – appointments which demonstrated in every case that, professionally, those officers were now dead men.

Meanwhile, the ship awaited their successors, and in particular the new Commander. The officers who remained in *Leviathan* had expected another Dempster, another upper-deck prophet with the caste mark of high promotion written on his forehead. They were surprised, and almost relieved, when a man was appointed whom nobody could possibly have expected.

Commander David Robert Markready RN, the new Commander, Executive Officer and Second-in-command of HMS

Leviathan, was not by any definition a brilliant naval officer. 'Steadiness' was the quality most often mentioned in his confidential reports. He had realised his own limitations early in life, at Dartmouth, where in a vintage intake which included several men who were now Captains it had soon been made clear to Bob Markready that his place was not amongst the captains and kings but amongst the hewers of wood and the drawers of water. He was now forty-five years of age and he privately doubted whether he would ever reach the rank of Captain. He was a dogged man, who put one foot carefully in front of the other until his object was reached. He did not pause on the way, nor did he belittle his own judgments, once they were made: once his foot was placed on the ground, his whole weight rested upon it. Thus he had reached his present position while others, who had perhaps promised more, had fallen by the wayside. His contemporaries thought Bob Markready old-fashioned, conservative, not flexible enough, too intolerant, too stubborn and incapable of the delicate touch needed to control the varied talents and clashing temperaments of a large aircraft carrier's wardroom. But, his contemporaries conceded, *Leviathan* was a golden chance for him. If he succeeded in making the ship work only moderately successfully, Bob Markready was a made man.

The new Commander was well aware of his opportunity. Furthermore, he disbelieved the stories of *Leviathan*'s bad luck. In his opinion, the ship's misfortunes were more likely to have been caused by bad management. He believed that *Leviathan* could be made to work successfully, and he believed that he was the man to do it.

If *Leviathan* was to be changed, there was no time to begin like the present. For instance, the quarterdeck guard-rails were slack.

The Commander looked about him. The quarterdeck was empty. The officer of the watch and the quartermaster had been present when Tony Dempster left the ship but now, less than five minutes later, they had both disappeared. The Commander felt a surge of irritation.

'Officer of the Watch!'

'*Yes.* What is it?'

The Officer of the Watch came out of the small watchkeepers' compartment built in the after screen. He had a cigarette in his

7

hand but seeing the Commander he flicked it over the ship's side. 'Yes sir?'

While the Officer of the Watch stood at attention, the Commander studied him. He had dark hair bunching untidily under his cap, which had been put on askew. His tie was not properly pulled up to his collar-stud. He looked sulky and resentful. The Commander remembered that Tony Dempster had introduced him earlier in the day; he had some name like Burge or Briggs. He could not be more than twenty-two or twenty-three years old and the Commander wondered why he had been sent to *Leviathan;* an officer of his seniority as a lieutenant would have been better off in a small ship.

'Have these guard-rails tightened. They're hanging all over the place.'

'Aye aye sir, but the duty part of the watch are having their supper, and I'm afraid I haven't got any hands to do it just now . . .'

'Hands?' The Commander's irritation was turning to anger. 'What do you want with hands? Your quartermaster's been sitting on his arse for the last two hours. He can do it.'

'Yes sir, but . . .'

'What's your name?' The Commander's rage, pure and violent, mounted inside him.

'Bird, sir. We have met, sir. This morning.'

'Mr Bird, I would be obliged if you would order the quartermaster to tighten the guard-rails. At once.'

The quartermaster was not a fool. He had recognised the savage edge in the Commander's voice. He had already found a marling spike and was bending by the first guard-rail stanchion.

The Commander nodded towards the after screen door. 'Come with me.'

They stood together in the passageway inside the screen door, between two rows of officers' cabins. The cabins were empty and unfurnished, and the passageway was grimy. Dockyard workmen's tool-boxes were stacked by one bulkhead and beyond them was a pile of a dozen small valves, each with a red label tied to its handwheel. Temporary power cables, stopped up with pieces of twine, hung in uneven loops overhead. The plastic deck covering was scuffed and littered with scraps of paper, strands of oily

8

rope, cigarette butts, and a pieces of fluff. The passageway and its connecting flat smelt sour, of dirt and stale air. The Commander made a mental note to have the place cleaned up in the morning. The ship might be in dockyard hands, but that was no reason for letting her go completely untended.

He looked at Bird again. The main tide of his anger was already dissipated, leaving behind a sore residue of tension. He tried to speak calmly.

'I don't know what you thought of that exhibition out there, Bird, but I thought it was pretty poor. I'm not in the habit of bawling out officers in front of ratings. But when I give an order I expect it to be carried out. At once . . .'

'But sir, I thought as we were in dockyard hands . . .'

'I don't care what you *thought!* I gave you an order and that's that.'

'Yes sir, but . . .'

'And I don't want any more back-chat! That's enough!'

'But I must say, sir . . .'

The Commander's rage ignited again, exploding and expanding until he knew that he must bend this man to his will or strike him to the deck.

'Mr Bird if you say one more word I'll have you off this ship so fast you won't know what hit you! And you won't be coming back!'

Bird's mouth half-opened to speak, so that the Commander involuntarily clenched his fists and tipped his weight forward on to his toes, but then Bird hesitated. He had been about to retaliate, to tell the Commander that nothing would please him more than to leave *Leviathan* for ever. He had joined the ship under a cloud of official displeasure; his current conduct was still being reported once a quarter to the Admiralty. One more incident could result in him being discharged from the Navy. He had already considered applying to resign. But that was not an action to be precipitated by a quarterdeck tiff with the Commander. He composed his voice in its most neutral, inoffensive tone.

'I'm very sorry, sir. Carry on, please, sir?'

'No, it's *not* all!' In his rage the Commander misheard. 'When the quartermaster has finished taking up the slack on the guard-rails, tell him to fetch out a broom and sweep up this flat! It's in

9

a disgraceful state! And while you're officer of the watch you remain on the quarterdeck, on duty, where I can see you, at all times! And you don't skulk away for a quiet cigarette while you're on watch, do you understand?'

'Aye aye, sir.'

The Commander returned to his own cabin, trembling, and disgusted with himself. Bird had been his first brush with the old *Leviathan* and her ways. He had exhausted his temper and lowered his dignity in a public wrangle with a Lieutenant. Certainly, the quartermaster would now take the news forward that the new Commander was a man to beware of. Perhaps that was not such a bad thing. Nevertheless, the Commander knew how near he had come to striking Bird. The great ship had almost succeeded in slipping under his guard at the first encounter.

In the day-cabin, the Commander's steward was unpacking suits from a black tin trunk and carrying them through to the wardrobe in the sleeping cabin next door. Two more tin trunks lay by the door. A wooden packing case had been placed in the far corner, under one of the cabin scuttles. The lid was open and the Commander warmed at the sight of the books inside. He had never collected souvenirs of his service; he had no ship's crests, no ornaments except a square green glass ashtray, and no pictures except a small framed photograph of his father, in a Commodore's uniform. But his books had always travelled with him. He had the regular naval officer's chameleon-like ability to adjust himself to his surroundings. His cabin was unfamiliar now but in a month's time he would feel that he had lived in it half his life.

'Leave the books, Mulligan. I'll unpack them and put them up myself.'

'Yes, sir.'

Mulligan was a squat, barrel-chested man with ginger hair thinning on the crown of his head. In spite of his name he spoke with a trace of a Devon accent and he looked like a seaman or a bosun rather than a steward. His nose was large and red and bibulous, but Tony Dempster had reassured the Commander that he was both a teetotaller and a good steward.

'In the meantime, see if you can find my mess undress and a stiff shirt amongst all that lot. I'll be dressing for dinner every night from now on, except when I'm going ashore.'

10

The Commander always changed for dinner, wherever he was, not only as a matter of habit but as a demonstration of good manners and politeness towards his fellow officers. It made no difference to him that the ship was in dockyard hands, that only part of the wardroom was in use and that the meal itself would be little more than a makeshift supper. When he reached the ante-room, he was surprised and disturbed to see that he was the only officer who had changed. A few others drinking coffee by the club fender were wearing reefer jackets and straight ties. They were all duty officers, embarrassed by the Commander's starched shirt and bow-tie, and having each greeted the Commander cautiously, they left to go on watch or to do rounds.

The Commander looked dispiritedly round the ante-room. Perhaps when all the officers had joined the room might take on a more cheerful appearance. With only himself present, it was a cheerless and depressing compartment.

Leviathan's wardroom and her two adjoining ante-rooms were each vast compartments intended to accommodate the ship's full complement of officers which would be nearly three hundred when the squadrons were embarked. The ante-rooms were designed for the officers' relaxation and recreation, but they had been furnished without taste or imagination. The bulkheads were panelled in a pale blue formica, which gave the rooms a hard, forbidding appearance, like the waiting rooms of a gigantic clinic. The headroom, already low, was further reduced by a labyrinth of pipes, rod gearing cover, ventilation trunkings and electrical cables, so that in many places a tall man could not stand upright. Fluorescent lighting units were fitted in the deckhead wherever the irregular pattern of the piping allowed. Neither ante-room had any pictures, except the signed portraits of the Royal Family above the fire-place in the forward ante-room. The small arm-chairs and the two long divans on either side of the fire-place were upholstered in a shiny blue imitation leather; later their bleak and slippery surfaces would be hidden under patterned chintz covers, but until commissioning day they would remain uncovered and unwelcoming. The deck was furnished with a darker blue carpet, which stopped a few feet short of the bulkheads. The carpet edge nearest the bar was torn and the margin stained. The back of the fire-place was sheeted with copper which, the Commander

11

noticed, was unpolished. In the fire-place an electric fire with three heating elements was bolted to a metal bracket. A long green baize notice-board ran beside the double water-tight doors which gave access to the ante-room. The forward ante-room, by some naval constructor's quirk of mind, also had a short annexe, giving the compartment the shape of an L. In the annexe were a piano, two high letter-racks and table covered with newspapers and magazines.

The bar was no more than a serving hatch and the Commander foresaw that it would be seriously overloaded when the full commission began. The bar steward was waiting for the Commander's order.

'Pink gin, please.' He signed the chit-book with his name and the number one, the traditional mess number for the president of the mess – just as number nine belonged by tradition to the Surgeon Commander.

'Large one, sir?'

The Commander looked up. 'What do you mean, a *large* one? This isn't a chi-chi roadhouse. When I want a *large* one I'll ask for it.'

'Very sorry, sir. The last Commander always had large ones, sir.'

The remark for some reason irritated the Commander. 'What's your name, steward?'

'Leading Steward Connolly, sir.'

Connolly's appearance might have been precisely calculated to prejudice the Commander against him. He looked like a gigolo, with black, grease-shiny hair and long sideboards. Connolly was a Liverpudlian, a city boy born and bred, and his urban upbringing showed in his wary eyes, his complexion and his quick, pick-pocket's movements. He had volunteered to be a bar steward. The hours were long and the task thankless, but Connolly took a cynical pleasure from seeing the officers in their unbuckled moments. On the steward's messdeck, Connolly's opinion of an officer was definitive.

Connolly brought an empty glass to the bar and poised the bitters shaker over it. 'Bitters, sir?'

'Three shakes.'

Connolly shook in the bitters, poured the measure of gin, and brought the glass back to the bar. 'Ice, sir?'

'No, never.'

Connolly began to add water carefully from a small china jug. 'How much water, sir?'

'That's it.'

The Commander found himself obscurely pleased by Connolly's attentions. He knew that Connolly would now remember the Commander's recipe and pass the information to the other bar stewards.

'How long have you been in this ship, Connolly?'

'Since the first commissioning day, sir.'

The Commander caught the defensive note in Connolly's voice. Again, he sensed the guardedness of those who had served in *Leviathan*'s previous commission. Furthermore, he was oddly aware that it was impertinent of him to enquire.

'Good evening, sir. I'm sorry to see you all by yourself on your first evening.'

The Senior Engineer was stepping over the door-sill into the ante-room. He was a very tall man and he had to stoop to make his way to the bar. As second-in-command of the Engine-room Department, the Senior was a man of many cares. The first year in *Leviathan* had been a mechanical nightmare; the Senior had been called from his bunk most nights when the ship was at sea and even now, when the ship was alongside and power was supplied from the dockyard, he seemed to hold his head cocked expectantly, as though he were anticipating yet another urgent summons from the Engineers' Office. He was wearing what looked like his oldest and shabbiest reefer jacket. The Commander could smell a faint odour of oil.

'Do please excuse my rig, sir. I haven't got around to the routine yet.'

The Commander was instantly mollified by the apology. 'That's quite all right, Senior. Been busy?'

'Fairly. Lot of main condenser trouble last year and we're replacing a fair amount of tubes during this refit period. I thought I'd just hang on for a bit tonight and see how the tests made out.'

The Senior had a permanent frown-mark engraved between his eyebrows, and there were many more lines around his mouth and his eyes.

13

'How are things generally?'

The Senior grinned. 'Difficult to say. I've given up making firm pronouncements around here. This ship's rather like that bit in *Alice Through the Looking Glass*, where Alice and the Red Queen have to run like hell just to stay in the same place. That's exactly what we have to do here.' The Senior noticed the expression on the Commander's face. 'At least, sir . . .' he cleared his throat, '. . . that was our experience last commission, sir.'

'I'd like you to show me round down below some time, if you would, Senior.'

'I'd be glad to, sir.' The Senior looked as though he had just realised that the Commander was a formidable personality, and he was taking the chance to counter-attack. 'But I expect Commander (E) would like to show you round everything himself, sir.'

'Of course.' The Commander took the point of protocol. The Commander should be shown round the Engine-room Department by his fellow Head of Department.

'There seem to be very few officers on board in the evenings?'

'This is very much a married man's ship, sir. You won't normally find anybody except the duty officers on board after four o'clock when we're in harbour. Are you married, sir?'

'No, I'm not.'

This information was of importance. The ship's company preferred their senior officers to be married and to be living locally. Their home life kept them off the ship and out of the way in the evenings and at week-ends. The news of the Commander's bachelor status would now be passed to the ship's company, through Connolly, and to the rest of the wardroom by the Senior. It would be one more piece of the portrait of the new man which the ship was trying to build up.

'You dining on board tonight, Senior?'

'No sir, I was just going to have a quick drink and then home to pacify my wife. She's keeping supper for me. But . . .'

The Senior's dilemma was plain on his face. He was looking forward to going home, but if that meant the Commander would be dining alone on his first night, then perhaps he should stay and keep him company.

The Commander was about to reassure him, when there was a

deep, bull-like roar from outside the ante-room, where the First Lieutenant was hanging up his cap.

'One whisky-water Connolly, and chop chop!'

The First Lieutenant was the senior executive watch-keeping officer, the senior seamen's divisional officer, the ship's damage control officer, and he was in charge of working anchors and cables on the fo'c'sle when the ship entered or left harbour. An aircraft carrier First Lieutenant's duties required an experienced officer, but the appointment was not normally an avenue to promotion. There were a number of senior lieutenant commanders in the Navy List to whom such an appointment could be given. The Commander knew the type well. They were usually jovial and sociable men, who made excellent messmates. They were always willing to organise the Summer Ball, or a children's party, or the ship's sporting fixtures. They were competent enough naval officers but somewhere in their service careers, either through bad luck or indolence, they had missed their main chance.

Leviathan's First Lieutenant could have been the archetype of them all. He was a stout, pot-bellied man, with round brick-coloured cheeks and bright blue eyes. His hair was sandy and grew in sideboards longer than Connolly's. He walked with a slightly pigeon-toed gait, wheezing breathlessly wherever he moved. His baggy reefer jacket had three rows of war medals, headed by the blue and white ribbon of the DSC. As a concession to his position as duty lieutenant commander of the day he had put on a bow-tie. The Commander was sure that but for his own presence on board the First Lieutenant would have eaten earlier, with the other duty officers.

The Commander and the First Lieutenant dined together. They were the only officers dining and it was a strained and awkward meal, beset with mutual suspicions. The First Lieutenant was still warily gauging the mettle of his new superior, while the Commander was repelled by the First Lieutenant's disinterested manner and was privately wondering whether he could ever achieve his main purpose in *Leviathan* with such a First Lieutenant, whether indeed he should apply for a replacement at once. They had never served together before and it seemed that they had few friends in common in the Service. Their conversation did not come alive until the end of the meal.

'Hasn't the mess ever had any pictures, Number One?'

'Oh yes, we did have some, some jolly good ones. But they belonged to Tony. He took them away with him.'

The Commander winced. This was a most revealing indication of the circumstances in which Tony Dempster had left *Leviathan*. In any other ship he would surely have presented his pictures to the mess when he left. Tony must have been deeply hurt, to have gone to such lengths to leave no trace of himself behind.

The First Lieutenant had guessed the Commander's thoughts. 'It was symbolic in a way, sir. I don't blame him. He was absolutely right to take them.'

The bitterness in the First Lieutenant's voice warned the Commander to leave the subject.

'How long have you yourself been on board, Number One?'

The First Lieutenant sighed. 'Since the bitter beginning, sir.'

The Commander scowled. 'Just what do you mean by that?'

'Just that. From the beginning of last commission. I was even there when this ship was launched, although I was just a happy laughing spectator then, with not a care in the world. Little did I dream that one day I would actually be appointed to this vessel. It was just one more in a chapter of accidents.'

'I don't follow you?'

'Oh, a workman was killed during the launching. Some dockyard matey or other. I forget how it happened. He must have got in the way of something. It was all in the papers. They were always reporting the goings-on in *Leviathan*. I think it was worth their while to keep somebody permanently on board. There was always something happening.'

'What sort of thing?' The Commander knew that the conversation had already gone far enough, but he could not contain his curiosity.

The First Lieutenant shrugged. 'Fellows injuring themselves. Things going wrong *all* the time, not just some of the time. Somehow they managed to seal up a live black cat in a watertight compartment next to one of the boiler rooms. It was ten days before they heard it. When they took the lid off, the cat came out like a mad thing and it had enough strength to claw out somebody's eye. The newspapers called us the "Jinx Ship". I think they had a point. Still have, for that matter.'

16

'I'll accept that remark tonight, Number One, but never let me hear you say that again.'

'Oh, I shan't say it again, sir. I'm only telling you all this because you asked.'

Clearly the First Lieutenant did not care in the least what the Commander thought of him. Like many officers who had been passed over, or who were on the brink, the First Lieutenant had learned to be philosophical. He no longer concerned himself over one more senior officer's good opinion.

'The cat was just an omen, of things to come.'

Both now knew that the conversation should stop. There was nothing to be gained by resurrecting the past. The First Lieutenant was willing to let it drop, but the Commander felt impelled to go on, to forearm himself with knowledge of what had happened to Tony Dempster.

'Tell me what happened finally.'

The First Lieutenant shrugged again. If the Commander wished to torment himself with the details of his predecessor's fall, that was his own business.

'It's been common gossip for some time . . .'

'I haven't heard it. I was on my way home and I've only heard garbled rumours.'

'Well, it really was the most stupid thing. One of the young pilots, a particularly innocent young fellow, came upon two stewards in what the newspapers might call a compromising situation.'

'Oh good God.'

'If I'd been him I'd have turned right round and pretended I hadn't seen a thing.'

'Would you?'

'Yes I would.' The First Lieutenant looked the Commander challengingly in the eye. 'And as things turned out, I'd have been dead right. The pilot told the two men to report to the quarterdeck. They both cleared off like greased lightning and by the time the pilot got to the quarterdeck himself he was just in time to hear the older of the two stewards complaining to the officer of the watch that he, the pilot that is, had sexually assaulted him. And he had the younger steward as a witness. He'd never have got away with it, of course, but it did serve to confuse the issue.'

17

'Were there any other witnesses?'

'No.'

'Who was the Officer of the Watch?'

'Young Bird.'

'I see. Go on.'

'Well, things began to snowball from there on in. There didn't seem to be any proper statements taken at the time and it was devilish difficult to find out afterwards just exactly what did happen. It turned out by sheer coincidence that particular pilot had been involved in a similar sort of case before. Before we knew what was happening the whole ship began to take sides. There'd always been a bit of bad blood between the ship and the squadrons anyway, for one reason or another. One thing led to another and before we could say "Jaggers Troup" we were all involved in a sort of witch-hunt. Not only that, but you never knew quite what would happen when you gave a sailor an order. It was the opposite of that thing in the Bible, you know, where one character says to another Go, and he goeth, and to another Come and he cometh. It got to the stage where if we said unto a sailor Go, there was quite a chance he would turn round and tell us to get knotted. The Admiral himself came on board and told the Captain that the whole ship stank rotten.'

'How do you know that?'

'Tony told me. He was there. The Admiral maintained he could feel there was something wrong the moment he set foot on board. That may be a bit of an exaggeration . . .'

'Probably it was.' But the Commander knew that it was not. He had felt the same, when he had first stepped on board *Leviathan*. 'What happened then?'

'Well sir, there was a lot of coming and going. Sinister-looking fellows from the Admiralty kept on arriving unexpectedly, and before we knew what had hit us we were paid off into refit. Modifications to the catapults, they said.' The First Lieutenant smiled maliciously.

'Wasn't that true?'

'Oh yes, we needed modifications to the catapults all right. Or so I'm told. But we needed something else much more than that. We needed a complete change of heart.'

'By God, we're going to get it, too!'

18

'Let's hope so, sir.'

'There's no *hoping* about it!'

The First Lieutenant dropped his eyes, in as clear an expression of disbelief as though he had actually said the words. 'It's very nearly time for rounds, sir. Shall I report them to you here, or in your cabin?'

'Yes please, in my cabin.'

On his cabin desk the Commander found a long brown envelope containing several sheets of foolscap paper closely written on both sides. It was a letter from Tony Dempster. The Commander sat down at the desk and began to read.

'Dear Bob,

I knew I'd be in such a hurry that I wouldn't get a chance to tell you half the things I meant to, so I've written out a few turn-over notes which might be useful to you. I'll leave them behind so they can be delivered to you after I've gone. Perhaps you can read them when you get the time.'

The turn-over notes contained comments on the ship's life during the first commission, thumb-nail sketches of some of the senior ratings in the ship's company, and details of some of the problems Tony had faced and the way in which he had solved them. It was valuable information, Tony Dempster's last professional will and testament, and the Commander was grateful.

'... But I expect the main thing you want to know is, What Went Wrong? I wish I knew. You've probably heard all about that affair with the stewards, but I think that was just the fuse which set it all off. If it hadn't been that it would have been something else equally stupid. We were riding for a fall the whole time, I see that now.

'I think the main trouble is that we're now dealing with a new Navy and nobody seems to be aware of it. In those old music hall performances they always waved a Union Jack at the end of the finale, so it didn't matter how awful the show had been, everybody ended up cheering patriotically. I think we've been doing that in the Navy. No matter what went wrong, no matter how badly we misjudged the situation and the sailors, we simply waved the old White Ensign and everything was all

19

right again. The trouble nowadays is that sailors, like audiences, are getting more sophisticated. They just don't buy that sort of stuff any more.

'God knows we tried hard enough to get things going. We organised football matches, cricket matches and every kind of sporting fixture until we were blue in the face, but nobody would play. In a bitter sort of way the lack of support was almost comical. We tried to get a concert party going and although we *knew* there was bags of talent on board they just *wouldn't* show an interest. When we went to Oslo last summer for a jolly we laid on coach tours and sight-seeing trips. The coaches were all empty. Nobody went on them. All they were interested in was getting back to the UK where they could pop off on week-end leave and see their wives and floosies. A chap would come on board after a fortnight's leave and the first thing he'd do would be to put in a request for week-end leave. Quite frankly, it baffled me and rather frightened me.

'I forgot to ask you whether you'd ever served in a carrier before. If you haven't, you must prepare yourself for some shocks when the squadrons embark. Some of their officers are first class, as good as you'll get anywhere. But some of them are very shaky indeed. They're mostly short service commission fellows. They've been taught how to fly and that's about all. When the squadrons went ashore in plain clothes it was difficult to tell which were officers and which were ratings! If anything, the ratings were better dressed!

'I don't know who you'll get in the new wardroom. A lot will depend on the new Commander (Air), of course. Some-how, the last one and I never seemed to hit it off. Senior is a good fellow, and so is Chief. Number One is a very capable fellow, take my word for it – *if* you can get him to show an interest! The Captain's Secretary was a tower of strength. You'll just have to ignore his cynical little mannerisms. If you can get him to stay on for this commission you'll be fortunate. Sam Barnes, the Deputy Electrical Officer, is another valuable man. Commander (L) you've met. The electrical boys tend to live in a world of their own. In fact this is the great danger and it might be part of the solution of what went wrong. Everyone tends to get absorbed in his own problems. It's a very difficult ship to run and they're all so damned busy hoeing their own little rows, nobody has time to look around and see what the whole field looks like.

'I hope these notes will help you. I wish you the very best of luck and if you can just keep *Leviathan* out of the newspapers for a few months you'll have achieved more than I ever did! And if you could drop me a line sometime whenever you have a moment and let me know how the old ship's getting on, I'd be *most* grateful.

Yours, Tony.

The Commander laid the letter on the desk and smoothed it out with his fist. The Senior Engineer had compared *Leviathan* to *Alice Through the Looking Glass.* The First Lieutenant had called her a 'Jinx Ship'. Reading between the lines, even Tony's letter was steeped in the inevitability of defeat. The Commander had braced himself to change *Leviathan.* Already the main battle-ground was clear. His chief struggle would not be in the ship, but in the minds of her officers.

2

The Captain's Secretary in *Leviathan* was a dapper little man, with carefully brushed silver-grey hair and pointed, almost vulpine, ears. His brow was constantly furrowed, as though he were permanently preoccupied with affairs of state affecting the administration of the ship. He was intelligent, cynical, witty and, like almost every other Captain's Secretary in the Navy, he played an excellent game of squash racquets.

When his fellow officers came to know him better, they discovered that the Secretary's chief preoccupations were with matters of gossip and scandal. Intrigue, innuendo and rumour fascinated him: he would have made a superb Parliamentary lobby correspondent on a national newspaper. He enjoyed the spectacle of his fellow officers' frailties and his duties gave him ample opportunities to indulge himself. As the Captain's private assistant and adviser, every confidential document concerning the most intimate parts of the ship's life passed through his hands. He had refrained from attaching himself as Secretary to one particular senior officer, and allowing himself to be borne up to promotion in that officer's train – 'on the hog's back', as the Service saying had it. He preferred to free-lance and to perfect his own individual techniques of gaining friends in high places and of becoming so intuitively adept at judging the moods of the officers that he could inform his Captain, whose position forced him to stay remote, on the least change in the wardroom's temper.

The Commander and the Captain's Secretary respected each other. The Commander knew that the Secretary could be a valuable ally, while the Secretary for his part was intrigued and awed by the determination with which the Commander was attacking the problems of fashioning *Leviathan* into an efficient ship. The Secretary often called at the Commander's cabin, simply – as he put it to himself – to watch the irresistible force grappling with the immovable object.

'Busy, Bob?'

The title 'sir' was a form of address used by the Secretary only when speaking to Post Captains and Flag Officers whom he disliked.

The Commander looked up from the papers on his desk. 'Yes, but no more than usual. Come in, Scratch.'

'Just heard a buzz about our new Captain. It's not official yet, but my sources tell me he's been nominated.'

'Good. Who is it?'

'McTigue.'

'*Tosser* McTigue?'

'That's him. D'you know him?'

'I know *of* him. Well, I'll be damned.'

The Secretary was pleased by the effect of his news. 'He's a turn-up for the book, all right. You two are going to be quite a contrast to the last pair.'

The Commander nodded. It was a fair comment. Measured against their brilliant predecessors, the new Captain and himself would be a very homespun couple. After a diet of champagne, which had evidently proved too heady for the ship, the Admiralty were falling back on home-brewed beer. Tosser McTigue had first made his name as captain of one of the Navy's most successful rugby football teams. He had progressed, amiably and competently enough, from one appointment to the next but nothing in his subsequent Service career had ever quite equalled that early success on the football field. As the Secretary had implied, in any book on prospective Captains for *Leviathan,* Tosser McTigue would have been among the longest-priced outsiders.

The Secretary had a spiteful look on his face. 'I'll bet there was the hell of an almighty shake-up in the Captain's list and McTigue happened to be the name that came out of the hat. He's probably the only one who could come at such short notice.'

The Commander knew that it was reprehensible to exchange views on their future Captain this way but the temptation to pump the Secretary was too strong.

'What's he like?'

'Tosser?' The Secretary grimaced. 'He's an honest plodder. I served with him once and got to know him quite well. I doubt if he's changed much.'

'Will you be staying on yourself?'

'I doubt it. I expect Tosser will bring his own Secretary with him.'

'*Would* you stay on, if he asked you?'

'You bet I would!' The Secretary beamed, like a ring-sider at the prospect of a knock-down. 'I wouldn't miss the next few months in this ship for all the tea in Pompey dockyard! If what I think is true, you seem to be making all the noises of a man who's going to try and sort this ship out. It should be quite a contest.'

'It should indeed, Scratch.'

'By the way, my wife and I are having a few people in for drinks before lunch on Sunday. We wondered if you'd like to come along?'

'Certainly. I'd be very pleased to. What time?'

'Oh, about noon. Any time will do.'

'I'll be there.'

The Secretary paused in the cabin doorway. There was a mischievous expression on his face. 'Do you good to get out of the ship, Bob. You don't want to get too involved, you know.'

'Don't I?' The Commander longed to tell the Secretary that he was quite wrong. *Leviathan*'s only hope was that somebody should become involved in her, should commit himself utterly. Already, too many men had served in her for what they could gain, and not for what they could give. But this was not the time to put the point.

'I'll look forward to Sunday, Scratch. Thank you very much.'

The Commander had spoken no more than politely but as the week-end approached he found himself looking forward to Sunday with genuine anticipation. It was February and the week-ends in *Leviathan* were cold and uncomfortable. Most of the officers and ship's company had not yet joined and the great ship was still more than half empty. Many of her messdecks were uninhabited and unfurnished. Her long deserted passageways and vast compartments were unheated. The ship's domestic services were on a makeshift basis. There were skeleton staffs on duty in the wardroom and in the ship's company's dining hall. The hot water supply, heated by steam from two donkey-boilers on the jetty, was often only lukewarm or dried up altogether. Electric power, supplied by cables from the dockyard, fluctuated erratically; lights and electric fires throughout the ship were frequently extinguished without warning. Snow fell on Friday evening, while the dockyard workmen and week-end libertymen were leaving the ship. The men remaining in *Leviathan* existed on board like the first settlers in a hostile territory, inhabiting isolated colonies of light and warmth scattered about the ship.

The Commander spent the solitary hours of the week-ends working in his cabin, reading files of past correspondence and daily orders, examining the course of the last commission and laying down his own plans for the future. If it were true that the great ship's history might pursue her, then the new ship's company might be only too easily discouraged; at the first setback they would say amongst themselves that obviously they could not succeed where everyone before them had failed. The Commander intended to be forearmed with knowledge of the past, ready to point out why the previous commission had failed and how therefore the new commission might profit from the example.

On Sunday morning, the Commander arrived late at the Secretary's house. He had been delayed by an irritating incident, itself a legacy from *Leviathan*'s past. The port guard boat had not been challenged when it passed *Leviathan* on its way down river during the middle watch. The officer of the guard had, quite rightly, landed, crossed the after gangway unobserved, and had signed *Leviathan*'s quarterdeck log. To his surprise and irritation, the Commander had discovered that nobody was properly to blame. The fault was in *Leviathan*'s organisation. In the ship's present decommissioned state the practice had grown up, unknown to the Commander, of allowing the officer of the middle watch to keep his watch, dressed and awake, but in the wardroom anteroom. Similarly, and also unknown to the Commander, the quartermaster was allowed to leave the quarterdeck to brew cocoa in the watchkeepers' mess. Thus neither the officer of the watch nor the quartermaster had been on deck to hail the guard boat. The Commander's irritation had been exacerbated by the commiserating smile on the face of the Assistant Queen's Harbour Master, when he called on the ship later in the forenoon. His manner was that of a man not at all surprised that *Leviathan* had been caught out. She was too easy a mark to be worth comment. The officer of the guard had, it seemed, signed the log more in sorrow than in anger.

The Secretary and his wife lived in Old Portsmouth, in one of a terrace of three-storied Victorian houses facing a playing field. The Commander could not park his car nearer than two hundred yards from the house; clearly, the Secretary had invited more than 'a few people'.

The Secretary himself swung open the front door as the Commander walked up the steps. 'Good morning, Bob. Trouble?'

'No, no. Just a bit cold, that's all.' The Commander spoke hastily, annoyed that he should apparently have brought *Leviathan*'s problems with him, written so plainly on his face.

'Come in, come in. Let me take your coat.'

The Secretary noticed the Commander looking at the gloomy hall, the giant Victorian coat-stand, and the long, dark green plush curtains which hid a space for boxes and trunks by the staircase. He shrugged apologetically.

'We only rent this. It's a furnished house. Fanny, come and meet Bob Markready, our new Commander.'

'Oh, so *you're* the new broom! How do you do?'

'Yes, that's me. How do you do.' The Commander shook hands, and cleared his throat, a little disconcerted by the Secretary's wife. He thought her an unlikely woman for the Secretary to have married; he should have married someone witty and worldly and faintly malicious – someone, indeed, to match himself. But Fanny was rather plump and fussy and had a high, florid complexion which she had partly quelled with powder, so that her face glowed an improbable pink. There was only one adjective for Fanny: suburban. The Commander could imagine her as a denizen of that weird, mid-afternoon half-world of wandering mongrel dogs, and policemen, and babies in prams outside supermarkets. He could see Fanny, with her flower-patterned headscarf drawn tightly over her hair, her sheepskin-lined coat, her hip-bulging trousers, wheeling her shopping basket and trailing a tartan-jacketed cairn terrier on a tartan lead.

Fanny stood in her living-room doorway and waved a hand vaguely, visibly bracing herself for the effort of launching a new guest into her party. 'Now let me see ... Oh, you're *bound* to know everybody here anyway. Go in, and help yourself to a drink.'

The living-room was full, and Fanny was very nearly right: the Commander did know a great many people there, although the Captain's Secretary had an unusually wide range of acquaintances. At these Sunday morning sessions the host normally invited some of his fellow-officers of the same branch and seniority, who came with their wives, and talked desultory shop amongst themselves, as though they were still on board. There would also be a few neighbours and their wives, who exchanged gossip about lawn-mowers, and childrens' schools, and motor-cars, and plumbing, much as they would have chatted over the garden fence. These two constituents were certainly present, but there was also a third and rarer element. They were officers of the C-in-C's staff, from the dockyard, and from a few ships and training establishments, who made up an indefinable inner circle within the port and the command. Their gossip was always professional, their jokes were pointed, and their innuendoes harmful. For these officers, the Secretary's house was evidently part of a recognised circuit which they regularly travelled and dredged for information, as fishermen rowed round their lobster pots. The Commander at once sensed that he was a figure of special interest for them. They had all watched the collapse of *Leviathan*'s commission and they had been waiting, in comfortable immunity, to see who would be appointed to pick up the pieces. Now he had arrived, not only unabashed but confident of success. The word had passed round that there was now in *Leviathan* a man who proposed to set her to rights. It was a startling, almost an unheard-of, proposition. They were all agog to meet the man who was going to try and demonstrate it.

'Here you are, Bob.' The Secretary appeared at the Commander's side. 'One very large pink gin. That should keep the cold out. Do you know Tam here?'

'Indeed I do.' He nodded at a man who had already been edging towards him. He knew him. He had once served with him. Tam was two years younger than the Commander but had been promoted a year earlier. He was now on the Commander-in-Chief's planning staff.

Tam had been waiting, anxious to talk to Bob Markready, and he seized the Secretary's cue as eagerly as though he were being introduced to the fabulous unicorn.

'I haven't seen you for *ages*, Bob. What have you been doing with yourself?'

'I've been out in the Far East.' The Commander was aware that Tam knew very well what his last appointment had been.

'And now you're back just in time to get yourself lumbered with that great big bastard down the river there.'

'Lumbered?' The Commander was puzzled by the word. 'I've never thought of myself as being *lumbered.*'

'You wait until you've been in it a bit longer. For one horrible week I thought *I* was going to get that job. I tell you, I was terrified. You're on a hiding to nothing there, boy. That ship's a widow-maker.'

The Commander recognised that he should now make some suitably flippant reply, to disengage himself, but after three years away in the Far East he was out of touch, halt and lame in this quick-silver company. At one time he could have held his own but now he felt like a man who knew the tune well enough but had forgotten the most effective words.

Tam was still probing, feeling for a tender spot. 'I hear you had a slight contretemps with the guard boat last night?'

The Commander bit his lip, knowing that the remark had been intended to goad him, to make him reveal himself. He was furious that the incident should already have become common gossip; in these matters, the port was like a whispering gallery.

'Yes, we did. But it was nothing much. It won't happen again.' Suddenly, he could bear no more of this talk about *Leviathan.* He could not confide any of his hopes to this man; it would be equivalent to publishing them in a command bulletin. Tam was clearly primed and ready to listen, but he would not give such a man any more ammunition.

He looked around the room. There were three young men standing in a group by themselves in the window. They were, the Commander could see, slightly drunk. He stared at them, trying to place them. They were not *Leviathan's* officers. It was unlikely that they were Scratch's neighbours and they certainly did not move in Tam's world.

'Who are those three over by the window, Tam, do you know?'

Tam frowned. 'Dunno. Never seen them before in my life. They don't look like friends of ours, do they?' The Secretary was just passing, and Tam stopped him. 'Who are those three comedians in the window, Tony?'

The Secretary sucked his teeth disgustedly. '*Those*, are three flyboys from Rupert's squadron. They're at Lee on Solent for the week-end and they were all at a bit of a loose end so Rupert rang up this morning and asked if he could bring them along. Like a *fool*, I said yes. It looks as though all they're going to do is get as tight as they can, as quickly as they can, on *my* liquor. Have you met Rupert Smith, Bob? He's the CO of one of the squadrons we're getting later on.'

'I'd like very much to meet him.'

'Hang on, I'll go and find him.'

Having never served in an aircraft carrier before, the Commander had had almost no contact with the Fleet Air Arm. He studied the trio in the window more closely. These were the type of officer, some seventy or eighty of them, who would be joining *Leviathan* when the squadrons embarked later in the commission. They were standing together, absorbed in their private conversation, and there was something in their attitudes, in the very compactness of their little group, which repelled outsiders. It was as though they deliberately turned their backs on all who were not pilots. One of them had not bothered to change into a suit and was wearing a pale lemon-coloured cardigan and a pair of slacks. As the Commander watched, he threw his head back to laugh at some remark one of the others had said so violently that he slipped on the floor and nearly fell.

The Secretary returned, bringing with him a short, slightly-built man with fair hair and very white teeth. 'This is Rupert Smith, Bob. He's the CO of Rupert's Heavy Foot.'

The Commander shook hands. 'Rupert's Heavy Foot?'

Rupert Smith grinned. 'That's the nickname of my squadron, sir.'

The Commander guessed that Rupert was well over thirty, but his fresh complexion, round cheeks, and his smile made him look at least ten years younger.

'Do I know your face from somewhere, Rupert? Have we met before?'

'Could be, sir. I was a term officer at Dartmouth for a time, and then I was Jimmy of a destroyer out in the Far East.'

'Which one was that?'

'*Charlemagne*, sir.'

29

The Commander nodded. 'That would be it. I've just come back from three years in Singapore myself.'

In conversation, the Commander probed Rupert Smith's background. He was a General List officer and had chosen to fly as his specialisation, as others in his Dartmouth term had chosen navigation or gunnery or communications. He was a professional naval officer, who was only secondarily a pilot and he had shrewdly realised that in the modern Fleet Air Arm there were few chances for individual panache in the air; the Air Direction Rooms kept all aircraft under tight control from launch to recovery. A squadron COs first duty was to lead and drill his pilots until they were technically competent in the air, but some of his most difficult and important tasks were in the administrative and divisional field on board the carrier. Here, Rupert Smith had a clear advantage over his short-service commission contemporaries, most of whom had little wider experience of the Navy and who were embarrassed and irritated by their new duties when they became Senior Pilots or Commanding Officers of squadrons; they tended to long for the good old days, when they had no other responsibility but to fly their own aircraft.

Rupert Smith was anxious to leave a good impression with the Commander. He knew that public relations would be a vital part of his job on board. The Old Guard, like *Leviathan*'s Commander, were only too ready to condemn pilots as, to put it candidly, 'not quite gentlemen'. Aircrew officers had a reputation for brashness, for irresponsibility and defiance of accepted wardroom conventions – a reputation which Rupert was uneasy to see his three officers in the window doing their best to uphold. He would have liked to have introduced his officers now but glancing once more over his shoulder he decided against it.

The Commander was impressed by Rupert Smith. He and his squadron were working-up ashore and would not be joining *Leviathan* until later in the year, but Rupert was obviously impatient to complete shore training and begin serious carrier flying. If the rest of the squadron CO's were like this man they would be an asset not only to the wardroom mess but to the ship as a whole.

Rupert Smith stepped back and narrowly missed treading on the toe of a woman standing behind him.

'I'm so sorry . . .'

'I wondered when you were going to notice me, Rupert.'

'*Annabel!* My goodness, it's been a long time. How are you?'

'I'm very well.'

Rupert gave the woman an affectionate but, the Commander noticed, brotherly kiss. 'Annabel, I don't think you've met Commander Markready . . .'

There was a crash of broken glass by the window. The pilot in the cardigan had fallen against a stool and was lying on the carpet, laughing drunkenly, with his legs in the air. In the momentary hush, the voice of one of the others carried resonantly.

'Get up Alfred, you stupid old bugger!'

While the whole room cringed, Rupert Smith finished his drink quickly and set his glass down on the sideboard. 'Excuse *me* a minute, please.'

Annabel had merely raised her eyebrows, and turned back to the Commander. 'It looks as if somebody's had a little too much.'

The Commander admired her calm. Hers was the infrangible poise of the true naval wife; if the man she were talking to suddenly fell dead drunk at her feet she would simply step over him and carry on talking, without a break in her voice, to the next man.

'Which ship are you in?'

'*Leviathan.*'

'Oh, *you're* the man. I've heard of you. Aren't you the man who's going to try and put that big ship in order?'

'Yes, I'm trying.'

She had not only heard of him, she had noticed him as soon as he came into the room. His height and his hair, which was almost entirely grey, made him prominent in a crowd. She had paid him the compliment of wondering who he was. He was a new face and he looked too straightforward to be one of Tony and Fanny's usual friends. She guessed that he was not clever – she had seen him looking bewildered and defensive when he was talking to Tam – but he had something more, some tougher quality which none of these other men had. If this one ever failed it would not be for want of trying. He looked a decisive, hot-tempered and dangerous man, with his broad, square face, heavy-lidded eyes, and the deep lines at the sides of his mouth. But he also looked vulnerable, at bay. Even now, standing in the middle of the party, he wore a lonely and rather perplexed expression, as though he were at the party but not a member of it. She wondered if he had brought his wife with him.

'I'm sure you'll succeed. I know it's naughty of them, but some of the wives are beginning to bet on whether you'll make it. Lady Metcalf was saying she's going to make a book on it.'

He pricked up his ears and looked more closely, curious to know more of this woman who was apparently on such intimate social terms with the wife of the Commander-in-Chief. Her dress was plain black, with a row of short pleats gathered in the front of the bodice. She wore one brooch, a small naval crown in marcasite and tiny diamonds, pinned on her right shoulder. She held her glass in a touchingly protective manner, holding it in both hands high in front of her. She had a trick of tilting her head back when she talked to him, to exaggerate his height. She flattered him by looking steadily at him while he was speaking, without letting her eyes stray as though hoping someone more entertaining would appear behind him. Her forehead was too broad, her nose too long, her features generally too cold and fine for her to be called a beauty but looking at her the Commander experienced that identical giddy feeling of expectation and achievement, that same lift of the spirit, as when he walked to the top of a hill and first felt the breeze and saw the view below him.

'If anyone offers you a bet, you take it.'

'You're as certain as that?'

'Yes, I'm certain.'

'Well, it's nice to meet someone really confident for a change.'

He looked down at her left hand. She followed his glance, but he went on with his question. 'Is your husband here?'

'No, he's not.'

He waited, to give her an opportunity, but it seemed she had no more to say. Her husband was probably away at sea. Fanny had done her duty and invited her that morning. The wives often performed such a service for each other. Later, it might be Annabel's turn to repay the favour and invite Fanny, when Scratch was away.

'Do you know Fanny well?'

'Quite well. We're neighbours. I live only just round the corner. Oh dear, I think those three little men are being made to leave.'

The three pilots were on their way to the door, being urged onwards by a grim-faced Rupert Smith. The one wearing the cardigan was a round-shouldered, sharp-featured young man with mousy brown hair, a broad nose, and wide upturned nostrils. His neck and chin were scarred with the messy aftermath of a pimply acne rash. He was sweating, and staggering slightly, and evidently in that state of half-intoxication where all inhibitions are removed. When he saw the Commander with Annabel he stopped, despite Rupert's prodding finger. He looked from Annabel to the Commander and a knowing smile spread over his face.

'Got the old ball and chain with you, I see, sir?' He belched. 'God bless you, sir.' He patted his mouth genteelly.

The remark and the approach were so offensively familiar, from an officer so vastly junior who had not even been introduced, that the Commander's breath was quite taken away. It was a moment before he grasped the man's meaning.

'The old ball and chain...?' The Commander stepped forward until he towered over the young man, his face so thunderous and menacing that Annabel put a hand to her breast, in alarm. 'Look here, I don't know your name, and I don't know where you learned your manners, but let me tell you this. I'm not married and even if I were I'd hardly use such language to describe my wife. Before you come on board, you'd better learn how to act like a gentleman, as well as just wearing the uniform. Do you understand me? Now get out. Get off with you!'

The young man's mouth dropped open; he seemed genuinely astonished that he had given offence. The other two pilots had closed up behind him and together presented a combined front of hostility. The Commander had the first uneasy inkling that he might have been far more insulting than he had intended. Their faces showed that he had hit them hard; even Rupert, in the rear, was flushed a deep red. The Commander had said more than he knew; he had meant to be rude, but he had apparently been unforgivably rude.

The Commander outstared them all, until their eyes dropped down. 'Get off with you. And think yourself lucky I'm not your host.' He turned round, to see an expression of joy, mixed with consternation, on Annabel's face.

'I'm really very sorry about that, Annabel. I'm sorry I talked so pompously. It was very bad-mannered of both of us.'

'I didn't mind. The old ball and chain . . .' She said the words over again, as though savouring the phrase. 'It's a very good description. I haven't heard it before. In some cases, it could be very apt.'

She had been more interested than shocked. Her chief curiosity about him was now satisfied, and she had seen his expression change when he turned from that poor tight little man back to her. If she had been that young man, she was sure she would have been far more frightened than he had appeared to be.

'That, I am afraid, was one of our officers to be. A pilot, needless to say.'

'You don't like pilots very much?' She was quick to take up the implication.

'Oh no, I shouldn't have said that.' He realised that he had spoken rashly. 'It wasn't fair of me to say that. I've hardly met any pilots yet, so I can't judge. I'm sure most of them are going to be quite all right. But . . .'

'. . . But you think one or two of them won't fit in?'

'Possibly.' He accepted the remark meekly. She was too quick for him. She had the words out of his mouth almost before he had said them.

They talked desultorily for a few more minutes, but the Commander felt that he been cheated. His vanity asked that he entertain this woman, that he impress and charm her, but the intervention had broken his mood, leaving him unsettled and preoccupied. He had lost an important chance. The incident had also cast the first shadow of a problem the Commander had never anticipated; he remembered Tony Dempster's comments in his turn-over letter, and for the first time became aware that there might be difficulties of personality and temperament in *Leviathan*'s wardroom which were peculiar to aircraft carriers.

He had, however, talked to Annabel long enough for the Secretary's sensitive social antennae to detect them.

'I see you've met La Belle Annabel, Bob. Or did you know her before?'

'No, I've never met her before.' He watched her, with her coat, saying good-bye to Fanny at the door. 'What's her surname? I only know her as Annabel.'

34

'Powell. She's a neighbour of ours. If I were you, I'd take a great deal of care how you go on, Bob. Drying a widow's tears is one of the most dangerous pastimes known to man.'

'I didn't know she was a widow!' It was no wonder she had said no more of her husband. 'Was he in the Service?'

'Oh yes. Tom Powell was one of the brighter pilots in the trade, until one day his aircraft blew up when he was testing something or other. Don't you remember, somebody took a picture of it which was in all the newspapers? There was a bit of a barney about it between Their Lordships and the Press Council. About the publicity and the effect of it on the poor bastard's family.'

'I don't remember anything about this?'

'Happened just over two years ago, nearly three now. Probably you were in Singapore. Everybody expected Annabel to take a new boy friend but Tom's death must have knocked her right back. She's been pretty quiet. I'd say she's just about due to come out of her lair and start stretching her claws and looking for more meat.'

'How old is she?' There were times when a man with Scratch's knowledge was invaluable.

'Thirty-one, thirty-two, something like that. I'm not sure. She's got a couple of kids at boarding school.'

'What does she do with herself all day?'

'In the old days I would have said that Annabel spent her time looking for men. But now, I don't know what she does. She lives just round the corner from here. Tom must have left her the house or something. But if I were you, I'd take all seaman-like precautions, Bob. She's high octane stuff, on an empty stomach.'

'How do you know my stomach's empty?'

The Secretary laughed. 'Isn't it?'

3

The Secretary's finely-tuned social instinct had detected a possibility, a hope for the future, of which the Commander himself was dimly aware but as the tempo of preparing *Leviathan* for her new commission accelerated, the Commander put such thoughts behind him. If Annabel was to win the bet he had so confidently recommended, if that condescending, pitying look was to be wiped from the Assistant Queen's Harbour Master's face, if all those who smiled behind their hands when *Leviathan* was mentioned were to be confounded, then the task would need all the Commander's time and energies.

The Commander was just beginning to comprehend how testing indeed the task would be. Like every newcomer to *Leviathan*, he had been taken aback by her sheer size; it was a weary joke in the wardroom that every new officer joining the ship tied a thread to the handle of his cabin door to guide him, like Theseus, back through the labyrinth. *Leviathan's* size made even routine ship's tasks into major problems of space and time and numbers. In *Leviathan*, it was as though the naval constructors had been given licence to plan and extend and ornament as they pleased. In *Leviathan* every ship's statistic was raised to a higher power, and every system and ship's service enlarged and duplicated. Her two aircraft hangars were each as large as a normal carrier's single hangar. As the First Lieutenant said, *Leviathan* had more of everything, from galleys to radar sets, and from armoured plate to soda fountains. Her nine hundred foot length was sub-divided into twenty-seven sections by massive watertight bulkheads which extended vertically through her eleven decks and horizontally across her hundred foot beam. Each of the twenty-seven sections was itself composed of a steel honeycomb of a hundred smaller compartments sealed by their own watertight doors, but each capable of complex linkings and regroupings and cross-connections to minimise the effect of action damage.

The Commander could not begin his task without a knowledge of the fantastically rich variety of *Leviathan's* compartments and

36

equipment. He was surprised by the warmth of Commander (E)'s response when he asked to be taken on a tour of the ship's machinery spaces.

'It's more than your predecessor ever did, Bob. He never came near the machinery spaces. I often wondered what he thought used to happen below the main deck. Would you like the sixpenny Cook's Tour, or the full Grand Tour?'

'Well, I'll never have a chance to see your empire again, Chief, so I'd better have the whole works.'

'Have you got a spare day?'

'Not a *whole* day, surely? In that case I'd better just have an abbreviated tour.'

'We'll do the main machinery spaces and a few of the oddments like the steering gear. You'd better put your running shoes on, Bob. We've got about five miles of ladders to climb up and down.'

The ladders were one of *Leviathan*'s characteristic features. At intervals, the main deck bulkheads were cut back into recesses enclosing the hatch-ways. Chains, stretched between stanchions, fenced off the openings from careless passers-by. Gusts of warm air rose from the shafts, carrying the subdued hum of machinery and the smell of oil and sea-water. The Commander had often looked over the edges and down the brightly-lit shafts, some of which plunged down fifty or sixty feet to the bottom of the ship, where he could see a segment of polished steel grating, or an intricate tangle of piping, or sometimes the movement of a man's hand or head. More hatches were fitted where each shaft passed through a deck level; when the hatches were shut, the shaft became a vertical column of separate miniature compartments, each containing a short length of ladder.

One hatch was set vertically in the bulkhead. The heavy lead shielding, the air conditioning trunkings, and nearby air filtration unit and the tell-tale Geiger counter dials, denoted a compartment of special significance.

'What's that, Chief?'

'The Nuclear Bomb Room airlock access. This ship's got a nuclear capability.'

'Have you ever had it on board?'

'No. We didn't get that far last commission. I expect we shall this time.'

The Commander could have climbed down any shaft and entered any compartment to satisfy his curiosity. But he had an executive officer's shyness of unfamiliar machinery compartments, which was caused partly by a reluctance to trespass into another man's department, and partly by the unadmitted fear that he might be presented with some sudden emergency which needed an officer's direction but which his technical ignorance would prevent him from solving.

Leviathan's machinery spaces confirmed the same paradox as the rest of the ship: *Leviathan* was a huge ship, but there was no room in her. The Commander had expected to see large machinery spaces, to match the ship's size. *Leviathan*'s engine-rooms and boiler-rooms were comparatively tiny, each just large enough to contain the machinery and a platform for the watch-keepers. The low deckheads, the stifling heat, and the bulkheads rising up immediately beyond the furthest piece of machinery gave the compartments a curiously claustrophobic atmosphere, as though the stomach wall of the ship's body had been pressed back sufficiently for the purpose and was awaiting the opportunity to close in again.

It was while touring the Engine-room Department with Commander (E) that the Commander first encountered that attitude of the ship's company which had so enraged and alarmed his predecessor, that protective shell which every man in *Leviathan* grew after he had been in the ship a few weeks. The Commander was infuriated by the engine-room ratings' indifference. The watch-keepers seemed wholly absorbed in their duties, concentrating as though any private, unscheduled action would betray them. They acknowledged the presence of Commander (E), as the Head of the Engine-room Department and the ship's senior technical officer, but of the Commander himself they seemed oblivious. In one turbo-generator room the watch-keeper was a young stoker, wearing blue overalls, with a white sweat band tied round his forehead. He was holding a pose of almost classical concentration, one foot resting on a polished copper pipe, both hands grasping the steel rail in front of him, and with his head tilted away towards the gauge-board on his left. Although his visitors were standing by the ladder, within a few feet of him, he gave no sign that he had noticed them.

Commander (E) ran his eyes expertly over the gauge-board and, as speech was difficult over the generator noise, nodded towards the ladder.

He waited for the Commander on the main deck. There were four ladders to the top and the Commander was sweating hard.

'That chap seemed to be concentrating pretty grimly?'

'Oh, he knew we were there all right.'

The Commander was puzzled. 'Shouldn't he have said something then?'

'We wouldn't have heard a word he said.'

'Maybe, but shouldn't he have made some sign, instead of just goofing into space?'

'He wasn't goofing into space, he was looking at his gauges.' Commander (E) laughed apologetically. 'What's the point? At least he wasn't asleep, that's something to be grateful for.'

'Do you get a lot of that? Sleeping on watch?'

'We did last time. I expect it'll be the same this time.'

The Commander was furious that the Chief, one of his fellow Heads of Departments, should already be assuming that the new commission would follow the same course as the old.

'Was that lack of supervision?'

'Supervision! How *can* you supervise them, I ask you! If you tried to supervise all the watch-keepers all the time, that would defeat the object of having watch-keepers. Besides, the system would be unworkable. No, you've just got to rely on the goodwill of the blokes down there. They're not too bad, by and large.'

'Delegation of responsibility, as they used to say at Dartmouth.'

'Ah yes, delegation's the word, mate.'

Delegation of responsibility was particularly hard for a man like Commander (E), who had joined the Navy as a boy artificer and who had won a commission through a great deal of hard work and a happy knack of being able to express himself well at interviews. He was a practical man, used to working with his hands, and although he was proud of his rank – a rank which many engineer officers who had started with the advantages of Dartmouth and Keyham did not achieve – it carried the disadvantage of remoteness. He itched to go below, but was seldom able to do so; an emergency which required the physical presence of the Engineer Officer was an emergency indeed. Commander (E) was often forced into the position of having to provide the Captain with up-to-date information without himself being able to demand frequent reports from the Senior Engineer. During the last commission he had spent hours in his office, tormented by doubts and anxieties, waiting for reports from his subordinates, and many nights lying awake in his cabin, waiting for the Senior to telephone him. He had blessed the good fortune which had given him a Senior Engineer who reported fully and frequently.

'You must have had some anxious times in the past, Chief?'

'Some.'

'Did it ever get you down?'

'Not really. It's better if you think of it as a piece of metal. Or several hundred thousand pieces of metal. They're designed to work, and they've just bloody well got to be *made* to work.'

'But there's more to a ship than that.'

'You're obviously a romantic, Bob. No, this ship is several hundred thousand pieces of metal which have got to be made to work.'

'Oh come off it, Chief!' The point was so fundamental that the Commander determined to press it. 'It's more than a collection of bits and pieces of metal. It's got a personality, a life of its own.'

Commander (E) shook his head. 'Not this ship, Bob. I should forget any ideas like that, if I were you. This ship is several hundred thousand pieces of metal, which have just got to be made to work.' Commander (E) repeated the sentence as though it were a talisman which had many times saved his sanity. 'Bob, if I can give you some advice . . .'

Commander (E) paused, embarrassed and remembering that he barely knew Bob Markready. The new Commander represented the broad mainstream of the Navy, which began at Dartmouth and ended in Whitehall, and there were still occasions when Commander (E) felt very much the raw stripling artificer, the outsider, with his sharp cockney accent and his unwilling awe of officers. Even now, after years of living in wardrooms, Commander (E) still felt a twinge of self-consciousness when he first addressed a man like the Commander by his christian name.

The Commander had noticed his embarrassment. 'Any advice you've got, Chief, I'm willing to listen.'

40

Commander (E) had quite recovered his composure. 'I was going to say, it's better not to get involved. Your predecessor let himself get personally involved. Anything that affected the ship, affected him personally. It broke his heart.'

And his career, the Commander added, to himself. 'I said I was willing to listen to advice. I should have said any advice but that.'

Commander (E) ducked his head. 'Please yourself. It's up to you. But I don't want to see you being wheeled away under a cloud like poor old Tony.'

The Commander could no more have taken that advice than he could have cut off his arm. He could not disregard the existence of *Leviathan*'s personality. He was by habit an early riser and it became his custom to walk the upper decks and the jetty beside the ship every morning before the hands were called. Except for the gangway sentries and the quarterdeck watch, he had the ship to himself and he used this time for reflection and for planning his day's programme. It was when he stood on the jetty in the bitter February mornings, when there was ice on the puddles between the dockyard railway lines and the windscreens of the cars parked by the gangways were sheeted with frost, that he felt most profoundly the strength of the great ship's presence. *Leviathan* was vast and intimidating and seemingly indifferent to the men on board her. Her massive steel sides rose from the water like the slopes of an invulnerable fortress. More able men than he had dashed themselves against those formidable walls. The shapes of her boats, her cranes and life-rafts, her gangways, the jagged silhouettes of her flight deck sponsons, irregularly shot with light and dark from the bleak upper deck lighting, all seemed to form the very patterns of resistance to order and discipline. And yet it was at such times that he was most assured that the great ship was willing to be dominated: if the man appeared, the ship would surely follow.

The question of personal involvement arose again, when the Commander toured the messdecks with the First Lieutenant. Most of *Leviathan*'s messdecks had been ingeniously planned and cleverly decorated to make them as comfortable as possible and to save man-hours in cleaning them. But the problem of providing the whole ship's company with proper messdecks had been too much for *Leviathan*'s designers. Nearly a fifth of the leading and ordinary

41

rates lived wherever space could be found, in messdecks which had no enclosed identity, which were scattered about the ship wherever there was room to fit the lockers and stow the hammocks.

One messdeck was no more than part of a broad passageway which led to the boiler-room. Lockers had been fixed in gaps between equipment on the bulkheads. A hammock stowage had been improvised in a space behind a large ventilation trunking and hammock bars welded in uneven lines overhead. Three mess tables jutted out from the ship's side. The centre of the messdeck was dominated by an electric hull and fire pump which, when the Commander arrived, was stripped for overhaul.

The Commander was indignant. 'They call this a messdeck?'

'Yes, sir.'

'For how many men?'

The First Lieutenant looked at the list in his hand. 'Thirty-seven, sir.'

'*Thirty-seven!* Good God, whose messdeck is it?'

'One of the squadrons, sir.'

'Did they object when they saw it?'

The First Lieutenant chuckled. 'Very strongly indeed, sir. The squadron CO even took the matter up with Commander (Air).'

'And what happened?'

The First Lieutenant blew merrily through pursed lips, as though still relishing an old joke. 'Usual thing, sir. Wings took it to Tony, who couldn't do anything, so Wings took it to the Captain, who couldn't do anything either. The squadrons have their fair share of the good messdecks. It was just that particular squadron's horrible luck that they got this one. It was no good pointing that out to them, of course. That only made it worse.'

'Where does that hatch go to?' A heavy armoured hatch, kept open by its counterbalance weight, obscured most of the bulkhead at the forward end.

'Down to one of the boiler-rooms, sir.'

'Of course.' The Commander realised, with shame, how little of Chief's tour had stuck in his memory.

'That's part of the trouble, sir. Stokers going on and off watch have to come through this messdeck and you can hardly expect them to have spotless shoes after four hours down a boiler-room. The place always used to look so scruffy the messdeck dodger got discouraged and just jagged it in.'

The ship's side bulkhead was coated with thick insulating material painted over with pale blue gloss paint. The Commander poked the lower edge of the insulation and a large powdery lump fell away.

'Good God. Couldn't we give them some incentive? A cake or something, for the best messdeck on Captain's rounds?'

The First Lieutenant smiled the tolerant smile of a doctor when a colleague, fresh to the case, suggests an obvious remedy, already tried and already discarded. 'We did just that, sir. We presented a cake to the best messdeck after Captain's rounds. But it was always won by the same messdecks. You can rub over some of them with a damp cloth two minutes before the Captain arrives and they'll come up as good as new. *This* place...' The First Lieutenant made a gesture of contempt. '... You could have a dozen hands working here for a month and it would still look like a shit-heap.'

The First Lieutenant sympathised with the Commander. He, too, had passed through the same stages of shock, indignation and determination when he first arrived on board. The Commander had yet to reach the ultimate and inevitable stage, of resignation.

The Commander sensed the First Lieutenant's sympathy, and resented it. 'So what's the solution?'

'There isn't one, sir. The sailors get used to it and realise it won't last for ever.'

'What a *fantastic* attitude to start a new commission with!'

'Yes sir, but there it is. There's no point in getting personally involved in something you can't alter.'

'Personally involved!' The trigger phrase turned the Commander's frustration into anger. 'It's our *business* to be personally involved! How the devil can we expect anything from the ship's company if the officers are not *personally involved?*'

'Aye aye, sir.' The First Lieutenant's voice was non-committal.

'Something will have to be done before we commission.'

'I'll give it some *more* thought, sir.'

The Commander had rounded on the First Lieutenant, head lowered as though to charge him, before he became aware, with a stab of surprise, that *Leviathan* had almost slipped under his guard yet again. He caught himself up. The First Lieutenant was

43

already proving himself an opponent, and a colleague, worthy of anybody's respect. He had a knack of expressing a problem in a way which exposed its core. He knew what made the sailors tick. He was as imperturbable as he looked, and would not be browbeaten. He must already have wrestled with the problem of the messdecks. If there had been a solution, he would have found it. The messdecks had been built into the ship with the rest of her and there was no help for them now.

'I'll give it some thought myself.'

'Aye aye, sir.'

But as the work of preparing *Leviathan* for her new commission began to accumulate, the Commander had no time to spare for the messdecks. Until the Captain joined, he was the senior executive officer on board and carried responsibility for the ship, in addition to the daily domestic trivia which were his normal concern. His personality tended to breed more work, because men were encouraged to bring problems to him. The word had percolated through the ship that the new Commander was willing to listen and to suggest a solution and, furthermore, that he had the one quality which the ship's company prized above rubies: he could make up his mind.

Many of the new ship's company's difficulties were legacies from the past. There were signs everywhere in *Leviathan* of the state of mind which had prevailed in the ship during the final days of the last commission. The last ship's company had made what amounted to a mass evacuation. They had been so eager to quit the ship that they had shrugged off their responsibility like a detested overcoat and let it drop, not caring where or how it fell. Officers and senior ratings of the previous commission had left the ship with vital information which should have been passed to their successors. Ship's funds accounts were found to have been hastily audited. Hundreds of locks were forced, because the previous custodians had taken the keys with them. Stores had not been properly mustered and the definitive muster lists could not be found. In theory, the Commander was empowered to use official remedies; defaulters could be recalled to the ship to account for deficiencies and omissions. But he believed that there was nothing to be gained by mounting a witch-hunt against the old commission. *Leviathan* needed a fresh start.

The new Captain joined a week earlier than he was expected, and his arrival took the Commander by surprise. Fortunately he chanced to be walking along the upperdeck when he saw the taxi at the after gangway. The giant figure in the overcoat and the pork-pie hat who had climbed out of the taxi and was standing looking curiously up at *Leviathan* could be none other than Tosser McTigue.

When the Commander reached the quarterdeck he saw that the officer of the watch was Bird, who was chatting to the quarter-master with such an expression of moon-calf unawareness on his face that the Commander longed to strike him. Bellowing 'Captain's joining!' as he ran across the quarterdeck, he had just enough time to collect himself, grasp his telescope firmly under his arm, and salute as the Captain reached the top of the gangway.

'Good morning to you, Commander!'

'Good morning sir, and welcome.'

Tosser McTigue's hand-shake was friendly but crushing. It was clear that he had once been a rugby football player. His features naturally suited a scrum-cap. His nose was broad and flat, and had at some time been broken. One ear was permanently calloused. But unlike many former athletes he had not gone to fat. His figure had thickened but his step was light and resilient.

'Sorry I couldn't give you more warning, Commander.'

'That's all right, sir.'

'As I was early, I thought I'd telephone from the station to let you know I was coming and then go and call on the Chief of Staff before coming on here. I hope that gave you enough time.'

The Commander could not prevent himself looking accusingly at Bird. The Captain had warned the ship, and Bird had taken no action at all. Bird's awakening expression betrayed that the Cap-tain's telephone call had entirely slipped his mind.

The Captain noted the exchange, but he turned away and sur-veyed the quarterdeck, which was as untidy and filthy as when the Commander himself had joined. With half an hour's notice, the Commander could have had most of the dockyard debris cleared away.

'These mateys do make a mess of a ship.' The Captain moved towards the ladder leading down from the quarterdeck, assuming that it led, as in most ships, towards his cabin. The Commander forestalled him.

'That one goes to a cabin flat, sir. Your cabin is on the next deck above, sir.'

The Captain laughed awkwardly. 'I'm not used to these flat-topped monstrosities. Everything's arse about face.'

The Captain's suite had been unoccupied and neglected since the last Captain had left the ship. Dust lay on the polished mahogany dining table in the day-cabin, and there were newspapers spread over the blue carpet. The chintz covers had been removed from the armchairs and the sofa and were piled, still dirty and creased, on the deck. The cabin air was stale and there was a musty smell from the pantry. If the Paymaster Commander and the Chief Steward had been given warning, they would certainly have drafted in a team of stewards to make the Captain's suite more habitable.

The Captain sniffed, and opened a scuttle. He tried a drawer in the desk. The wood was damp and the drawer stuck. Lifting his knee, the Captain slammed the drawer back in place with a force which shook the desk and the cabin bulkhead. 'Not bad at all. Very much bigger than I expected. Don't worry about anything Commander, my steward will be joining in a couple of days to get things straightened out.'

The cabin was very cold. The Commander switched on the main electric fire. As he half-expected, there was no warming glow from the bars. The fuses had probably been removed during the refit. If only Commander (L) had been warned.... The Commander gritted his teeth. Most of the ship's Heads of Departments would be interviewing young Bird later in the day.

The Captain sat down on the sofa, still wearing his overcoat. 'Don't worry about that, I'm still here unofficially. It's my own fault for taking the bit between my teeth and coming down here unexpectedly.'

There was a knock at the door.

'Come right in, don't knock, I haven't got a woman here! Ah, hello Tony!'

'Hello Tosser, how are you?'

The Commander wondered how the Secretary had come to know so quickly of the Captain's arrival.

'I'm very well indeed, Tony, and it's nice to see a familiar face.

46

Are you Captain's Secretary in this mighty vessel?'

'That depends on you, Tosser.'

'D'you want to stay?'

The Secretary glanced sidelong at the Commander, as he bowed formally. 'If you have no Secretary appointed, sir, I shall be happy to act in that capacity.'

'Good. You're hired. That's that.' The Captain looked apprehensively at the papers in the Secretary's hand. 'There's nothing vital in there, is there?'

'There is this one.'

'Oh dear.' The Captain's expression sobered when he saw the ominous heading at the top of the form. 'Who's the lucky lad?'

'A Lieutenant Julian Everest Bird.'

'Who's he, Commander?'

'One of the junior watchkeepers, sir. He's a seamen's divisional officer and also in charge of boats, laundry and a couple of other oddments.'

'I see.' The Captain nodded. 'Laundry and Morale Officer.'

The Secretary laid the papers out on the sofa. 'This is really a left-over from last commission. He's under confidential report and the next three-monthly instalment is overdue now. I'm sorry to bounce this on you the minute you get here, Tosser, but I wanted to tell you about it because if we leave it much longer C-in-C will be getting bolshie. I've had one reminder already.'

The Captain sat back in the sofa and studied the form. 'Well, *I* don't know the fellow from Adam. What do you think, Commander?'

'I've only been on board three weeks myself, sir.' The Commander cleared his throat. '*But . . .*'

'*But,* you don't go much on him?'

'He was the Officer of the Watch when you came on board, sir.'

'Ah yes.' The Captain took the point. 'So you don't think we should keep him then?'

'No sir, I most certainly do not.'

The Commander gave his opinion without hesitation, although he might have been tempted to be charitable. A new commission should mean a new start and with new personalities in the wardroom and the knowledge that the past had been forgotten, Bird could turn over a new leaf. But the Commander did not intend to take the chance, or rather, he did not intend to allow the ship to take the chance. Only a lunatic attempted a difficult climb with equipment known to be faulty. And if he had ever felt any goodwill towards Bird, that morning's tragi-comedy on the quarterdeck had dispelled it.

'I'll go further than that, sir. I think we ought to get rid of him as soon as possible.'

A fleeting expression of respect, almost of fear, crossed the Secretary's face. This man really did mean business, even to reviving the ancient custom of launching a new ship with human sacrifices.

'Right Tony. You take all this away and draft out something to the effect that we don't want him. Bring it back, I'll sign it.'

The Secretary's eyebrows arched. This report would almost certainly result in an officer being discharged from the Navy, his services no longer required. Every other Captain the Secretary had ever served under would have spent days composing such a report, considering every word of it, guarding it jealously from his Secretary and only giving it up to be typed with shame and reluctance. As he gathered his papers together and passed the Commander on his way to the door the Secretary's expression said clearly, 'I knew you two were going to be different, but behold, the half was not told me.'

The Captain waited until the Secretary had left. 'He's a useful fellow, Tony.'

'Tony? Oh Scratch, you mean, sir. I'm sorry.' The Commander was so accustomed to the Secretary's trade nickname that his Christian name still fell oddly on his ears. 'I think you made the right decision in keeping him as Secretary, sir.'

'When I last served with him I remember he used to have a sort of built-in early warning radar set, so he could tell the Captain what the wardroom were thinking almost before they thought of it themselves. That can be bloody useful to a Captain. By the way, I don't like to stand on formality when we're in private. My name, as everybody knows, is Tosser. D'you call yourself David or Robert?'

'Bob, sir.' The Commander reddened with embarrassment. The relationship between a Captain and his Executive Officer must necessarily be a close one, closer than their mere professional duties demanded. But the Commander did not have the Secretary's casual social manner. He simply could not bring himself to call the Captain 'Tosser'.

'How did *you* come to get this appointment, Bob?'

The Commander blinked. Evidently Tosser McTigue was not a man to beat about the bush. 'I don't know, sir, to be quite honest. It came out of the blue.'

'And mine, by God!' The Captain's glance conveyed subtly that he had noted the Commander's refusal of Christian name terms. 'I was on my way to join Flag Officer Scotland's staff, in fact we'd even bought a house up there. Of course, the last commission here came such a hell of a crunch I suppose it caught everybody on the wrong foot. What do you make of it all, Bob?'

'I think that perhaps there was a lack of leadership last time, sir.' The Commander chose his words carefully. 'Perhaps not a lack of leadership, but certainly difficulties in command. Plus more than their share of bad luck, maybe. They seemed to do quite a lot of the routine things quite well, but there was some spark missing somewhere.'

'Would you say a *lack* of leadership?' The Captain obviously dismissed the theory. 'I would have said exactly the opposite. From what I hear, there was a damned sight too *much* leadership going on. Far too many bright lads buzzing about exercising their officer-like qualities at each other's expense instead of working together and paying attention to the things sailors really care about. Too many Chiefs, and not enough Indians, that was the trouble. Sailors are realistic these days, Bob. You see that they get their leave and their mail and enough hot water to do their dhobying and the rest will follow, mark my words.'

The Commander studied the Captain's face intently. With his wide blue eyes and his candid expression, sitting there hunched in his overcoat on the sofa, Tosser McTigue looked as guileless as a beagle pup. Did he really believe what he had just said? Could he really believe that as long as there was hot water in the bathrooms and a regular boat for the postman, all would be well? It seemed that he could, and did.

'Naturally, we'll try and do the small things well, sir. That must come first and a lot more will follow. But not everything, sir. I believe there's more to it than that.'

The Captain snorted, and looked at his wrist-watch. 'That's all very well for the recruiting posters, but it doesn't cut any ice with the modern sailor. Now, I think I'd like to meet the Heads of Departments, if that's possible, and any other officers on board. This place is a bit gloomy. Would you mind if I came down to wardroom. . . .'

'By all means, sir. I'll have a pipe made to get all officers in the wardroom . . .'

'Oh no, don't do that. This is purely informal. I'll meet them as they come in.'

The Commander led the way down to the wardroom. The great ship was living up to her reputation of being able to surprise those who believed that they had begun to understand her. The Commander had thought that he had calculated his chances very well, but it seemed that he had overlooked the personality of the Captain, which was one of the most important factors of all.

The weeks leading up to *Leviathan*'s commissioning day were the most exciting and professionally the most absorbing of the Commander's career. He shelved most of his paper work until the evenings, so that he could walk around the ship during the day and watch her slowly, miraculously, taking shape before his eyes. He was impressed by the ship's immense store of unobtrusive talent; all over the ship, men working singly or in small parties, were carrying out their specialised duties with little or no supervision. They had never attracted the attention of the Executive Officer before, and they were delighted and flattered by the Commander's interest. After nine months in dockyard hands *Leviathan* was rusty, in structure and in organisation. Hundreds of seized valve hand-wheels were freed, disused machinery brought forward into service, and neglected compartments cleaned and painted. A score of disbanded specialist working parties were reconstituted and retrained, and lapsed duty rosters reorganised for sentries and patrols, and for duty officers and men of every specialisation.

The flight deck and the island were scenes of continuous activity, from early morning until long after midnight. In the island super-structure several of the giant radar aerials were already turning; unless there was a serious defect or a total electrical power failure in the ship, most of them would not now stop rotating until the commission was over and the ship once again paid off. On the island and flight deck gun sponsons, the Ordnance Department were bringing the ship's anti-aircraft armament to life, patiently training the mountings right and left, elevating and depressing the multitude of gun barrels, training and reversing, elevating and depressing, again and again and again. Amidships, abreast of the island, a mountain of sacks, boxes, cartons, drums, packing cases, carboys and crates lay spread across the flight deck like the base depot of a colossal mountaineering expedition. Ratings and officers from several departments climbed the mountain, identifying and checking the several million items of spare gear and naval stores which the ship and her aircraft would need during the coming commission. The mountain never diminished, the ship's port side crane adding fresh items from the dockside as fast as the working parties and fork-lift trucks could manhandle and ferry the stores away to the flight deck lifts.

Forward, the flight deck had been cleared for catapult testing, where dockyard workmen and the Flight Deck Engineer Officer's party were launching catamarans into the water ahead of the ship.

The catamarans were the size of furniture pantechnicons, and they had four huge wheels and massive, deep-treaded tyres. One of them, painted a blazing fluorescent yellow with the name *Nelly* roughly splashed in black on its side, was in position for launching on the port catapult.

The Flight Deck Engineer Officer, in white overalls and black flight deck beret, crouched beside a glass-sided howdah in the deck some feet from the catapult track. He acknowledged the thumbs-up signals from the rating who scrambled out from beneath the catamaran and from the look-out stationed forward on the flight deck, and then rose to his feet, raising both arms like a conductor gathering the attention of his orchestra.

He dropped one hand and the catamaran jerked, accelerated up the track and with a rumbling whirring of its wheels was hurled off the flight deck. It hung in the air, and then vanished. A moment later, a towering column of water rose above the level of the flight deck, and subsided again. It was a dramatic spectacle and the Commander, one of a small group of fascinated onlookers, joined in the murmur of appreciation and pleasure.

Forward of *Leviathan* a circling dockyard tug, flying a red flag to warn passing river traffic, took *Nelly* in tow to the dockside where a crane waited to hoist her back on board. As *Maria*, the next catamaran, was being wheeled into position the Flight Deck Engineer Officer caught sight of the Commander.

'Good morning, sir. Enjoying our show?'

'Good morning, Joss. This is better than a three-ring circus.'

'I reckon it must satisfy some deep psychological urge, sir. Everybody wants to hurl large lumps into the sea now and again and watch the splash.'

Like all the flight deck crews, Joss Parkhurst's face was burned by wind and open air; when he pushed back his beret, he uncovered a clear line of white untanned skin across his forehead.

He was a tall, lean man, with a long, gloomy jaw and the faint cicatrice of a scar by the side of his mouth. He was only slightly junior as a lieutenant commander to the Senior Engineer and after a harrowing year as Flight Deck Engineer Officer in the first commission he had asked for, and was entitled to a change of department. But Commander (E) had persuaded him to stay. Nobody understood *Leviathan*'s flight deck machinery better than Joss, and Commander (E) anticipated that his interest would rekindle in time. Commander (E)'s hopes had been fulfilled; Joss Parkhurst was once more so engrossed in the problems of bringing the catapults up to operational readiness that he would now have resented any suggestion of a change. The Commander recognised that he was speaking to yet another of the ship's specialist experts.

'Are these hydraulic catapults? They are, aren't they?'

'Yes, sir.' Joss Parkhurst looked anxious, afraid of taking the Commander's ignorance for granted. 'Did Commander (E) show you round, sir?'

'He did indeed. But I'm just an ignorant fish-head, Joss. You'll have to explain it to me again, if you wouldn't mind.'

Joss was only too ready. 'We've got some very large hydraulic pumps right down in the bottom of the ship, sir, and they pump some equally large hydraulic rams backwards and forwards. To put it simply, the rams are rigged up as pulleys and the pulley-wires end up at that shuttle there.'

Joss pointed at a thick metal stub, curved like a bent thumb, which projected from the catapult track. 'When the ram moves to and fro, that shuttle moves up and down the catapult track. You hook your aircraft to the shuttle with the wire strop and when the shuttle goes, the aircraft goes. That's when it's working, of course.'

Joss jerked his head towards *Maria*. 'This is a convenient way of testing the gear, while we take readings. The cats simulate an actual aircraft, and they float so we can boost them off and recover them again without too much trouble.'

He rubbed his chin, and the Commander noticed that his fingers were heavily nicotine-stained. While he was speaking, Joss looked warily about him, from the catapult to the look-out, and from the look-out back to the howdah. The Commander guessed that he was in a state of high nervous excitement. The state of the catapults literally decided whether or not the ship could operate

53

aircraft, because none of the aircraft the ship would be carrying could take off from the flight deck without catapult assistance.

'I'm told you had some trouble with them?'

Joss pulled nervously at the lobe of one ear. 'Oh yes, we had a lot of trouble. There were times when I used to wake up at night sweating, dreaming that the interlocks hadn't worked and we'd just given somebody a cold shot into the sea. The real trouble is that these boosters are too big. There's a limit to how far you can go with any given design and we've reached that limit. It's like the old dinosaurs. They grew so big, eventually they fell flat on their faces. As it is, these boosters are only just big enough for the kind of aircraft we're going to have on board this time. The next step up is the steam catapult. But of course, we're not fitted with those.'

'So our catapults are obsolete?'

Joss' lip curled. 'I'll *say* they're obsolete.' He had been looking over the Commander's shoulder and had caught the signal from the catapult crew. 'They're ready again, sir, excuse me.'

The Commander watched *Maria* take her spectacular leave of the ship, and walked past the stores mountain to a clear space aft of the island where a party of aircraft handlers were practising their art with a spare aircraft especially brought on board for their training. Dressed in blue overalls, gym shoes and blue skull-caps, the handlers moved like a team of expert dancers, whirling and spinning in unison, rehearsing the formation team-work which in due course would enable them to roll an aircraft across a heaving flight deck and park it to within an inch.

The Flight Deck Chief, a bull-necked man with a spade-shaped bronze beard, was acting as choreographer and artistic director. He was producing as good a show as the catapult crew, and with a better script.

'Keep your heads *down* when I tell you! *I* don't want to see your ugly faces. I want to see your ugly arses. When in doubt, lie flat, keep still, wait for the wrath of God to fall on yer.'

When a handler made an error, the Flight Deck Chief placed his hands on his hips and raised his voice half an octave.

'You stupid little ballet-dancer, you! You stepped right across that tail-pipe, *didn't* you? You'd have been frizzled, like a little herring on a little griddle, *wouldn't* you? I've never lost a man on

54

a flight deck yet and I'm not starting with you lot! Now get your head down and *move*, or Jesus Christ'll be drawing your *tot!*'

The Commander found himself becoming self-conscious of his role as spectator. It struck him that as a 'salt-horse' executive officer with no particular expertise he was already watching too much of the ship's life from the side-lines. He had been chastened to discover how little of the daily life of the ship came under his own personal direction. The work of the ship was almost entirely in the hands of the technical and armament departments. There was a second great paradox of *Leviathan*: she had more men on board her than any other ship in the Navy, but none of them were ever available. The Commander was often placed in the position of arbitrator between conflicting demands for men.

The clashes between the ship's various commitments were difficult to reconcile. The First Lieutenant hoped to hold the first tentative damage control acquaintance drills, only to find that the Senior Engineer required all the engine-room personnel for basin trials on the main machinery. The Mate of the Upper Deck complained to the Commander that he could not finish painting the outboard ship's side because of the traffic of fuel, water and stores lighters almost permanently secured there. The Gunner asked for extra hands to strike down small arms ammunition and pyrotechnics on the same morning as Bird had arranged to collect the ship's boats from the dockyard boat pool. A lorry with naval stores consigned to the Naval Storekeeping Officer would arrive at the same time, and at the same gangway, as a lorry with parachutes and Mae Wests for the Air Safety Officer. *Leviathan* was too vast for intimate control by one man but when the Commander found that there was little or no liaison between the departments he addressed himself to the task of becoming the ship's link-man. As the weeks passed he began to compare his position on board to that of general manager of a large commercial concern. He was reminded of the comparison whenever he watched the ship's company, who now included the squadron advance parties, coming on board for work in the mornings. Less than ten per cent of the ship's company wore uniform ashore and, as they parked their cars and motor-cycles and streamed up the gangways in their civilian clothes, the Commander was impressed by their resemblance to the employees of a large industrial organisation.

55

The leading and ordinary rates, corresponding to the shop-floor and domestic staff, arrived first, followed half an hour later by the junior management and office personnel, represented by the Chief and Petty Officers. Last of all came the officers, in managerial and executive posts, parking their cars in a separate enclosure and boarding by a separate gangway entrance. Watching them, the Commander sometimes had the unnerving thought that perhaps *Leviathan* never intended to go to sea; perhaps the ship herself considered it her only proper function to act as a floating, but stationary, factory and office block for more than two thousand employees of the Crown.

New officers were arriving every week. The Commander met them all personally on their first day. Although wardroom membership had doubled since he himself joined, the number sitting down to lunch every day had not increased in proportion. He was puzzled by the discrepancy until he stumbled upon the solution by accident, when he was walking through a cabin flat at lunch-time and happened to look through an open cabin door.

The Commander stopped in his stride, astonished. A young officer, one of the junior engine-room watchkeepers, called Fisher, was sitting at the cabin desk, reading a newspaper and eating a sandwich. There was a thermos flask and an open packet of sandwiches on the desk. A civilian sports coat, trousers and a shirt were piled on the bed. Clearly, Fisher used his cabin only as a changing room when he came on board in the mornings, and as a place to eat his sandwiches during his lunch hour.

Fisher was getting to his feet, urgently swallowing his last mouthful.

The Commander waved a hand, embarrassed that he had apparently trespassed. 'That's all right, Fisher. You carry on with your dinner.'

On a sudden impulse of curiosity, the Commander looked in three more cabins in the same flat. All three had startled occupants, who had been sitting by themselves with their newspapers, their sandwiches and their thermos flasks.

The Commander went down to the wardroom, oddly disquieted and resentful. Sitting alone in a cabin, drinking tea from a thermos flask, eating sandwiches and reading a newspaper – all were activities totally alien to his own conception of wardroom mem-

56

bership. Lunch-time was the traditional hour for gossip, for discussing business with someone one had been too busy to find all morning. In most wardrooms, more ship's business was done at lunch-time than at any other time of the day. The Commander was so concerned that he broached the subject to the First Lieutenant.

'This business of sitting eating sandwiches in your cabin instead of coming down to the mess. How long's this been going on?'

The First Lieutenant hid his surprise at the Commander's innocence. 'It's always been going on, sir. They're all on Ration Allowance. Living ashore. RA members have to pay for their lunch, sir.'

'Yes, I *know* that.' The Commander shook his head testily. 'But they don't pay all that much. Not half what they'd have to pay for the same meal ashore.'

'I quite agree, sir, but they obviously prefer to get their wives to make them up some sandwiches. It's the same up forrard, sir. If you went into any of the messdecks now you'd find it full of sailors eating wedges and drinking tea.'

'Don't they like the food in the dining hall?'

'I don't know, sir.' The First Lieutenant was mystified by the Commander's concern; that people brought sandwiches on board to eat at lunch-time could hardly be news, even to the Commander. 'I don't think there's anything wrong with the food. It's certainly looked all right whenever I've been up there. They just prefer their wedges.'

'It's fantastic! I must have another look at that dining hall.'

The ship's company's dining hall was well forward in the ship, a huge echoing and dismal compartment, situated where the ship's sides began to narrow towards the bows, which the First Lieutenant had once likened to the great hall of some poverty-stricken spartan king. Every amenity which might have improved the dining hall's appearance had been sacrificed to the functional purpose of serving meals to a very large number of sailors in a short time. The tables were bolted to the deck in lines so close together there was barely room for benches in between. When two adjacent benches were full, the sailors sat literally back to back. Six fluorescent lighting units, fitted along the centre of the deck-head, illuminated the whole compartment. The dark green linoleum on the deck was

57

cracked, and where the bare deck metal showed it had been battered and polished to a dull shine by the passage of thousands of shoes. The bulkhead paintwork was scuffed and smeared, and at the serving hatches where the sailors collected their meals, the paint at elbow level had been entirely worn away.

The dining hall was organised on a cafeteria system and when the Commander arrived a queue of sailors in working clothes and carrying mugs, cutlery and partitioned aluminium trays, was shuffling towards the serving hatches where the dining hall staff were slapping the ingredients of the meal into the tray partitions. The Commander read the menu pinned to a notice-board by the hatch. Roast pork, boiled potatoes, and runner beans, or steak and kidney pudding; chocolate pudding and sauce, or ice-cream. The meal sounded inviting enough and though he could see it being served with little finesse, it seemed to him quite palatable.

While the Commander had been watching the ship's company dinner being served, Commander (S) had come into the dining hall, accompanied by the Duty Supply Officer and the Officer of the Day.

Leviathan's Commander (S) had been known since his Dartmouth days as Delicious Joe. With his fastidious expression, the inches of cuff showing from his jacket sleeves, and the white handkerchief carefully folded in the breast pocket, Delicious Joe cut a curiously anomalous figure in the ship's company's dining hall, like a Regeny buck standing in an abattoir. Delicious Joe had the proper amount of indolence in his nature for a successful Supply and Secretariat officer; he sincerely believed that nothing ruined a ship more quickly or irretrievably than an energetic Supply Officer. He had learned to apply in practice a principle which many naval officers never discovered, namely that most problems will solve themselves if allowed time to do so. Delicious Joe had a venomous tongue, in spite of his elegance and his appearance of moving through his Service career as a gifted dilettante; he seemed never to notice details, but many a subordinate supply officer had been brutally reminded that Delicious Joe had been watching all the time.

Delicious Joe was well aware of the Commander's presence, though he pretended to be absorbed by the scene in the dining hall. He tensed himself for the meeting. He had not yet taken the

Commander's measure, being unable to decide whether Bob Markready was a genuine fanatic or merely criminally naïf.

'There doesn't seem much wrong with the food, Joe?'

Commander (S) carefully formed a smile on his lips. He had been expecting just such an opening remark. 'Of course there's nothing wrong with the food.'

'Then why do all the sailors bring sandwiches? And the officers. I've seen 'em at it. Munching away at their scruffy little wedges, instead of having a decent dinner.'

'Maybe they just prefer to have sandwiches.'

'But it's like having a job at a factory.'

'In a lot of ways, it *is* like having a job at a factory.'

'Oh balls.'

Delicious Joe had a quicker temper even than the Commander. 'I don't know what you're trying to achieve with all this crap . . .'

'*What* crap?'

'Where have you *been* these last few years?'

'I was in Singapore for about . . .'

'Oh my God.' Delicious Joe twisted his head, to look away from the Commander. 'I don't mean that. I mean the last ten years, *fifteen* years, while the Navy's been changing. Ever since you joined this ship you've been behaving like somebody who's been away, been asleep, like Rip van Winkle. Now you've woken up and it's all been changed. The Navy *is* a job now.'

They were standing by the main doors. Sailors passing on their way to dinner were staring curiously at the Commander and Commander (S), apparently arguing in public. The Commander noticed that the Duty Supply Officer and the Officer of the Day had moved aside, to conceal their embarrassment.

'I don't think this is the time or the place to discuss this, if you don't mind.'

'All right! Discuss it or not. As you please.' Delicious Joe glared at the Commander, as though Bob Markready embodied all that he most feared in the Navy. The last commission had admittedly been bad, but the Supply Branch had performed quite adequately; the last thing they wanted was a man like the Commander, boring and bulling his way in, disturbing a reasonably comfortable and efficient routine. Delicious Joe summoned himself to sting and to wound.

'But let me tell you this, since nobody else is likely to. *You* may think the last commission was a load of rubbish. But we weren't *all* incompetent, we weren't *all* booted out of the ship and we don't *all* need some self-appointed Lord High Executioner to tell us how to do our jobs! And unless you drop some of your crack-pot Nelsonian ideas about the Service and particularly about this ship, *you're* in for some nasty shocks, I can tell you!'

'That's as may be. But I must ask you to refrain from expressing such opinions in the presence of junior officers.' The Commander knew that Delicious Joe always made him talk pompously. He knew it, but could do nothing to remedy it. 'If you must use such language then I suggest you keep it for the Heads of Departments' meetings.'

'Oh *God*, you're as bad as your predecessor!' Delicious Joe's voice was sneering. 'Whenever anything came up, he would always say "Keep it for the Heads of Department meetings."'

'It was very good advice, and I can only repeat it.'

The Commander was neither stung nor wounded by Delicious Joe's attack. The incident confirmed that Commander (S) was not an ally, but he was still a competent officer, who could be relied upon to run his department efficiently. Leave Joe alone, and the Supply Department would come home. It was not the open dissenters like Joe who were the Commander's problem, but the others, who paid lip service and laughed behind their hands.

The Heads of Department's meetings had been instituted by Tony Dempster, to give himself and his fellow Commanders an opportunity to discuss ship's affairs at their own level and in privacy. It was an excellent idea which had been allowed to run to seed. More and more officers had been summoned to attend and, having attended once, felt themselves bound to continue. When the Commander approached the Aircrew Lecture Room, where the meetings were normally held, he was surprised to hear the roar of conversation carrying down the passageway. Inside, the Lecture Room was thick with tobacco smoke and the room was full of officers, sitting two deep round the table. Some of them, the Supply Officer (Cash), the Hangar Control Officer, and Joss Parkhurst, could not by any means be termed Heads of Departments.

The hubbub died as the Commander advanced to the chair left

for him at the head of the table.

'Gentlemen, there seems to have been some misunderstanding about the purpose of this meeting. I called a meeting of Heads of Departments. To me, that means myself, Commander (Air) who is head of the Air Group, Commander (E) who is head of the Engine-room Department, Commander (L) who is head of Electrical Department, Commander (S) who is head of the Supply Department, the PMO who is head of the Medical Department, and the Air Engineer and Air Electrical Officers and the Instructor Commander, when they join. Other officers, such as the Shipwright Officer, the Captain of Royal Marines and the squadron COs, may be invited to attend from time to time. Now, I'd be obliged if any officer I've not mentioned as a Head of Department would excuse himself.'

Some of the middle-management officers, such as the First Lieutenant and the Senior Engineer, at once headed for the door, their expressions making it clear that they had better things to do with their time and they were only too delighted to be excused. But others, such as the Gunnery Officer, appeared reluctant. The Gunnery Officer indeed paused on his way to the door; he had always believed that he was, to some extent, a Head of Department.

'Sir, the last Commander always liked everyone to be here...'

'*Mister* Davenish.'

The title of 'Mister' was correct, though unusual, for all officers up to the rank of lieutenant commander and was technically no more remarkable than a barrister's use of 'My learned friend'. But the Commander's emphasis on the word, and the intonation of his voice, made the intended insult unmistakable.

'... The last commission and its ways are neither here nor there. I've told you who should be attending this meeting.' The Commander leaned forward, with his palms on the table. 'Now, *get out.*'

He glowered at the door until the Gunnery Officer had shamefacedly followed the rest of the officers out of the room. Then he straightened up and smiled.

'I'm sorry about that.' He waited until they were all looking at him, to make his apology plain. 'Nothing irritates me more than to be reminded of last commission. Commander (Air) not coming?'

'You won't find Wings on board much when we're in harbour.'

Commander (L) held a match to his pipe and puffed vigorously, until the Commander understood who was responsible for most of the tobacco haze in the room. 'You were quite right, Bob. These meetings were getting more like a bear-garden every time.'

Commander (L) was a small, rather corpulent man who sat hunched forward in his chair so that the lapels of his reefer jacket ballooned out under his chin. His name was Daffyd Llewellyn Gwynne-Jones. Like most Welshmen, he could not sing, nor did he play rugby football. His father was the RSPCA Inspector in a Welsh mining town, but 'Jones the Cruelty's boy' had travelled a long way from his background. He was one of a new breed in the Navy, one of the first generation of electrical officers to have any proper knowledge of their duties. The Electrical Branch was the youngest technical branch in the Navy and its early years had been blighted by a lack of competent senior officers. Former Torpedo Officers, and others with even sketchier qualifications, had eagerly transferred to the new branch because of the certainty of less competitive promotion prospects. Dai Bach, as he was inevitably known in the wardroom, was one of the first professional electrical engineers to reach a rank which carried any power. He was too generous, too impulsive, and probably too intelligent to reach the highest ranks of the Navy, but he made an excellent Commander (L) of an aircraft carrier. He was not above donning a pair of overalls and superintending the rewiring of a large generator armature himself, and his staff had respected him since the day he cured a defective wireless transmitter by giving the base of the console a sharp kick.

Dai Bach took a dog-eared and often folded sheet of paper from his wallet. 'Now that we're under new management, so to speak ...'

Commander (E) recognised the sheet of paper. 'Oh no, Dai, not that one again, please?'

'... Now that we're under new management, I want to raise a point about the Daily Orders which I raised last commission, with no success. This is a copy of the Daily Orders from one day last commission. We *all* know the Daily Orders are produced by the *Gunnery* Office ...'

The Commander was baffled by Dai Bach's preliminary oratory. 'What's all this leading up to, Dai?'

'I'll explain in one minute, Bob. These are the Daily Orders for one day last year. There are five items of information. Four of them concern the Gunnery Branch. Here, in block letters mind you, nine o'clock Able Seaman Daniels and Able Seaman Fraser, report to the Gunner's Store, collect webbing equipment. And right at the bottom, in lower case, twelve o'clock, ship's company muster for payment. Now I ask you, is that reasonable? Four items in block letters concerning *only* the Gunnery Branch and one little item at the bottom which concerns the *whole* ship's company. What would it be like if we all did that? If Chiefy here put it in the Daily Orders when he wants Stoker Bloggins and Stoker Snooks to collect two wheel spanners from the Engineer's Ready Use Store? Or if I myself put it in the Daily Orders whenever we wanted the Upper Deck Lighting Party to go to the main electrical store and draw fuses? The Daily Orders would be two *editions,* with a supplement!'

Commander (S) had been gazing at the deckhead, as though he had heard it all before. 'Dai, your trouble is that you were bitten by a Gunnery Officer at the age of two.'

Dai was indignant. 'I have the greatest respect and admiration for the Gunnery Branch! Some of my best friends are Gunnery Officers! It's their *attitude* I don't like, their attitude of moral superiority! When Moses brought the tablets down from the mountain he took them to Whale Island and nowhere else, that's their attitude. That's what I object to!'

'I take your point, Dai. I'll see the Gunnery Officer about it.'

'Thank you very much indeed, Bob.' Dai Bach tucked the sheet of paper away in his wallet.

'Can I have that copy?'

'Ah no, that's my evidence.' A glint of Celtic cunning showed in Dai's eye. 'I may need that *next* commission, who knows.'

The Commander realised that under the triviality Dai Bach had been hinting at a far deeper significance. The normal content of the Daily Orders contained many anachronisms. They were a relic of the days when the seamen formed by far the largest part of a ship's company. In *Leviathan* the seamen were in the minority and it was illogical to restrict the Daily Orders mainly to their movements and routine. It was important that the ship's literature should recognise the existence of the technical branches.

'I've taken your point, Dai. But now I want to get on to the

63

first main item for discussion. The ship's company dining hall.'

The other Commanders looked significantly at each other. This, too, was an ancient bone of contention.

'. . . When I went up there the other day I couldn't help noticing that the whole place needed a bloody good chamfer up all round. I intend to have it painted out as soon as possible and I'm going to see what the dockyard can do about replacing some of the worst bits in the deck covering. There's not much time left now, but perhaps we can replace some of it as the commission goes along. In the meantime, part of the trouble is the staff. It seemed to me they were uninterested, scruffy and inefficient. And they look unhygienic into the bargain.'

Dai Bach held up a hand. 'They're the ullage of the ship. But let's be honest, Bob. The Electrical Department have to send a certain number of ratings up there because it's a departmental commitment. We all have to do it. But we'd be foolish, surely, to send a good rating up to work in the dining hall when we can just as easily send a bad one? After all, he's only going to sling hash up there.'

Delicious Joe stirred in his seat. 'Not hash, Dai. Hardly hash.'

'A figure of speech, Joe, you know that.'

The Commander turned to Commander (E). 'What about you, Chief?'

'I'm with Dai, I'm afraid. I've told the Senior to send all the deadwood up there. Not that he needed any telling. You must admit, Bob, it's a little easier for the seamen.'

Commander (E) was amplifying Dai's original point. The seamen were the most expendable branch in the ship. Probably a case could be made out for saying that the least inconvenience would be caused to everyone if the dining hall were staffed entirely by seamen.

'All right then. I've heard all you've got to say. But I still intend to carry on painting out just the same. They may work better if their surroundings are improved.'

In spite of themselves, the others began to warm to the Commander. A meaner-spirited man might have used his offer of improving the dining hall to blackmail them into sending better staff. But Bob Markready was cast from a bigger mould. He had his plans for the ship and he intended to carry them out, with or

64

without assistance. The other Heads of Departments once more felt that in dealing with the Commander they were trying to divert an elemental force of nature from its path.

Commander (L), unwisely generous as always, hastened to offer some concession. 'I'll tell you what I'll do, Bob. I'll have another look at the blokes I've sent up there and I'll see what I can do.'

'Thank you, Dai. I can't ask more than that. Chief?' The Commander might not descend to blackmail, but he could exploit a tactical weakening in the opposition when he saw it. 'What about you?'

Commander (E) looked at Dai Bach as though he had been betrayed. 'All right, I give in. I'll see what I can do.'

Delicious Joe regarded the Commander with reluctant respect. Tony Dempster had tried in vain for a year to wring such concessions from these very men. Meanwhile, the Commander was passing on to the next subject.

'Fair enough. Now, the next thing. Commissioning day.'

'Ah yes.' The others looked up expectantly.

'We'll have the normal Commissioning day routine. The Commissioning party will parade on the Barracks parade ground if dry, in the drill shed if wet. The ship's company will march down to the ship with the Royal Marine band. The Captain will take the salute on the jetty by the after gangway. We shall have a service of dedication in the upper hangar, conducted by the Chaplain of the Fleet. The following Sunday I propose to have full divisions on the flight deck if dry, in the upper hangar if wet.'

The Commander had expected opposition, and he was not disappointed.

'*Divisions!*' Delicious Joe sat bolt upright. 'On *Sunday?*'

'Sunday is the traditional Service day for divisions.'

'Not any longer it isn't and certainly not in this ship it isn't! What about the sailors' week-ends?'

'There will be no week-end leave that Sunday. Not for anybody.'

'No week-end *leave?*' Commander (E) was laughing nervously, imagining the faces of his Regulating Chief Artificer and Chief Stoker when the news was broken to them. 'You can't stop the sailors' week-end leaves! Not for *divisions!*'

'I can, and I will. They've all had dozens of week-ends since we've been here. It won't do them any harm to miss the first one

65

of a new commission. All the ratings joining on commissioning day will just have come off commissioning leave, so they won't have any drips.'

'Won't they indeed!' Delicious Joe had decided that Bob Markready's naïvety had been humoured far and long enough. 'I can just see their faces. They join a new ship they've all been hearing terrible stories about and the first thing they're told when they get on board is that they're having divisions on Sunday. Just as though they were back doing their basic training again. And you say they won't have any drips!'

The Commander lowered his head, tensing his jaw muscles, and Dai Bach, who was the most perceptive of the others, understood that their battle was already lost.

'I can't see that they have anything to complain about...'

'Bob, we're not at war, you know. Nor are we training new entries at Shotley or Torpoint. We're already having more or less a full divisions on commissioning day. If you particularly want another, there's absolutely no reason why we shouldn't have divisions on Friday afternoon, as usual, and pipe week-end leave immediately afterwards.'

'No reason, except that I've decided to have divisions on Sunday.'

'But Bob, surely you can see...' Delicious Joe's voice was pleading, coaxing a simpleton child. 'Why, even Tony Dempster didn't...'

'Didn't what?' The Commander bristled at the apparition of the old, familiar bogey. 'Didn't *dare* to have divisions on a Sunday? I've already told you that what happened last commission is of no interest to me. Different ships, different cap tallies. And this is going to be a different ship.'

Delicious Joe's face now wore a mocking smile. 'And shall we all wear our Chief Cadet Captains' lanyards then?'

The Commander caught the drift of the remark, without understanding its full implication. 'Just what do you mean by that?'

'I mean that if we're going to *behave* as though we were back at Dartmouth, surely we ought to *dress* the part?'

The Commander's true adversary, the old *Leviathan* and her way of thinking, was in full view. He stood up.

'Joe, you seem determined not to understand what I've tried to tell you several times. Let me tell you again. I don't want to make too much of the last commission. But things are different now. *I* am now in the chair. I am *going* to make this ship work. I have *plans* for this ship. And I'm going to carry them out. With you. Or without you.'

Commander (E) and Commander (L) were profoundly impressed by the Commander's words. But Delicious Joe was wilfully determined to have the last word, and so to diminish himself in the eyes of the others.

'Well, all I can say is I hope it keeps fine for you. But if I know anything about this ship you won't get away with it. Something will happen to ball it up. It always does. If you get through your splendid commissioning day routine *and* your Sunday divisions without at least one major shambles, I tell you it'll be a bloody miracle!'

5

After the Heads of Departments' meeting, the Commander was reassured to find support where he most needed it. The Captain fully agreed with the intention to hold Sunday divisions.

'You must start as you intend to go on, Bob. I know it's thought reactionary and anti-social in this modern Navy to disturb the sailors' sacred week-ends but I'm all for having Sunday divisions.'

'It will only be this Sunday, sir.'

'I know. But I'm told the idea wasn't exactly unanimously approved by the other sergeants?'

'No sir, it was not.' None of the other Heads of Departments would have discussed their meeting with the Captain: the Captain's Secretary's grapevine must therefore be in working order already.

'Well, you know you can count on my fullest support, Bob.'

'Thank you, sir.'

'By the way, Bob...' The Captain's expression changed, becoming wary, as though he expected to be challenged. 'I've changed my mind about young Bird. I think we're being too harsh on him. A new commission should mean a new start. So I've scrubbed round my original draft. I hope you don't mind?'

'Not at all, sir. I expect that was the fairest thing to do.'

The Commander no longer had any strong emotions for or against Bird. A few weeks earlier he would have been angry that his advice had been rejected, after it had once been accepted, but now that *Leviathan*'s commissioning day was almost upon them, the issue seemed insignificant. He mentally filed the problem, as something which might one day require attention.

'Sunday will be a good opportunity for you to speak to the ship's company, sir.'

'I've already thought of that one and I'll certainly talk to them. Everything else fixed?'

'We're just about ready, sir.'

'My God, I hope it goes off all right.' The Captain gnawed at one knuckle and then flung the hand out, as though warding off

68

a blow; it was a curious gesture, of a man who desperately needed reassurance. 'You know, I've commissioned a good many ships over the years. I should know all about it by now but I've never had this feeling of being so much in the limelight before. I'm always nervous beforehand, like first night nerves, but this is different. I get the feeling the whole bloody Navy are watching us, waiting for us to make fools of ourselves.'

'I expect they are, sir. But that should only put us on our mettle.'

Like the Heads of Departments, the Captain felt himself warming towards Bob Markready. By some incredible fluke of officers' appointing, *Leviathan* had been given a Commander worth ten men.

'You're a comforting fellow to have around, Bob. I think we'll go a long way together.'

Either by chance or by wise intention, the Navy laid down a procedure for commissioning one of Her Majesty's Ships which was a superb gesture of mutual support against the hardships and dangers of an uncertain future. The officers and men who would live and fight in the ship first mustered on shore, marched down to their ship and boarded her together, as one company, and as one company they took part in a short service of dedication.

In *Leviathan* the purpose of the commissioning day ritual was partly defeated because the commissioning party of some four hundred men were mostly supernumaries, men whose presence on board was not necessary until the last moment, and they were greatly outnumbered by the men who had already joined the ship.

Matched against *Leviathan*'s size it seemed a small and rather forlorn company who wound through the dockyard on their way to the ship. A moist gusting April wind blew away the music of the Royal Marine band as the commissioning party approached the jetty nearest the ship. Although the railway lines, large pools of rainwater and the uneven surface of the dockyard roads made correct marching difficult, the Royal Marine detachment stepped out as though they were on a parade ground. But behind them the main party, headed by the Gunnery Officer, were hampered by their raincoats and small brown attache cases and by their distance from the band. The sailors furthest from the music were shuffling and often changing step. Nevertheless, when the commissioning party marched under the flight deck overhang and into *Leviathan*'s lee, the music swelled more confidently, the stragglers picked up the step and lifted their heads, and there was not an officer standing behind the Captain's saluting base who did not, for a brief moment, share in the Commander's hopes for *Leviathan*'s future. Perhaps this commissioning day truly was an omen of better things. Perhaps the great ship was about to shake off her past after all.

The Dedication Service was held in the upper hangar and to enable a large congregation to see and follow the service *Leviathan*'s chaplain had conceived the idea of bringing the altar up from the ship's chapel and placing it on the after hangar lift, which was normally used for transporting aircraft to and from the hangars and the flight deck. The lift had been raised and locked in a position a few feet above the upper hangar deck level. Lecterns with microphones were placed on either side of the altar, for the Captain and the Chaplain of the Fleet. The polished teak board bearing the battle honours of previous ships of *Leviathan*'s name had been brought from the quarterdeck and placed against the lift, facing the congregation.

The Commander took his place in the front of the congregation in a state of extreme nervous exultation. This was the moment in time when *Leviathan*'s commission officially began. The great enterprise on which he had set his heart was now properly under way. But one man could not succeed alone. The Service of Dedication was a token that no man in *Leviathan* was alone, its purpose to demonstrate publicly that the officers and ship's company were entitled to one another's support.

Others had come to support *Leviathan* on her great occasion. The congregation included representatives from the county, the town and the port, from the dockyard and from other ships in company. Beside the Commander in the front row were the Lord Lieutenant of the County, the Admiral's Chief of Staff, the Mayor and Mayoress, the Admiral Superintendent, the Sheriff, the Chief Constable, the Chief Naval Constructor, the Manager of the Engineering Department and other senior dockyard officers, the Town Clerk, and the Captains and First Lieutenants of other ships and shore establishments. Behind them were *Leviathan*'s officers and their wives and behind them, in rank after rank of faces as far back as the first hangar fire curtain, were *Leviathan*'s Ship's Company. The Commander looked at the faces with longing and with determination. He could see that they were restless, un-impressed, even cynical. But they only needed to be shown, to be led, and unless he could mould these men, unless he could win them, all his work would be as the sounding brass or the tinkling cymbal.

A pale shaft of sunlight from the flight deck unexpectedly illu-minated the after lift-well, as the Chaplain of the Fleet began the service with the traditional address.

'... Brothers, seeing that in the course of our duty we are set in the midst of many and great dangers, and that we cannot be faithful to the high trust placed in us without the help of Almighty God, let us unite our prayers in seeking His blessing upon this ship, and all who serve in her, that she may sail under God's good providence and protection, and that there may never be lacking men well qualified to offer in her their work and skill for His greater glory, and for the protection of our realm and empire.'

Leviathan's chaplain announced the hymn 'Lead Us, Heavenly Father, Lead Us' and the Royal Marine band, formed up in a corner of the hangar facing the congregation, played over the first bars. The ship's company cared nothing for the intricacies of descant or harmony. They required only a solid brassy foundation to their singing, and the Royal Marines provided it.

As he sang the words, which he knew by heart, the Commander recalled the last time he had sung this hymn at a commissioning service. He was a guest on board a destroyer commissioning in Singapore dockyard and he could remember now the white uniforms, the heat under the awning, the brilliant glare of the sunlight and the rank vegetable smell of mud and smouldering wood from the low green shores beside the Johore Causeway. He was half a world and more than a year from that commissioning service but once again he felt most vividly that same sense of participation in a venture which was new and hopeful and honourable.

After the hymn, the Captain stepped forward to call on the ship's company, using the ancient form of bidding, to ask for blessing on their ship.

'I call on you to pray for God's blessing on this ship. Bless our ship.'

The Captain was clearly nervous. The Commander guessed that he had only just restrained himself from testing the microphone

71

by blowing into it.

'What do ye fear, seeing that God the Father is with you?'

'We fear nothing.'

The Captain was reassured by the responsive murmur from his ship's company. 'What do ye fear, seeing that God the Son is with you?'

'We fear nothing.' The ship's company, growing accustomed to the collective sound of their own voices, began to answer with firmness and conviction.

'What do ye fear, seeing that God the Holy Spirit is with you?'

'*We fear nothing!*' The ship's company shouted the third antiphon in a mighty voice, which resounded round the hangar like a great and confident chorus.

The singing of Psalm 107 was less certain, the ship's company being happier with a proper tune. The Commander himself merely recited the words, flavouring their familiar magnificent cadences.

'... They that go down to the sea in ships: and occupy their business in great waters: these men see the works of the Lord: and his wonders in the deep. For at his word the stormy wind ariseth: which lifteth up the waves thereof ...'

With a sudden jangling of alarm bells, the after lift began to rise towards the flight deck. The two microphones reached the extent of their wires and were dragged off and fell on to the hangar deck. The honours board toppled backwards and dropped down the lift-well. The singing faltered and died away. The Royal Marine band stopped playing. The congregation lapsed into an astonished silence to watch the lift ascend, pause a few feet below the flight deck level, and descend again.

The Chaplain of the Fleet was a man of considerable presence and had the lift returned to its proper position at once he could have restored the solemnity of the Dedication Service. But, accompanied by the same clanging warning bells, the lift continued its descent past the upper hangar level, down into the lower hangar.

The disappearance of the Captain, the Chaplain of the Fleet and *Leviathan*'s chaplain was too much for the ship's company. Their first astonishment turned to smiles and to whispering, scraping of chairs and open sniggering laughter. Muffled and indistinct shouting could be heard from the flight deck. Men's silhouettes ran across the deck edge level, stopped and pointed, and ran back. At the height of the uproar, when the lift had vanished and the service was in confusion the Commander, mortified and furious, turned round to quell the most blatant of the whisperers and the sniggerers. He saw the malicious pleasure on Delicious Joe's face; Joe had prophesied disaster and his prophecy had been fulfilled beyond his furthest imaginings. Behind him, the nearest rows of the ship's company were exchanging delighted glances, and hiding their smiles with their hands, and only partly sobering their expressions when they saw the Commander looking at them.

There were too many people laughing. The whole solemn framework of the service had been dissolved. Tears sprang into the Commander's eyes and as he turned away, blinking and shamefaced, he noticed Annabel Powell, wearing a broad black straw hat, standing in the row behind Commander (S). He was struck by her expression of pity and sympathy; it was as though she were the only other person in that hangar who appreciated the shamefulness of what had happened, and though he normally resented sympathy, the Commander was suddenly grateful to her.

The warning bells rang again, and the after lift returned almost to its original position. The Chaplain of the Fleet, appearing unperturbed, could be heard resonantly singing the psalm alone, from the line where the service had been interrupted. The Royal Marine bandmaster picked up the time from him and slowly, with smothered giggles, the rest of the congregation joined in the singing.

The Captain, still brick-red with embarrassment, read the lesson. The service continued, but its purpose had been destroyed. The significance of *Leviathan*'s dedication was lost in the steady undertone of amused whispering and the half-hearted singing of men tightly straining to keep the smiles from their faces.

After the service, when the guests were drinking coffee in the wardroom, the Commander sent for the Flight Deck Officer who, expecting the summons, had already found out the cause of the disaster.

The Flight Deck Officer had thought the incident very amusing, until he saw the expression on the Commander's face, when he became apologetic and crest-fallen.

'It was one of the flight deck sentries, sir. You see, it says in my standing orders that flight deck sentries are to raise the lifts to flight deck level when it's raining. It looked as if it was going to rain so . . .'

'But for God's sake!' The Commander could barely believe his ears. 'Didn't he know there was a commissioning service going on underneath?'

'He did, sir, but he says he completely forgot about it at the time. He just didn't think.'

'But wasn't the lift *locked* or anything?'

'It was locked, sir, indeed it was.' The Flight Deck Officer now realised that the Commander was truly in earnest. 'But as I say, he completely forgot about the service, unlocked the spindle and raised the lift. It wasn't until he saw the Captain and the two bible bosuns coming up towards him . . .'

'What the devil do you mean, *bible bosuns*?' The Flight Deck Officer's choice of words added to the sheer surrealist improbability of the incident so that even now the Commander could barely persuade himself it had actually happened.

'I'm sorry sir, I meant the Chaplain of the Fleet and the Padre, sir. He says, that's the sentry says, that someone on the lift shouted at him to get them back to the lower hangar quick. So he did, but the service was in the *upper* hangar, sir. By that time he didn't know whether he was coming or going. And that's how it all happened, sir. And I'm extremely sorry about it, sir.'

'You're sorry.' The Commander could not remember ever disliking a man more than he now disliked the Flight Deck Officer. He was overweight, slothful, inefficient and to the Commander looked capable of having designed the accident as a practical joke.

'The whole *mess* shows the Flight Deck Department up in a very poor light. It shows a lack of training, of supervision . . .'

'He was brand new to the ship, sir . . .'

'He can be straight out of the egg, for all I care! I shall expect to see that man up at my table as a defaulter.'

'I don't see how, sir.' The Flight Deck Officer looked uncomfortable, but determined. 'It's in his orders, sir, and in fact in a way he was quite right. It's actually raining now, sir . . .'

'I don't care if it's shitting bricks out there! There must be something in your orders which says he must check the lift is clear *before* . . .'

The Commander abruptly checked himself. His anger was not

gone, but he could see that prosecuting the sentry would turn the whole matter sour. The Flight Deck Officer had come expecting the Commander's wrath, on behalf of his department. He had received it, and that should be an end.

The Commander sighed. 'Well, perhaps there isn't much point in going any further. If somebody had been injured, that would have been a different matter. Perhaps you'll impress on your sentries they must use their heads a bit more in future.'

'I'll certainly do that, sir.'

The Commander had collected the full facts of the after lift debacle before going to see the Captain, because he expected that Tosser, like any other Captain, would require a complete explanation. The Commander anticipated that the Captain would be as indignant and as mortified as himself and he prepared to smooth the incident over. He was surprised to find Tosser in philosophical mood. Far from being annoyed, Tosser was apparently shrugging the accident off.

'We just spoke too soon, that's all, Bob. It was unfortunate, but it doesn't *matter*.'

'I suppose not, sir.'

'It was partly my fault, anyway. When we got near the flight deck, there was a sailor up there messing about with some sort of handle and I shouted at him to get us back to the lower hangar. I meant to say the upper hangar but he took me at my word. So, *down* we went. You can't blame him. It must be a bit of a shock to see your Captain and two senior-looking sin bosuns suddenly appearing out of the depths, eh?'

The Commander swallowed. 'How did the Chaplain of the Fleet take it?'

'Oh, he was a bit put out, but he saw the funny side of it. We ought to be grateful to him that the whole thing didn't degenerate into a Fred Karno comic. It wasn't far off, at that. But he did tell me a funny thing. Did you happen to notice what the next lines of that psalm were, as we were going up and down?'

'No, sir?'

' "They are carried up to the heaven, and down again to the deep: their souls melteth away because of the trouble." Bloody appropriate, I thought it.'

Tosser slapped his knee and bent over and bellowed his laughter

75

at the carpet. But the Commander could not be consoled. By now, the news would be spreading that *Leviathan* was still up to her old tricks, that she was still mocking the men who served in her. He and the Captain would be pitied, on a day when they should have been proud. Recalling that scene in the hangar, the Commander felt his stomach knotting in agony, and his hands clenched in an involuntary spasm of shame and humiliation. Even he had to admit that such a thing could only have happened in *Leviathan*.

The Captain had been watching his face. 'Oh come on, Bob, don't take it to heart so. It wasn't anybody's *fault*. It was just one of those things. It could have happened to anybody.'

But, the Commander thought, it happened to us. He wondered at Tosser's resilience. How could he treat it so lightly? Did nobody else feel anything for the ship? Was he the only one who was ashamed? *Leviathan*'s commissioning service would be one of the stories of the year. His and the Captain's contemporaries at Dartmouth would be relating the story, with their blend of malice and affection, for months to come. And the Captain thought it just one of those things.

Turning away from the Captain, he came face to face with Annabel. Once more they exchanged a look of keen, authentic sympathy. But this time the Commander dropped his eyes. He was now ashamed of the weakness he had betrayed in the hangar. He had allowed a stranger to trespass and though he was aware that she was aching to speak to him, he tried to brush past. But she stopped him.

'Don't go. I just wanted to say how sorry I am about what happened at that service. It was the most awful thing to have happened.'

Her straw hat was tilted back on her head. It had a black silk ribbon tied loosely in a floppy bow at her throat. The effect was extraordinarily gay and carefree. She was clearly enjoying her occasion but she had, the Commander remembered, been the only sympathetic face he had seen in that hangar. It was boorish and unreasonable of him to try and ignore her.

'It's very kind of you to say that.' He found that he could only repeat the Captain's words. 'It was just one of those things. It doesn't really matter.'

'But it *did*.' She had seen his face, then, and now, when he remembered it. 'After all the hard work you must have put in.'

The Commander laughed, genuinely relieved; her concern seemed to lighten his own. 'Well, it's all over now. Are you being looked after? Somebody getting you something to drink? Some coffee, or something?'

'Oh yes, thank you. Jimmy Galbraith brought me in his party.'

'Who?'

'James Galbraith. He's the air staff officer on the C-in-C Home Fleet's Staff.'

'I see.' The Commander had never heard of him. He felt the first twinges of jealousy. Annabel's naval acquaintance, through her late husband, was much wider than he had supposed. But there had been nothing to prevent him inviting her to *Leviathan*'s Commissioning as his guest. It had simply never occurred to him. Once more, the Commander was conscious of an opportunity lost.

'One day you must come on board in *my* party.'

'I will. I'd like that very much.'

The Captain's Secretary was approaching them, carrying two cups of coffee, and looking quizzically from the Commander to Annabel. The Commander hastened to change the subject convincingly.

'What did *you* think of that episode in the hangar, Scratch?'

The Secretary leaned back, as far as the coffee cups would permit him, and raised his eyebrows in a gesture of despairing resignation. 'What the hell can you expect? If there's any way that things *can* go wrong in this ship, you can be sure they *will*. What about your divisions on Sunday, Bob? Are we going to get through them without some frightful drama?'

'Of course we are.'

The Commander spoke more confidently than he felt, but his confidence genuinely returned on Sunday morning, when he stepped out of the island door on to the flight deck and the spectacle of *Leviathan*'s ship's company falling in for divisions made him catch his breath, and stand, and look about him for a few moments, astonished and pleased.

Even he would not have believed that the great ship carried so many men. *Leviathan*'s divisions formed a regiment of white caps and blue uniforms which stretched away down the flight deck for a hundred yards on either side of where the Commander was standing. The Gunner's Party had placed metal markers on the flight deck beforehand, but many of the sailors were unfamiliar with their positions: the Gunner himself and the Chief GI booted and gaitered, marched critically to and fro across the flight deck, marshalling the divisions into their places, moving up a rank there, dropping back a rank here, so that when the Captain mounted his small dais he would see the divisions in an exact geometrical design of two halves, each facing him, just as the Gunnery Officer had planned it. Meanwhile, the flight deck was a hubbub of shouted commands, and the shuffling of feet as the sailors took up the dressing in their ranks, and the voices of divisional chief petty officers calling the rolls.

The Commander mounted the dais to receive reports. In front of him the divisions hardened into their set-piece patterns and the flight deck was quieter while the divisional officers made their own inspections. Soon they began to march one by one towards the Commander, forming a small queue in front of him which moved up steadily as the officer at the head of the queue reported his division, saluted, and marched away. *Leviathan* had so many divisions that the Commander had not attempted to memorise them all. A few paces behind, the Gunner stood with a list, to report when all the divisions were correct.

When it seemed to him that every division must be ready the Commander waited for the Gunner to make his report. The flight deck had become still and expectant, while the ship's company awaited the Captain's arrival. Sounds floated from the world outside the ship. The noise of a motorboat travelled slowly up the starboard side. The ferry secured with a clanking of chains ahead of the ship. A train rumbled into the harbour station. Seagulls dipped and swooped over the after edge of the flight deck and their squabbling cries came up from the quarterdeck below.

The Gunner had not reported. Behind him the Commander could sense the row of unattached officers, who had no divisions, growing restless, knowing that the delay had lasted long enough.

Still the Gunner had not reported. The Commander spoke over his shoulder.

'Gunner!'

'Sir?' The penetrating timbre of the Gunner's hoarse *sotto voce* whisper seemed to carry all over the flight deck.

78

'All correct?'

'No, sir! First Part of Starboard Watch of Seamen not reported yet, sir!'

'Who's their divisional officer?'

'L'tenant *Bird* sir!'

The Commander knew at once what had happened. Bird had lingered too long over his inspection. By the time he had finished, every other division had been reported and he had been unable to face the long, terrifying march up to the Commander on his own, while the other divisions were silent and motionless. So he had omitted his report, hoping that it would not be noticed. But for the Gunner's list, he would have been successful.

It was a very human omission and for a moment the Commander was tempted to let it pass. But these were the first divisions of the new commission.

'Lieutenant Bird?'

'Sir!' The thin, lonely voice answered from one of the seamen's divisions to the Commander's left.

'Report your division please, Mr Bird.'

'Aye aye, sir.'

Unhappily Bird's shoes had steel-tipped heels and in the stillness of the flight deck every step of his solitary march towards the Commander was advertised by the ringing taps of his heels on the metal deck plates. As he marched round the nearest division and approached the Commander, the other officers standing behind, safe and glad of their own obscurity, knew with a sudden collective premonition that Bird was about to fumble his sword drill.

The movements of halting while carrying a sword were at best awkward and unnatural. Even practised and confident officers had difficulty. When Bird halted in front of the Commander his sword slipped from his hand and swung away to the full extent of the sword-belt, while the scabbard tip grated noisily across the deck. Still keeping his eyes to the front, Bird bent from the knees, groped for his sword, and grasped it, only to lose it again. Again he groped, and again he missed. At last he looked down, took the sword in both hands and held it upright, before straightening to make his report to the Commander.

But the Commander was merciless. 'Next time you report your division call them to attention first. They're still standing at ease.'

79

If Bird's halt had been bad, his marching-off was a travesty of sword-drill, such as Whale Island instructors dreamed of, to demonstrate how a sword should not be handled. Again the movement was an awkward one. Bird saluted and turned, stepped off and hitched up his sword, trying to shift his grip from the hilt to the scabbard. The sword clattered along the flight deck and swung between Bird's legs, forcing him to halt, while a gasp of dismay rustled along the line of officers behind the Commander.

When Bird bent to retrieve it, the sword became possessed of an impish volition of its own, pivoting around on the radius of the sword-belt with every frantic movement of Bird's hips as he tried to catch it. By the time Bird had retrieved his sword and returned to his place, the Commander was sincerely sorry he had ever summoned him to report his division, and had made a mental note to dispense with the Gunner's list in future.

The Captain had been watching from the top of the ladder which led down to the island door.

'You'd better tell Guns to give that young man some instruction in sword-drill, Bob. I've never *seen* such an exhibition.'

'I'll do that, sir.'

The Captain paused on his way down the ladder and peered out of a scuttle. 'By God, they make a splendid sight, don't they, Bob? Do you know, I'd no idea there were so many of them.'

They divided the inspection between them, because it was physically impossible for one man to walk round all the divisions in a reasonable time. The Captain and the Heads of Departments inspected the forward half, while the Commander with the deputy heads of departments, known collectively as the 'Second Eleven', walked aft.

The Commander had often suspected that the average sailor disliked the prospect of divisions more than he disliked the event itself. Once he was up on the flight deck amongst his fellows, rigged in all the finery of his best uniform and gold badges, the sailor secretly enjoyed the vanity of a parade. Long practise had taught the Commander how best to indulge the sailors' vanity. He must walk quickly, because he had nearly a thousand men to inspect, but he must not walk so quickly that he gave the ship's company the impression that he was only going through the motions of inspecting them. Furthermore, this was the closest he had been to most of them and he knew that they wished to have a good look at him.

Nobody except ratings actually on watch or on essential duty was excused divisions, and thus the Commander was able to see for the first time the full complements of many special and esoteric trades, the shipwrights and the ordnance artificers, the blacksmith and the plumber and the painter, the photographers, the meteorological observers, the safety equipment ratings, the physical training instructors and the regulating petty officers, the sailmaker and the navigating officer's tanky. To a layman's eye, *Leviathan*'s divisions would have appeared as a homogeneous body of men, so many platoons of identical sailors, but the Commander was sensitive to the departmental differences and jealousies which separated the branches. Though they were formed up in adjacent divisions, the cooks and the stewards, the office writers and the stores ratings, had nothing in common with the naval air mechanics and the aircraft handlers. The engineer mechanics and engine-room artificers were divided not only by many decks but also by an utterly disparate way of life from the signalmen and the telegraphists. The seaman branch itself was divided and sub-divided and included gunlayers, quarters armourers, boom-trained ratings, underwater weapon and control ratings and radar plotters. There was no longer any such rating in the Navy as a plain ordinary seaman.

The Commander noticed, as he walked round, the scarcity of medal ribbons. Some of the senior chief petty officers had the full multi-coloured display of the '39–45 Star and campaign medals. Here and there a sailor wore the blue and yellow ribbons of Korea, or the red and white Naval General Service medal, but most of the ship's company, and their officers, wore no medals at all. The war had been over for twenty years and this was a new generation, who had never known it.

The Commander expected the appearance of the First Part of the Starboard Watch of Seamen to match his opinion of their divisional officer. He was amazed, and repentant, when he saw that their turn-out was well above the average, indeed much smarter than either of the two seamen's divisions he had already inspected. Bird had been quite right to linger: appreciating and commenting upon a smart appearance were more important than reprimanding slovenliness. As he followed the Commander along the ranks, Bird's own demeanour showed that he was clearly anxious the Commander should not miss a single point in his men's favour. The Commander acknowledged his own mistake; he had expected Bird to be a sawdust divisional officer, who barely knew his men's names and who took no action on their behalf except a token word of recommendation or mitigation when they appeared as requestmen or defaulters at the Commander's table. The Commander began to wonder whether Bird was one of that tragically-handicapped minority of officers, some of whom were passed over every year, who could only show their best face to their sailors and who always appeared at a disadvantage before their senior officers.

Paradoxically, the Commander yearned to find fault with Bird's division. He passed along ranks of shining shoes, neatly-cut hair, clean cap-ribbons and smartly brushed uniforms, and his resentment mounted. He was not appeased until he reached the second last man in the rear rank. The Commander could not remember the precise permitted measurement of the tapes tied in a bow in front of a sailor's jumper, but he knew the correct length when he saw it, and this man's tapes were too long.

The Commander pointed them out with relief. 'Tapes far too long.'

'Aye aye, sir.'

'But apart from that, it was a very good turn-out indeed. I congratulate you and your division.'

Bird saluted. 'Thank you, sir.'

The Commander had actually begun his inspection of the next division before he faltered in his step, realising that Bird had almost certainly trapped him with the oldest trick in the book: one small fault was deliberately left for the inspecting officer to find. He had used the trick himself, when the inspecting officer was new to him, or was suspected of being a tartar; it was, in an obscure way, a left-handed compliment to the inspecting officer. Once again, the Commander acknowledged that he might have been mistaken about Bird.

He had judged his inspection carefully, to finish at the same time as the Captain, and while he stood the ship's company at ease, the Captain climbed on to the dais and blew experimentally into the microphone. The sound of his breath, amplified many times, travelled round the flight deck in a series of short, shattering roars. Commander (L), standing beside the Commander, stiffened indignantly; it was a permanent source of grief to him that nobody in the executive branch, least of all senior post captains, ever completely trusted electrical equipment. The Commander heard Dai Bach muttering to himself. '. . . Why must they always *blow* on it like that? It's not a *birthday* cake . . .'

Just as at the Dedication Service, the Captain began nervously but found confidence as he continued.

'First, let me apologise for not inspecting you all today. As you can see, it's just not possible. The Commander and I are going to take it in turns so at least I shall see everybody every other divisions. I also intend to mention the best turned-out divisions in each half. Today, in my half, it was the Royal Marines. In the Commander's half, that's the after half of the flight deck, it was the First Part of Starboard Watch of Seamen.'

A murmur of approval passed down the line of officers standing behind the Captain. Delicious Joe whispered in the Commander's ear. 'That was generously done, Bob.'

The Commander scowled. Clearly, everybody believed that he commended Bird's division out of remorse, as some form of apology for that nightmare sword-drill. That was not so. Bird's division had simply been the best turned-out. No other considerations mattered.

'. . . Now I want to tell you something about our programme for the future as far as it's been settled. First, let me dispel any buzzes about where we're doing our work-up. We are not, repeat *not*, working up in the Mediterranean. We should have gone out there but now for some reason we're not. We shall do our work-up here at home, and we shall not be going out to the Med at least until the autumn.

'We shall go down harbour at eight o'clock tomorrow morning and secure to a buoy, where we'll embark avgas. After that we'll carry on out into the Channel and spend a week at sea for a shakedown cruise. We'll do drills, damage control exercises, a full power trial, radar calibrations, and anything else that occurs to us. We'll spend next week-end here and the following week we shall embark some aircraft from shore to test our catapults and flight deck machinery. The next Monday after that we'll embark our squadrons and our *real* work-up will begin. We're expected to be worked-up and fully operational in time for a big NATO exercise in the North Atlantic in July, followed by a visit to Norway and Sweden and then we'll be back here to give summer leave sometime in August. So much for our programme.'

The Commander foresaw that Tosser MacTigue would be popular with the ship's company. He was not clever, but that was no disadvantage; cleverness often encouraged an officer to be witty, and witticisms often turned to the deadly sin of sarcasm. A sailor could accept a plain reproof. Sarcasm rendered him defenceless and resentful. The ship's company, with their infallible talent for summing up an officer, already knew that Tosser was a little nervous and awed by the ship. But so were they all. Tosser had a directness and an honesty which appealed to the sailors: they would know how he would react, what would please him and what anger him. The Captain had four stripes on his sleeve, but he was one of the boys.

'... I'm not going to beat about the bush with you today. The last commission left this ship with a very bad name. There's no point in glossing that over. But different ships, different cap tallies, and the last commission has nothing to do with us. This is a new commission now, with fresh faces and a fresh way of looking at things. We're the biggest ship in the Navy and we can be the best. You can be sure that the rest of the Navy will be very curious to see how we get on. I think it's fair to say they'll be expecting us to make a balls-up of everything we do.'

The Captain pitched his voice a little higher, so that it carried boldly and clearly across the flight deck.

'But I suggest to you that we disappoint them all! I propose that we give the rest of the Navy the biggest shock of their lives by making this ship work and work well. It can be done. I *know* it can be done. But if it is to be done it will need a hundred per cent effort from every one of us, all the time. This is a big ship and people tend to disappear in it. It's very hard to resist the feeling that nobody will ever know what you're doing, that you're just another ant in a big ant-hill and nobody will ever notice a few ants more or less. That's not true. Never get the feeling that your efforts are not being appreciated, because I can assure you they are. If we all give our best there's no reason why this commission shouldn't be the best any ship ever had. I believe that. It's up to all of us to make it so. That's all I have to say to you today.'

Just as the Captain finished speaking, the safety valves on the auxiliary boiler lifted and a plume of steam billowed out from the top of the funnel. For more than a minute every other sound was drowned in the roar of escaping steam. As the Senior Engineer later explained to the Commander, the Captain's speech had been relayed over the ship's broadcast and the stoker petty officer on watch had been straining to hear the Captain's voice over the noise of the boiler-room fans. He had not noticed a reduction in steam demand until it was too late.

It was an uncommon error, which would probably never happen again throughout the commission. But to the Commander, by now hyper-sensitive to any symptom of disaster, it was as though *Leviathan* herself had listened to the Captain and promptly answered him with one gigantic hoot of derision.

Early the next morning, on the day *Leviathan* was due to go to sea, the Commander was woken by the sound of his cabin telephone ringing. He switched on his bedside reading light and looked at his watch: just after four o'clock in the morning, and improbable that anyone genuinely wanted him; more than likely it was a wrong number.

'Commander here?'

'... Bob, this is *Chief!* We've had a bit of trouble down here. The same old thing with bloody gauge glasses. Some maniac's run amok with a wheel spanner and smashed every gauge in the place!'

Commander (E) was talking rapidly, breathlessly, his words tumbling out as though speaking to the Commander provided him with a safety valve for his feelings.

The Commander blinked, and shook his head. 'I'm very sorry, Chief, but what was that again?'

'Some *maniac*, Bob! Smashed up all our gauges! Exactly the same as last commission! The whole place is a bloody shambles!'

'Have you told the Captain?'

'Just about to. I thought you ought to know.'

The Commander shut his eyes, and slowly massaged his eyelids with the thumb and forefinger of one hand. 'D'you want me to come down?'

'Not unless you feel like it. If you want to see the results of all this fine talk about it being a new commission ...'

'I think I will come down.'

'All right, just as you like. It'll shake you when you see it. He's made a proper job of it this time.'

A sudden doubt crossed the Commander's mind. 'This won't stop us going to sea, will it?'

'No, that's the stupid part about it. It's only one engine-room. We can always go to sea on the other three shafts. I'll see you when you get down. You can have a look for yourself then.'

The Commander got out of bed and put on his uniform jacket and trousers over his pyjamas. He was out of practise; it was a long since he had been shaken in the middle of the night and he still had only the barest grasp of Commander (E)'s message. His actions in getting up and dressing were instinctive responses to the urgency and fury in Commander (E)'s voice. He wound a blue muffler round his throat and tried to make some sense of the telephone call. It seemed to him incomprehensible. Why would anyone smash up the ship's machinery a few hours before she was due to sail? What could be the point of that? He longed to climb back into bed, turn out the light, and imagine that the telephone call had never happened.

He paused on the upper deck to look at the weather. The night was cold for April and a light steady rain was falling. The dockside was bleak and deserted under its yellow metallic lighting. This was the lowest hour of the night. The Commander yawned and straightened his back and then stopped, realising that he had no idea where Commander (E) had been speaking from. He could be anywhere in that labyrinth of machinery compartments.

The upper deck was empty in both directions. The Commander was standing, perplexed and annoyed by his own stupidity, when a sailor in blue overalls and a blue jockey cap climbed up one of the ladders from below. He was wearing gym shoes and carried a torch. He had a Damage Control armband on one sleeve and the name 'Dusty' in white paint across the top pocket of his overalls.

'Just a minute there, do you happen to know where they're having trouble with the gauge glasses?'

It was a fantastic question to ask a sailor in the middle of the night but, incredibly, the man knew.

' "B" Engine-room, sir. Down through the workshop flat, sir.'

'Thank you very much.'

The oblong of bright light from the engine-room hatch guided the Commander past the shapes of the lathes and milling machines in the dimly-lit workshop. He climbed down the ladder, feeling himself enveloped in the huge steam pipes which wound and curved about him in their thick white cladding. At the bottom, he heard a cautioning voice.

'Mind the glass! It's all over the deck.'

He turned and looked about him.

The glass had been swept from the centre of the control platform, but drifts of it still lay twinkling and glittering at the edges and in every ledge and projection of the gauge panels. Some of the gauges had been struck with such force that their faces had been driven back into the panel housing. One gauge had been wrenched from its fitting, laid on the step and hammered shapeless. The glass pane over the engine telegraph repeater was starred, and one triangular fragment had fallen out. There were more than a hundred gauges on the instrument panels near the main throttle valves, and not one had been left intact.

Commander (E) was standing by the register desk, with the Senior Engineer, Ben Krieger the senior engine-room watchkeeping lieutenant, and two other watch-keeping lieutenants in overalls. When Commander (E) stepped forward, his feet crunched on the broken glass. A larger segment dislodged itself from the deck plating and splintered in the bilges below.

'Well, what do you think of it, Bob?'

The Commander stared about him. 'It's unbelievable, Chief! He must have been a madman! How did he manage to do it?'

Commander (E) took a heavy wheel spanner from a rack by the desk and stooping, smashed it down so that the polished steel deckplates rang and splinters of loose glass tinkled into the bilges.

'Just like that. You could do all this in ten minutes if you put your mind to it.'

'When did it happen?'

'We don't know exactly. This place was visited by a patrol at three o'clock this morning and again at half past. It was all right then. The first man of the watch below came down here to start raising steam at about ten or five minutes to four. And it had been done by then.'

'You had patrols every half hour?'

Commander (E) smiled tolerantly at the Commander's innocence. 'We've been in this ship a bit longer than you, Bob. We've had this sort of thing before, particularly on nights before we went to sea. There were times last commission when we had sentries in every main machinery space *all night*. But we were optimistic enough to believe that perhaps this commission was going to be different.'

Commander (E)'s voice was bitter, and suddenly he smashed the wheel spanner on the plates again. 'It's so bloody *pointless!* It doesn't stop us going to sea. We can't put steam through this engine-room without gauges but there's nothing to stop us going to sea on the other three shafts . . .'

'The others are all right?'

'Oh yes. To keep us in harbour he'd have to do this to all four engine-rooms. That would have been stretching his luck too far. All this means is just a lot of extra work for everybody. It doesn't *prove* anything. It's not even original. Lots of ships have had this sort of thing. As I said, *we've* even had it before.'

'But why would anyone do this, that's what baffles me.'

'Family trouble. Chip on his shoulder. Didn't want to go to sea today and leave his wife behind for a week. Crazy mixed-up childhood. Bloody mindedness. Who knows, and who the hell cares?'

Commander (E) kicked viciously at a splinter of glass and sent it spinning across the control platform, to shatter against the opposite bulkhead. He seemed to tire of the conversation and gather himself to face the prospect of organising repairs.

'Senior, you'd better start getting all this cleared up. Find out what we've got in the way of spare gauges. See if we can't rig up some kind of jury rig so that we can put steam through here.'

The Senior Engineer and Ben Krieger were looking at the devastated instrument panels with expressions of utter hopelessness. The tiers of smashed gauges recalled their bitterest memories of the last commission. It seemed that nothing had changed, in spite of all their hard work, all their hopes and all their promises: this was precisely where they had left off before. Their expressions wrung the Commander's heart. He resolved that he would find and punish the man who had done this.

He noticed that the officers' manner contrasted oddly with that of the Chief ERA of the engine-room and the rest of his steaming watch who were standing, curiously remote and detached, in a group by the main throttle valves. They too were looking at the wreckage, but with closed, indifferent faces, as though the matter were entirely for the officers to settle and concerned themselves not at all.

Commander (E) nodded towards the ladder. 'Let's go and see the Captain, Bob.'

Tosser was sitting on the edge of his bunk in his dressing-gown, slowly rubbing his knees and looking as if he had been waiting for them since Commander (E)'s first telephone call. The Commander recognised his expression. Tosser was sleepy and bewildered and, like himself, not sure whether he had heard the message aright.

'Well, Chief?'

'Well, sir . . .' Commander (E) briefly described the discovery of the damage, its extent and his plans to repair it.

'When do you expect to finish?'

'It's very difficult to say, sir, until we've made a proper estimate of the damage. We'll certainly have to go down to the buoy on three shafts, but I hope that by the time we've finished embarking petrol, which should be about tea time, we'll be able to try something on four. That's with luck.'

'All right. I'll draft a signal now to C-in-C and the Admiralty, tell them what's happened. Do you want dockyard assistance?'

'Probably, sir. And we'll need a whole lot of spare gauges brought up in a hurry.'

'I'll mention that in the signal. Now I expect you want to get on with it.'

When Commander (E) had gone, the Captain looked directly at the Commander.

'*Now.* How are we going to catch this little bugger, Bob?'

The Commander cleared his throat. He was beginning to feel the after-effects of his sudden awakening. The skin felt tight and drawn on his face, and his eyes were aching. 'First, I'm going to have a wash and a shave, and then I'm going to sit down and find out who was up and about, why, what they were doing, and why they were doing it.'

'Do you want the police in? The local CID are probably used to this sort of thing . . .'

'Oh no, sir!' The Commander's rejection was a pure reflex action. This was the ship's private shame. He could not bear to make it public.

The Captain looked doubtful. 'We'll have to tell the dockyard police in any case, Bob. For all we know it might have been some intruder in the yard. Though that's very unlikely. Then there's the press . . .'

'Surely not, sir!'

'You can't keep this sort of thing entirely under your hat, Bob, you really can't. You've got to say something. If you stall them off it only makes them more curious. I'll put enough detail in my signal to let somebody up at the Admiralty push out some form of statement. And we'll hope for the best. This kind of sabotage is not a novelty any longer so we'll probably escape the front page. Now, off you go, let me know how you get on.'

The Commander's plan of action was a simple one. He intended to interview every man who had had any reason for moving about the ship that morning and any others who might have been seen on deck between three-thirty and four-thirty. Sailors were not normally expert dissemblers. The Commander was sure he would know his man as soon as he saw him.

But as so often in *Leviathan*, a simple basic proposition became confused by weight of numbers. The number of men who had legitimate reasons for moving about the ship early on the morning before she put to sea proved on investigation to be very much larger than the Commander had expected. The gauges had been smashed at a time when the middle watchmen were preparing to send messengers to shake their reliefs of the morning watch. On this particular morning, the normal auxiliary watch were augmented to the full steaming watch below, a total of nearly seventy men. At the same time the communications staff, the hangar and flight deck sentries, the damage control patrol and some of the electrical department were in watches. Others, including the galley and gangway staffs and a few late-returning liberty-men, also had reasons for moving about the ship. There were also scores of ratings whose existence and duties the Commander had forgotten: the gyro compass artificer, the aviation fuelling parties, the steering gear and turbo-generator artificers, and the radar plot and maintenance ratings, all had valid reasons for making an early start that morning. The ship which had seemed so deserted and lifeless to the Commander on his way towards the engine-room at four o'clock had at that very time actually been swarming with men. Summing up, the Commander could count nearly three hundred men who had been up, awake, and theoretically able to damage the gauges. Leaving aside all but the engine-room and electrical department ratings, there were still more than a hundred men who must have been passing and repassing the workshop flat while the gauges were being smashed.

It seemed scarcely credible to the Commander that none of the men he interviewed had seen anything out of the ordinary. Somewhere there must have been an empty bunk, an empty hammock which should have been occupied, an unexplained absentee from a watch or a working party, or an extra face which should not have been there. There *must* have been something, even if it was only an unfamiliar silhouette at the end of a passageway or at the bottom of a ladder. But the further the Commander probed, the more he felt himself entangled in a conspiracy of indifference. A malignant cell had broken loose in the ship that morning. Instead of rejecting it, the other cells were combining to ignore and so to shelter it. By breakfast-time the Commander had interviewed more than fifty ratings. None of them had any information to offer and none of them, he was sure, was the man.

The Commander ate a solitary breakfast in his usual place at the end of the main wardroom table. His breakfast was a ritual meal, arranged and supervised by the Chief Steward himself who knew that he could perform no greater service for the ship's company than to start the Commander's day with a satisfactory breakfast. The Chief Steward saw to it that no other places were laid near the Commander's chair, that there was a copy of *The Times* in the Commander's paper-stand, that his napkin was in position, and that there was a steward available to take away the Commander's plate, fill his coffee cup and bring him more toast and marmalade as necessary. The Chief Steward was normally admirably successful, but this morning his ministrations were too late. The Commander's day was already irretrievably disturbed. Nowhere in his investigation had he surprised the least sign of personal involvement. The ship's company were tacitly permitting one of their number to damage the ship; the investigation was apparently a matter which concerned only the man himself and whichever member of the wardroom made it his business to investigate.

At eight o'clock the work of the harbour paused for a few minutes at the spectacle of *Leviathan* at last putting to sea. Dockyard tugs drew the great ship away from the jetty she had dominated for so long. The dockyard buildings she had dwarfed reappeared in their proper proportions once her bulk had been withdrawn. The early rain had cleared to a mild windy April morning. Great white clouds sailed across a blue sky, sending harlequin patches of sunlight and shadow racing along *Leviathan*'s crowded sides. From the bridge the sailors lining the edges of the flight deck looked like miniature figurines, a row of tiny blue and white dolls on a huge green table. With the water churning under her square stern, her numeral pennants streaming in the wind, and the bugle notes saluting the flags of the Commander-in-Chief and the Admiral Superintendent, *Leviathan* pointed her massive hammer-shaped bows towards the sea.

The first voyage of the new commission was an anticlimactical trip to a buoy outside the harbour. By nine o'clock the aviation fuel tanker had been secured alongside and the Captain's signal had had its predictable impact ashore. From the landing stage, a fleet of motor boats ferried senior dockyard managers, officers of the dockyard police and members of the Commander-in-Chief's engineering and operational staffs out to the ship.

Later in the forenoon, the Captain rang the Commander before speaking personally to the Commander-in-Chief over the ship-to-shore radio telephone link.

'I'm just about to speak to the Admiral, Bob. Any news for me to tell him?'

The Commander had been badgered by callers all morning, each one more enfuriatingly sympathetic and with more helpful suggestions than the last. The effort of preserving a front of politeness had made him testy.

'No sir, I'm no further forrard now than I was at four o'clock this morning.'

'I see. Never mind. I'll tell the Admiral we're still working at it. Have you asked Number One how they did it last time?'

'Yes, sir.'

The First Lieutenant had merely confirmed the Commander's own opinion. 'You'll know him when you see him, sir. We didn't actually *find* the fellow last time. He admitted it, as soon as we asked him. We just hadn't asked him before, that was all.'

'He's not still on board, is he?'

'Oh no.' The First Lieutenant chuckled. 'Good gracious me, no. *He's* still serving his two year sentence inside.'

'You don't think we ought to have called in the CID after all, do you?

The First Lieutenant recognised that the Commander was, un-

93

characteristically, asking for reassurance. 'I don't think so, sir. They'd only do what you're doing now and they wouldn't have your local knowledge. It's too late now, anyway. If it's the same Detective Sergeant as last time I know he'd get all shirty because he wasn't called in at the beginning. They like to start when the trail's hot.'

'So do I.'

'So do we all, sir. You think to yourself "Christ, if only I'd been there a minute sooner". Last time I was sure I knew who did it, but it turned out to be somebody else entirely different.'

By lunch-time, the Commander had interviewed every member of the middle and morning watches in the engineering and electrical departments, but he was convinced that he had not yet set eyes on his man. The most important witnesses were the patrolman who had been the last person to see the engine-room undamaged, and the engineer mechanic of the steaming watch below who had been the first to discover the damage. Although they were interviewed three times neither of them varied their stories substantially, and the Commander believed them.

He desperately craved a cigarette during his investigations, but no smoking was allowed anywhere in the ship whilst the avgas tanker was alongside. The aircraft jet engines burned a form of kerosene, less volatile than petrol, but the helicopters and the long-range piston-engined search aircraft used a high octane aviation gasolene, known on board by its service abbreviation of avgas. Avgas was potentially the most dangerous substance on board. It was secreted away, like a source of plague infection, in isolated tanks deep below the water-line and cut off from the rest of the ship by cofferdams of air and water. When it was pumped to the flight deck, avgas was handled as delicately as though it were nitroglycerine by specially-trained working parties equipped with rubber-soled shoes, shielded lighting units and special non-ferrous tools to prevent sparks. Avgas explosions had killed and maimed men in the past, and wrecked whole ships. Compared with avgas, nuclear warheads and the hundreds of tons of high explosive in the ship's magazines were as harmless as butter.

The avgas tanker was slipped after tea and by that time the Commander knew that his enquiries had gone cold. He was now interviewing ratings whose duties rarely took them near the machinery spaces. Some of them indeed were not sure where *Leviathan*'s engine-rooms were. He had not asked any sailor point-blank whether he had seen anything suspicious, knowing that he would at once deny it. But even when he wrapped up his true objective in a screen of common-place questions on when the sailor got up, where he had been and whom he had seen, the Commander had still failed to uncover any information of value. None of *Leviathan*'s ship's company had seen or heard anything suspicious. As the ship was preparing to go to sea again, the Commander went up to the bridge to report his failure.

The Captain was not perturbed. He had never had many expectations that the Commander would find anything.

'Never mind, Bob. We'll keep at it discreetly. Sooner or later he'll overreach himself, and then we'll have him. Have you seen this signal from C-in-C?'

He handed the Commander the signal log. The top signal in it was routine, unclassified, from the Commander-in-Chief to *Leviathan*.

'The very best of luck to you all in your new commission. The Book of Job, chapter forty-one, verses one through six, refer.'

'Job forty-one?' The Commander shook his head. 'I don't know that one.'

'Nor did I, but I've looked it up. It's damned appropriate. The Admiral must have been boning up on his home-work.' The Captain took a Bible from the shelf above the chart table and the Commander saw that there was a marker already in place.

The Captain began to read aloud from the Bible.

'Canst thou draw out leviathan with an hook? or his tongue with a cord which thou lettest down? Canst thou put an hook into his nose? or bore his jaw through with a thorn? Will he make supplications unto thee? will he speak soft words unto thee? Will he make a covenant with thee? wilt thou take him for a servant for ever? Wilt thou play with him as with a bird? or wilt thou bind him for thy maidens? Shall the companions make a banquet of him?'

The companions are here, the Commander thought, but would there be a banquet for them?

The same thought had occurred to the Captain. He put down the Bible and threw his arm round the Commander's shoulders.

95

'We're the companions, Bob, but how about the banquet?'

The Commander smiled. 'How about it, sir.'

For *Leviathan*'s first week at sea, the Commander had prepared a comprehensive and concentrated working-up programme, knowing that the first week was the foundation-stone of the commission. Much depended on the quality of planning and the supervision when the sailors first attempted their drills. Habits, principles and routines firmly laid down in the first week stood a chance of enduring throughout the commission. But if drills were not approached correctly, or were supervised slackly, not carried through to their proper ending, or if mistakes were not pointed out at once, then every evolution would be doubly harder to work up later in the commission.

The Commander acknowledged that *Leviathan* had problems peculiar to herself, but there were still a great many evolutions common to all warships. The ship's company began simply, with exercises and tests of ship knowledge, first-aid drills, changing over emergency steering methods, exercising collision and fog stations, darken ship, man overboard, sending away the sea-boat, mustering and exercising the fire and emergency parties. Later, they graduated to firefighting and damage control on a major scale, exercising spraying the hangars, shoring up damaged bulkheads, rigging emergency lighting circuits, pumping out flooded compartments, counter-flooding to compensate for damage, and closing down the whole ship in defence against nuclear fall-out. Each department took the limelight in turn, the engine-room for the full power trial, the gunnery branch during the 4-inch and bofors shoot at a drogue target, the Royal Marines when the landing parties were sent ashore in the ship's boats, the seamen when laying out the gear for towing and for transferring stores at sea by light and heavy jackstay, while throughout the week the Air Direction and Radar Room crews practised their complicated three-dimensional exercises in detecting, controlling and dispatching aircraft at different heights, speeds and distances from the ship.

From the first day at sea, the Commander found himself battling against the insular departmental outlook of the ship's company. The sailors were all reluctant to look beyond their own branch responsibilities. Most of the evolutions were standard for all HM Ships on commissioning and many of the ship's company, particularly those who had served in the last commission, looked on them as routine, immutable, and certainly not worth fresh thought. This attitude of mind was quickly corrected by the Commander. No exercise was too minor, no drill too obscure, no evolution too routine for him to ignore it; wherever the hands were working, there was the Commander with criticism and encouragement, examining ways of performing the drill in less time and with fewer hands, always challenging 'the way we did it last time'. The First Lieutenant, for instance, disputed the Commander's proposal to cut down the number of men who attended a fire.

'I don't agree with that at all, sir. We don't know how bad the fire is. Any fire is an emergency, sir.'

The Commander held up a hand. 'Half a minute. Let me get my breath back.' The Commander stood with his hands on his hips, taking deep breaths. Evening Quarters had just finished and he had just led a perspiring and cursing ship's company, all wearing gas-masks, at a brisk double round and round the flight deck, while the Royal Marine band played 'You Must Have Been A Beautiful Baby'. The First Lieutenant had brought up the rear, also in a gas-mask, and had run as hard as anyone but the Commander noticed, with annoyance, that Number One was showing no signs of distress.

The Commander shook the perspiration out of his gas-mask. 'I don't think we'll do that again. I agree that a fire is an emergency but most fires are small, at least to start with. The last time I attended a fire exercise there were forty people there. *Forty!* And thirty-eight of them were doing bugger-all except stand about chiyacking and getting in each other's way. If it had been a real fire we would have put it out by sheer weight of numbers. The fire wouldn't have had a chance to breathe!'

'What do you suggest then, sir?'

'Cut the fire party to the absolute minimum. Ten men and one in charge is quite enough. If they need any help they can always sing out for it. And there's no need for all those duty officers to attend a fire.'

'Right, sir. I'll fix it.'

'And another thing. When we went to action stations this morning I noticed a hell of a great chaos on the ladders. Queues of sailors fighting to get up while another mob tried to get down.

Neither of them making much headway. Next time I want you to try a new scheme. Have the starboard side of the ship for those who want to go forrard and the starboard side ladders for those who want to go up. Have the port side for those who want to go aft and port side ladders for those who want to go down. Starboard side forrard and up, port side aft and down. You try it, see how it works.'

'Aye aye, sir.'

Occasionally, the confusion of numbers was compounded by ignorance of the ship's equipment. On his way to watch the first rehearsals of laying out the gear for refuelling at sea, the Commander found the passage leading to the fuelling bay jammed with sailors, standing with their hands in their pockets. The Mate of the Upper Deck and the Chief Bosun's Mate, looking hot and bewildered, were in the centre of the crowd.

'What are all these hands doing here?'

The Mate of the Upper Deck jumped involuntarily at the sound of the Commander's voice. His main responsibility on board was Assistant Direction Officer; Mate of the Upper Deck was a secondary and, in his opinion, very subordinate part of his duties. All the executive officers took turns in supervising fuelling at sea: it was just his horrible luck that he happened to be in charge of the fuelling bay on a morning when the Commander so obviously had a full head of steam.

'They're waiting to hose the haul . . . *haul* in the *hose*-line, sir.'

'By *hand!*'

'Yes, sir.' The Mate of the Upper Deck looked for confirmation at the Chief Bosun's Mate. 'That's the way they did it last commission, sir.'

'I'll bet they didn't! Haven't we got a winch?'

'No, sir.'

'What's that behind that grille there? That looks to me very much like a winch.'

'That's an ammunitioning winch, sir.'

'Couldn't it be used for hauling in the hose-line?'

'I don't think so, sir.'

'You don't think so. I bet it can. Get hold of somebody from the electrical office.'

The electrical officer in charge of high power equipment, which included the disputed winch, was a very young Lieutenant (L), fresh from Cambridge. He was a pale young man, with spectacles and red hair, and he looked to the Commander the sort of fellow who would have been happier as a boffin in a research laboratory. *Leviathan* was his first ship and nothing in his previous academic existence had prepared him for the experience. But he was already finding his feet and had indeed taken the sensible precaution of spending his first fortnight on board touring the ship, sighting every item in his charge and learning its purpose.

'There you are, Simmondson! Come and tell us about this winch!'

Simmondson blushed as he came forward through the crush of sailors. He was not accustomed to being called for his professional opinion so publicly. Nevertheless, he recognised the winch at once.

'It's a winch for refuelling at sea, sir, and for transfer by heavy jackstay when you're not able to use the flight deck. It's got a tally on it somewhere.' Simmondson bent over the winch drum and ran his fingers over the paint-work. 'It looks as if the tally's been painted over, sir. But that's what it's for, sir.'

'Not for ammunitioning?'

'Oh no, sir. All the ammunition winches are two decks below this, sir.'

The Commander bore down on Simmondson, intending to fluster him. 'How do you know that?'

'Because I've checked them, sir.'

'Well done.' The Commander looked at the Mate of the Upper Deck. 'There you are then.'

The Mate of the Upper Deck was not convinced. 'I'm not sure a winch is safe for this, sir. It doesn't give you enough control if something goes wrong.'

'What d'you say to that, Simmondson?'

'This is a special type of winch, sir, with fine adjustments on the controls. And it's self-rendering, sir.'

The Commander beamed at Simmondson. He himself was not sure of the meaning of 'self-rendering', but he recognised a knock-down, unanswerable technical phrase. 'There you are. Self-rendering! We can get rid of all those hands cluttering up the place. How long's this winch been here, Simmondson?'

'Since the ship was built, sir, as far as I know. It's on the original drawings.'

'By God, and all last commission they did it by hand!'

The Air Department had taken only a minor part in the evolutions of the first week. The second week, however, was organised almost entirely for their benefit. As soon as the ship cleared St Catherine's Light on Monday morning six aircraft from shore kept a rendezvous with the ship and the ship's company went to flying stations while the aircraft, flying in pairs, took off and landed again, one after the other, for eight hours a day throughout the week.

The pilots were known as The Clockwork Mice and they were among the most experienced in the Fleet Air Arm. They had already survived more carrier flying than was statistically probable and they were each respectively the only survivors of their original training classes still actively flying. They had all carried out more than five hundred deck landings, and one of them had completed over a thousand. Years of practise had refined their deck landing techniques to a pitch where they could not only guarantee a correct landing every time but they could select a particular arrester wire as requested.

The Commander met the Clockwork Mice in the wardroom and found them theatrically bored, cynical, and quite uninterested in the ship or her officers. To them, one aircraft carrier was much like another: the flight deck drill was good in some, bad in others. Their lives, they assured the Commander, were heavily insured. All they aske dof the ship's officers was that they should have their arrester wires tensioned and their ship heading approximately into the wind, with a modicum of wind speed over the deck. The Clockword Mice were not disturbed if the mirror landing sight failed while they were on their final approach, nor did they fret if there was no batsman to guide them on in its place. Except perhaps in rough weather or in poor visibility, the Clockwork Mice regarded such deck landing aids as irrelevant distractions. After a flight deck mishap which would have had younger pilots sweating with fear, the Clockwork Mice merely passed, and flew round again, and again, and if necessary yet again, until the flight deck crew were ready. And if a defect had ever occurred in their aircraft they would not have stayed to investigate but would have ejected at once, and would have been rude to Commander (Air) if the seaguard helicopter had not been on the spot to pick them up the moment they hit the water.

The Clockwork Mice only showed signs of irritation when they were delayed on the catapult. Waiting to be catapulted was a nervous period for any pilot, however experienced. It was a time when his every nerve and muscle were braced for the launch, anticipating the violent acceleration along the track and the rapid sequence of control corrections which would be necessary as soon as the aircraft was airborne. Nothing disturbed a pilot's concentration more than to be ready in body and mind for launching and then to receive a thumbs-down signal from the flight deck and to be forced to relax while his aircraft was manhandled off the catapult and transferred to the other.

Both *Leviathan*'s catapults gave constant trouble during the flight deck training week. The delays were not serious, because only two aircraft were operating at a time and one catapult could normally be kept serviceable while the other was repaired. But the signs were ominous for the future, when the squadrons would be embarked and when both catapults would be essential to launch sorties at the combined rate of three or four aircraft every minute.

The catapult defects precipitated the first direct clash between Commander (Air) and Commander (E). The row had been brewing all week and finally flared into the open during the Heads of Departments meeting, held on Saturday morning, when the ship had anchored for the week-end.

The Commander did not pretend to understand the technical details of the argument. For once he found himself in the position of a mere spectator while the exchanges waxed warmer and warmer. His own sympathies lay with Chief, because he mistrusted Commander (Air)'s motives. Commander (Air) worked as hard as any officer on board but the Commander suspected that he did so only for reasons of personal advancement, because a successful carrier commission brought almost certain promotion for her Commander (Air). The Commander himself wished *Leviathan* to be successful for her own sake, as a gift to the gods. Commander (Air) only looked upon her as a possible promotion platform.

Commander (Air), or Wings as he was known on board, was still a handsome man, but his good looks were fading. His blond

101

hair was receding, his lean cheeks becoming chubby. Once, as a young pilot, his photograph had appeared in a magazine feature on the Fleet Air Arm. It had been the high point of his life. He was frightened by the deterioration in his appearance and his reflexes; envy sometimes made him rude and harsh towards younger pilots. He could be charming, when he wished, and consequently he was almost always disliked by ship's companies, who knew a Popularity Jack when they saw one. He was jealous but also contemptuous of Dartmouth officers like the Commander, not realising that they could, and would, destroy him without even noticing what they had done. He himself had joined the Navy on a pilot's short service commission but on being offered a permanent commission he had transferred eagerly to the General List. He was one of the few pilots who had commanded their own ships; his last appointment had been as captain of a frigate and he had commanded her for eighteen months without driving her ashore or colliding with another ship – an achievement which few modern destroyer or frigate captains in the Navy could claim. He was unaware that he had already reached his ceiling in the Service and his term in command had whetted his ambition. He believed that his record as a commanding officer, if it were added to a successful Air Group in *Leviathan*, would assure him of post captain's rank. Ambition had made Commander (Air) intolerant, suspicious, impatient of delays, and capable of spreading malicious gossip to harm his contemporaries. He saw Commander (E)'s difficulties with the catapults as a deliberate attempt to thwart him.

'... You've had eight months to get those boosters sorted out, Chief. Eight bloody months! And we're still having trouble. Neither of them did more than three launches on the trot last week without going US. The starboard catapult hasn't been serviceable since Thursday night!'

'Well, what of it!' Commander (E) was well used to defending his department against the attacks of executive officers, although his opponents were seldom as sarcastic or as persistent as Commander (Air). 'You can't expect them to spend that time in dockyard hands and then work perfectly straight off the bat. That's what the working-up period is *for*, to sort these things out.'

'And even when the boosters *were* working, the drill wasn't all that hot.'

'Well, for Christ's sake, what d'you expect? They're all as green as grass!' In the past, Commander (E) had listened resentfully to Commander (Air)'s sneers at the Commander. Now, his combative instincts were rising. He welcomed the opportunity to put this jumped-up cab-driver in his place. 'Your fly-boys have *three months* to practise their precious little party tricks. My boys get one *week*, and you expect them to be on top line before they've even had that week. They're only bloody human! It takes weeks to get catapults and their crews on top line.'

'But there's no plan or system about anything you do. As fast as you come up and announce that everything's OK again, something else goes wrong.'

Commander (E) rolled his eyes towards the deckhead, as though he were confronted by a supreme example of Air Group idiocy. 'I keep telling you, Wings, though you seem to be too *thick* to take it in, you *cannot* do maintenance work as an evolution. This is a basic fact of engineering practice. Nor can you repair defects to a strict time schedule. It just doesn't happen like that. I wish to God it did!'

'*I* think it can.'

'I'm *telling* you it can't! And if you're upset about last week then you've got some rough times ahead of you, mate. You're going to spend hours chewing your nails up in that little chicken coop of a Flyco, I can promise you.'

Commander (Air) had a sulky look on his face. 'We'll see about that.'

Commander (E) took the implication at once. 'If by that you mean you'll be complaining to the Captain about the state of the catapults, then you're wasting your time. I can prove to him in two minutes that we're doing our best. *He's* a reasonable man, at least.'

Commander (E) made one last attempt to mollify his oponent. 'Just take my word for it, Wings, I know it's bloody annoying but we are doing our best. Do you think we *like* it when both catapults keep going US on us as fast as we can mend them?'

'I don't accept that you're doing your best.'

Commander (E) sat back in his chair. 'Well then, you can just go and take a running fuck at a rolling doughnut.'

The Commander had been prepared to support Chief if Wings

had made some outrageous remark about the ship, but he now saw that Chief was quite competent to look after himself. He made a mental note that if he himself ever had a point at issue with Commander (E), he must avoid the direct frontal attack.

When the meeting broke up, the other Heads of Departments, looking at Commander (Air)'s face, expected him to take his case to the Captain at once but when the Commander next saw the Captain he did not mention the argument over the catapults. Wings' certainty that he was in the right had evidently left him. The Captain spoke only of the fortnight just past.

'What did you think of it all, Bob?'

'It wasn't too bad, sir. Some things could have been improved, but I've known much worse.'

'I'm glad you said that. Because I thought that considering everything it was a cracking good start.'

The Commander caught the oddly defensive note in the Captain's voice. He conceded that Tosser, too, was out of practice and needed reassurance. There would be a hundred minor matters, the addressing and classification of signals, the ship's routine, even the handling of the ship, which must still make the Captain pause and think. In a month's time the Captain would do them automatically, but now he was still feeling his way.

The Commander had deliberately understated his opinion of the first fortnight of the commission. In spite of departmental rivalries, he believed that somewhere in the turmoil of those two weeks, in the mess of ropes and water and hoses and the eddying shambling bodies of men, a tiny part of all his hopes had been born. He could not point to anything tangible. His only evidence was a gleam in an eye, a back bent willingly, a sailor standing on his toes ready to move, or a valuable suggestion from an unexpected quarter. He could not say that the companions had begun their banquet, but he believed that at least they had laid the places.

7

'Any more developments about those gauge glasses, sir?'

The Commander's brows knitted. He did not like to be reminded of the subject. 'No, nothing yet.'

The First Lieutenant skipped a pace, and fell in step again. 'Ah well, I expect something will turn up.'

'It will.'

The Commander and the First Lieutenant were walking on the flight deck on Sunday evening, half an hour before sunset. *Leviathan* was anchored at Spithead, swinging to a light westerly wind and an east-running tide. Ahead of the ship a red sunset wash had spread across the sky and astern, to the east, grey and honey-coloured and violet clouds were massing, bringing the night with them. In this last abnormally clear light of the day, landmarks stood out with striking clarity – to port the houses and the pier of Ryde, to starboard the submarine escape training tower at Gosport and the power station in Old Portsmouth, and further astern on the starboard quarter the big wheel of Southsea funfair.

Many of the ship's company were also taking the air on the flight deck, some of them walking up and down, in groups and in couples. By the island, five or six deck-hockey players were flicking a rope puck from one to another with amazing dexterity. Sunlight burst through the western cloud and flooded the flight deck with such golden radiance that the running and walking figures were startlingly illuminated, their features picked out in relief with the glowing solidity and detail of a Flemish painting.

The Commander looked down at the flight deck as he walked, studying it and marvelling at such a monument to the naval constructor's abhorrence of an empty space. From a distance *Leviathan*'s flight deck appeared to be a featureless metal plain but a man actually walking upon it had to pick his way between arrester wires and the shrouded metal spools which housed them, crash barrier stanchions, and bomb-lift hatches, and fuelling connections, and coiled firefighting hoses, and parked flight deck vehicles. Every yard of the deck was recessed for deck rings or for

105

retractable prewetting water connections, and every junction of the deck plates felt uneven and rutted under foot. To the unwary pedestrian, *Leviathan*'s flight deck was as difficult walking as a ploughed field.

The First Lieutenant wondered whether to pursue the topic of the smashed gauge glasses. There had been a touch of malice in his question. He knew very well that there had been no fresh developments. The saboteur had still not been discovered. The First Lieutenant had heard that the opinion was growing amongst the Admiral's staff and up at the Admiralty that the Captain and the Commander should not have kept the investigation within the ship but should have asked for police assistance.

At the time, the First Lieutenant had half-expected that the Commander would find the saboteur within a few hours. He had been relieved, and almost glad, when the Commander had failed. It would have been intolerable if he had succeeded. Such a feat, with all that the Commander had already achieved, would have proved that the citadel of the great ship was at last about to fall. The First Lieutenant, and many others in the wardroom, would then have been in the position of men who had prophesied that a peak would never be scaled and who had the mortification of watching while another, bolder, man climbed it. The First Lieutenant felt himself diminished by the Commander's presence. If he did succeed in taming *Leviathan,* what would then become of those who had stood back and said that it could never be done? The First Lieutenant, like most of the wardroom, had not yet grasped the truth which the ship's company had known from the Commander's first day on board. The wardroom had learned to avoid the Commander's touchy subjects, just as they would have taken care to avoid a gouty foot. But they had yet to be convinced that the Commander intended nothing less than to have the ship eating out of his hand within a year.

He looked the man to do it. His very manner of walking the flight deck, his deliberate tread, hands clasped behind him and his cap under one arm, head bent forward boring into the wind, emitted an aura of power and command and confidence. The Commander moved everywhere in the ship with shoulders hunched and head lowered, as though he expected to batter down opposition. Several times during the last fortnight, when he had seen

106

the Commander approaching along a passageway, the First Lieutenant had caught himself involuntarily turning aside, like a man with a guilty conscience. It was a childish impulse which the First Lieutenant had not experienced since he was a junior midshipman, when he had often had a guilty conscience. The First Lieutenant was immediately ashamed of it, but he had been unable to prevent his body making what amounted to an animal movement of self-preservation.

The Captain's Secretary was standing at the after end of the flight deck with his arms folded. He was staring at the tarpaulin cover which shrouded the mirror landing sight.

'I sometimes think I ought to be bowing down and worshipping that thing, Bob.'

'Do you know how it works?'

'Not a clue. That would spoil it. I only know it works in mysterious ways, its wonders to perform.'

'One of the Squadron COs was telling me last time...' The First Lieutenant paused, and saw the others looking at him attentively. 'He told me how the chap who designed it first tried the idea out. They asked the girl in their office to prop up her handbag mirror against a book on the desk. They drew a line in her lipstick horizontally across the mirror and stood the lipstick case up on end a little way from the mirror. Then they told the girl to walk towards the desk, keeping the mirror reflection of the top of the lipstick case in line with the horizontal lipstick mark all the way. As she walked towards the desk, so she had to bend lower and lower to keep the reflection and the line together. Eventually she came down a perfect glide path and her tits hit the deck at about number four wire!'

The Commander threw back his head and laughed out loud. 'How about that! And they really designed it from that?'

'So he said, sir. They substituted a row of coloured lamps for the lipstick line, a source light for the top of the lipstick case, added a few gyros and things to keep it level, made it adjustable for different types of aircraft, and there you are. It's a good story, anyway.'

'It is indeed.'

The Secretary pretended to be disappointed. 'You've spoiled one of my great illusions, Jack. I always thought it was Buddha or somebody under that tarpaulin. My God, talking of all this, I've just had a horrible thought! I've been trying to forget it all week. Tomorrow's the big day isn't it, when the Goths and Visigoths arrive?'

'The squadrons arriving, you mean?'

'Yes.' The Secretary sucked his teeth and sighed deeply. 'What a bloody performance. About seventy new officers all joining at once. The whole wardroom utterly disorganised for a week. Never enough newspapers to go round at breakfast-time, never enough coffee cups after lunch. You can't get near the bar to get yourself a drink. And they're such yobbos, some of them.'

'*Yobbos?*' The Commander formed the word on his lips, as though tasting it. He remembered the three officers at the Secretary's house. 'That's a new one on me.'

'It describes some of the pilots perfectly, Bob. Take my word for it, yobbos is what they are. I suppose I must be a snob, but last commission I used to look at some of those aircrew and think to myself, Ye gods and little fishes, where do they *come* from? Where does the Navy *get* them?'

The squadron baggage and rearguard parties came off by boat early the next morning before the ship sailed. As soon as the ship had cleared the land, the ship's company went to Flying Stations and the squadrons flew on later in the forenoon and early afternoon. When the Commander arrived in the forward ante-room just after six o'clock that evening, he was at once reminded of the Captain's Secretary's description.

He stopped on the threshold of the ante-room, bewildered, with the sensation that he must somehow have trespassed into somebody else's mess. There were more than fifty strangers in the room and their presence had somehow transformed the atmosphere from a gentlemen's club almost to that of a frontier saloon bar. The air clamoured with their alien conversations which seemed to the Commander to be spoken in some foreign language. The bar was besieged by a crowd of unfamiliar faces six deep along its length. Groups of ten or a dozen pilots, some of them still in flying overalls, were sitting at the tables, pounding with their fists and shouting 'Why are we waiting?' and 'Let's have some bloody service!' and 'For Christ's sake, steward, what's keeping you?'

Their faces were young and cocksure and insolent, and the

Commander glared at them. This was a wardroom, not a backstreet pub in Barrow; sitting at tables and expecting their drinks to be brought to them, where the devil did they think they were? The Commander had the naval officer's traditional preference for drinking on his feet; he would no sooner have thought of taking his liquor sitting down than of eating his meals standing up.

The Gunnery Officer, the only ship's officer at the bar, was being jostled from side to side and elbowed away by a press of aircrew officers.

'Thin out a bit, you fly-boys, *please*. Let's have a look at the bar!'

The nearest pilots turned on him, with an unequivocal answer. 'Thin out a bit yourself, fish-head. We've been waiting longer than you.'

'Yes, but don't all congregate at once . . .'

'Drop dead, fish-head.'

The pilots turned back towards the bar, where Leading Steward Connolly and a junior assistant steward were doing their best under a burden of exhortations of 'Chop chop, steward!' and 'Jesus wept, what a dank ship! Can't even get a bloody drink.' The Commander stood at the back of crowd for some time before Connolly noticed him, waved the pilots aside and served him.

The Commander's object in coming early into the ante-room that evening had been to give the squadron commanding officers an opportunity of introducing themselves and their officers. As President of the Wardroom Mess, it was the Commander's duty, and his pleasure, to meet and to welcome all new members. He himself would have felt uncomfortable in a strange mess until he had made the acquaintance of their President. The aircrew clearly had no such scruples. Again and again they looked coolly at the Commander over their shoulders, noted the three gold stripes and the lack of wings on his sleeve, and turned their backs on him.

The Commander took rapid sips from his glass, noticing that his hands were trembling. A slow red flush mounted his neck and cheeks. Any ship's officer could have warned the aircrew that an explosion was approaching which would blow them all out of the ante-room.

'Commander, sir? May I introduce myself again, sir, please?'

109

'Why yes, indeed!' The Commander wheeled about, delighted. 'It's Rupert Smith! I'm delighted to see you again.'

Rupert Smith wore the rings of a lieutenant commander, the Korean medals, and pilot's wings on one sleeve. He had aiguellette hoops on his shoulder, the insignia of some past appointment as a Flag Lieutenant. He was at ease in the wardroom, having no need to behave in the noisy, exaggeratedly extrovert way of most of the aircrew – behaviour which the Commander now understood, with a return of charity, was probably motivated by self-consciousness.

The Commander shook hands warmly. 'Have they fixed you up with everything? Messdecks, cabins, and all that?'

'Oh yes, sir, thank you. Everything was laid on. Sir, I wonder if I could introduce the officers of my squadron now?' Rupert Smith had intended to introduce his officers after dinner, but seeing the look on the Commander's face as he stood by the bar, he had decided to act at once. He was rewarded by the Commander's immediate smile of relief and pleasure.

'By all means introduce them. I'd like very much to meet them.'

Rupert Smith nodded unobtrusively, and a tall gangling pilot, with red hair, high prominent cheekbones and very large protruding front teeth left the crowd by the bar and joined them. The Commander was pleased by the manoeuvre, subtly flattered that Rupert should have taken the trouble to gather his officers together and have them ready to be introduced.

'Lieutenant Geoffrey Goodall, sir, my Senior Pilot.'

While he was chatting, asking the conventional questions, the Commander noticed Goodall's uniform. There was something about a pilot's reefer jacket which distinguished it, even without the wings on the sleeve. It was an unfamiliarity in the cut, in the way the jacket hung from the shoulders, the line of the lapels and the spacing of the buttons, even in the texture of the cloth. Every pilot looked as though he had bought his uniform second-hand from the same second-rate tailor.

Rupert's Heavy Foot, *en masse,* were a phenomenon quite outside the Commander's previous experience. He was astounded by their lack of curiosity. Their manner made it clear to him that they were not interested in *Leviathan* as a ship. They were like young circus performers, examining an unfamiliar Big Top, asking only how it would support their act. In the Big Top itself, how it was constructed and who were the men who erected and maintained it, they appeared totally incurious. *Leviathan* was simply a movable stage from which they could practise their art, a bar from which they could get a drink, a table where they could eat their meals, and a cabin where they could sleep and hang up their clothes.

The Commander sensed that Rupert was not particularly popular with his squadron officers. They were afraid of him, nervous in his company, because as a General List officer he was judging their performance and their conduct by other, broader Service standards. When each pilot had been introduced and released he returned to the squadron group by the bar whence, a moment later, a great burst of private laughter aroused in the Commander an intensely melancholy feeling of being left outside a closed circle. He foresaw that despite the best of intentions on both sides, from now on there would always be two wardrooms in *Leviathan*.

Rupert Smith, a little apprehensive, was introducing his next officer. It was the young man who had made such an exhibition of himself at the Secretary's house.

'Sub-Lieutenant Alfred Stiggins, sir.'

'*Stiggins?*'

It was an impossible name for a naval officer. The Commander could not prevent himself repeating it aloud in astonishment. Alfred Stiggins. He was probably called 'Alfie' in the squadron. It was a name for a band-leader: Alfie Stiggins and his Novelty Mandoliers. Or for a character part in a radio comedy: Alfie Stiggins, the jaunty milkman, with a cheery word and a pinch on the bottom for every housewife.

'That's right, sir. Stiggins is the name. Pleased to meet you.'

The Commander blinked. *Pleased to meet you?* Stiggins spoke with a noticeable Birmingham or possibly Liverpool dialect twang, similar to Connolly's. Indeed, the thought struck the Commander that in only slightly different circumstances he might now be welcoming Sub Lieutenant (P) Connolly to the wardroom mess, while Leading Steward Stiggins served behind the bar.

'How old are you . . . Stiggins?'

'Twenty, sir.' Stiggins smirked. 'Not got the key of the door yet, sir, you might say.'

111

Key of the door, you might say?

Rupert Smith had anticipated, ever since the Secretary's party, that Stiggins might not make a favourable impression on the Commander at their first official encounter. The interview was proceeding even more unhappily than he had feared. 'This is Stiggins' first ship, sir.'

'That's right, sir. First time out on the briny.'

On the *briny?* The Commander winced, and closed his eyes, and turned his head away, hardly believing his ears. The memory of their previous meeting lay like a shadow between them but, while still remembering, the Commander had been prepared to let bygones be bygones and begin again, on an officially correct basis. But Stiggins was evidently troubled by no such preoccupations. Because he had met the Commander before he continued to chat with a kind of ghastly affability, not as a very junior officer talking to a senior, but as a neighbour gossiping over a back-garden fence. The Commander submitted with growing rage, while longing to be rid of Stiggins.

'. . . I'm happy to have met you, Stiggins. Thank you.'

'Not at all, sir. Thank *you*. The pleasure's mine. Cheeribye, sir.'

Cheeribye. It was too much. The Commander had struggled to be charitable, to remember that this was the young man's first ship. But this was too much. He leaned forward, his lower lip jutting as he drove each word into Stiggins' face. 'What the devil do you mean, *cheeribye!* The pleasure's *yours*. Pleased to *meet* you. Where do you think you are? Where do you come from, with your . . .' The Commander began to stutter in his rage. '. . . with your extracts from a C-cockney p-pantomime . . .'

Stiggins had believed that he had been keeping his end up with the Commander very well; he retreated, amazed and hurt, to the squadron group. While he talked to the next officer, the Commander was aware of the atmosphere behind him. When he next turned round, he saw their faces: Rupert's squadron were standing in a row, shoulder to shoulder, united in a common unwavering hostility towards himself.

The squadrons' first task on board was Deck Landing Qualification, during which the pilots satisfied Commander (Air) and their squadron COs of their competence by carrying out a

112

set number of successful deck landings. Freshmen Trials, as they were called, were the pilots' first chance to demonstrate their skill to the ship. Some of them far surpassed their previous form, responding to the challenge of actual deck landing conditions, and to the stimulus of the huge galleries which crowded every vantage point in the island, with flying well above their standard in training ashore. Others, who had perhaps shone in training, betrayed that they could not raise their game. The flight deck quickly found them out. Freshmen Trials were notorious for accidents. Pilots and flight deck crew were still raw and neither entirely trusted the other. Amongst themselves the squadrons had a saying, of an uncertain pilot, 'He'll be all right if he gets through DLQ's.'

The first day's weather was calm and misty, with so little wind that *Leviathan* was forced to steam at high speeds to create enough wind over the flight deck for flying. The Channel lay as placid as milk, shrouded in hanging curtains of mist in which the ship tore great ragged holes, emerging into sudden blindingly clear patches shot with bolts of streaming sunlight. In places the mist rested in shallow layers so that the great ship swam through a ghostly, cotton-white sea which spilled from the bows in wisps and trailers back across the flight deck. Towards noon, the banks of mist rolled back uncovering white cloud towers reaching up like columns to the central arch of blue sky, while *Leviathan* drove on down broad avenues of flat, gleaming sea.

At high speeds *Leviathan*'s after cabin flats were made almost uninhabitable by the sound and vibration of the ship's tearing passage through the water. The booming propeller note was transmitted through the ship's structure, every plate and frame adding its own frequency, until the decks throbbed and shivered underfoot. The thunder of the screws was reinforced by the rumble of catapults from forward, the crash and impact of an aircraft landing overhead, the drawn-out groan of the arrester wire taking its load and from time to time the thrashing, almost agricultural, sound of the sea guard helicopter flying to and from its station off the quarter.

In the Commander's day cabin there was a private hubbub of smaller sounds. A tooth-glass tinkled in its rack. Pencils clicked together in the box on the desk. Books inched themselves out of their shelves and fell on the carpet. A loose electric light shade

113

rattled enfuriatingly. The Commander leaned his elbows on the desk, put his fingers in his ears, and tried to concentrate upon the problem of the squadron messdecks. As the First Lieutenant had forecast, the squadron COs had begun to complain almost as soon as they set foot on board. The Commander had discussed minor improvements with the Shipwright Officer but there was no general solution. Some of those spaces should never have been used as messdecks.

Suddenly, the Commander became aware of quietness. The shaft revolutions had slowed. The sounds of flight deck activity had died away. He got up from his desk and looked out of the cabin scuttle. The ship had almost stopped, and was swinging slowly to port. The mist had cleared, the sun was shining and a brisk wind was ruffling the surface of the sea with patterns of tiny waves.

There was no reason why the ship should not have slowed down, but the Commander knew intuitively that there had been an accident. Taking his cap from its hook, he went down to the quarterdeck.

Two or three seamen and the Royal Marine lifebuoy sentry were clustered by the quarterdeck rail, staring out to starboard. A mile away on the starboard quarter the seaguard helicopter, the bird of mourning, was hovering over the sea. As the Commander watched, it rose, and then hovered, and then rose again, as though satisfied, turning and heading back towards the ship. The Commander heard the Captain's Secretary's voice behind him.

'Here we go again, Bob.'

'What's happened?'

The Captain's Secretary inclined his head towards the helicopter which was now large and clamorous almost overhead. 'There's a laddie down in the sea.'

'Killed?'

'Must be. The chopper's been over there for about twenty minutes and they didn't look as though they'd picked anybody up. Probably sank like a stone.'

'Who was it, do you know?'

'Fellow called MacLachlan.'

Lachlan MacLachlan. The Commander remembered him well. He was one of the pilots Rupert Smith had introduced. Mac-

114

Lachlan had told the Commander that he came from the Highlands. His accent had been underlaid with the trillings and lispings of Highland speech and there had been some quality in his face which reflected the Highlands, their silences, the twilights and the distances. His face had had a brooding rebellious look; the Hanoverians hunted down men with such features like vermin after Culloden.

'What happened?'

'I don't know. I've just come down from seeing the Captain but I didn't see what happened. All I heard was that someone had gone into the 'oggin and his name was MacLachlan.'

There were formalities to be observed after the death of any serving officer or rating. A board of enquiry would be convened as soon as possible. In the meantime, the Admiralty and the next-of-kin had to be informed, arrangements made for the funeral or for a memorial service, and for the disposal of the man's private effects. The squadron would have the arrangements in hand but the Commander called on Rupert Smith in his cabin.

'I'm very sorry indeed to hear about MacLachlan, Rupert.'

'Thank you, sir. We're all feeling a bit low. It was the very worst possible kind of start.' Rupert was sitting at his desk, staring at a pad of writing paper. 'I like to get this part over quickly. I hate delaying it. It only makes it harder.'

'Have you had to write them often?'

'This is the first in this squadron. We didn't lose anybody while we were working up ashore. I'm writing to his father, actually. The mother died some years ago. He's a Church of Scotland minister somewhere over in Wester Ross. Rather a splendid old bird, one of those hell-fire and brimstone preachers who could convert a barn-door if he put his mind to it. He came to a Burns Nicht while we were at Lossiemouth. Spouted Rabbie Burns by the hour and drank enough whisky to sort out a rhinoceros.'

'Do you want any assistance with the arrangements, or anything?' The Commander was not sure how to phrase his offer.

'No thank you, sir. We can fix it all.'

'Does anybody know what happened?'

'We think it was a flame-out. He'd just joined the landing circuit when it went out and he wasn't able to re-ignite. He was too low to eject although I don't know, I think if I'd been him I'd have

115

given it a shot rather than ditch. He didn't say a word to anyone after he'd given his fuel state, so we'll never know what went wrong. I didn't see it personally. I was just about to join the circuit myself and had lots to think about but Little F was watching from Flyco and he said it looked to him like a flame-out.'

'Was MacLachlan a good pilot?'

'So so. About average I would say. If anything he was a bit slapdash. Typical clansman, all fire and fury. He was a bolshie sort of fellow, you never knew quite what he was thinking. He's the first. I hope to God he's the last.'

'Well, if you want any assistance from the ship, if you want me to bring pressure to bear, just let me know.'

'Thank you, sir. Thank you very much.'

The Commander had not expected *Leviathan*'s wardroom to be morbidly preoccupied with MacLachlan's death, but he was unprepared for the way in which the subject was apparently forgotten. In every other wardroom he had ever served in, the death of a member, however junior or obscure, would have diminished them all. In an aircraft carrier it seemed that a pilot's death was a topic of conversation only at the meal immediately following the accident. By dinner-time in *Leviathan*, it was as though MacLachlan had never existed. His name had been known for a few hours on board, by a few people, and now he had returned to the obscurity in which he had joined. There was to be no mourning for MacLachlan. No piper would stand at his grave-side, no pibroch would play the mourners down off the hill.

After dinner and rounds, when the ship was anchored for the night in Sandown Bay, the Commander paid his usual evening call on the Captain. It was a custom they both valued; it was a convenient time to discuss the day past and the days to come.

The Captain was also writing to MacLachlan's father. 'Nearly finished, Bob. This was a hard one. Not that they're ever easy. But I'd never even met this chap. I've met quite a lot of them, but it would have to be one of the ones I haven't met. Did you know him, Bob?'

'Hardly, sir. I met him briefly when he joined last night. I know he was a Highlander, but that's just about all.'

'Never mind.' The Captain signed the letter and blotted his

signature. 'That's that. Now I'll get the Secretary Bird to vet this before I send it off. He's my legal eagle.'

The Commander nodded. A letter of condolence from the Captain of one of Her Majesty's Ships ranked almost as an official document; it was important that the letter should not contain in its sympathy any suggestion of negligence in the ship nor any statement which could be construed as an admission of Admiralty liability.

'The Padre tells me he's writing, too. He didn't know the lad either but when he heard the father was a minister he thought it would be appropriate. Strange, isn't it? Now his son's dead the old man's being showered with letters from men who never knew him.'

Returning to the ante-room, the Commander was surprised to find it still crowded with aircrew officers. He had heard that the squadrons always eschewed alcohol and went to bed early on nights before flying, but the small annexe containing the piano was full of pilots. Geoffrey Goodall, Rupert's Senior Pilot, was sitting at the piano, playing solitary chords. Another of Rupert's pilots, Chuck Beasley, a short fat man with a copper-red beard, stood fingering a guitar.

The Commander was disgusted that MacLachlan's own squadron should choose this night, of all nights, for a sing-song. His disgust was shaded by bewilderment when he noticed that none of the pilots were drinking nor talking amongst themselves, and that Rupert Smith himself was sitting in the centre of the group.

Chuck Beasley plucked a running scale on his guitar, Geoffrey Goodall joined him, and all at once the pilots began to sing.

> 'All the birds of the air fell a-sighing and a-sobbing
> When they heard of the death of poor Cock Robin,
> When they heard of the death of poor Cock Robin.'

Rupert Smith himself led the verse.

> 'Who killed Cock Robin?
> I, said the flame,
> I'll take the blame,
> *I* killed Cock Robin.'

117

The Commander admitted that the squadrons sang very well, bravely, and with a pure elegiac solemnity which invested the words of the absurd nursery rhyme with the sincerity of a lament.

'Who saw him die?'
'I, said the Fly,
With my little eye
I saw him die.'

The squadrons continued the rhyme, each taking a part, their voices harmonising and blending as closely as a trained choir. At the last line Geoffrey Goodall changed key and they all swung immediately into the tune of 'The Yellow Rose of Texas', the singers beating the time with their heels. The melody was jaunty and the words irreverent but they came like light after dark, like waking after sleeping, indeed like Reveille after the Last Post.

'When St Peter says 'Gor Blimey,
Good God, what have we here?'
You can tell him you're a pilot
And you've come to fetch the beer...'

The Commander thought the squadron singing an emotionally debased and tawdry exhibition, but he was moved in spite of himself. He stood with the handful of ship's officers present in a respectful silence, recognising that Lachlan MacLachlan was having his funeral pibroch after all.

From his first day on board the Commander had made a point, amounting almost to a fetish, of being available to anyone who wished to see him. Once, as a junior watchkeeping lieutenant, he had himself served under an eccentric Commander who had literally hidden himself from the ship's company. He had been so elusive and so irritable when he was at last run to earth that eventually the ship's company had ignored him and the ship had functioned, unhappily and inefficiently, without him. Watching, and noting the example, the Commander had made up his mind that if he were ever promoted to be Executive Officer of a large ship he would ensure that he was properly accessible. In *Leviathan* it became known that except at the time of requestmen and defaulters, or any other ship's appointment mentioned on the Daily Orders, the Commander could normally be visited in his cabin throughout the working forenoon.

The Commander believed in paying attention to detail. Like Autolycus, he was a snapper-up of unconsidered trifles. The First Lieutenant, who was one of the Commander's most frequent visitors, soon ceased to be surprised by the range and scope of the Commander's enquiries.

'By the way, what do you think of the notice boards, Number One?'

The First Lieutenant was used to the Commander's seemingly random opening gambits, and was at once on his guard.

'Which notice boards, sir?'

'The ship's company ones.'

Trying to keep one leap ahead of the Commander was part of the First Lieutenant's job, but the question puzzled him. 'I can't say I've looked at them lately, sir.'

'*Exactly!*'

The First Lieutenant realised, with dismay, that he had fallen into the trap, whatever it was.

'... *Nobody* looks at them! *I've* been having a look at them recently and they're not working. For a start, there are too many

119

old out-of-date notices still hanging up on them, some of them from last commission. That's my office's fault and I've already told my writer to start weeding out all the dead-wood. But what do you think of the actual physical positions of the notice boards?'

'They seem all right, sir. One in the canteen flat and the other in the main lobby beneath the island. People are always passing there.'

'Ah. They're always *passing,* but they're not stopping to *look.* You stand by one of them and you'll see what I mean. The main times when sailors can read notices are, stand easy, the dinner hour, immediately after secure from work, and at supper-time. But those are exactly the times when the canteen is open and there's a great queue of sailors right in front of the notice board. You can't see the notices for sailors. And the board in the island lobby is right by a hatchway. Anybody trying to read the notices has to keep making way for people going up and down the ladder.'

'That's quite true, sir.' The First Lieutenant did not have a high opinion of the Commander's intelligence; he was afraid that Bob Markready's 'bull and bash' methods would inevitably lead to the same kind of explosion as in the last commission. But the First Lieutenant was forced to admit that the Commander did sometimes have ideas which were too simple to have occurred to anybody else.

'. . . In any case, two main notice boards are not nearly enough for a ship this size. I've asked Chippy to make me a dozen more. They should be ready in a week or so. In the meantime I want you to go round and choose twelve likely spots. Anywhere where there's a clear bit of bulkhead where sailors can stop and have a look.'

'I'll certainly do that, sir. Could we do something to brighten the notices up? At the moment they seem to be dozens of closely-typed sheets of paper.'

'That's a good point and we've already laid in a stock of stencils and coloured inks in my office. We're going to town on notices in a big way. Have more notice boards, with fewer and brighter notices on them.'

The proposal was, the First Lieutenant reflected, probably better than the Commander himself knew; by improving ship's publicity they might well be forestalling one of the most disheartening features of the previous commission, the ship's company's boycotting of ship's activities. It was possible that many sailors had not been intentionally absent but had simply been unaware that anything had been taking place.

The Commander was watching the First Lieutenant's face. He guessed Number One's opinion of him and it amused him to be able to prove sometimes that he was not as earnestly thick-headed as he looked.

'Anything else?'

'No sir, I don't think so.'

In fact, there had been something else. The First Lieutenant had intended to remind the Commander of his promise to find some solution for the more makeshift of the messdecks before commissioning day. He knew that there was no immediate solution and he knew that the Commander now also knew it. He had wanted to hear the Commander admit it, to watch him wriggle. But it would be more gracious now to leave the matter where it was, understood but unspoken.

'Did you see anybody else waiting out there?'

'Yes sir, REA Lethcombe.'

'Right, send him in. Oh, and Number One ... I'm afraid there doesn't seem much I can do about those messdecks, in spite of my promise. I'm sorry.'

The First Lieutenant gritted his teeth; this was known as heaping coals of fire.

Outside his departmental duties, Radio Electrical Artificer Lethcombe was also producer and programme planner of Radio Leviathan. The Ship's Welfare Fund paid him a small fee for the work, although Lethcombe was keen enough to have done it for nothing. On the air, Lethcombe affected the nasal mid-Atlantic twang of a professional disc-jockey; the Commander had heard him compering programmes with a breezy, cheery delivery and a rapid flow of spontaneous quips and comments. Most of Radio Leviathan's broadcasting time was relayed directly from the BBC or from Radio Luxembourg, but Lethcombe had already begun to introduce the ship's own programmes – record requests, quizzes, and a brains trust. The Commander was interested in Radio Leviathan's possibilities: a lively ship's radio, like a winning football team, was a valuable aid to morale.

'You want to see me, sir?'

'Yes Lethcombe, I've got a bright idea for your programme. Sit down.'

'We're always glad to get ideas, sir.'

'Well, how about this one. You know as well as I do that half the people in this ship haven't the faintest idea of how the other half lives. What would you say to a programme of interviews in which you took people from various departments and asked them questions about their work, their daily routine, what their chief difficulties are, and so on? You could get the fellow to choose the records he likes and play them between the questions.'

'You mean a mixture of "Desert Island Discs" and "What's My Line", sir.'

'That's it. That's it exactly.'

Lethcombe stroked his chin. 'We could do something like that, sir. It's a very good idea. We could actually call it 'How The Other Half Lives'. Or 'Down Your Hatch' or something. How would you like to be the first person to be interviewed, sir?'

The Commander grinned. He should have guessed that Lethcombe would be sharp enough to ask. 'I don't think it would be a good idea if I was on the first programme. But you get it moving amongst the ship's company and then I'll be very happy to take part later on. I'll look forward to hearing it. There are quite a number of people in this ship I've always wondered about. REA's, for instance.'

'We're a very hard-working lot, sir.'

'I'm sure you are, Lethcombe. Let me know how you get on.'

'Yes, sir. The Master-at-Arms is waiting to see you, sir.'

'Ask him to come in.'

There was a popular theory, firmly held by many naval officers, that Masters-at-Arms were, by definition, the salt of the earth, the backbone of the Navy, with their fingers on a ship's every pulse. The theory was companion to the sentiment which led divisional officers to award yearly character assessments of 'Superior' to all their Chief Petty Officers, not because they were necessarily superior but merely because they were Chief Petty Officers and because it seemed a pity to break their previous sequence of 'Superior' assessments.

The Commander did not subscribe to the theory, because he

had observed that it was unsupported by the facts; the confidential reports on the several incidents of indiscipline and one case of open mutiny in HM Ships since the war had showed that on no occasion had the ship's officers received any prior warning of trouble from the regulating staff. The ship's police had either been unaware of or had acquiesced in the disturbance. The Master-at-Arms was the senior rating on board, a man of power and consequence, and the Commander valued his opinion but he constantly bore in mind that the Master's opinion of the ship was as accurate, no more and no less, as a Chief Constable's opinion of his county borough.

Leviathan's Master-at-Arms was comparatively junior in his rate; *Leviathan* was only his second ship as Master. But he was competent, energetic, and thoughtful. The Commander suspected, though he would never have attempted to prove it, that many cases did not reach his defaulters' table because the Master had already forestalled them, applying his own nameless penalties.

Yet the Master-at-Arms had one exasperating idiosyncrasy. He read Queen's Regulations and Admiralty Instructions, all Admiralty Fleet Orders, and all port and ship's standing orders closely and thoroughly. If there were a catch or a loop-hole, the Master could be guaranteed to spot it. But he could not be relied upon to pass his knowledge on. He seemed to gain a perverse pleasure from hugging his extra knowledge to himself, as though by so doing he was putting himself one up on the Commander. Whenever he discussed ship's business with the Master-at-Arms the Commander felt that he was sitting down to play chess against a man who had taken the trouble to read all the small print in the rules.

'Come in, Master. I know what you want to see me about. Next week-end.'

'Next week-end it is, sir . . .'

'Sit down, Master . . .'

'I won't, sir, thank you. I was just passing and I thought I'd check the leave times. Bearing in mind the railway strike, sir.'

'Bearing in mind the railway strike, as you say, Master. Well, I don't see how we can allow it to make any difference. It's timed to start at midnight on Sunday, but it may not come off. We shan't know until Sunday and they'll all be on week-end by then.'

'So we grant long week-end leave as usual, sir?'

'Have to. We can't muck about with the sailors' sacred week-ends. That would be like killing a cow in India . . .'

The Commander broke off. Sarcasm was probably just permissible with the Master-at-Arms, but it was still a dangerous weapon to use with any rating.

'. . . I've asked the Barracks Commander what they're doing and he says they're treating it as a normal Whit week-end, except that they're going to warn everybody that it's their own responsibility to get back on time and no excuses to do with trains will be accepted. We'll do the same. Week-end leave from time of arrival on Friday evening to seven-thirty Tuesday morning for junior rates, eight o'clock for Chiefs and petty officers.'

'It will be an aggravated offence if they're adrift, sir.'

The Commander opened his eyes wide. 'So it will. So it will. The ship'll be under sailing orders so if they're adrift it will be an aggravated offence, as you say. Make sure every libertyman knows that before he leaves the ship and make doubly sure they know that excuses about trains are no use.'

'Aye aye, sir. There's an officer waiting outside to see you, sir.'

'Ask him to come in, Master, thank you.'

The next visitor was the Instructor Lieutenant Commander, a thin, spare man, with sparse grey hair and, as his nickname 'Beaky' suggested, a sharp beaked nose. His appointment as *Leviathan*'s assistant instructor officer hardly ranked as a post of high academic distinction but Beaky had the almost comical mannerisms of the true pedagogue. He spoke with pedantic care, picking his words with precision. His uniform jacket looked as though it was permanently impregnated with chalk dust. He had false teeth which sometimes rattled when he was pronouncing certain labial and dental consonants. The Commander wondered what prompted Beaky, and other instructor officers like him, to carry on in the Service. He understood that teaching was not only a profession but a vocation, but he could see little inspiration in coaching sailors to take elementary educational tests for advancement to Leading Seaman. Perhaps, like some naval medical officers, Beaky had been seduced by the lotus fruits of a professionally uncompetitive career, financial security, and the supply of duty-free liquor and tobacco. Beaky was never likely to be given one of the more challenging posts for instructor officers at Greenwich or Manadon. He had not even added another string to his bow by taking a course in meteorology. Beaky would never be promoted to Instructor Commander, but would continue to serve in one humdrum appointment after another until he was old enough to retire on pension. Meanwhile, he was a useful member of *Leviathan*'s wardroom, because he was one of the few officers who had the time to take on the duties of Mess Secretary.

'What can I do for you, Beaky?'

'I wished to inform you of the party in the ante-room on Saturday night, sir.'

'What sort of party?'

'Drinks. Buffet supper. And dancing to records, sir.' Beaky clipped off each word precisely, as though enumerating a list of exceptional orgies.

'Good. What's the rig?'

'Informal, sir. Plain clothes or uniform. The squadrons are taking this opportunity to bring their wives on board, sir.'

'Good for them. I'll be there.'

'Will you ask the Captain, sir?'

'I'll ask him, but I know he's going away for the week-end. What time does this mighty thrash start?'

'Eight p.m., sir.'

'It'll have to end by eleven-thirty, you know that, I suppose? The dockyard police don't like ladies in the dockyard after midnight.'

'It is scheduled to end at eleven-thirty, sir.'

'Good. O.K. then, Beaky, off you go.'

'Thank you, sir.'

On Friday afternoon, the Commander saw the Captain off at the after gangway. Tosser had his golf clubs with him, and his wife was waiting in the car at the bottom of the gangway.

'I'm off now, Bob. Got the weight?'

'Yes, sir.'

'The Officer of the Watch has got my telephone number if you need me. In the meantime, call me when it's stopped coming on to blow.'

The Commander grinned. 'I'll do that, sir.'

Tosser took a couple of practise swings with an imaginary club.

'It does seem a pity to leave you here all on your tod. Laura was saying the other day she feels a bit guilty about you. I think she's got plans, Bob, so watch out for yourself. When the women-folk start getting ideas about your social life it's time to take to the hills. See you Tuesday morning.'

While the Commander stood at the salute, the Captain shouldered his golf clubs and went down the gangway. His wife waved from the car as they drove off.

The Commander stayed on the quarterdeck for a time, watching the evacuation, which was on the scale of a mass exodus, of officers and men leaving the ship for the week-end. The probability of a strike on the railways evidently carried no threat for the ship's company. *Leviathan* was emptying of men like some vast commuters' train, and indeed the jetty beside the ship resembled the forecourt of a suburban railway station, with its line of taxis, and private cars driven by wives collecting their husbands, and crowds of hurrying men on foot. Every officer and man wore or carried his blue Service raincoat. It was an excellent demonstration of what the First Lieutenant had once described as the Navy's Raincoat Syndrome: all over the globe, in all climates and temperatures, the Royal Navy took raincoats, without which they would have felt naked and exposed. Certainly, the Commander himself had once witnessed British naval ratings going ashore for the evening in New York, at the height of summer in Manhattan, each with his raincoat neatly folded over his arm.

Walking back towards the wardroom, the Commander could feel the emptiness of the cabins on either side. An occasional late leaver burst from his cabin, carrying his raincoat and his brown travelling bag, jamming his hat on his head as he raced for the quarterdeck, but the flats and passageways were otherwise deserted. It was like a school during the holidays.

Stirring his lonely cup of tea and eating his solitary buttered toast in the wardroom, the Commander thought over the implications of the Captain's parting words. There was a grain of substance in them. Perhaps his private life did need some radical change. He had often heard the ancient malicious gibe that any unmarried officer over the age of forty must have homosexual tendencies. He knew it to be true, in a few cases. However, in the majority, which included himself, circumstances rather than personalities had prevented marriage. It was only too easy to remain a bachelor in the Navy and, after the early susceptible years, it became easier still. The monastic structure of the wardroom mess, and the self-orientation and insularity of shipborne life suited a bachelor: it was the married officer who had continually to compromise between his domestic and his professional life.

Nevertheless there was enough residual truth in the accusation to make bachelor officers of the Commander's age sometimes feel uneasy and deprived. Curiously, it was not at Christmas, the traditional festival of loneliness, when the feeling of deprivation was strongest; every wardroom arranged compensating celebrations for officers living in at Christmas. It was at ordinary week-ends throughout the year, when the married officers went home to their families, that the Commander felt most keenly the lack of some private destination ashore. The younger bachelors had their own company and could go ashore together. The number of officers with whom the Commander could spend an evening ashore was restricted by his rank. Furthermore, he had been careful to prevent the formation in *Leviathan*'s wardroom of any clique which could be called 'the Commander's set'; he had once experienced the disastrous atmosphere in a wardroom where the President of the Mess held his own court, complete with jester.

After tea on Saturday afternoon, the Commander made his way thoughtfully towards the quarterdeck. There was one way in which he could enliven his private life. Having made up his mind, he walked on the quarterdeck with a mixture of a skip and a change-step which made the quartermaster and Bird, who was officer of the watch, look at him in surprise.

'Good evening, Bird. Lovely evening, isn't it?'

'Good evening, sir. Yes, it is.' Bird's voice was cautious. It was not like the Commander to be so affable. This could be the smile on the face of the tiger.

'Are all the dinghies booked for tomorrow?'

'No, sir, I've just checked the Sailing Book. I was thinking of taking one out myself tomorrow afternoon, sir.'

'Good, good. Put me down for a boat from eleven o'clock onwards.'

'Aye aye, sir. Shall I arrange to have it rigged for you at the time, sir?'

'That's a splendid idea, Bird, if you would.' The Commander rubbed his hands together gleefully. 'A simply *splendid* idea.'

The quartermaster's eyebrows rose towards the peak of his cap; a little more of this, and the old bastard would be breaking into song.

'Mind if I borrow your shore telephone?'

'Not at all, sir. It's the one with the dial, in the cabinet, sir.'

There was a directory by the telephone and he knew that he would recognise her number as soon as he saw it. The address would be in Old Portsmouth, since she was a neighbour of Scratch's. The Commander had not felt this moistening of the palms of his hands, this anticipatory trembling in his throat, not since he was a sub-lieutenant.

'Hello ... This is Bob Markready, do you remember we met at ...'

'Of course I remember you, Bob.' Annabel's voice was breathless, helping her to hide her pleasure that he had taken the trouble to find out her telephone number. 'I'm sorry I'm a bit out of breath. I heard the telephone and I had to come running all the way down the stairs. I was upstairs looking out a dress.'

'A *dress*? Are you going out somewhere tonight?'

'Why yes. I'm going to a dinner party. Why?'

He felt the evening sun going behind a cloud and all the joy drained from him.

'Why, were you going to suggest something?'

'Well, we're giving a party on board tonight and I was going to ask you if you could come. I know it's rather late ...'

'Oh, if only I'd known *sooner*!' She was annoyed that he had suggested so much more enjoyable an evening only when it was too late. 'I'm only going to make up the numbers tonight, as a sort of spare woman. But now I've said I'll go I *can't* let them down now.'

'Of course you can't. But what about tomorrow? I've got a dinghy in the morning. I thought we could go out and sail round the harbour.'

'Oh Bob, if only you'd given me more warning. I'm going down to see the boys at school tomorrow. I'd loved to have come out sailing. I could have brought some lunch and we could have made a day of it. But I must go and see the boys. They're expecting

128

me. But what a *disappointment.*'

She really did sound disappointed. Perhaps he could suggest Monday, which was also a holiday. But perhaps that would be urging too fast, too soon. Perhaps she might suggest Monday herself.

Annabel, too, had thought of Monday but perversely did not suggest it. Any man who had the perseverance to find out her telephone number must also have the patience to wait. She paused, knowing that he was wrestling with the decision of whether or not to mention Monday.

'Oh well, perhaps there'll be another time.'

'You must give me a ring the next time you're in, Bob.'

'I will.'

'Now I must go, I'm afraid. I've got a lot to do. Good-bye.'

'Good-bye.'

Bird and the quartermaster were quick to sense the change in the Commander's mood when he reappeared from the telephone cabinet. He stood staring at the deck for a few moments.

'You can cancel my booking for the dinghy tomorrow. I shan't be needing it now.'

'Aye aye, sir.'

Although Bird carefully guarded his expression the Commander detected enough sympathy in his voice to be sure that the quarter-deck staff must have overheard and understood at least the gist of his conversation with Annabel. He wished that he had made the call from the privacy of his cabin: it irritated him that his private disappointments should become public knowledge.

The Commander's eye roamed the quarterdeck. The guard-rails were taut. The brightwork was shining and the deck scrubbed clean. The quartermaster, the Royal Marine bugler, and Bird himself were correctly and smartly dressed.

The duty part of the watch of seamen were mustering on the port side of the quarterdeck. The Commander looked unseeingly at the end sailor in the front rank.

'You. Get your hair cut.'

'Aye aye, sir.'

The Commander turned and stamped up the ladder towards his cabin, while Bird, the quartermaster and the Royal Marine bugler stared after him with interest. The ship's company would be glad to know that The Bloke had woman trouble, just like anybody else; somehow, it made him almost human.

At the party in the ante-room, while talking to some of the wives he had met on previous occasions, the Commander reflected on the old and well-beloved naval legend that there was a particular type, almost a biological sub-species, of Naval Wife. It might have been true before the war, but the post-war generations of naval officers had tended to marry healthy, unembarrassed middle-class girls who were good letter-writers, who could hunt for a house and set up a home on their own, who could handle the children and deal with tradesmen, girls who could, in a phrase, hold the fort while their husbands were away. If they had a common characteristic then he believed that it was their provincialism. The faces he could see around him in *Leviathan*'s ante-room could have belonged to members' wives at a provincial golf club dance, or to the guests at a 21st Birthday party given for his daughter by some prominent Conservative businessman in the provinces.

Nor did he believe the second favourite legend, that an officer's career could be vitally affected by his wife. Of the half-dozen of his own Dartmouth term who had already been promoted to Captain most, in his opinion, had married coarse, common women. A girl would have to be outstandingly farouche in her appearance and her behaviour to prejudice her husband's career.

The squadron wives, he could see, were different. They were younger, and prettier, and more determined. Their faces showed that they would not be left at home to mind the baby. They were going along with their husbands, or they would make trouble. When the pressures of family and children became too great, their husbands would be made to leave the Service. They were not, in fact, naval wives at all; they had merely married young men who had afterwards become naval officers.

Talking to the wives of the other Heads of Departments, the Commander tried to conceal his restlessness. These were all worthy women, and probably good wives, but their conversation wearied him. They were so clearly conscious that they were talking to the Commander: they saw him in plain clothes, but they were looking at his uniform. Commander (L)'s wife was drinking plain ginger ale, but cackling with laughter as though it were neat whisky. Her name was Gwyneth and she was small and dark and Welsh. Dai

Bach obviously had some reputation as a wit at home, because Gwyneth was always ready to break off her conversation with the Commander and listen to her husband, with her head cocked and eager, ready to laugh. The Commander had the impression that Gwyneth was still marvelling at her husband's progress in the Service; for her, the novelty of appearing in a wardroom would never fade, the gold braid on her husband's cap never tarnish.

Commander (E) had married long before he had a commission and the Commander could see that Doris, his wife, had never quite advanced at the same pace as her husband. Behind the mature figure of the Chief's wife there was still the shy, fluttering girl who had married the young ambitious artificer. She was a tall woman, taller than her husband. Her features, pretty in her youth, were now hard and angular and she wore a brown silk dress which made her look taller and more angular. She had glossed over her background and her accent but the Commander guessed that left to herself she would still tend to turn forward rather than aft when she reached the top of a gangway.

Commander (S)'s wife, whom the Commander had not met before, came as a refreshing surprise to him. Where Joe was cynical, Mary his wife was charitable. While Delicious Joe was elegantly dressed, exquisitely turned out of a bandbox, Mary had locks of hair astray, and an earring missing, and her lipstick was slightly smudged. The Commander was warmed and refreshed by the way she talked to him. She had, he discovered, been a kinder-garten teacher before she married and she enquired about the ship in the same tone of voice as she would have asked her son about his progress at cricket. To Mary, naval officers and naval affairs were clearly funny, and touching, and altogether fascinating. Delicious Joe was a hard man to serve with; without Mary, he would have been impossible.

The Commander's arm was suddenly jogged from behind, so that his gin slopped over his hand and wrist.

'My dear *man*, I'm so *sorry!*'

The Commander irritably mopped his sleeve. 'That's quite all right.'

She was a very young woman, wearing a close-fitting black wool dress, a tiny black pill-box hat, and a short black veil. When she caught the Commander's arm in apology, her wedding ring showed through her thin black net gloves. She appeared a little drunk and in a mood for an argument. She looked the Commander boldly up and down, so that he was quite aware of her meaning: she was wondering, almost aloud, what he was like in bed.

'You look like an important-looking sort of man. Is this ship as bad as they say it is?'

The Commander coughed. 'That depends on who says it's bad and how bad they say it is.' Perhaps he had been premature in deciding that a man's wife made no difference. How many promising careers had been shrivelled by a wife's tactlessness?

'Bloody horrible.' The girl smacked her lips. 'That's what my husband says, and he should know. He's served in one or two.'

'Who is your husband, may I ask?'

'Julian Bird. Do you know him? He's Laundry Officer, Boats Officer, Seamen's Divisional Officer...' She was ticking the titles off her fingers. '... chief bottle-washer and general d-dogsbody.' She stumbled over the word 'dogsbody' but her voice was otherwise neutral and classless. The Commander tried unsuccessfully to place her background. Did she come from a family who regarded a naval officer as a catch, second only to a trades union official? Or had her mother been disappointed, and only consoled by the ephemeral glamour of a naval wedding?

'I know your husband very well.'

'What's he like at his job?'

'Very good indeed, I believe.' He answered reluctantly; it was no part of his philosophy to discuss an officer's professional ability with his wife.

'That's *good*, because I want him to be an admiral. He doesn't want to be an admiral. *He* wants to retire. But I won't let him.'

The Commander was startled. This was a new variation; normally it was the wife, and particularly a young wife, who wanted her husband to retire.

'Don't you ever find that moving house gets you down a bit?'

The girl raised her shoulders in an elaborate gesture of fatalism. 'I knew about all that when I married him.'

The Commander saluted such pragmatism. The possibility seemed fantastically remote, but if this young woman really was determined, and he had no reason to doubt her, then Bird might well become an admiral.

Bird was approaching them, carrying two glasses, and disconcerted to see his wife chatting intimately with the Commander.

'Good evening, sir. You've met my wife Monica, sir.'

'Yes I have.'

'I've *met* him, darling, but I don't know who he *is*.'

Bird looked apologetically at the Commander. 'This is Commander Markready, darling. The Commander.' Bird's voice betrayed his anxiety over what his wife might have been saying.

'We've been having a most *interesting* conversation, darling.'

Bird looked even more uneasy. 'If you'll excuse us, sir.' He transferred both glasses to one hand and took his wife by the arm. 'Darling, I think we ought to put our drinks over there and go and dance. Will you excuse us please, sir?'

'Why certainly.'

Monica put her face up close to the Commander and hissed at him. 'I'm being *dragged* away!'

The Commander was left with the suspicion that he had been the target of a calculated public relations effort. There was an old, and true, Service saying that it was better to be notorious than to be unknown. With such a wife, Bird was unlikely to remain unknown.

On the other side of the ante-room the Commander saw Stiggins, with a blonde girl in a blue strapless dress of some shiny material and a white crochetted shawl over her arm. Something familiar in the tripping eagerness of her walk reminded the Commander of the many tortured evenings he had endured at ship's company dances. Her face, her dress, her way of walking behind Stiggins towards the dance floor, recalled vividly for him those droves of patient faces lining the walls, that strained syrupy music played by a six-piece band in plum-coloured smoking jackets, the musky smell of cheap scent, the jagged light splintering off the mirror facets of the ball revolving above the dancers, and all those sweating sailors doing the tango, with cigarette packets tucked in the fronts of their jerseys.

The Commander heard Wings' voice behind him.

'There you are, Bob. Angie, come and meet the Commander.'

Commander (Air)'s wife was not yet the queen – an elevation delayed until her husband was promoted Captain – but she was one of the wardroom's senior ladies-in-waiting. She was big, and blonde, and her face showed the excavation marks of a thousand facial treatments: Stiggins' little blonde, the Commander thought, would look like this in twenty years' time. She moved only from the hips when she walked, holding her shoulders rigid and her breasts forward, like the figurehead of a ship. Her dress seemed unnecessarily elaborate for the occasion, being made of layers of tulle, with misty recesses of pink, and hollows of blue, and frothy clouds of net swirling around her plump, freckled bosom. The piled blonde hair, the pinkly-painted face, the stiff china-doll posture, the formal dress, all filled the Commander with a wild sense of satisfaction that justice had been done: Wings *deserved* such a wife.

Angie offered the Commander two fingers of her hand to shake, and began to talk in a manner both condescending and domineering. The Commander was well aware that Angie was interested in him only because of his rank and his position in the ship. A plain bachelor of forty would otherwise have been beneath contempt. His abhorrence of the abominable Angie so obsessed him that he searched for some pretext to disengage himself. He could ask her to dance, which might stop her talking, but that would be a desperate solution indeed. When he saw a steward coming towards him, obviously with a message, the Commander turned to him as to a lifeline.

'Shore telephone call, sir.'

'For me?'

'Yes, sir.'

'Where?'

'Main exchange, sir. If you ring them, they'll put you through.'

'Of course, of course.' This time he would make no mistake. He ran to his cabin and sat down at his desk, the blood thudding in his ears.

'. . . Bob? It's me, Annabel again . . .'

His heart leapt up. 'Yes?'

'I've just come back from *the* most dreary dinner party. It's just occurred to me, if you're really not doing anything tomorrow, would you like to come down to the school with me? It would be company for me and . . .'

'I'd love to, Annabel.' He was already considering the implications; according to port regulations, he and the Captain should

134

not both leave the port area at the same time. 'Just one thing. Can you give me the telephone number of the school? I have to let the ship know where I'm going.'

'Yes, I've got it written down here.'

'When will you be setting off?'

'Oh, about ten o'clock. Is that too early?'

'No fear. I'll be there!'

The gangway staff were taken aback, but secretly relieved, to see the Commander in plain clothes and clearly going ashore so early on a Sunday forenoon. The Commander fancied he caught the shade of relief in their expressions; there was no doubt the Ship's company preferred their senior officers to be ashore at weekends. There must have been some consternation throughout the ship when they heard that he was a bachelor.

'Who's the duty lieutenant commander today?'

'The Gunnery Officer, sir.'

'Tell him I'm going ashore now and I won't be back until late this evening. Here's the telephone number if he needs me.'

The entire gangway staff understood from the Commander's expression that if the Gunnery Officer did telephone, it should be for nothing less than a Red Warning of an imminent nuclear attack on the ship.

He had not asked Annabel directions because he had her address from the directory and by a coincidence he knew the house. Friends of his had once lived in the same street a few yards off the High Street and going to dinner there he had noticed the narrow, three-storied Georgian house opposite, with its white front, bow window, the pillars on either side of the black and white painted door, and the potted geraniums on the steps. The little house had been a merchant's or a doctor's home in Old Portsmouth's heyday as a sailors' town, when the High Street was the busiest and rowdiest street in the kingdom. He had often wondered who lived there now.

Annabel was waiting on the top step outside her front door. She was wearing a wide-rimmed Breton straw hat, a cotton skirt and a white blouse, and a blue jacket cut like a blazer, with broad brass nautical buttons. When she came out of the shadow of the porch into the sunlight in her straw hat and her blazer she looked like a school girl or a very young games mistress.

'Good morning, marm.' He raised his hat, grinning and delighted to see her again so soon and so unexpectedly.

Annabel smiled, with pleasure that he had not been too proud to accept an invitation made at the last minute. 'Do I look as school-marmish as that?'

'Of course you don't. It was just that I could hardly believe you've got two boys at school.'

She looked at his car. 'What a lovely, opulent-looking Jaguar, Bob.'

His car was his only indulgence; as a bachelor Commander, he could afford it. 'You don't think it a bit ostentatious?'

'Not a bit. Can we go in it?'

'Naturally.'

'Well, then, you drive, and I'll direct you.'

She had a string-bag with her, containing a large biscuit tin.

'That looks pretty exciting.'

'Oh, it's just a cake for the boys.'

'I expected a tuck-box, or something.'

'No, they've got a shop where they can buy things. It's money they always want, not food.'

He took the bag from her, and then paused. 'It's not *Speech Day* today is it?'

'Lord no. I'd be wearing a proper hat and be all dressed up like a dog's dinner if it was.'

He was wearing a grey linen suit, made for him in Hong Kong, and a panama hat. Suddenly he had misgivings about them. 'You don't think I'm too formally dressed?'

'You're just right, Bob. It's going to be a scorching hot day, for a change. It normally rains today, because it's the cricket match against the masters. So it's not really a day out for the boys. They get five exeats a term, when we can take them out, but today's not one of them.'

Cricket against the masters. Exeats. Mama bringing a cake down in a tin. He helped her into the car, sighing nostalgically. 'This brings it all back for me, Annabel. It's like going back thirty years. I didn't know all this was still going on. Do they have a father's match?'

'Not as such but they haven't got enough masters to make up a full team so one or two of the fathers will be playing today. Would you like to play?'

'I'm not a father.'

137

'That doesn't matter.'

'And I'm not a cricketer, either. But I'm a very good spectator, I will say that. Where are we off to?'

'Make for Devizes, and I'll tell you where to go from there.'

He drove as he did everything, carefully and methodically. His share of the conversation dwindled as he concentrated on working through the dense coast-bound traffic on the outskirts of Portsmouth and on the roads fringing Southampton. Watching him, when his replies had become few and monosyllabic, Annabel saw that he was treating the drive as he seemed to treat everything in that ship, as a personal challenge to his skill.

'What time have we got to be there?' He spoke as one whose own life was mapped out by routines and who could not bear to be late.

'We haven't got to be there by any particular time.' Her voice held a note of sharpness. 'So you can relax.'

'I'm sorry.' He let his shoulders drop, and took one hand off the steering wheel to scratch his head. 'I'm letting myself get personally involved again. A thing I should never do, they tell me.'

'Is that what they tell you on board, not to get personally involved?'

'More or less.'

'I wonder why. It's a fault on the right side.'

'But it's not a fault at all!' He countered with an answering sharpness which startled her. 'It's essential.'

'Yes, I suppose it is, in your sort of job.'

She turned in her seat so that she could study his profile unobtrusively while he drove. He really was an attractive man, if only he would not look so solemn and stuffy whenever anyone mentioned The Ship. She would never know why she had asked him to come with her. She had merely obeyed the impulse, when she came back to her empty house, still hearing the disappointment in his voice. She had hardly expected him to accept but now that he was here, beside her, she felt a moment of alarm; maybe she had unthinkingly begun on a venture which could not be so carelessly abandoned. As a naval wife, married to Tom for eleven years, she had met all kinds of professional naval officers, but this man was an original. In any other appointment, in any other ship, he might

138

have been fair and willing game but there was some quality in this present ship which had captured him and made him immune. She had been faithful to her husband through their marriage, though she had been tempted, but now she was aware of the first stirrings and promptings of an old challenge.

'Was your father in the Navy, Bob?'

'Oh yes.' He spoke casually, as though she could have taken that for granted. 'He retired as a Rear-Admiral just after the war. He died ten years ago.'

'And your mother?'

'She died about a year later.'

'I'm sorry.'

'It happens. One goes, and the other follows soon after. My mother didn't pay much attention to things after my father died.'

'So what do you do with yourself on your leaves? Where do you go?'

'It's a good question.' He remembered his own question of the Captain's Secretary; it was ironical that they should both wonder what the other did with the days. 'I sometimes go abroad. Sometimes I stay in London. I've got a sister there. And I sometimes stay with friends. It all depends. I must say the question of leave hasn't cropped up lately. I didn't take any in Singapore, except the odd bit of station leave to thumb a lift in a ship going up to Hong Kong. I had a lot due to me when I came home, but I couldn't take it because I had to come straight to this ship.'

'How long were you in Singapore?'

'Just over three years.'

'So you haven't had a proper holiday in nearly *four* years?'

'No.' The point had not occurred to him before. 'Now that you mention it, I haven't.'

'I'm sorry I'm asking all these questions, Bob. But I've just realised I know almost nothing about you. Are you lonely?'

'Sometimes.'

He had not meant to answer so honestly. His reply had been jarred out of him by the question's unexpectedness. From a stranger, it was a spectacularly percipient question. For a woman who claimed to know nothing of him, Annabel already had a dangerously complete knowledge, and he had a warning premoni-

139

tion that she might be about to make unusual emotional demands on him.

They were clear of Salisbury, on the long straight roads and great swelling hill-sides approaching the Plain. Annabel sat comfortably in her seat; it was a long time since she had had a man to drive her. When they reached Devizes, she stirred herself to give directions.

'Take the Chippenham road, Bob.'

'It's a relief to be with someone who knows the way.'

She was flattered by his acceptance of her directions. Tom had always been restive when she was directing him, doubtful that her knowledge could be correct.

'We're nearly there. There's a big gate and a lodge on the left, about half a mile from here. We turn into that.'

They turned into the drive and at once they were travelling through a pale green, breathless world, a submarine tunnel lit by quick splashes of sunlight dappling the car bonnet. A double row of lime trees, still in their first spring shadings of individual greens, lined the drive and the car wheels whipped up whirling clouds of the yellow husks and furry debris of spring which covered the road. They crossed a cattle-grid at the end of the drive, drove round a wind-break of flowering red and pink rhododendron, under the branches of a bottle-green cedar tree, and on to the gravel of the open space in front of the house.

Bob Markready parked his car at the end of a line of others. He helped Annabel out, and looked around him.

The house faced south and was built of a warm, orange-brown Cotswold stone. The main façade had a massive appearance of bulk and size but it was tempered by the proportions of the main door in the Palladian style, by the positioning and spacing of the windows and the line of the stone balustrade running along the roof. There had clearly been additions to the original fabric. At the eastern end a complete wing had been built in a different stone : the baroque clock tower, the castellated roof-line, and the elongated gothic windows demonstrated some Victorian's enthusiasm for the semblance of war.

Bob Markready pointed at the mock arrow-slits in the east wing. 'If this was mine, I'd knock that whole wing down. But the rest of it's gorgeous.'

Looking closer, he noticed unobtrusive and whimsical details which had been added to divert the eye. The angle of one wall was filled out by a short stubby tower with a conical roof, like a dovecot. Ivy spread like a rich green birth-mark around a vertical sun-dial set in the western masonry. A tiny bronze mermaid sat in her fluted niche, formed like a palmer's shell. Two pointed cypress trees grew in square stone cisterns on an ornamental balcony.

'Robert? Is that Robert Markready?'

A small man with a shining, nut-brown face and white hair stood at the top of the steps by the main door. In his white duck trousers, white canvas shoes, blazer, silk square and his round straw hat, he looked an oddly archaic figure, like an elderly Edwardian roué about to take the air on the Promenade des Anglais.

Bob Markready mounted the steps two at a time to shake him by the hand. 'Good morning, sir, how very pleased I am to see you! How are you, sir?'

'It *is* you, Robert. You're looking well.'

'So are you, sir. I'd no *idea* you were here! Are you. . . . You're not the Headmaster, sir?'

The little man gave a grating, nasal chuckle. 'I'm the Bursar, boy. The keeper of the bloody bullion bags.' He shaded his eyes with his hand. 'Is that *Annabel* there?'

The little man descended the steps, doffed his hat, and kissed Annabel on the cheek. 'If I were a younger man, Annabel, we'd get married tomorrow.'

'That's very gallant of you, Bowler.'

'It's not gallantry, my dear, it's lust. Have you seen your two little men yet?'

'Not yet, we've just arrived.'

Bowler drew a breath. 'Jago!'

The hall-porter, another elderly man, in a black jacket and striped trousers, appeared at the main door.'

'Powells Major and Minor, Jago.'

Jago touched his forehead in an indeterminate salute. 'Aye aye, Captain.'

Bowler flinched. 'Aye *aye,* Captain.' He sucked his teeth disgustedly. 'What sort of an acknowledgement is that? Just because I was in the Service Jago thinks he's got to talk like something out

141

of the Mutiny on the Bounty.'

Bob Markready had lost touch with John Bowler since his father's death. John Bowler had been one of his father's greatest friends in the Service. He had been Commander of the ship in which Bob himself had first gone to sea as a midshipman and he had been his Captain in his first ship as a watch-keeping lieutenant. He had learnt much from Bowler, indeed his philosophy in *Leviathan* was based on John Bowler's early example.

For his part, John Bowler had always taken an avuncular interest in his friend's boy. As Nick Markready's son, Robert deserved well of the Service and Bowler had been delighted, though astonished, to read of his appointment to *Leviathan,* just as he was astonished, but delighted, to see him with Annabel. In Bowler's opinion, Robert had always stood in his father's shadow. He had never shown that he could be the man his father was. But now it appeared that things were coming right for Robert at last.

More parents were arriving, and boys were coming down the steps to meet them, among them Annabel's two sons. David, the elder boy, was in cricket flannels but the younger boy, Jeremy, was in a grey uniform school suit, just as he had come from church. Bob Markready was at once struck by their family resemblance; they were so clearly brothers, and Annabel's sons. He was surprised to see them both kiss their mother; at Dartmouth such a demonstrative form of affection would have been unthinkable. Towards himself, they both showed a proper formality, shaking hands and speaking with a composure which pleased him and yet made him envious. He thought of his own shyness and sulky boorishness when his parents came to visit him at Dartmouth. His father had descended on the College as though from Parnassus and everybody accompanying him, even John Bowler, had been invested with the same terrifying, Olympian splendour.

Bowler was marshalling the party. 'This way, this way. Lunch is in the marquee on Big Side.'

Annabel and the two boys drew ahead. Bob Markready, walking behind with Bowler, thought that if he had been told she was the boys' elder sister, he could have believed it.

'I remember going to visit you when you were a nipper, Robert.'

'Yes, I remember, sir. I don't think I had quite the self-possession of those two.'

142

'No, I don't think you did, Robert. But they've had to grow up fast in the last couple of years.'

Bowler himself had hardly changed since the last time Bob Markready had seen him. He had lost none of his Service prejudices.

'You haven't met the Head, have you, Robert? Typical pongo. He was in the Grenadiers during the war.' They were walking along a covered colonnade by the wall of an orangery built on the west wing. 'Nice fellow, but...' Bowler nodded at the wall '... as thick as that bulkhead.'

The Headmaster was circulating amongst the visiting parents in the marquee like a giant, flamboyant fair-ground barker. He came out to greet Annabel with a hug which made her gasp.

'Do put me down, George. You make me feel as though I'm visiting a grisly bear.'

'Just the impression I wanted you to get, Annabel.' The Headmaster had a deep, booming ferry-boatman's voice. He was indeed a hairy, friendly bear of a man. Ginger hair stood up in a dramatic plume on his head. He had a sandy, tobacco-stained moustache and tufts of biscuit-coloured hair grew on his cheeks in what were called in the Service 'bugger's grips'. More and spikier tufts sprouted from his ears. His complexion was a dark plum red which clashed unhappily with the shocking yellow and orange of the MCC square knotted round his neck. Yet Bob Markready could see from the grins on the boys' faces that the Headmaster was popular in his school in the same way and with the same kind of personality as Tosser McTigue was popular with the ship's company.

If the Headmaster felt any surprise at Bob Markready's presence, he concealed it when Annabel introduced them.

'Very glad you could come down and visit us, Commander.'

'And I'm very glad to be here, Headmaster. I can't think of a better way of spending a fine Sunday.'

'Nor can I, nor can I.' The Headmaster's voice was brusque, as though the remark had been too obvious to be worth making. 'Now come and have some food, all of you.'

Bob Markready ate his lunch with an extra sauce of nostalgia. There was a timelessness about an English middle-class preparatory school. The fathers were not so tall, the mothers not so

143

fat, nor the lunch so delicious as it would have tasted to his school-boy palate, but nothing else had changed; that small boy in the short trousers and the broad-striped black and purple blazer might have been himself at the age of eleven, before he went to Dartmouth. No doubt there were record-players now in the common rooms, guitars and models of lunar space probes in the studies, but matron would still have her nightly bath-roster, the Hall Porter would still be taking round lists of the names of boys who were to see the Headmaster, breakfast would still be porridge and fried bread and sausages, and milky weak school tea.

So many of the other parents assumed that he was Annabel's husband that after the first disclaimers Bob Markready allowed himself to be so nominated. He enjoyed the scraps of school gossip vouchsafed to him in his new capacity. The boys pointed out to him the parents who were very rich, or who were divorced, or owned racehorses. He learned that David was in his last term and a king in the school, Senior Monitor and Captain of the School; he was also a considerable athlete, and Captain of the Cricket and Football Elevens. Jeremy, he learned from the parent of another small boy in the same form, was more artistic and had recently become notorious for a witty rhyme about the Headmaster and his hair.

The side flap of the marquee nearest the cricket field, which was known as Big Side, had been rolled up and he could see the rest of the school already filling up the seats around the ground. Three or four boys in front of the pavilion were tossing a ball about from one to another. Two groundsmen, one very old and the other still a boy, were returning the roller to its place behind the pavilion. He looked for Annabel and saw her walking towards the pavilion with Jeremy and several other small boys; it was clearly part of Annabel's duties as a visiting parent to be reintroduced and renew her acquaintance with some of Jeremy's particular friends. Bob Markready settled himself in a deck-chair, while David and the Headmaster were walking out to the pitch to toss.

It was a day of golden heat, a perfect summer's day such as the inventor of the Beaufort Scale must have had in mind for the number zero. The far trees and the sight screen wavered in a shimmering heat haze. A bumble bee slammed past his ear; the

144

Air Engineer Officer had once told him that a bumble bee was aerodynamically impossible. With that shape it should not be capable of flying an inch. A wood-pigeon broke with a clattering of wings from the sycamore behind and fled in its tumbling startled flight to the single oak tree on the far side of the ground.

Having lost the toss, David led the School into the field. The Masters' batting was opened by John Bowler and by the Headmaster himself who, almost at once, was given out lbw after attempting an improbably oblique leg glance.

Bob Markready heard the deck-chair next to him creaking as the Headmaster settled his weight in it.

'The same damned shot as last year, Commander. I must learn not to try it so early in the innings.'

'If you'd connected it would have been four runs cut and dried.'

'Ah yes, *if* I'd connected.' The Headmaster's wistful voice distilled the cricketer's eternal longing that one day, if only for one shot, his execution would match his imagination. 'Do you enjoy watching cricket, Commander? It's not a game one associates with the Navy somehow, although John Bowler's batting very well, for a nautical.'

The Headmaster joined in the applause for a smartly-struck four by Bowler and Bob Markready appreciated that Service rivalry was a running battle between them, much enjoyed by them both. He wondered whether Bowler's presence in the school had ever encouraged a boy to join the Navy; John Bowler was quite capable of some discreet recruiting.

'How many of your boys join the Navy, Headmaster?'

'Can't say with any certainty. Doesn't concern us so much now they've washed out the thirteen-year-old entry. It's the public schools' job to worry about that, these days. We used to send a few to Dartmouth. Funnily enough, I always used to think they were of two types. There was the rather dreamy romantic boy who thought he'd enjoy the life. And then, nine times out of ten, there were the boys with parental pressure behind them.'

Bob Markready took the point. His own father had never directly advised him to join the Navy; he had merely made it seem unthinkable that his son should ever do anything else.

'Their Lordships have never given credit where it was due, Commander. We used to say that one determined mum was worth a thousand recruiting posters.'

'You're probably right. Are you getting the same type of boy as you always did here?'

The Headmaster looked across sharply, as though scenting a loaded question. 'If you mean, are we getting the same type of *parents* I would say by and large, yes. Lord knows how some of them can still afford it. I suppose you can always afford something if you want it badly enough. Well hit, Bowler!'

There was a commotion amongst the crowd on the midwicket boundary, and the umpire was holding up his hands to signal a six.

'Tell me, Commander. Do you know Annabel well?'

'As a matter of fact, I've hardly spoken more than a few words to her before today.' He was himself astonished by the admission; it seemed hardly possible that he had known her such a short time.

'Ah well. This is the first time she's come down here with anybody else since her husband's death and of course we're all very pleased to see it. I imagine you knew her husband?'

'I never met him, I'm sorry to say.'

'I liked him very much. It was a great shock. We only had the older boy here then. We let him off school for a few days. Annabel came down to collect him. It nearly broke our hearts to see her. My wife and I were very upset. We're very glad to see you, Commander.'

The Headmaster's voice contained no trace of a match-maker's coyness. He was stating his plain opinion, expecting Bob Markready to draw the proper inference.

'Oh Bowler, that was unnecessary.' The Headmaster had been keeping his eye on the game. Bowler was starting towards the pavilion, tucking his bat under his arm. A fielder on the far boundary tossed the ball back to the wicket.

'Caught on the boundary. Must go and clap him in.'

Bob Markready stood up to join in the clapping for Bowler, whose face was flushed with the happy after-glow of the successful batsman. He sat down in the deck-chair vacated by the Headmaster and began to unbuckle his pads.

'That was a good knock, sir.'

'Good for the image, Robert.' John Bowler was out of breath. 'Thirty runs for the Masters against the School is worth two hundred in a Test match.'

'You obviously enjoy this life, sir.'

'I do. I was damned lucky to get the job and I've enjoyed every minute of it. Some of my contemporaries who got the Golden Bowler at the same time as I did weren't so lucky. Our trouble was that we all left the Navy with a whole way of life showing in our faces. You can't serve a life-time in the Navy and finish up as a Captain without having some kind of air of command about you. It goes with the job.'

Bowler took off his pads and laid them on the grass behind the deck-chair. 'It wasn't our fault. But it put prospective employers off. They were taking on a new employee, not a new chairman of the board. There wasn't much we could do about it. You can't shake off the manners of a life-time in two minutes, just for an interview. One thing I wanted to ask *you*, Robert. How are you getting on in that great ship of yours?'

Bob Markready heard the subtle change in Bowler's voice. He was no longer making idle conversation.

'Better than I expected, sir, so soon. We've got a long way to go yet, of course. The ship had a terrible commission last time . . .'

Bowler nodded. 'It shouldn't have happened to a *dog*.'

'But I'm convinced we can have a good one this time. The actual running of the ship's not difficult. A computer could probably do that as well as I, or better. The really hard thing is to persuade everyone on board that a good commission is on the cards. Once they're convinced, they'll go off and do it. Most of them don't believe me at the moment. But they will.'

'I was never in a carrier. I'm told they can be awkward sods. The squadron fellows complicate things.'

'They can, but they'll come round, with the rest. I'm sure of it.'

'So you think you can make a go of it?'

'I know I can, sir.'

Bowler grasped him warmly on the knee. 'By God, I'm damned glad to hear you say that!'

For the first time, Bob Markready became aware that his work in *Leviathan* was watched by a great host of silent witnesses. Bowler's questions had been put on behalf of a vast, mute, and totally involved audience. They seldom wrote to the Admiralty, or to the newspapers, or even to each other, but their collective

opinions made up a powerful pressure group. They were the elderly
retired officers, most of them living quiet lives at home, working
in their gardens, running the parish council and helping their wives
with village affairs, but all considering themselves as much a part
of the Navy in retirement as they had ever done while serving.
The Navy's gains were their gains, and when the Navy lost, they
were all losers. The stories of *Leviathan*'s first commission must
have come upon them as a succession of family disasters. He wondered whether the new generation would be as concerned when
their time came. Would Bird, or Fisher, or Simmondson or any
of *Leviathan*'s younger officers feel lighter at heart, put an extra
half-crown in the plate on Sunday, because the Navy had acquitted
themselves well in the Persian Gulf? Would Stiggins, when he
was sixty and retired, cuff his dog and ignore his wife at breakfast-
time because a socialist Member had challenged the Navy
Estimate Vote for new ship construction? Would any of them take
the Commander of a ship aside at a school cricket match and ask
him, as a matter of urgency, how goes the battle? And would they
by so doing reassure him that he was not alone and their prayers
were with him?

Bowler was applauding his successor at the wicket. 'Good shot,
Clem boy.'

Clem was the classics master, and he also coached the Eleven.
He had played for Sussex Gentlemen in his time and he was still
worth a place in most club sides. The game had taken on a more
tense atmosphere since Clem had come in to bat; in the Master's
match, it was a point of honour for Clem to score runs, as it was
for David and his side get him out cheaply.

'Are you going to marry Annabel, Bob?'

'Good gracious, sir, we're almost strangers!' Bowler had put it
baldly but now of course, as Bob Markready admitted to himself,
it was not such a preposterous notion.

'I see. I just asked because I know you so well and because this
is the first time she's come down here with anybody else. I suppose you must have come across Tom Powell?'

'No, I didn't, sir. To be honest, I'd never even heard of him.'

'I hear he was quite a swell in his own line of business. I met
him one Speech Day down here and I was most impressed. He
told me he'd just transferred to a permanent commission and I

148

remember thinking this was one occasion when Their Lordships had got a good bargain. Annabel's been unnaturally quiet since he went. She's a good-looking woman, and an impulsive one. She might have thrown her cap over the moon out of sheer boredom and frustration . . .'

A howl of exultation rang around the ground. Clem was taking off his batting gloves and grimly walking away from his shattered wicket. Several of the fielders were capering with joy. David was congratulating the grinning bowler.

'Clem boy, we were relying on some runs from you.' Obeying that self-defensive urge to huddle together which affects all batting sides in time of emergency, Bowler got up and went off to join the rest of the Masters' team in the pavilion.

In the lull between incoming and outgoing batsmen, Bob Markready studied the boys nearest to him on the boundary, conscious that he was watching a section of a micro-civilisation, almost a miniature ship's company. They had their leaders and they led, their own routines, their customs and taboos. No success in later life, not even success in *Leviathan,* could be sweeter than success at school. Turning over the pages of one public school's centenary book, he had once chuckled at the biography of a very famous Old Boy. His school career was given in full, his prowess as Under-16 Long Jump Champion and Captain of the First Tennis VI printed in heavy bold type, while the information that he had been Prime Minister and First Lord of the Treasury and afterwards elevated to the peerage had been included, almost as a postscript, in much smaller and thinner print. But perhaps he had been wrong to laugh at that. Perhaps the school's priorities had been absolutely right.

'You're looking very thoughtful, Bob.'

'Oh hello, Annabel.' He blinked as he got up from his deck-chair, horrified to feel his eyelashes wet. 'I was feeling quite maudlin. It must be the Englishman's "nostalgie d'école".'

'I don't know what that is, but it sounds jolly painful.'

With Annabel sitting beside him, Bob Markready reflected on how his knowledge of her had deepened even in the time they had been at the school. Surely it was an unusual woman whose future could so preoccupy two men as dissimilar as John Bowler and the Headmaster. They had both been glad to see him, for her sake. Their conversation had enlightened him, by illuminating her with

149

two spotlights from different angles.

They sat together, watching the Masters' batting recover from Clem's dismissal. It was a long, dour recovery, led by the French master and by the father of one of the Eleven, which lasted until the Masters were bowled out for 120 runs just before tea.

After tea, when the School were batting, David came and sat with them while he was waiting to bat. Bob Markready was warmed, and humbled, by the respectful looks given their small party by passing parents and boys. A man could visit a school as First Sea Lord and Chief of Naval Staff but if he were sitting with the Captain of the Eleven there was no doubt who was the celebrity. When the first School batsman was out, Bob Markready took a vicarious pleasure in the cheering which accompanied David's advance to the wicket.

David batted sensibly and undramatically, supported by the remaining opening batsman, and the School did not lose another wicket, although Bowler, Clem, the French master, every member of the fielding side, including the Headmaster himself, all bowled. By six o'clock the School had won a famous victory, by nine wickets.

John Bowler was amongst the crowd in front of the school to see the departing parents off. 'Goodbye, Robert. I hope you're right about that great ship.'

'I know I'm right, sir.'

'Good, good. Take care of Annabel.'

'I shall.'

Annabel was quiet until they reached the bottom of the drive. 'How much did you tip them, Bob?'

'I gave David seven and sixpence and Jeremy four shillings.' The amounts had been decided by the loose change he had in his pocket. 'Was that too much?'

'It was a bit generous, but it's all right. My father always gives them far too much.'

'What does he do, your father?'

'He's got a factory in Birmingham. They make precision parts for motor car engines, or something like that. Dad always wanted a son-in-law to help with the business but I married a naval officer and my sister married a school-teacher and neither Tom nor Colin would touch the business with a barge-pole. So poor old Dad has to keep on running it all by himself.'

They stopped for a meal on the way home. The hotel lounge was dusty and still warm from the heat of the day. The chairs were covered in cracked brown leather and there were Spy cartoons and racing prints on the walls. Two elderly women, each with a blue roan clumber spaniel on a lead, stood like tweedy caryatids at either end of the small bar.

They sat at a table in a corner, while they waited for their meal. The silence extended, until the room was full of fly-buzzing, clock-ticking quiet. The spaniels settled again on the floor but their owners continued to look knowing and tolerant and a little pitying, in the way, Bob Markready realised at last, people looked at lovers.

10

The national strike on the railways began as planned at midnight on Sunday, and no trains ran anywhere in the country until midnight on Tuesday, when a settlement had been reached. On Tuesday morning, before *Leviathan* sailed, the Master-at-Arms came to the Commander's cabin, looking like a man drawing Priam's curtain, to tell him half his Troy was burned.

The Commander came straight to the point. 'Well, what's the damage?'

'Five hundred and fifty-nine absent over leave, sir.'

'Good *God!*'

The Master at Arms shook his head, half dismayed, half wondering. 'It must be some kind of record, sir. I don't think any ship's ever had so many leave-breakers in one day, sir.'

The Commander had expected an irresponsible minority of the ship's company to break their leave, using the railway strike as an excuse. The Master-at-Arms' figure showed that a third of the men who had left the ship during the week-end had broken their leave.

The absentees included two pilots who had given themselves barely enough time to drive down from London and who had missed the ship because their motor car had a puncture on the Portsmouth Road. Their misdemeanour was unconnected with the railway strike, but to the Commander it was the ultimate disappointment. He had been confident that the wardroom would support him, confident that when he came to punish the ship's company's leave-breakers he would have behind him the powerful argument that at least the officers had all returned to their leave. Now, every defaulter who came before him would be able to mitigate his offence in his own eyes because the officers, too, sometimes overstayed their leave. The Commander sent for the two pilots, with their squadron CO, when they rejoined the ship on Tuesday evening.

Their names were Collins and Dryburgh. They were both sub-lieutenants, both very young, and sure of themselves. Neither of them appeared abashed by the Commander's summons. The puncture had been inconvenient, but no more than that. Roger Calvados, the CO of their squadron, looked far more out of countenance than either of the culprits. The Commander set himself to scourge off their complacency.

'... There are two hundred and thirty officers in our wardroom. Most of us went away for the week-end. All of us got back on time, rail strike or no rail strike. All except two, that is. *Mister* Collins and *Mister* Dryburgh, both as *wet* as piss, were adrift. Lieutenant Commander Calvados has told me why you were adrift and frankly it's the sort of excuse I expect to hear from some poor little boy seaman who doesn't know any better. "Please sir, I had a puncture." There's a drill shed in Chatham Barracks where the bulkheads are plastered with old excuses we've all heard before. Punctures are one of the original ones, with alarm clocks that don't go off, and losing your railway ticket, and *wetting your pants*. That's the sort of excuse we expect from small boys just out of the egg. I can see that neither of you has been in the Service more than half a dog-watch but I don't expect to hear that sort of drivel from *any* officer, I don't care how junior he is. You as officers don't have to keep to strict leave times. You can go ashore whenever you're not required on board for duty. That's your privilege. But it's also your *responsibility*.'

The colour had left their faces. Collins was biting his lip.

'I'm just about to punish more than five hundred of the ship's company for doing exactly what you did. When they get up in front of that table they're all going to look at me and think to themselves. "What's he getting at us for? The officers are just as bad. Why doesn't he have a go at them?" The whole wardroom, all of us, are going to be put at a disadvantage and all because two half-baked sub-lieutenants who haven't got the nappy wrinkles out of their pink little bottoms didn't have the elementary wit to leave themselves enough time to get back to the ship. You think about that before you go ashore again.'

The Commander guessed that if he had judged Calvados correctly, Collins and Dryburgh would have a great deal of time in which to ponder his words before they ever set foot on shore again. He himself intended to take no further action; the Air Group were best left to settle such matters amongst themselves.

Roger Calvados was a stern man, jealous of his squadron's reputation. The Commander heard later that he had stopped both sub-lieutenants' leave for two months – a stiffer penalty than the Commander himself would have imposed.

Meanwhile, the ship's company leave-breakers could not be dealt with so summarily. The number of cases awaiting investigation threatened for a time to disrupt the normal routine of the ship: there were so many defaulters that *Leviathan* would be operating virtually at two-thirds complement while their cases were being heard. On Wednesday morning, the line of defaulters stretched forward from the keyboard flat, through doorway after doorway, and along passageway after passageway, until the men at the end of the queue were several compartments forward of the keyboard flat, level with the hatch leading down to the wardroom ante-rooms. The petty officers and leading patrolmen of the regulating staff, wearing the awe-struck expressions of fishermen who had taken a miraculous draught, were fully extended in marshalling the queue, checking names against the Master-at-Arms' list, and keeping silence in the passageways. The Royal Marine keyboard sentry, who normally occupied the flat alone, was pushed, with his book and his keys, into one corner by the press of investigating and divisional officers who stood eight deep beside and behind the Commander's table.

When the Commander himself arrived he saw that the proceedings were being debased into farce. The staggering numbers of men involved were destroying the gravity of the occasion. Hours, perhaps days, would pass before the men at the end of the queue reached his table. In the meantime, they could be doing their normal work about the ship.

He beckoned the Master-at-Arms. 'Are they all here?'

'Yes sir, all here.'

'But do we need them all? It's going to be some time before I see the ones at the end. You'd better keep fifty, say, and tell the rest to carry on. Then as time goes by you can muster parties at the Regulating Office and bring them down here twenty or thirty at a time.'

'Aye aye, sir.'

First, the Commander dealt with a few sailors who had routine minor requests, to discontinue shaving, or to take turn of leave out of watch, or to change from 'Temperance' to 'Grog'. Then, he began on what came to be known in *Leviathan*'s wardroom as The Bloody Assizes – Bloody not because of the severity of the punishments, which were strictly prescribed in naval law, but because everyone concerned was utterly weary of them in body and mind long before they were finished. The Commander heard the evidence of the first case at nine-thirty on Wednesday morning. He gave his judgment on the last case at six o'clock on Friday evening.

During the three days of The Bloody Assizes, the Commander's table became the focal hub of *Leviathan,* round which the whole life of the ship revolved. The leave-breakers had returned, and indeed were still returning over so long a period that every member of the officers' quarterdeck watch-keeping roster was involved in the preliminary investigations. Their roster was repeatedly disrupted as officers were relieved, and relieved again, to give their evidence to the Commander. The senior regulating petty officer kept watch on the tail of defaulters and, as the line shrank, mustered a further party and added them to the end of the queue. The Chief Quartermaster, the Regulating Chief Stoker and Chief Electrician, the Flight Deck Chief and every ship and squadron rating with regulating responsibilities were kept at full stretch to find ratings as they were required and to arrange reliefs for those who were on watch. Divisional officers went about their duties in the ship with one eye on the clock, afraid to be absent from the Commander's table for more than half an hour, lest a member of their division should be called. Officers who had cabins near the keyboard flat found their desks and beds piled with the thick envelopes containing ratings' service documents, dumped there by divisional officers so that they could conveniently be picked up on the way to the Assizes.

By the afternoon of the second day, the Master-at-Arms' voice was hoarse and strained. His rendering of the ritual description of the charges had by constant repetition lapsed into a parrot gabble, in which he accentuated only the period of time absent over leave.

'... commit an act prejudicial to good order ... naval discipline ... in that he did remain absent over leave *eight hours, five minutes,* sir, namely from zero seven three zero ... this being

155

an aggravated offence, he having been warned the ship was under sailing orders . . .'

The investigating officers, shuffling the pages of their notebooks, stepped up to the Commander's elbow, saluted, and they too made their formal recitals.

'I investigated this case, sir . . . stated that the first train from Nottingham left at four in the morning . . . reported to the Barracks Regulating Office at three o'clock on Wednesday afternoon, sir . . .'

Some ratings had made genuine and whole-hearted attempts to return in time. A leading stoker had hitch-hiked from Scarborough and had only missed the ship by half an hour. A naval airman in Roger Calvados' squadron borrowed his small daughter's bicycle and set off in the middle of the night to cycle back to the ship from Oxford, reaching Basingstoke before being knocked off the bicycle by a passing lorry. He had grazes on hands and knees to prove his story and a note from the Basingstoke police certifying that he had produced the remains of the bicycle at the station; the police had provided a car to take him from the hospital to the ship which had missed sailing time by ten minutes.

The Commander had schooled himself over many years to be objective when examining defaulters; he knew, without conceit, that he rarely allowed his personal feelings to prejudice him. But when, towards the end of the Bloody Assizes, the leave-breakers were senior petty officers and chief petty officers, who were traditionally examined last, the Commander had to conceal his disgust. These ratings were intelligent and highly-trained men. Most of them had technical qualifications which were greatly valued in industry. These men seldom troubled their divisional officers with their domestic affairs. They were quite capable of organising their own lives. They had cold-bloodedly weighed up the penalties of being absent over leave against the inconveniences of attempting to get back to the ship, and they had deliberately chosen to stay at home. They knew that the Navy's scales of punishment for leave-breaking were old-fashioned and minimal deterrents, based on a code framed at a time when the ordinary bluejacket was socially and financially no better than a second-class citizen. They knew that the Commander was like a man punishing modern offences with archaic penalties. They wished to be treated as responsible men on board, but also to shelter be-

156

hind the legend of the sailor's traditional irresponsibility ashore; in short, they wished to have their cake and to eat it. The Commander had no doubt that if he had been empowered to fine these men twenty pounds for the offence and ten pounds for every hour's absence, every last one of them would have been on board when the ship sailed on Tuesday morning. The Commander discovered that he was face to face with the higher representatives of the New Model Navy, and they disgusted him.

The rest of the wardroom agreed that The Bloody Assizes were a personal triumph for the Commander. He was as patient at the end of the day as he had been at the beginning. He listened as attentively to the evidence of the three hundred and first case as he had to the evidence of the first. Many sailors had identical stories, but the Commander did not betray to any accused man that his excuse had been used by the last dozen men before him. The Commander's performance throughout the week had been, the whole wardroom conceded, a model demonstration of how to keep one's temper when there was every justification for losing it. Most of them had attended the Commander's table at some time during the three days and all of them mentally tipped their hats to him. He had done something they admitted none of them could have done as well. The Captain spoke for all the officers.

'I don't suppose you're in the mood for compliments just now, Bob, but that was a damned fine piece of work. A smaller man would have lost his temper long before the end. My Secretary tells me he's never seen such a session in all his time in the Service.'

'Thank you, sir. Don't forget it's your turn next week.' Persistent offenders, and leave-breakers above the rate of leading seaman, were punished by the Captain himself.

'Don't I know it. And I'm not looking forward to it. Still, it's all in the game. Never mind.'

The Commander was reluctant just to let the subject go. 'I really thought we were achieving something, sir. But this has shown me we haven't begun to start yet.'

'Oh nonsense, Bob. This is just the rub of the green. At last we can say we do things in a big way here. That must have been an all-time record for the number of leave-breakers in one day.'

'Yes, sir. But it's the sort of record I'd prefer somebody else had.'

157

Once again, the Commander was baffled by Tosser's insensitiveness. *Leviathan* had had enough men absent over leave on one morning to provide the full complement of a pre-war light cruiser, and Tosser called it just the rub of the green. Tosser McTigue had a reputation as a bluff, simple seaman, but the Commander wondered whether he was as cloddish as he liked to appear. The promotion selection boards were capable of some odd aberrations, but surely no man as apparently stupid could rise to Captain. The Commander himself had sincerely believed that he had been achieving at least a little in *Leviathan*. The aftermath of the Whitsun week-end seemed to prove that he had been deluding himself. Nor was there any comfort in knowing that other ships had had similar troubles. The Secretary had made enquiries and had reported that, while no ship could approach *Leviathan's* total, others had higher percentages of leave-breakers in their ship's companies. One of the frigates berthed ahead of *Leviathan* over the week-end had been unable to sail until noon on Tuesday morning, when enough of her ship's company had returned from leave to make up a quorum to take her to sea.

On Friday evening, when the last defaulter had been dismissed, the Commander went back to his cabin and stretched himself face down on the bunk. He was exhausted and depressed and for the first time found himself hating *Leviathan*. There seemed no end to her brightly-lit passageways, no escape from the noise of the ventilation fans, the footsteps, the incessant idiotic chatter from the loudspeakers and, underlying every other sound, the constant whirring and rumbling of machinery. He felt a claustrophobic sense of being surrounded by hundreds of human beings, all pressing upon him their demands on his time and his nervous energy.

He turned over, sat upright, and reached for his telephone. There was, just possibly, somewhere quiet he could go.

'... Of course you can come round, Bob.' The mere sound of her voice revived him. 'I'd love to see you again.'

'I was hoping I could take you out to dinner somewhere.'

'I've got a better idea. Have you had a hard day at the office?'

'Not at the office, but it's been a long day, all right. A long week, actually.'

'I thought so, by your voice. You come round here and I'll make some supper. Would you mind a quiet evening here?'

'There's nothing I'd like better. I really would like that. What time?'

'Any time. I'll be here.'

'I'm going to have a bath and change, and then I'll come.'

'Right, you do that.'

She was wearing flame-red tights, and a black sweater knitted of some heavy ribbed wool, and black pointed slippers with an almost Turkish rake to their tips. She had a locket on a gold chain round her neck, plain gipsies' ear-rings, and a gold bangle round one ankle. Her hair was tied up in a top-knot and secured by a band of black tortoise-shell engraved in white with elephants, and men with spears, and crouching tigers, and helmeted warriors on horse-back. Altogether, he thought, she presented an exotic appearance for Old Portsmouth on a dull, windy summer's evening.

'Well, how do I look?'

'I'm sorry, I must have been gaping.' He was recovering from his first surprise. 'I like it. But I feel I ought to be bringing you some incense or some slaves, or something.'

'Yes, I know just what you mean. This is what Tom would have called my House of Assignation rig. Come in. I've never asked you how you knew where I lived?'

'Oh I knew the house. I used to visit the Marriotts when they lived in that house opposite.'

'You knew them? Where are they now?'

'In America, I think. Steve got some job on the staff in Washington.'

'They were just moving out when we came back here. Just as well. *He* was all right, but I don't think she and I liked each other very much.'

He could well imagine it. He thought it unlikely that any wife would welcome the spectacle of Annabel, in flame-red tights, living opposite.

Annabel led the way into her living-room, and he saw at once that she must have some income of her own. Naval families took with them their clothes, their pictures and their ornaments, and their small furniture, relying on furnished houses or Admiralty married quarters to provide the main pieces. Annabel's living-room demonstrated a level of taste and income much higher than the

159

normal naval family home. That grey-and-white striped wallpaper was never Admiralty issue, nor was the sea-grey carpet, nor the armchairs in their saffron coloured covers. No Naval Storekeeping Officer had ever delivered the veneered walnut kneehole writing desk, nor the two octagonal small tables with engraved tops, nor the camphorwood chest under the window. Above the fireplace, there was a painting of an orange-hulled fishing boat at rest on a calm luminously blue sea and, on the bookcase, a framed portrait photograph in colour of a Lieutenant Commander in uniform.

He was in full fig, with sword and medals which included the rose and pearly blue-grey ribbon of the MBE. Bob Markready studied the face, the sharp nose, blue eyes and square jaw. He searched his memory again, but he had no recollection of ever having met Tom Powell.

Annabel was standing by a stained oak corner cupboard which held bottles and glasses. 'What will you have, Bob?'

'I think I'd like some whisky. But let me do it.'

She picked out a square glass decanter. 'Drat it, it's empty. It's a long time since I had anyone here who drank whisky. I'll get some.'

'Let me get it!'

'No, you stay where you are. I know where it is. There's a bottle out in the back somewhere. Won't be long.'

Beside the portrait lay a leather-covered photograph album, with an elaborate monogram of the initals A and T stamped in gold.

The first photograph was of their wedding, taken just as they emerged from the church, under the arch of swords. Annabel looked about seventeen or eighteen years old, and Tom could only just have been promoted lieutenant. In her bridal dress, with her veil thrown triumphantly back and her bridesmaids clustered behind her, Annabel stood poised on the brink of her new adventure.

The guard of honour included some familiar faces; nearest the camera was Commander (Air), as a lieutenant, and next to him, but still a sub-lieutenant, was Roger Calvados. In the opposite rank was Rupert Smith and behind, next to the church wall, there was the profile of the Captain's Secretary. They were all grinning as they held up their swords, but the photographer had caught a moment of their common envy: there was not a man in that guard of honour who would not gladly have married Annabel himself.

There were several newspaper cuttings and photographs of the wedding; plainly Tom Powell must have been something of a Fleet Air Arm celebrity even at the time when he was married. Bob Markready turned the pages, eager for more pictures of Annabel. There she was on horse-back, on the beach, in a line of pupils at a ski-ing class, and in a family group holding a child after the christening. There were photographs of David and Jeremy, at stages in their lives from their christenings to their first school uniforms and there were more pictures of Annabel and Tom, arriving at the church for other people's weddings, hanging over the side of a sailing boat, sitting in a party at a ship's dance, crouching by the fire at a fancy dress barbecue.

The latest cuttings and pictures had not been pasted in. The cuttings all covered Tom's accident, and most of them were illustrated by the famous photograph. Bob Markready examined a print from a weekly magazine. From the angle of shot, the picture had obviously been taken from an accompanying aircraft and it recorded the instant Tom Powell's aircraft had ceased to fly, before it broke up into separated debris. The main plane of the starboard wing was strained upwards as though whipped by an enormous shock-wave travelling along its structure. A small panel was just breaking from the fuselage below the cockpit. The tail-plane, the port wing and most of the cockpit were concealed by smoke. Tom Powell's face could be distinguished, where the smoke was thinner; his eyes were shut tightly, his mouth hung open, in his last conscious expression before he and his aircraft were blown apart. It was a remarkable picture. No wonder the Press had printed it, and no wonder the Admiralty had objected.

'Sorry I've been so long. You looking at the story of my life?'

'Yes I was, I'm afraid.' He shut the album quickly, feeling that he had been caught spying.

'There's no need to feel guilty. Jeremy collected all those. Some of Tom's friends used to come here and spend hours just looking at that picture. I suppose they went away and talked about it amongst themselves and tried to think what could have happened.'

Some women might have taken consolation from the very

dramatic nature of their husband's death; they might even have been partly compensated by the thought that their husband had not died as other men died. But he could detect no shading of complacency nor false histrionics in Annabel's voice; to Annabel, it was understandable that her husband's friends should be professionally interested in the accident.

'You pour yourself some whisky, and mix me a gin and something.'

She took a cushion from the sofa, placed it on the carpet and sat down, her head against the arm, to watch him and to take pleasure in his small, methodical movements. She had heard from the wives, who had it from their husbands, that Bob Markready might actually be on the way to success in *Leviathan*, not by doing any great thing but by doing a thousand small things. Tom had once told her that the Navy produced many such men. In peace-time they were invaluable, although they tended to be given only limited command in war-time. The tragedy of such men, Tom had said, was that they spent their professional lives preparing for war and were replaced by others as soon as a war began.

He carried the glasses over.

'Thank you. Now tell me what's been bothering you.'

He shook his head. 'There's nothing bothering me.'

'Come *on*, Bob. There's something grinding away inside you. I can see it in your face. What have you been up to this week?'

'It's all shop, Annabel. I'm sure you wouldn't want to be burdened with it.'

'Try me. I don't know how many times Tom used to pin me in a corner, give me a drink, and batter away at me until he had something clear in his mind.'

'Well, it isn't any one single thing. This week it happens to be leave-breaking . . .'

He realised that he must have come subconsciously intent on telling her, because he slipped into his story as though he had rehearsed it. Annabel made a good audience. She was outside the Navy, but she had been a naval wife. She knew the language. Like most thoughtful officers, he did not despise a woman's opinion; some of the most penetrating and constructive criticisms he had ever heard of a ship had been made by the Captain's wife and that Captain, he now recalled, had retired as a full Admiral. He told

Annabel of his hopes for *Leviathan,* of his sincere belief that he was slowly winning. He told her of the warnings they had given the ship's company before the week-end and of his own certainty that there would not be an unusual number of leave-breakers. He told her of the part which had hurt him most of all, of his feeling of impotence when he heard the defence of the most senior ratings.

'. . . They just look at you. They know they've got quite a lot to offer a civilian employer and they know they can buy themselves out of the Navy any time they like. Or they think they can. They think you can't touch them.'

'But this is nothing new, Bob. Tom had the same thing when he got his first squadron. He used to come home *fuming* because some of his sailors were brainier than he was. But he got used to it.'

'I know it's nothing new. Maybe this is just the first time I've come across so many of them, all at once, in the same ship. I sometimes feel completely out of touch with what they're thinking. In the old Navy all a divisional officer had to do was to see that his sailors got their rum and their mail and their leave, make sure they put in for their next good conduct badge when they were entitled, and very occasionally he had to try and sort something out when their wives ran off with somebody else. But *now.* . . . Now a divisional officer spends his time vetting hire purchase agreements, and witnessing house mortgage documents and *passport* applications and *share* transfer certificates. They're not sailors, they're *tycoons!*'

Annabel concealed her smile, passing her hand quickly over her face. 'But is that such a bad thing? They're citizens, like everybody else.'

'I agree they're citizens, just like everybody else. But they're *not* citizens once they're on board. They're members of the ship's company then, just as I am, and they leave their citizenship at home, just as I do. They think they can come on board like any other civilian job and work at their desks or their blasted electronic black boxes, nine to five, five days a week and every week-end off. And they howl blue murder when I won't let them. But it *can't* be done like that. That's not how the Navy works. The other day I actually saw a Chief Petty Officer coming on board in the morning wearing a bowler hat! I'm told that particular fellow is a bit of a comedian and did it for a bet, but I thought

163

it symbolic. They think they can't be touched, but by God they can, and I'm going to touch them!'

He was like a great wild bull, ignoring the men with nets and stakes. He was depressed now, and tired, and bewildered, but that would pass: he would be back, breathing out strength and confidence again. Annabel hoped that *Leviathan* would not prove too strong, even for him. She would hate to see him humbled.

She brought in their supper on a tray: celery soup, and ham, and a cunning salad with hidden resources of tomato, whole boiled eggs, endives, slices of apple, and chopped banana and cubes of blue cheese. Afterwards, there was sherry trifle, and coffee with cream.

'If this is the sort of supper you put on when you're not expecting me, I must come one evening when you are expecting me.'

'I'm glad you liked it.'

'I did, very much indeed.'

There was no advantage in telling him that this was the meal she had prepared for two girl-friends, two wives whose husbands were away. Annabel had telephoned them both and although she had not put her dilemma in so many words, the girls had taken her meaning at once: for a woman in Annabel's position an engagement with a man, any man, automatically took precedence.

He had guessed at the circumstances of his magnificent windfall. He wondered again about her life here at home, with no husband, and her two sons away at boarding school.

'You once asked me if I was lonely, but how about you, Annabel?'

'What do I *do* with myself all day, you mean?' She did not resent the question. Such preliminaries were necessary. In her experience, there was seldom any such phenomenon as love at first sight: intrigue was almost always preceded by curiosity, and she knew, as though it were part of an ancient inherited lore, the magical series of degrees, like a picture coming into ever-sharper focus, by which an acquaintance became a lover.

'I wouldn't call myself lonely, exactly. I know a lot of people round here. The girls are always having coffee mornings, because they want a gossip or to raise money for something. And a spare, moderately presentable woman with her own transport is useful to make up the numbers sometimes. No, I wouldn't call myself lonely. And, of course, I do "Meals on Wheels" one day a week.'

'What's "Meals on Wheels"?'

'We take cooked meals to old people in their homes. Now *there* you've got real loneliness. Especially some of the old men living by themselves. It's not food they want so much, it's somebody to talk to. They're dying to talk about the Government or the football season.'

She paused, as though to consider what she had said. 'I will admit I still miss Tom very much. You feel so helpless as a widow. There are so many things your husband used to do which you suddenly have to learn to do yourself. I will admit I miss the Married Patch life, too. I know people always laugh and make jokes about the Married Patch, but it had its points. If you had children under school age there were always other children for them to play with. You always had company if you wanted it, when your husband was away. There was always somebody to help in an emergency.'

'Such as, if your husband was killed?'

She looked at him directly, again not resenting the question. She recognised that he was not being deliberately tactless. It was necessary to sweep the old facts away.

'I didn't really mean that, but such as that, yes. But it was an odd thing about that, it wasn't always the people you expected who needed help the most. I remember the Captain's wife at one air station we lived on. She was a wonderful person, a really wonderful woman. She was always ready to help, and if there was anything that needed organising she'd do it, or see that it was done. If somebody had a raw deal she'd pitch in and do what she could to put it right. She was an absolute brick. And then the Captain was flying one day. . . . You know they have to put in so many hours a year to keep up their flying pay?'

He nodded. 'Yes, I knew that.'

'Well, he was doing that and he was on one of these trips when they had an accident and he was killed. I went along to their house immediately with two of the other squadron CO's wives, to see her and see if we could do anything to help.'

He could picture them. It would have been news that threatened them all. The husbands would be away during the day-time and it would have been an all feminine society, gathering to console

165

the inconsolable, to help one of their number begin to face a future which was unthinkable.

'. . . She was just about hysterical. We had to more or less hold her down to stop her hurting herself. She kept shouting "It can't be us, it *can't* be us!" We had to take it in turns to stay with her for days afterwards, even after the funeral. She'd been married twenty years at least. She must have thought about it many times. When it actually happened it just completely unhinged her.'

He saw her wincing, as though the memory of that other woman's agony was now more vivid than her own.

'Some of the others were completely different. One pilot in Tom's first squadron was about twenty, and his wife couldn't have been much more than eighteen or nineteen when he was killed. They'd only been married six weeks. But when I went to see her she was absolutely as calm as ice. She hardly said a word to me and she'd already started to pack her clothes to go home. In a way, it was even more terrible than the Captain's wife. The girl went home to her mother's and we never saw her or heard from her again. I think that was the worst part of it, the way they used to just drop out of your life. One day they were married, and part of life, joining in things and being your friends. The next day they were widows and they just left. They took the children away and most of them never wrote or saw their friends again. They might just as well be dead, too. It made you think that women were only there on sufferance. If anything happened to their husbands, they had no right to stay, they had to go and leave it all behind, just as if they'd never been married.'

'But you didn't.'

'No, I didn't. I could have gone back to my parents but I decided to stay here. This is our home. I made up my mind to try and start a new life.'

'I'm very glad you did.'

'I'm very glad I did, too.'

Before he left, he kissed Annabel. It was the first time he had kissed her and it was a gentlemanly kiss, a formal gesture, like the climax of a figure in the Lancers. It was no more than a token, a talisman exchanged for the future, and as such Annabel accepted it. The matter on which she had set her heart would not be hurried. When he was ready, she would be there.

The Commander returned to the ship with a light heart and a brisk step. He had unburdened himself to a woman and so experienced, if only by proxy, one of the more blessed side-effects of marriage. Like Saul, he had taken his troubles to a witch and his brow was cleared. He went to bed and fell into a calm sleep from which, at three-thirty in the morning, he was aroused by the ringing of his cabin telephone.

'Commander here. Who's that?' His sleep-fuddled brain turned over memories of the last time his telephone had awoken him at such an hour.

'Is that the Commander?'

'*Yes*. What is it?'

'Nothing, sir. I just wondered if you wanted to go to the heads.'

'*What!* Who's that speaking? Who's there?'

'A well-wisher.'

The line clicked dead. The Commander rattled the receiver for some moments before dialling the main exchange.

'Who was that calling my cabin just now? This is the Commander here.'

'I can't tell you that, sir.' The operator's voice did not hide his surprise at hearing the Commander at such an hour. 'It's an automatic telephone exchange, sir. They could have been speaking from anywhere in the ship.'

'But did you happen to notice anything on my cabin extension?'

'No, sir.'

'All right. Never mind.'

The Commander lay back on the bunk. But after a time he got up, put on his dressing-gown, and went along the passageway to the senior officers' bathroom.

11

The Commander awoke in the morning, preoccupied by the absurd telephone call: although it could have been made by a drunken sailor returning on board, it was an odd time of night for a liberty-man to come off shore. The telephone call had further implications which were not at all absurd, which indeed were serious enough to be worth mentioning to the First Lieutenant.

The First Lieutenant was not surprised to hear of it. 'He must be working up the scale, sir. The Officer of the Watch had one, Fisher has had one, so has the Senior and so have I.'

'When did this happen? Why wasn't I told?'

'It happened last night, sir, when you were ashore.' The First Lieutenant had hoped to settle the matter quietly, without involving the Commander. 'Did he by any chance ask you if you wanted to go to the heads, sir?'

'Yes, and the damnable thing is that as soon as he gave me the idea I had to get out of bed and go.'

The First Lieutenant chuckled. 'That's the way of it, sir. You didn't happen to recognise the voice, I suppose?'

'No, I didn't. It could have been anybody. It certainly didn't sound like a voice I knew.'

'Would you have said it was an officer's voice, sir?'

'No. It sounded to me like a sailor.'

'That's what I thought, sir.' The First Lieutenant sighed. 'It looks as if we've got our joker back again. We had much the same thing last commission.'

'What's the drill then?'

'There's no drill, sir. There are more than two thousand blokes on board and more than five hundred telephones. It could be any one of the blokes, speaking from any one of the telephones. He'll either stop of his own accord, or he'll go on and make a mistake and then we'll nab him.'

'I'm not sure we can just stand around and wait for him to make a mistake. We'll see.'

The Commander's own hopes that he might be able to deal with the matter unobtrusively were dashed immediately after breakfast, when the Captain sent for him. He was puzzled by the summons, because he had just left the Captain after meeting him on the quarterdeck when he came on board, and the Captain could surely have mentioned any outstanding business then.

Tosser was in his sleeping cabin, changing into his uniform. He was dragging at the knot of his tie, and scowling into his mirror.

'There you are, Bob! Look, what the devil's going on in this lunatic ship . . .'

'I beg your pardon, sir?'

'. . . I'd just got up here when that telephone there in my day-cabin rang. When I answered it, someone said "Is that the Captain?" So I said "Yes it is, what do you want?" And then some madman said "Captain sir, this is a well-wisher, do you *masturbate?*" My God I was so flabbergasted, by the time I'd realised what he was actually *saying*, he'd rung off!'

'I'm very sorry about that, sir. Did you happen to recognise the voice?'

'Of course I didn't!' Tosser irritably shrugged on his uniform jacket. 'The people I know don't ring me up first thing in the morning to ask me if I abuse myself! If you really pressed me, I would have said it was a Birmingham accent, but I wouldn't get up in court and swear to it.'

The Commander himself had fancied he had caught the trace of an accent, but he could not name the region. It could have been Birmingham, or somewhere in the Midlands.

The day-cabin telephone rang again, and Tosser looked round at it in alarm. 'You answer that, Bob.'

'Who's that?' The Captain's Secretary's voice crackled in the earpiece. 'That you, Bob? Is Himself there?'

'One moment, Scratch. It's the Secretary, sir.'

'Thank God for that! I thought it was that madman ringing up again to ask me if I'd seduced my grandmother! Just leave it there, I'll take it. In the meantime you'd better get on to this fellow quickly, Bob. This is all very funny, but the next thing we know he'll be ringing up to report fires which don't exist. And the next thing after that, he'll be ringing up to report fires which *do* exist.'

The Captain had put his finger on the one serious implication of the telephone calls. The Commander was ready to admit, though not to enjoy, their comical aspect. The Well-wisher, as the Commander had already begun to think of him, had a warped but inventive sense of humour, but with malice and a few telephone calls he could quickly put the ship's security organisation into confusion. In a ship as large as *Leviathan,* the physical obstacles in the way of personal meetings were so great that the telephone was the normal medium of communication. Nobody would climb several ladders and cross several decks to speak face to face when he could use the telephone at his elbow. Although local networks of sound-powered telephones served the main machinery spaces, the flight deck and hangars, and the damage control organisation, the main automatic exchange was the only system which embraced the whole ship. Most compartments had a telephone, and abuse of the system was the most effective way of disturbing the ship's routine.

The Captain had accurately forecast the Well-wisher's progress. Later in the forenoon, when the Commander was pouring himself a cup of coffee in the ante-room, the rarely-used action broadcast speaker on the bulkhead above the notice-boards began to hum and crackle.

'. . . Fire, fire, fire! Fire in the Canteen Flat! Fire and emergency parties muster in the Canteen Flat . . .'

Slowly, the Commander put down his coffee cup. Fire in the Canteen Flat? It was not possible. It was ten o'clock, stand easy time, on a Saturday forenoon and the canteen flat would be so crowded there would hardly be the physical room for a fire. There could not possibly be a fire in the canteen flat at that hour of the day.

When the Commander reached the canteen flat, the fire and emergency party, led by a bewildered stoker petty officer, were enduring the witticisms and jeers of the queue of sailors waiting to be served at the canteen counter. Two of the fire party sheepishly held extinguishers, which they had snatched up on their way. A third had unreeled a fire-hose and was bashfully holding the nozzle end. In the crush of sailors behind were an engine-room artificer, an electrician, and a shipwright, each with a bag of tools, and a sick berth attendant with a first-aid box

170

under his arm. The fire and emergency party were present and correct; only the last essential requirement, the fire or the emergency, was missing.

The Commander forced his way through to the stoker petty officer.

'What's your name?'

'Petty Officer Harvey, sir. Damage control petty officer of the watch, sir.'

'Where's the fire then?'

'I don't know, sir. There's no fire here I can see, sir, and the lads over there say there's never been a fire, sir.' Harvey's voice was hurt and resentful; he was a young petty officer, who took his job seriously.

The Shipwright Officer came out of the side door of the canteen and pushed towards the Commander, holding his hands out in the shape of a ship's bows and shouting 'Gangway!'

'Are you the Damage Control Officer of the Day, Chippy?'

'Yes, sir. I've just been talking to the Canteen Manager, sir. He's been here for the last hour and hasn't seen or heard a thing. It looks like a mistake, sir.'

'Obviously it's a mistake. Who reported the fire?'

'It was reported by telephone, sir, to HQ One.' Petty Officer Harvey's voice had become defensive; at any moment he expected to be accused of dragging out the fire and emergency party, and the Shipwright Officer, and the Commander, on a wild-goose chase. 'I didn't stop, sir. I made the pipe from HQ One and came straight on up here, sir.'

'That was exactly the right thing to do, Harvey. Who was it? Who made the telephone call, I mean?'

'I didn't quite catch the name, sir. Wiltshire, it sounded like, but I didn't stop, sir, the fire was the thing I was bothered about...'

'That's all right, Harvey. Dismiss your fire and emergency party now.' The Commander could see the pattern: Wiltshire and Well-wisher could sound alike, in the heat and haste of the moment, and perhaps on a bad line.

The canteen flat was now besieged by sailors, clamouring and pressing in from the passageways on either side. Everyone loved a fire, and a fire in the canteen flat gave every member of the ship's company a legitimate excuse to visit it, on the pretext of buying something at the canteen. The First Lieutenant's voice was raised, somewhere at the back of the crowd.

'All right, all right! Gangway there! There's no fire, there's no excitement. So you can all go home. I'm sorry to disappoint you, but there's *no* fire. Nothing to see, so you might just as well all go away . . .

As the crowd thinned, the First Lieutenant joined the Commander.

'Our mutual well-wisher, I presume, sir?'

'Yes.'

'I guessed as much.' The First Lieutenant took care to keep any tinge of sympathy from his voice, knowing, like the rest of the wardroom, that sympathy would only infuriate the Commander. But it was wretched luck to meet something as ridiculous and as unsettling as this. Their well-wisher, whoever he was, had a perverted sense of humour. Never before had the First Lieutenant witnessed a fire and emergency party arriving to tackle a fire in a compartment they could barely enter for the press of bodies already inside.

'. . . Fire, fire fire! Fire in the steering gear compartment! Fire and emergency parties muster in the steering gear compartment!'

A roar of derision rose up from the sailors still in the canteen flat, which rang in the Commander's ears as he left. Breathless after running most of the length of the ship, he arrived in the steering gear compartment on the heels of the fire and emergency party.

The steering gear artificer was on the telephone. He had been in the compartment when he heard the alarm and he was ringing HQ One to refute it. Looking at the artificer's face, as he indignantly denied any knowledge of the fire alarm, the Commander caught the First Lieutenant's sleeve.

'That does it. Let's go and talk to Commander (L). I've an idea we can scotch this fellow. I'm *not* going to be messed about by this . . . this *comedian*.'

Dai Bach was in the ante-room, just finishing his coffee and looking forward to a week-end at home in his garden. He had not heard of the telephone calls and was taken aback by the Commander's proposals.

172

'... *Monitor* the main exchange! Ah now, Bob, you don't know what you're asking! I've only got four main exchange watch-keepers, on twenty-four about. I haven't the hands to monitor every call ...'

'Dai, I'm not asking you to monitor *every* call. The only numbers any good to this fellow are the quarterdeck, the bridge when we're at sea, HQ One, and possibly the Main Machinery Control Room, and perhaps Hangar Control and the Aircraft Control Room. That's six numbers. Can you do those?'

Commander (L) pensively stroked his chin with the tip of his forefinger. 'I suppose we could. We may have to double up on the watch-keepers during the day-time, but I suppose we could, yes.'

'And can you fix it so that the Captain's cabin telephone number and the Heads of Departments' numbers can't be dialled direct but have to come through the main exchange?'

'Another sort of monitoring, you mean. Yes we can do that. We had to do something like it last commission. It means you won't be able to dial numbers from your cabin. You'll have to make all your calls through the main exchange.'

'That won't matter. And tell me, is there anything you can do about wire-tapping those six numbers?'

'*Wire tap?*' Commander (L) looked up in dismay. 'Bob, you're taking this seriously!'

The Commander threw away the last restraints on his temper. 'Of *course* I'm taking it seriously, you *stupid* man, although everybody else seems to think it the funniest thing that ever happened. It may *be* funny, having us running round in little circles but soon the novelty of that's going to wear off and he'll start lighting *real* fires! And sooner or later someone's going to get hurt! *Now* do you see why I'm taking it seriously!'

'I'm sorry, I'm sorry.' Commander (L) held up his hand; Bob was obviously taking this to heart. 'I take your point, Bob. But we can't do anything about wire-tapping. We haven't the gear for it. You must admit, it's unusual in HM Ships.'

'But can we spread it about that we *are* wire-tapping, even though we're not?'

'Yes, certainly.' Commander (L) hoisted himself from his arm-chair. 'I'll go and see what I can do, and let you know.'

'Thank you Dai.' The Commander was already contrite. 'And

173

I'm sorry I lost my temper with you.'

'That's all right. It was my fault. I didn't know this was bothering you so much.' Dai Bach had his own reservations about the effectiveness of monitoring telephone calls: but if it made Bob Markready any happier, he was willing to arrange it.

'Will you be on board during the week-end, Number One?'

The First Lieutenant had been listening to the conversation with growing consternation. Now, he looked down at his feet, disconcerted.

'Well sir, I *was* hoping to . . .'

'Never mind. I'll be on board myself. I'll look after everything.'

The Commander had hoped to go ashore and see Annabel during the week-end. He knew that he could brief the duty lieutenant commander, turn over the situation to him, and leave the ship for the whole week-end and nobody would think it strange. But he could not leave *Leviathan* knowing that someone was free to move around in her and pick up a telephone whenever he liked. Success might make the Well-wisher careless. The Commander wanted to be on the spot when he made his mistake, while the incident was still fresh.

The Commander could not force himself to stay in his cabin, or in the wardroom, or in any one place, for longer than a few minutes. He jumped whenever a telephone rang, and he discovered that he was bracing himself on the edge of his chair, ready to move, whenever the ship's broadcast system hummed and paused before an innocent, routine announcement. On Saturday afternoon he prowled the ship restlessly, surprised to find how very difficult it was for any man to remain unobserved in *Leviathan*. On the starboard boat-deck, he stopped by one of the canvas-covered ship's motor-boats and at once a crane-driver walked from forward and mounted the rungs set in the base of the crane pedestal, climbing up to his seat to operate the crane. Murmuring voices came from the other side of the boat and, looking round its bows, the Commander saw four sailors sitting by the guard-rail, smoking, and reading newspapers in the Saturday afternoon sun.

Above the boat-decks, the ship's side contained a warren of tiny compartments and narrow passageways, short flights of steps, isolated platforms projecting over the water, and unexpected galleries which turned sharply outboard, ran along above the water

174

for a few feet, and turned inboard again. There were minute mess-decks on this level, for eight or a dozen men, remote workshops containing only a bench and a lathe, small-arms ammunition and anti-aircraft magazines, potato lockers, and other miniature com-partments, some no more than a door and a recess in the bulk-head plating, which chief petty officers used as make-shift cabins, keeping their personal belongings and writing their letters in them. As the Commander walked, he saw a sailor in every one of those tiny compartments and on every open patch of sunlit deck. Above, on the flight deck and on the gun sponsons, there were more sailors, gossiping, or reading, or watching traffic passing up and down the river. His own presence was apparently disturbing the normal make-and-mend atmosphere for so large a number of the ship's company that the Commander took off his cap, to demonstrate that he did not wish to be saluted nor any official notice to be taken of him.

The ship was as thickly populated below decks. The Commander had only to wait by an air-conditioning machinery space, obscurely tucked away behind the shipwrights' workshop – in which, he saw, two shipwrights were working – and in a few minutes a patrol-man had passed on his rounds and a watch-keeper had arrived to measure and log the hourly pressure and temperature readings. Next door a large compartment, loud with the noise from two rows of low-power generators, looked empty and vulnerable, but when the Commander paused outside the open door an electrical artificer, who had been lying on his back repairing one of the generators, sat up and stared at him. The lower hangar seemed deserted enough from the glass inspection port in the inner air-lock door, but when the Commander stepped through the door a belted and gaitered sentry appeared in the space between two rows of parked aircraft and looking up, he saw that he was also observed by a watch-keeper sitting in the glass-sided hangar control cabin perched in one corner of the hangar deck-head. Even on the flag deck, high in the island in a windy world of strumming halyards and turning radar aerials, he found the duty signalman, awake and watchful. The Well-wisher, whoever he was, must have superb protective colouring. The Commander had no doubt that if he himself had attempted an act of sabotage he would have been discovered at once; he had as much chance of damaging *Leviathan* and escaping unseen as he had of robbing the Bank of England in broad daylight.

On Sunday evening, after the week-end had passed with no activity by the Well-wisher, the Commander was feeling a familiar sense of anti-climax and of wasted opportunity when he telephoned Annabel.

'I meant to thank you again for a splendid meal last Friday.'

'I'm very glad you enjoyed it.'

'I did indeed. I've meant to telephone you all week-end but I've been tied up here.'

'That's all right.'

She made her voice sound so indifferent, so successfully concealing that she had been hoping he would call, that some of the exuberance went out of him.

'How are you? What are you doing now?'

'I'm sitting here in front of the telly, watching some ridiculous juggling.'

'It's a shame. There's a film on board here tonight which I was going to ask you if you'd like to come and see, but I just haven't had a chance.'

'Never mind, I've probably seen it anyway.' This time she could not entirely hide the pique in her voice: nothing was more maddening than to be told by a man that he had *nearly* invited you out.

'I would have very poor company for you this evening.'

'Why, what's been happening?'

'Oh, it's nothing very much. Just some pointless telephone calls which don't mean anything. Some sailor with a grievance. I've been hanging about all week-end trying to catch him.'

'I hope you do catch him.'

'I shall, sooner or later. In the meantime, can I call you when we get in next time?'

'Yes, do. I'll look forward to that.'

On Monday morning, Commander (L) was not surprised to hear that the week-end had passed without incident. 'Our friend probably went on week-end himself, like a sensible fellow. Or else he got to know about the monitoring.'

'Could he get to know about it?'

'Easily. You can't keep that sort of thing secret for long. Unless

176

your fellow is stupid, and from what you tell me I don't think he is stupid, he's bound to get to know. Do you want me to carry on with it?'

'Yes please, Dai. For a couple of days at least.'

The lull continued for two days, but no sooner had the monitoring stopped than the bosun's mates began to receive requests to make pipes which were either meaningless or directly misleading. The fire and emergency parties were led a futile dance about the ship, answering fictitious alarms. One afternoon at sea, the officer of the watch received a 'Man Overboard' message. The ship turned and stopped, the sea-boat was lowered, and the helicopter was in the air, before the Captain discovered that the quarterdeck life-buoys had not been jettisoned, the Royal Marine lifebuoy sentry knew nothing of the incident, and nobody could say who had first raised the alarm.

From telephone calls the Well-wisher progressed, as the Commander had anticipated, to minor acts of sabotage. Valves were found to have been opened after the ratings responsible for shutting them had shut them, and swore, at the Commander's table, that they had been checked shut. Fire-extinguishers were activated and left to spray decks and bulkheads with foam and water. Fuses were removed from a fuse-box outside the stewards' messdeck, putting both wardroom ante-rooms and two cabin flats in partial darkness.

The Well-wisher appeared to have a detailed knowledge of the ship's compartment layout, and an expert appreciation of the ship's alarm reflexes. There were certain calls for help which the Ship's Company could not ignore, no matter how often 'Wolf!' was cried. As the First Lieutenant said to the Commander, 'He can report a fire every hour, on the hour, and we've still got to go to every one.'

'Have we started up the monitoring again?'

'Yes, sir, but it's very difficult to mark down the suspicious calls. There are so many genuine ones we're getting bogged down. It doesn't seem to be deterring him this time. I've an idea one or two others are joining in the act now. I get the feeling it's not all the same fellow.'

'It's one particular fellow we're after, all the same. You'd better tell all the officers to keep their eyes and ears open. The more people we have looking out the better.'

The officers responded to the appeal with enthusiasm. Spy-catching mania spread through the wardroom. The officers were perhaps too zealous. Any rating who spoke indistinctly on the telephone ran the risk of being summoned before the First Lieutenant. Two seamen whom the Captain of Royal Marines found cleaning fire extinguishers on the upperdeck were taken in front of the officer of the watch as defaulters. Beaky pounced on a prowler outside his cabin late at night, only to discover that the intruder was the Third Engineer Officer of the Watch, a respectable Chief Engine-room Artificer on his legitimate rounds of the steering gear and shaft spaces. Meanwhile, the ship's company's mood was best expressed on Radio Leviathan by REA Lethcombe, ever the alert commentator on ship's affairs, who dedicated to 'All the ship's fire and emergency parties' a record of 'Where Are You Now, My Love?'

The Senior Engineer, too, was inclined to look on the brighter side. He pointed out to the First Lieutenant that pursuit of the Well-wisher brought unexpected fringe benefits.

'At least I'm brushing up on my ship knowledge. I've been to compartments I haven't been to for months. I'd forgotten half of them even existed.'

'Same here. And it's teaching everybody to speak up when they use the telephone.'

'Talking of that, I always thought you chose your damage control ratings for their unintelligibility? Whenever you got hold of some guttural Geordie, I always thought you said to him 'Come on lad, you'll do fine as a communications number.'

'Well, I like the way you say that! Whenever I talk to one of the engine-rooms I always get some boggy Irishman or an adenoidal Scouser.'

Overhearing the conversation at the wardroom bar, the Commander realised that the impetus of his search for the Well-wisher was dying away. If the Senior and the First Lieutenant, two officers most closely concerned, had begun to look upon it as joke, then the rest of the wardroom must be still more indifferent. Their interest would only be revived when the Well-wisher laid an actual fire and if, as the Commander feared, ridicule goaded him, an actual fire was only a question of time.

The moment the Commander had been awaiting arrived ten days after the first telephone calls. The ship was at sea, having remained at sea all night, and Flying Stations had just been sounded off. The Commander was shaving in his cabin when he heard the familiar action broadcast.

'... Fire in the Wardroom Bedding Store ...'

The Commander wiped the lather from his face and reached the door just as the First Lieutenant dashed by.

'It's a real one this time, sir, and no mistake!'

The wardroom bedding store was situated below one of the aftermost cabin flats, where the cabins, being small and dark and over the main propellers, were normally allocated to junior squadron officers and less important wardroom visitors. When the Commander reached the hatch and peered down through the smoke he saw that all the bystanders were aircrew officers, most of them, he noticed with annoyance, still wearing pyjamas and dressing-gowns.

'If you gentlemen have nothing better to do than stand about and goof, I suggest you do it somewhere else.'

The First Lieutenant's head appeared from the smoke below. He was coughing, and rubbing his eyes with his fingers.

'I can't get anywhere near the damned thing.'

'Is that the bedding store down there?'

'No sir, this is another cabin flat. The bedding store is at the end of the flat, on the starboard side.'

The Commander realised that he had probably been unjust to the aircrew officers; they had all been driven out of their cabins below by the smoke.

'Anybody down there now?'

'Three of the fire party, sir. It shouldn't be long now. It looks to me like more smoke than actual fire. Probably the blankets. One moment, sir, please.'

The Commander stood back to allow one of the firefighting party to pass. The man's face was shielded by the rubber mask of his breathing set. He was stooping under the weight of the air bottles on his back. His head and shoulders were covered by a grey asbestos cape and hood. The smoke had thickened and was now so dense that before the man had reached the bottom of the ladder there was no sign of him except his life-line trailing over the hatch coaming. The Commander and the First Lieutenant retreated to the end of the cabin flat, by the ladder, where a petty officer sat in the corner, his legs stretched out and his head between his knees. A sick berth attendant was squatting beside him.

The Commander jerked his head at the spreadeagled figure on the deck. 'What's the matter with him?'

'That's Petty Officer Steward Gibson, sir. He discovered the fire and like an idiot he tried to get down there through the smoke. He's probably feeling a bit sick and dizzy.'

'Gibson?'

Gibson lifted his head and let it fall back against the bulkhead. His face was pale and lines of sweat had run down his cheeks and neck, and inside his opened shirt. He was a thin, sallow man who had apparently been trying to grow a beard. His chin was partly covered in long straggling black hairs. The Commander remembered having granted his request to discontinue shaving some weeks before.

'Don't get up, Gibson. Tell us what happened.'

Gibson cleared his throat and swallowed. 'I was coming to get some bedding up, sir, and I just lifted the hatch . . .'

'Was the hatch padlocked when you got there?'

'Yes, sir.'

'The padlock was still all right?'

'Yes, sir.'

'Did you *find* the fire, or were you told about it? By telephone?'

Gibson was bewildered by the question. 'I just lifted the hatch . . .'

'And that was the first you knew about it, when the smoke came up?'

'Yes, sir, of course.'

'When were you last down here?'

'Yesterday tea-time, sir.'

'And everything was all right then?'

'Oh yes, sir.'

'Do you smoke, Gibson?'

'A bit sir.'

'Were you smoking down here yesterday tea-time?'

'Oh no, sir.' A shade of colour returned to Gibson's face.

'All right, Gibson.'

The smoke was clearing from the cabin flat. The furthest cabin doors and the ventilation fan casing on the far bulkhead were already visible.

'*Sir!*'

The First Lieutenant wheeled about. One of the fire-fighting party was standing with his head and shoulders through the lower hatch.

'Out?'

The man nodded and held up a thumb.

'Right. Start the ventilation fans again.'

Fresh movement of air shredded away the smoke in the lower cabin flat. The Commander followed the First Lieutenant down the ladder. The deck was streaked with foot-prints, where the fire-fighting party had trodden in the foam on their way to and from the fire. At the end of a short passageway another ladder led down to the bedding store, where piles of blankets, sheets, table-cloths and spare cabin door-curtains were stacked behind a wire-mesh grille. Three packing cases containing wine glasses lay by the foot of the ladder and in a corner formed by the grille and the bulkhead there was a table and a chair.

The fire had done its worst damage in the blankets nearest the chair. The First Lieutenant cleared the foam from the top blankets with the side of his hand. Fingers of smoke rose from the blackened cloth.

'Jesus Christ. What a bloody mess.' The First Lieutenant bent down and smelled a piece of charred blanket. 'Not much actual flame, I guess. But a hell of a lot burnt all the same. Blankets take a fair time to get going. I would say this lot's probably been burning all night.'

The Commander turned over a piece of blanket with his foot. Red embers still glowed in the remains of the fabric.

'Would any of the patrols come down here during the night?'

'I doubt it, sir. This flat's a dead end and anyway it's wardroom country. Somebody might have come down to look at the padlock. I can soon check that, though.'

'Don't bother.' The Commander was already convinced that the fire had been a genuine accident. It only remained to make Gibson admit that he had been smoking down there the day before.

'You'd better see that Gibson goes to the sick-bay. When the

PMO's finished with him, try and find out whether he really was smoking down here.'

The First Lieutenant laughed out loud. 'You took the very words out of my mouth, sir! I don't think for one minute this was our mutual friend.'

'Nor do I.'

The sound-powered telephone wailed on the bulkhead.

'I'll get it, sir. It's probably HQ One ringing up to find out what's happening about the fire.'

'Let me know about Gibson.' The Commander started up the ladder. 'I'm off to put the Captain in the picture.'

The First Lieutenant held out a hand. 'Just a minute, sir.' He took the receiver away from his ear. 'Flood, sir. And a real one, too, by the sound of it.'

'Where?'

'Number Two hangar spray pump space.'

'Where the devil's that?'

'It's the hatch at the after end of the boys' messdeck, sir, towards the port side. It's hidden behind some kit lockers.'

'I think I know the one. God Almighty, it's one damned thing after another.'

12

A flood did not have the dramatic attraction of a fire and there were no idle bystanders by the pump space hatch. The compartment was so remote that most of the ship's company, like the Commander himself, were hardly aware of its existence. When the Commander arrived, one stoker was standing by the row of kit lockers, holding a sound-powered telephone receiver in his hand.

The Commander looked over the edge. The intervening hatches were open and the access to the pump space was now a brilliantly-lit vertical shaft which dropped six decks down through the ship.

A face appeared at the bottom of the shaft.

'Up top! Tell 'em to stop pumping!'

The Commander was nonplussed by the shout, but the stoker standing beside him had obviously been expecting the order and was already repeating it into the telephone.

He swung himself over the edge, and began to climb down. The air became noticeably cooler and damper as he descended. At each landing water-tight doors led to compressor rooms, and naval stores, and magazines. At the lowest two levels the bulkheads were blank and here the ladder rungs were wet and slimy.

The pump space was lit only by the light from the shaft. Below him, the Commander could hear water swilling in the bilges, as the ship rolled. He was impressed by the pump's size; the compartment was only just big enough to contain it. The deckhead cleared the top of the motor by a few inches. There were six hangar spray pumps in *Leviathan*, fitted for a rare but vital purpose; although they might never be used in earnest throughout the ship's life, they were kept at instant readiness at all times. In the event of a major fire in a hangar, all six pumps would damp the flames in a deluge of sprayed water, ten times heavier than the most violent tropical storm. The Commander had heard sailors' tales that a man could not breathe if he stayed in a hangar while the sprays were in use.

The Senior Engineer, the Damage Control Engineer Officer and

183

two engine-room department ratings were crowded together on the railed gangway in front of the pump.

'Has Commander (E) been down?'

'Just left, sir. He's gone up to see the Captain.'

'How deep was the flood, Senior?'

'It was up to about eighteen inches from the top of the compartment, sir.'

'You've been damned quick about pumping it out!'

'Not really, sir. It's a small compartment and we had two big pumps on it.'

'Who reported it?'

The Senior flashed the beam of a torch on the compartment telephone, on a bulkhead bracket by the ladder. 'That telephone reported it.'

'Oh *no*, not again . . .'

'No sir, it was the oddest thing. About half an hour ago the watch-keeper at the main exchange noticed the switchboard light for this compartment extension flashing on and off. He tried to ring up and see what they wanted but he couldn't get any answer. Well, as you can imagine sir, all the main exchange watch-keepers are a bit sensitive about any funny business on the telephone these days. So he didn't mess about. He rang the Engineer Officer of the Watch, who sent somebody down here. They found the place flooded. The light flashing on and off must have been caused by the water, when it reached the level of the telephone on the bulkhead.'

'I can't quite see how the water got in.'

The Senior swung his torch downwards on to a small open-ended pipe projecting from the pump impeller casing. Water was still dribbling from the pipe, whenever the ship heeled.

'Through that pipe. It's supposed to seal the pump glands with water. Somebody disconnected it.'

'You wouldn't think you'd get enough water through that?'

'Oh yes you would, sir. That's a three-quarter inch diameter pipe and we're about twenty-five feet under the water-line here. With that size pipe and that head of water you can get a surprising amount of water through in quite a short time.'

'This place is visited in the normal way, I suppose?'

'Once a day in harbour, once a watch at sea. I'll be checking up to see who came down here during the morning watch and what time.'

'You're sure this was deliberate, Senior?'

'Absolutely certain, sir. And so is Commander (E).'

In a way, the Commander was almost relieved to hear it. Here, at last, was an unmistakable act of sabotage. The fire in the bedding store could have been an accident. Removing fuses, opening and shutting valves, larking about with fire extinguishers, even the telephone calls, were merely mischievous and difficult to prove. This was a clear criminal act, wilfully designed to damage the ship.

'It looks as though it must have been done by somebody with a bit of technical knowledge.'

The Senior Engineer turned swiftly, like a man espying danger out of the corner of his eye.

'It needn't necessarily have been an engine-room rating, sir. Almost everybody gets some form of technical training these days. The pump suction valve is always left open and there's always a head of water in the pump. There's a row of spanners in that rack there. All he had to do was disconnect the pipe and see what happened.'

'I suppose you're right, Senior.'

Nevertheless, as he made his way up to the bridge to see the Captain, the Commander was unconvinced. It seemed to him incredible that a non-technical rating should venture into an unfamiliar machinery space and disconnect a pipe, on the off-chance that he might thereby flood the compartment.

The Captain was sitting in his high, straight-backed 'Father's Chair'. *Leviathan* was turning out of the wind, having just completed a landing serial, and the Gunnery Officer, who was Officer of the Watch, was conning the ship on to her new course. *Leviathan*'s bridge was wide and spacious, with large clear windows, banks of telephones and instruments. The First Lieutenant had once called it 'The Sun Lounge' and the Commander found it hard to associate the compass platform with the same ship that also contained the dark, humid pump space he had just left.

The Captain had heard the technical details from Commander (E). He had another point to put to the Commander.

'Is this chap getting you down, Bob?'

185

'Not getting me down exactly, sir . . .'

'But you're not getting anywhere very fast?'

'No, sir. We don't know about the fire in the bedding store this morning. That could have been an accident. Personally, I think it was. Of course, we're not arson experts . . .'

'I know you're not. And that's the point I was going to make. I think it's time we did have some experts on board.'

'You mean the police, sir.' The Commander realised that he had incautiously presented the Captain with the perfect cue.

'I mean the police. I know how you feel about having outsiders to settle our own problems for us, but this whole affair is taking a turn I don't like. I can't afford to mess about with this fellow much longer. I'm giving you until the week-end, Bob. If you haven't found him or made some reasonable progress by then, I'm going to ask for police assistance.'

The Captain's ultimatum forced the Commander to hurry forward a plan he had been considering for some days. He called a conference, attended by Commander (E), Commander (L), the Senior Engineer, the Deputy Electrical Officer, the First Lieutenant, and the Gunnery Officer. They gathered in the Commander's cabin, knowing that the affair of the Well-wisher was now approaching its climax.

'Firstly, have we found out anything new about the flood this morning Chief?'

'A little. The compartment was visited by the Second Engineer Officer of the Watch fairly early on this morning.'

'Who visited it?'

'Dobell.'

'Good.' Sub-Lieutenant Dobell was one of the most reliable officers in the Engineering Department, with many years' watchkeeping experience as an officer and as an artificer behind him.

'Jim Dobell says he got there shortly before five o'clock and everything was all right. No floods, nothing leaking. The flood was found at about a quarter to nine, that's roughly four hours later. We can't be exact but we've worked out approximately that you'd get *about* four or five tons of water an hour through that size pipe with that head of water behind it. There must have been nearly twenty tons of water in the compartment when we pumped it out so it looks as if the place must have been flooding for almost the whole of that four hours. Just as if somebody had gone down there and started it going the minute Jim Dobell left.'

The Commander shook his head. The Well-wisher seemed to be able to spirit himself about the ship, remaining invisible while he waited his opportunity. He took several papers from his desk and held them up for the others to see.

'We're obviously going to have to be a bit more cunning. These are copies of a list I've made of every incident and all we know about it, every telephone call, the date, time, place, who took the message, what was actually said, and any other facts we've managed to get. I've been trying to work out some sort of common factor about the incidents. I admit I've not been very successful but the main idea is to try and get a mental picture of the man we're after . . .'

'Just a minute, sir.' The Gunnery Officer interrupted. 'Shouldn't Commander (S) and Commander (Air) be here?'

The Commander restrained himself from telling the Gunnery Officer that if he had wanted Commander (S) or Commander (Air) to be present he was quite capable of asking them. 'I don't think we're looking for anybody in the Supply Branch or the Air Group. I've a hunch our man is in one of the departments represented here. I'm willing to lay odds he's either a seaman or in the electrical or engineering departments. I'll explain why.'

The Commander looked round the group, to catch and fix their attentions. The success of his plan demanded that they be convinced.

'Our man's quite intelligent. He had enough wit to pack it in when we started monitoring, until he saw how effective it was going to be. He's got some nerve, too. It's not every sailor who'd telephone the Captain or myself, even anonymously. He's certainly a skate, with a chip on his shoulder. I'm sure he's been in the rattle since he's been on board, probably for leave-breaking, or insolence to a superior officer, or slack in obeying an order, or something of that kind. He's got a first-class knowledge of the ship and the ship's routine. He might well have been on board last commission. This is why I've ruled out the Air Group. Their ship knowledge is not normally as good as this. Whatever his job is, it gives him a damned good protective colouring. It's a job which allows him to move about the ship at odd hours of the day

187

and night without anybody taking too much notice of him. I'm sure he's a watch-keeper of some sort. This is why I'm discounting the Supply Branch. Anybody with any nous at all would have smelled a rat by now if they'd seen a cook or a steward going down one of the machinery compartments late at night. And there's another interesting thing. I know the Senior doesn't agree with me it's all that significant, but there seems to me to be a *technical* bias to his activities. That fuse-box. I know there's nothing much to taking a few fuses out, but you'd be astonished how many people are scared of electricity and wouldn't dream of touching a fuse-box, whether it was live or dead.'

Commander (L) grinned. 'Just like me, man. I'm dead scared of electricity. Never touch the stuff.'

'. . . While I'm going through all the dreary business of finding out who was up and about this morning and why, I want you to think about the ratings in your departments and make me out a list of those you think *might* be the man. It doesn't matter if you haven't got any proof. The fact that you even suspect him is enough. Go through all your defaulters' books, your leave books, your watch and station bills. See who *could* have done it. You'll be able to eliminate a lot of them at once. Some will have been ashore or on leave at the material times. Some will have been on watch in places where they're under supervision the whole time. Or they might have been in the sick-bay or away on courses. There may be somebody you think might have done it but there's nothing tangible to suggest him. Put him down all the same. He might be the one.'

The Senior Engineer looked up. 'You're sure it's only one bloke, sir?'

'Positive. Oh, I don't say that some of those telephone calls weren't made by part-time jokers trying to improve the act. But it's only one man we're really after, I'm certain of it.'

'You realise one thing, Bob.' Commander (L) had been disappointed by the Commander's cold reception of his last remark, and was anxious to redeem himself. 'With a net as wide as this, you're going to have an awful lot of names on those lists.'

'I don't care how many names I get. I'm quite prepared to interview every single member of the ship's company and go through this list of incidents with him if necessary. But I want some names to start with first. Any more points?'

'How about this Birmingham accent, sir?' It was typical of the First Lieutenant that he should raise what was perhaps the only piece of real evidence of identity.

'It's certainly a point worth bearing in mind. I don't want to put too much emphasis on it because it might be misleading. But it's worth noting. Now, I've told you what *I* think we should do. What about you, Chief?'

'No, I think something on the lines you suggest is our best chance, Bob. I'm a bit dubious about all this stress being laid on the technical side of it. Every Tom, Dick or Harry gets some form of technical training these days.'

'I take the point, Chief. I may be quite wrong about the technical angle. All I say is, it's likely. Dai?'

'I'm with you, Bob. Up to now he's been more of a nuisance than a danger. This flood means he's getting more ambitious.'

'Guns?'

'I'm sure you won't find a saboteur in the Gunnery Branch, sir.'

'And I'm *sure* you're right, Guns, but I still want to check up on it. I expect a list from you just like everybody else.' The Commander wondered why it was that the Gunnery Officer, so patently an honest and worthy officer, should still have this never-failing ability to set his teeth on edge.

'When do you want the lists, sir?'

'There's some urgency about them. Today's Wednesday. We're getting in tomorrow afternoon and we've got a day in harbour on Friday. I'd be very grateful if you could get your lists completed by the time we get in tomorrow and that will give us the whole of Friday to comb through them. Remember, if you're in any doubt, put him in!'

When the meeting broke up, the Commander was satisfied that he had convinced them and it was a measure of the control he had established over the wardroom that the meeting had agreed to take so much trouble for so long a chance of success. The Commander himself still believed he would know his man the moment he clapped eyes on him. He hoped that the activity of this investigation into the flood, and the uneasiness which was bound to spread through the ship while the lists were being compiled, would flush the Well-wisher into the open.

189

The Commander's scheme might have been successful, if it had been given a chance. At midnight, it was overtaken by events. The Commander had the details from the First Lieutenant when he arrived on the scene.

A leading airman in Rupert Smith's squadron, returning to his messdeck after working late, had found a pile of oily rags and cotton-waste burning in the passageway which led from the messdeck to the nearby bathroom. The fire had been laid directly outside the door of a petrol stowage space, one of several small compartments scattered about the ship which were used by the aviation fuelling parties while transferring avgas or kerosene to the flight deck.

The squadron rating had acted with speed and resource. Without pausing to give the alarm, he had taken a pair of blankets from his bunk and smothered the fire. Then, bundling blankets, rags and cotton-waste together he had pitched them into a shower stall and turned on the water. When the fire and emergency party arrived, the constituents of the fire had been reduced to sodden and blackened scraps littering the deck of the shower stall.

As he had feared, the Commander found the Captain's mind already made up.

'I'm sorry, Bob. I was willing to go along with you so far, but when funny little men start lighting fires near petrol it's time to call in the professionals. I've already sent a signal asking for the police to board us when we get in. We shan't be going alongside as planned this evening. We'll stay at anchor at Spithead while the police get down to it. I want you to have lower deck cleared immediately after we've anchored and I'll speak to the Ship's Company.'

'Aye aye, sir.'

'Perhaps *I* can convince them that we're no longer amused by this.'

After the ship anchored, the ship's company mustered by divisions on the flight deck, wearing their working clothes. The ship had been buzzing with rumours all day. Some of the ship's company had been concerned in the enquiries. Most of them had heard garbled and distorted stories about the Well-wisher and his feats. All of them could see from the expression on the Captain's

190

face that he had not cleared lower deck to award prizes.

'I may as well come straight to the point. I've cleared lower deck this evening to tell you we have on board this ship at this moment a man who has tried to kill some of us. Last night a fire was discovered outside a petrol stowage compartment. That fire was not an accident. It was deliberately laid by someone on board. But for the prompt action of Leading Airman Manvell, of Number Fourteen Squadron, some of you might not have been here this evening. You would have been dead. Anyone who has ever seen, as I have, the effect of an avgas explosion in an aircraft carrier will know what I mean. The last one we had in the Navy killed nine men and maimed forty more for life. During the last war whole carriers were lost as a result of petrol explosions. Petrol is dangerous enough in itself. But when you mess about with it you're messing about with your shipmates' lives. This sort of thing is no longer funny. That fire last night was only one of a long series of stupid and dangerous incidents . . .'

Standing behind him, the Commander noticed how Tosser had grown into the job. The nervousness of the start of the commission had entirely disappeared: Tosser was now the Captain, standing up to tell his ship's company exactly what he thought.

'. . . The joke is over. This man *must* be caught. To catch him, we must have your help, all of you. I must ask you to report anything you see or hear which seems suspicious. Don't be afraid to tell somebody. It's much better to sing out and be wrong than to look the other way and let this *outlaw*, because that's what he is, an *outlaw*, succeed in what he's doing. The police are coming on board this evening to start their investigations. There will be no week-end leave, no leave of any kind, until they've finished. Nobody, not even the postman, is to leave this ship until the police are satisfied. That's all I have to say to you.'

When he had dismissed the ship's company, the Commander found the First Lieutenant at his elbow.

'The Feet are on board, sir.'

'Where've you put them?'

'In the guest-room.'

'Good, I'll go down there now. Have you got those lists?'

'All except the Gunnery Branch, sir. The Gunnery Officer's just making out a fair copy of his.'

191

'When you've got them all, bring them to the guest-room with you.'

'You want me to be present, sir?'

'Good God yes! I want some moral support when I start dealing with the constabulary.'

The wardroom guest-room was an excellent choice for an investigation room, being quiet and private and away from the ship's main thoroughfares. It was a large cabin converted into a dining-room where officers could entertain ladies or give private dinner parties without subjecting their guests to the hurly-burly of the main wardroom meal. The room was furnished with a long dining table, covered with a green cloth, a dozen chairs, a hot-plate, and two low sideboards. The guest-room also contained the wardroom television set, because the Commander and a group of senior officers had banished it from the ante-room, and, for some reason, the wardroom reference library. A tall, glass-fronted bookcase contained such volumes as *Who's Who, Wisden's, Kelly's* and two shelves of the *Encyclopaedia Britannica*.

There were four policemen, three in plain clothes, and the fourth an Inspector of the Dockyard Police in uniform.

'Good evening, Inspector. I can't truthfully say I'm glad to see you again.'

'Naturally not, sir. I'm like the bailiff, sir. Bad news.' The Inspector had come on board during the investigation into the smashed gauge glasses when the Commander, without mincing any words, had told him the ship's officers were quite competent to look after their own affairs. Now, the ship had admitted defeat and the Inspector was back, in a position trebly strengthened. But he was a generous man and did not intend to make capital of his advantage.

'These are CID officers, sir, from the city police. Detective Sergeant Gillespie, Detective Constable Morton, and Detective Constable Fisher, sir, the fingerprint expert.'

The Commander shook hands with the Detective Sergeant, and nodded to the other two. They were all wearing cream-coloured shirts, dark woollen ties, and shiny grey double-breasted suits bought, the Commander guessed, off the peg. Their jackets were unbuttoned and they were all plainly wearing braces. They had each brought a rain-coat and a trilby hat, which they had piled

192

together on the end of the table. The fingerprint expert was holding a small brown suitcase which the Commander presumed contained the tools of his extraordinary trade.

All three CID officers presented a subtly alien, hostile appearance which made the Commander long to tell them to pack themselves off. They were something new to him and much more menacing than the plain dockyard officers. He could not help himself resenting them and looking upon them as opponents. They had already sensed his antagonism and he took a seat opposite them in an uncomfortable silence.

'Well, gentlemen . . .' The Commander attempted a smile. 'I expect you've been told why you're here.'

When he spoke, the Detective Sergeant's voice was surprisingly melodious and beguiling. The Commander remembered that this man probably spent hours of his normal working day, just chatting.

'As we understand the position, sir, we're here to carry out a preliminary investigation into alleged acts of sabotage and arson, together with certain other acts liable to cause a breach of the peace.'

'Yes, I expect that describes it. Now, I want you to look at these.'

The Commander passed round copies of his list of incidents, giving one copy each to the Dockyard Inspector and to the three detectives. As he went through the list with them, answering their supplementary questions, he began to see how childish the affair of the Well-wisher must appear to anyone outside *Leviathan*. The ship had asked for police assistance because the officers believed the ship was in danger. But now, the Commander felt like a headmaster explaining that he had called the police because one of his pupils had been insubordinate. The Dockyard Inspector knew something of naval routine and the disciplined society in a ship, and he could be expected to understand the disruptive effect of even one member who failed to conform. But while he was describing one ludicrous telephone call after another, the Commander despaired of ever convincing the CID officers.

Yet strangely the Detective Sergeant also appeared to understand the Commander's meaning at once. This so-called Well-wisher had allegedly broken the law. People who had allegedly broken the law provided the Detective Sergeant's bread and butter and of course he took them seriously. When the Commander had

193

finished his summary, the Detective Sergeant leaned forward, placed his elbows on the table and put the tips of his fingers together, peering at the Commander over the arch thus formed by his arms.

'Now all we need to ask you, sir, is "Who did it?" '

'Who *did* it?' The Commander had compelled himself to treat the remark as a joke, in very poor taste, before he appreciated that the Sergeant intended a serious question. 'We don't *know* who did it. What do you think we asked you here . . .'

'There's always someone who is suspected, sir.'

'Ah, I see.'

The First Lieutenant had slipped into the chair nearest the door while the Commander was speaking. He pushed a large brown envelope across the table. 'There are the lists, sir.'

The Commander withdrew the sheaf of papers from the envelope and spread them on the table.

'Sergeant, over the last twenty-four hours we've been compiling lists of the names of all the men on board whom we think *might* be the man we want.' The Commander shuffled the papers. 'I can see there are a lot of names . . .'

'We've got all night, sir.' The Detective Sergeant leaned back and put his thumbs in his braces. 'And all tomorrow, and all the next day if need be. If we can have those lists, sir, and interview everyone on them? If he's there, we'll *know*, and we'll tell you.'

The Commander believed him. For the first time, his attitude towards the Detective Sergeant mellowed a little.

'Here . . .'

The Commander stopped. The top name on the second sheet of engine-room department ratings had made him pause. He felt a prickle of memory, a thrilling, stirring sensation as a forgotten fact swam up again to the conscious surface.

'Engineer Mechanic Miller, by God! *Dusty!*'

'What's that, sir?'

'Number One, you remember the night the gauge glasses were smashed? On my way down there that night I *met* a sailor who knew all about it! He actually *told* me how to get to the engine-room. He had "Dusty" written on his overalls, I remember now. But he wasn't one of the men I interviewed afterwards because he wasn't on watch and he wasn't just coming off watch. So what

194

the devil was he *doing* down there? How did he know?'

The Senior Engineer had appeared in the guest-room doorway.

'Senior, just the man! Get hold of an Engineer Mechanic J. Miller for me. He's a damage control rating.'

The Senior looked like a man whose important piece of news had been poached. 'That's very funny, sir, I've just been talking to the leading hand of Miller's mess down in the Engineer's Office and I came to tell you about it. He's been thinking over what the Captain said and he says that Miller's been acting a bit odd lately.'

'What does he mean by "odd"?'

'Getting up in the middle of the night. Not there when people expect him to be there, and so on.'

The Commander pounded a clenched fist on the table. '*Exactly* the sort of information we've been looking for! *Why* didn't he speak up before? Where is Miller?'

'That's just it, sir. We've piped for him but we can't find him. We've got a search going.'

'You find him, Senior, and bring him here.'

'Yes, sir.'

The Detective Sergeant was sitting with his head bowed, having seemingly withdrawn himself from the conversation. He had seen it happen in this type of case many times before: often his mere presence acted as a kind of catalyst, precipitating some unexpected and vital constituent in the investigation.

The Dockyard Inspector was looking puzzled. 'I don't see how you associate the name "Dusty" with Engineer Mechanic Miller, sir?'

'Oh come on, Inspector, Dusty's a traditional Service nickname for people called Miller. Probably outside the Navy too, for all I know. Dusty Miller, Nobby Clark, Bungy Williams, there are dozens of them.'

The Commander placed one fist in the palm of the other hand. The facts all fitted. 'Of course he would have a good knowledge of the ship. Of *course* he would know the times and routines of all the patrols. While the fire and emergency parties were dashing about all over the ship he could have been sitting quietly in HQ One directing them! He's a technical rating and with a damage control armband on his sleeve he could go anywhere in the ship and nobody would take any notice. Talk about protective colouring! The one thing that never occurred to me, a damage control rating.'

'What's the particular significance of that, sir?'

'These men are supposed to look after the ship, Sergeant, to *stop* damage being done. It's like a policeman on the beat being caught shop-breaking. How would you feel about that, Sergeant?'

The Sergeant's face showed that the shaft had gone home.

'If *only* I'd remembered.' The Commander tipped back his chair and swung his legs on to the table. 'I'll kick myself for the rest of my life for not remembering that I saw that fellow. None of this need have happened.'

'You're of the opinion that Miller is the Well-wisher, sir?'

'I'm quite certain of it, Sergeant. I suggest we wait here until they find him. I don't think we need look any further. Number One, you'd better get off and give Senior a hand with the search.'

The Commander arranged for some cans of beer and some coffee to be sent up to the guest-room, and he telephoned the Captain to tell him of their discovery. Meanwhile, there was nothing he personally could do and he composed himself to wait. He attempted conversation with the policemen but found the effort too much. His thoughts insisted on returning to the search for Miller, and his ears were constantly pricked for the sound of approaching footsteps.

The Detective Sergeant spent the waiting time making notes from the Commander's list. He was a painstaking officer and he did not have the Commander's grounds for being certain that Miller was their man. The Inspector took 'Jane's Fighting Ships' from the bookcase, opened it at the page devoted to *Leviathan*, and studied it with absorbed interest. The fingerprint expert took a wallet chess set from his pocket and, to the Commander's astonishment, he and the other Detective Constable settled down to play.

It was an hour and ten minutes before the First Lieutenant returned.

'Got him?'

'Yes, sir.'

'Where is he then?'

'The last time I saw Engineer Mechanic Miller, sir, he was being carried towards the cells by four very large Royal Marines.'

196

'He *what?*'

The First Lieutenant's eyes glistened. He had a good story to tell and relished the prospect of telling it.

'We found him hiding in the port outer stern gland space. I don't know what he thought he was doing there, it's one of the places that was bound to be searched. The Senior went down to talk to him, but Miller made a rush at him so the Senior hopped it quick. No point in adding striking an officer to the other things he's going to be charged with. Then the Regulating Chief Stoker went down there and Miller did thump him good and proper. So the Senior called up the bootnecks and they went down with a Neil Robertson stretcher.'

The Commander nodded. The stretchers were designed to carry a badly-injured man out of a confined space: they would, where appropriate, make excellent strait-jackets.

'Did he say anything? Miller, I mean?'

'Never stopped, sir. I heard some of it myself. Shouting that we'd have to come and get him. That he'd fooled all us stupid pigs. That he hadn't half finished yet.'

'I think he has. I think friend Miller's race is run.' Now that the Well-wisher's identity was known, the Commander's impatience with the police returned. 'Inspector, you can leave this to us now. You'll be hearing from us officially in due course. Thank you for your help, Sergeant. I think the mere fact that you came on board helped to bring all this to a head. I'll show you to the quarterdeck.'

The Commander fought to control his itch to rid the ship of the police. He could hardly hustle them to the quarterdeck and down into their boat quickly enough. When he was standing at the quarterdeck rail, watching the boat leave, he reflected that at least the day had held one good omen. The ship's company had responded to the Captain's appeal in a way they might never have done in the previous commission. The Captain had appealed not to Caesar, but to the citizens of Rome, and they had answered him.

'Like the Mounties, Bob, you always get your man.'

Commander (S) was standing behind him, also watching the police launch leaving the ship.

'I didn't get him. The ship's company got him. That's the

197

one good thing about this. The sailors are at last beginning to show a bit of public spiritedness. Perhaps that fire last night brought them to their senses.'

Delicious Joe smiled in a way which chilled the Commander with a premonition that the bubble of his well-being was about to be pricked. 'Bob, there was nothing particularly dangerous about that fire last night. If it had been *in* the stowage compartment, instead of outside it, that would have been different. It was no more dangerous there than anywhere else in the ship.'

The Commander was in no mood to try debating points. 'Oh go to hell, Joe.'

Commander (S) chuckled. 'Bob, you really must try to grow up and leave the Boy Scouts, you know. The ship's company aren't interested in public spiritedness. They're terrified of losing their week-end leaves.'

The Commander's neck muscles tightened against his collar, but he controlled himself, so as to be able to speak soberly. 'That's the most despicably cynical thing I've ever heard any officer say. If you really think that, you've no business to be an officer in this ship, or in any ship.'

Commander (S) seized the Commander's sleeve with such violence that the Commander staggered. It was a rare show of emotion for Delicious Joe. 'I'm not being cynical, Bob, do believe me. If you can't get this straight in your head you're riding for the biggest fall anyone ever had! I don't want to see you come a cropper, *believe* me.' He held the Commander's arm tightly, so that the Commander could not get away. 'Listen to me. While that fellow was making a nuisance of himself and the officers were running round in ever decreasing circles trying to catch him, the ship's company didn't give a *damn*. It was something for the officers to sort out. Kept them out of mischief. But as far as Jolly Jack was concerned, it didn't mean a thing. But when you announced there would be no week-end leave, now that's quite another matter. That *does* affect them. That's *serious*. It showed you meant business and once the ship's company woke up to the fact you weren't fooling, they *soon* put a stop to it.'

The Commander wrenched his arm away and began almost to run across the quarterdeck.

'Sir, sir! Just a minute, please sir!'

The Master-at-Arms, understandably, wished to know about leave.

'Leave as from now until the normal times tomorrow, Master. I'll see about an MFV to come out from shore as soon as I can.' The Commander spoke automatically. These were standard responses he could have made in his sleep.

'Week-end leave, sir?'

'As usual.'

'Thank you, sir.'

'Just a minute, Master.' This was one aspect of the ship's company on which the Master-at-Arms was an authority. 'Why do you suppose somebody told us about Engineer Mechanic Miller tonight?'

'Well sir, it was getting a bit close to the week-end to start messing about with the police.'

The Commander gasped, as though struck in the groin. The Master's reply had been given artlessly, without pause for thought, and so carried the crushing weight of the truth. The Commander headed for his cabin, as a wounded bull flees to its querencia. He needed time and space to think, but the Senior Engineer was standing outside the cabin, about to knock on the door.

'Come in, Senior. Come in and sit down. I suppose it's Miller?'

'I've just come from seeing him, sir.'

'Oh yes?' The Commander's mind revolved around the appalling truth he had learned on the quarterdeck. 'Who's his divisional officer?'

'Fisher. That was a clue in itself. Fisher was the first to get one of those telephone calls.'

'There were lots of clues, if we'd only seen them.' The Commander irritably drummed a pencil on his desk. 'He did everything but write us a postcard and tell us who he was. You'd think he wanted to get caught.'

'That may not be so far from the truth, sir. I've been through that list with him and he admits to smashing the gauge glasses and causing the flood yesterday and the fire last night, and one or two other incidents. But he says he didn't have anything to do with the fire in the wardroom bedding store . . .'

'I know that. Petty Officer Gibson was smoking down there.'

'He also says he didn't make all those telephone calls and he

199

had nothing to do with taking out those fuses. He's frightened of electricity.'

'Did he say why he did it?'

'He did say one odd thing, sir. He lit the fire because nobody was taking him seriously. He didn't mean to harm the ship.'

'Balls.'

'There's more to this case than meets the eye, sir. He's never been in the rattle before.'

'Hasn't he? Well, he's going to make up for that now. Don't tell me the gory details, Senior. Let me make some guesses about Engineer Mechanic Miller. My guess is that he's known on his messdeck as a bit of a screw-ball, an odd man out. He comes from a broken and unhappy home, poor little *sod*. He doesn't know why he joined the Navy. He only knows he doesn't like it now. There's a woman giving him trouble ashore somewhere. He's a poor, crazy, mixed-up kid and my heart bleeds for him. I hope he goes to prison for life. Unfortunately, he'll only get two years.'

The Senior was shocked by the bitterness in the Commander's voice. The Commander had summed up what was known of Miller's background with fair accuracy, but it was not like him to be so furiously sarcastic.

'You're a hard man, sir.'

'*Hard man!*'

The Commander whipped round in his chair, and the Senior was appalled by his expression of angry misery.

'Have you any idea what I'm trying to do in this ship, Senior? Do you know what it's like to come to a ship known throughout the Navy as a *shit-barge* and try and make it into something? And to do it in *spite* of a wardroom who think more of their private lives than the ship, and in *spite* of a ship's company who think more of their week-ends than the rest of the week? Have you any idea at all what I'm trying to do, and what it means to me to be bedevilled and buggered about by crazy little nut cases who ought to be locked up for good? Obviously, you haven't any idea.'

In the months they had served together the Senior had developed an affectionate respect for the Commander. He was horrified to see him naked in his rage.

'I do understand what you're doing for the ship, sir, and I

apologise for that remark.'

'Oh good God.' The Commander waved a hand wearily. 'Never mind, Senior.' He knew that once more his anger had trapped him into betraying himself. 'Go and help Fisher try and make something of the defence. Tell the duty lieutenant commander I want the case started tonight. And tell him for God's sake not to forget to caution Miller before he makes any statement up at the table. I want that man to go to prison and I don't want any mistakes on the way.'

'Yes, sir.'

'By the way, where does Miller come from? Where's his home town?'

'Smethwick, sir. It's the only reason I put him on the list.'

After such a day, the Commander did evening rounds himself. It was important that he gauge the latest temper of the ship's company; it was a process which John Bowler had once compared to a bee-keeper inspecting his bees. Preceded by the Royal Marine bugler blowing the note of G, the Commander walked along the familiar passageways and through the messdecks with every sense alive to the significance of a tone of voice, of the look in the messdeck sweeper's eye as he made his report, of the faces of the sailors standing at attention, but watching, in the background, of the shrouded shapes in the hammocks, and the very feel and resonance of the deck itself. More of the ship's company were on board than on a normal night because many of them had decided it was too late to go ashore by the time leave was piped. The conditions on board could have been right for unrest, but it was as Commander (S) had said: the Well-wisher was a matter for the officers. Even on his own messdeck, Miller had had his hour and was now, it seemed, forgotten.

The Commander was half-way through his rounds when he heard the 'Man Overboard' alarm. When he reached the quarter-deck it was already crowded with spectators.

The ten-inch signalling projector on the flag-deck was sweeping the water astern of the ship. The bow-lights of two of the ship's motorboats crept down the ship's side, the bowmen searching ahead with their Aldis lamps. A flare shone out and went black again, as the lifebuoy dipped between the waves.

'What's the tide doing?'

201

'Ebbing, sir. And sluicing out, too. He'll be out at the Nab by now.'

One of the Royal Marine escorts was talking to the Mate of the Upper Deck.

'We were just coming up on the quarterdeck, sir. Just got there, when he said something and got away from us. He ran to the guard-rail and then he was gone, sir. Quick as that.'

The Commander watched the lights of the boats moving further astern, away from the ship. He did not think of himself as a vindictive man but, as he mounted the ladder towards the Captain's cabin, his predominant emotion was disappointment that now he would probably never have to give evidence at the Well-wisher's court martial.

13

'I hear you got that man who was giving you so much trouble
Bob.'

'Got him, and lost him again.' He was driving along the Com
mercial Road, with Annabel sitting beside him.

'There wasn't much about it in the newspapers. Just that he'c
fallen over the side.'

'Maybe *Leviathan*'s not news any more.'

'What happens now?'

'About that fellow? We'll have a board of enquiry next week.'

She was chilled by the indifference in his voice. A rabbit run
over in the road would have concerned him more. Those sailors
in that ship did not know what sort of man they had on board;
it would be easier for them in the end if they did what he wanted
them to do now.

'Did you feel he'd done you out of a chance to get your own
back on him?'

He bit his lip, embarrassed and yet curiously gratified that she
could guess his thoughts so accurately. 'I did feel like that. I'm
ashamed to say it now.'

'It's quite understandable, Bob.'

'Understandable maybe, but still not excusable.' He braked to
avoid the pedestrians swarming across the centre of the road. The
citizens of Portsmouth seemed to jay-walk in the road as though
impelled by some sort of regional death-wish.

Annabel looked out of the window. The crowd on the road were
mostly young men, in tapered trousers, cuban-heeled shoes, and
bulky leather jackets with fur collars. One of them came close as
the car stopped. His face, leering and mischievous, bent by the
window.

'What a lot of peculiar-looking characters. Portsmouth always
seems to be full of them.'

'Those peculiar-looking characters are sailors in plain clothes.'

'Are they *allowed* to dress like that?'

'You can't stop them. They can go ashore in plain clothes in

203

any of the home ports, but the book doesn't say what sort of plain clothes. Provided they're not actually indecent, there's not much we can do about it.'

'Don't they go ashore in uniform any more? There's something about a sailor's uniform. Don't you touch a sailor for luck?'

'So they used to say. But it ain't fashionable to wear uniform any more. It's the mark of an employee. Citizens don't wear uniform.' He was satisfied that he had kept any bitterness out of his voice; he had recognised, just in time, that he had been approaching that subject, on which he was terrified of becoming a bore.

'It's funny, when I was a little girl I used to be a bit scared of sailors when I saw them in a train or walking along the street. And soldiers, too. I thought they all looked so hairy, and lewd, and kind of smelly. But these look just like errand-boys all dressed up.'

'I'll tell Connolly our bar steward that when I next see him. He always thinks of himself as a snappy dresser.'

'What sort of do are we going to tonight, Bob?'

'Usual thing. Dinner with the Captain and Mrs Captain. It'll be pretty quiet, I expect.'

Tosser had given him the invitation that morning, before he went home for the week-end. Tosser had been so transparently relaying his wife's instructions that the Commander had almost been able to hear the echo of Laura's voice: 'Ask him if he can bring a partner with him, to make up the numbers. If not, tell him *we'll* find somebody.'

'Where does your Captain live?'

'Have you not met him?'

'Not yet, no. I've met her two or three times, at people's houses. But I've never been to their house.'

'They live at the top of the Council Estate somewhere.'

'The Council Estate,' on the outskirts of Portsmouth, was a huge, rambling monument to the Admiralty's long-delayed and grudging admission that their employees needed housing for their wives and families. It spread like a medieval Italian city over a whole hillside, its close-packed rows of houses following the contour lines as neatly as a Japanese maize field. Tenants on the Estate were allocated houses according to an Admiralty caste system of Brahminic rigidity. The altitude of an officer's house on the hillside depended upon his rank: sub-lieutenants, and junior lieutenants and their families lived in the small semi-detached houses at the foot, while Commanders and Captains occupied the larger, detached houses at the summit. The distinctions of rank extended from the site of the house itself down to the number and quality of every household fitting, to the pile and thickness of the carpets, the design of the crockery, the colour and pattern of the curtains and wall-paper, even to the number and variety of garden tools. A tenancy on the Estate lasted only as long as an officer's current appointment and tenants were reminded, in many subtle ways, that their homes were on loan. Their stewardship was subjected to unobtrusive, but frequent, inspections. Incoming and outgoing tenants submitted to a jealous inventory-taking, where every scuff-mark was measured and every cracked cup counted. Although there were many domestic advantages in living on the Estate, hostesses still tended to apologise to guests visiting for the first time; to live in a married quarter on the Estate was tacitly a sign of defeat, of having taken the line of least resistance. Most wives felt obliged to offer excuses because she and her husband had not been more enterprising.

Driving up through the Estate towards the top, Bob Markready noticed the tell-tale signs of a nomadic life. More than half of the vehicles parked outside the houses were vans or station wagons, capable of carrying quantities of children and baggage. In some of the garages he could see a pile of cabin trunks and packing cases, kept ready, like a Bedouin's tents, for instant flight.

'There's something about houses which are not lived in by the people who own them. I don't know what it is. They look cared-for, and yet they look neglected.'

'I think they look very nice, Bob. Some of the gardens are beautiful.'

He had noticed the gardens, and had been struck by the care taken of them. A few had been roughly dug over, and no more, but most had been as carefully and imaginatively tended as though the occupants had bought the house. There was something touching about the gardens. They had shrubs, planted by people who might never see them flower, and potatoes, which might be eaten by the next tenants, and roses, which may have been pruned by one and would be picked by the next.

205

As they drove up, more avenues of houses opened on either side. 'Rows of little boxes. Frightening, isn't it? "Package Man", *en masse*. For years there's been a great *brouhaha* about the lack of married quarters. Now we've got a few of them, I wonder whether they were right to make such a fuss.'

'People have got to live somewhere, Bob. And they've got a lovely view, right across Portsmouth.'

He grunted. 'You're too charitable for a naval wife, Annabel.'

'Can I take that as a compliment?'

'You can.'

Tosser met them at his front door and began at once to make excuses for the remoteness of his house.

'Did you manage to find us without too much trouble?' He spoke as though he had been about to send St Bernard dogs to look for them.

'Yes sir. No trouble at all.'

Bob Markready wondered why so many hosts maintained the fiction that their houses were hard to find. The name of Tosser's road was clearly sign-posted. Tosser's house, like every other house in the road, had a number plainly visible on the front gate.

Tosser shook hands with Annabel. 'I think we *have* met before, you know. I certainly knew your husband when he was alive.' Tosser blushed at his own solecism and muttered to himself. 'A great loss, a great loss.'

Annabel had taught herself to disregard the embarrassment of people who thought they had been tactless about Tom. 'I think Tom went on some course or other with you, didn't he?'

'He did.' Tosser was beaming. 'He did indeed. What a memory you must have. It was the staff course, I remember.'

Bob Markready noted the information. It was a measure of Tom Powell's prospects in the Service that, as a comparatively junior aircrew officer, he had attended the same staff course as General List officers considerably senior to him. Or perhaps it was just an indication of Tosser's backwardness.

Laura was placing small bowls of peanuts and olives on tables in the living-room. Bob Markready wondered how Tosser had come to marry her. He was reminded of some carpets he had seen which looked unexceptionable once they were laid, but which he could not imagine anyone going into a shop and actually choosing.

And so with Laura: no doubt she was an adequate wife, but what had possessed Tosser to pick her especially, to have and to hold, forsaking all others? She was dressed in some woolly-brown material which matched her hair. Her face was pudgy and slightly vague. She wore spectacles. Her cheeks were round and apple-red, like a peasant-woman's. She spoke hesitantly and almost inaudibly, as though expecting to be challenged. It was possible that Laura had brought money with her when she married, but Bob Mark-ready could see none of those quiet signs that Tosser had an income other than his pay. The long living-room, which extended for most of the length of the house, was furnished in the standard Admiralty pattern laid down for officers of Tosser's rank and seniority. Their pictures, which might have been significant, were duplicated in hundreds of naval homes: a map of Devonshire, by Robert Morden, hung in a Hogarth frame above the fireplace, and on another wall there was a Japanese crayon of a prancing horse. Two rows of painted medallions, the crests of all the ships Tosser had ever served in, faced the fireplace. The books in the case were of one size and binding, published by a book club. They were shabby and looked neglected, as though nobody ever handled them, and there seemed just enough of them to suggest that Laura had subscribed to the club until she had sufficient volumes to fill a bookcase respectably.

Annabel was at the window, where she had gone hoping to be able to comment on the view. But the gradient of the hill flattened outside Tosser's house and the view was shut out by the house opposite. 'I've never been in one of these houses at the top before. I've often passed them and wondered what they were like inside.'

Laura hurried forward the traditional apology. 'We're not too keen on it ourselves, but we didn't have time to find anywhere else. Tosser got the job in a hurry, and this was vacant, so we ... just moved in ...'

Laura ended limply. Annabel, who had intended her remark innocently, was taken aback to find that she had unexpectedly drawn blood. 'Oh, I do think they're really very nice inside. Though they do tend to look all the same from outside, don't they?'

'They ought to be all right, considering how much they charge you to live in them.' Tosser was at the Admiralty pattern sideboard, pouring sherry from a bottle. 'Still, I suppose we ought to be grateful for anything at all. Not so long ago, you could have put your wife up in a bell-tent on Portsdown Hill for all Their Lordships cared about it.'

'I'm afraid we're going to be an odd number tonight.' Laura was clearly a compulsive apologist. 'The Chief of Staff and Mary have let us down at the last minute. But Aubrey McConnell rang us up this afternoon and invited himself along . . .'

'That's him now.' Tosser reacted to the sound of chimes from the front door. He gave everyone a glass of sherry and went out.

While Tosser was away, Bob Markready wondered why he felt uneasy at Aubrey McConnell's name. Aubrey was a Captain, of about the same seniority as Tosser, but the two men could not possibly be friends. Tosser had no friends at court. Aubrey was one of the principal courtiers. Bob Markready supposed that Aubrey had served the necessary time at sea for promotion, although he had never heard of him in a sea-going appointment. Aubrey was one of those officers who had indeterminate appointments on the staff, or in the Ministry of Defence. Sometimes, they appeared as liaison officers, or as naval attaches in foreign embassies. Their duties were always nebulous, their responsibilities undefined. They inhabited a world where a threat to an officer's reputation could be spawned in the air, could grow out of nothing more than the sudden silence which fell over a discussion. Like the Errinyes, men such as Aubrey were part of the machinery of retribution. They were especially active whenever the Navy was under pressure from Parliament or Press. Bob Markready wondered why Tosser McTigue, that most open and unpolitical of officers, should receive a visit from one of the Kindly Ones, from a member of Her Majesty's most ancient and honourable corps of hatchet-men.

Aubrey McConnell made his entrance, bouncing on his toes, with the ease of a practised actor and kissed Laura's hand with a flourish.

'Laura, my dear, how very pleased I am to see you again!'

'We're very pleased to see you, Aubrey. It's not often you come and see us.'

He was a chubby, pigeon-toed, boisterous little man, wearing an old-fashioned dinner jacket with wide, sharply-pointed lapels.

When he grinned, deep dimples appeared in his cheeks and his large bone-white teeth had gaps between them which, with his round turnip-shaped head, gave him the appearance of a Hallowe'en mask. He advanced upon Annabel.

'You've no need to introduce me. Annabel Powell. I know all about you. I knew Tom so well.'

Everybody, Bob Markready noticed, had known Tom well. A man like Aubrey would of course make it his business to know any officer likely to rise in the Service.

Aubrey seemed truthfully surprised and pleased to meet Bob Markready. 'How very fortunate to meet you, Bob. I hear you're going great guns in that ship of yours down there.'

Bob Markready was unsuspicious of any double meaning. 'It's very kind of you to say that, sir. We're trying, anyway.'

'A glass of sherry, Aubrey?'

'Thank you, Tosser. Here's to you, Laura. And to you Tosser, may your shadow never grow less.'

Aubrey made an admirable guest, and he exerted himself to do his duty by his hostess. They had tomato soup, followed by a joint of mutton, which Tosser carved without imagination, and the sweet was some concoction of ice cream and fruit salad. It might have been a trying meal, but with Aubrey there were none of those devastating and seemingly irretrievable silences which so often bedevilled naval dinner parties when there were ladies present. Aubrey could be relied upon to keep a subject spinning with informed comment or to turn the last remark deftly on to a new topic. Tosser and Bob Markready were both interested to hear his opinions, because he seemed to have the latest information and to have met everybody implicated in some controversy or scandal.

Yet the dinner party was not wholly a success. Aubrey was too exotic for Tosser and Laura's homely fare. His manner betrayed subtly that the food was passable but he was accustomed to keener and more astringent conversation. The others found themselves always waiting for Aubrey's comment, for Aubrey to cap their stories, or to lead off into another topic.

Nevertheless he was an entertaining performer and it was not until they were drinking coffee after their meal that Bob Markready was reminded of his first misgivings on hearing Aubrey's name.

'You were talking about civil servants, Bob. I wonder, Bob, if you and I are talking about the same sort of person?'

Bob Markready frowned. 'I don't understand you. Surely a civil servant is a civil servant is a civil servant.'

'Ah, now I'm not so sure of that.' Aubrey's expression showed that Bob Markready's comment was precisely what he would have expected from an ordinary, uninformed, ship-borne naval officer. 'The average naval officer pretends to have a sort of left-handed respect for civil servants. He calls them "Our Masters". But he doesn't really *believe* that. In fact, if anything, he despises them. When he thinks of a civil servant he's thinking of the little man who comes out to do the inventory when you're moving out of a married quarter. Or those dreary little men you meet in local government. The civil servants *I* mean, the sort of man *we* deal with, the *top* laddies, are not like that at all. Some of them are quite bright, a damned sight brighter than the average naval officer, let me tell you. They sit up there in their offices like mandarins and some of them are very hard to convince, you know. They're quick to take a point but not to concede one. It's often very difficult to make them see the point of view of the man on the spot, actually in the thick of things. The Board of Admiralty seem to be the same, after they've been up there for a time. They acquire civil service attitudes from the atmosphere, by a kind of osmosis. That affair you've just been having down in *Leviathan* for instance, where that idiot chucked himself over the side . . .'

Bob Markready suddenly felt cold and frightened. He knew now that he had been right to distrust Aubrey McConnell. Aubrey had at last made his objective clear. He was down there to find out what had been happening in *Leviathan*. He was not conducting an investigation. Investigations were clumsy, and misleading, and their evidence often obscured the truth. Aubrey would have been sincerely incredulous at the suggestion of anything so crude. Aubrey trafficked in the manner words were said rather than the words themselves, in the background to facts, in the shadows rather than in substances. If Bob Markready or anyone else had ever demanded to know by whose authority Aubrey McConnell was making enquiries, the C-in-C's staff and the Admiralty would have produced genuinely puzzled disclaimers. Aubrey's was a delicate business, and discreet as the hangman's inspection on the eve. Bob Markready thought with pity of his predecessor: in those final months poor Tony must have been visited by packs of men like Aubrey, gauging him, measuring him for the drop.

'There was a lot of interest in that affair up at the front office. We were all astonished we managed to get away with so little press publicity, particularly when you think of the ship's past record. You obviously handled it pretty well. But that man must have caused you a good deal of anxiety at one time. Would you say?'

Aubrey looked at Tosser.

'He did. But I was overruled most of the time. You tell it, Bob. It's really your story.'

The cue was unfortunate. It implied that there had been a disagreement between the Captain and the Commander, and that the difference had been settled in the Commander's favour. But that was not true. It had been the Captain's decision to call in the police. Was it possible that Tosser still believed that Aubrey had been at a loose end that evening and had called fortuitously? Bob Markready could not credit Tosser with such naïveté.

While he listened to the story of the Well-wisher, Aubrey played the role of the sympathetic fellow-officer, understandably anxious to hear the details, in case he too found himself in the same predicament. He repeatedly denied previous knowledge of events in *Leviathan* but his questioning betrayed that on the contrary he already knew a great deal of the affair. Aubrey had been thoroughly briefed.

Aubrey's disguise was so finished that Bob Markready himself was almost deceived, until Tosser broke while they were discussing the dilemma of whether or not to call in the CID.

Aubrey's prompting was smooth and compassionate. 'That must have been a difficult one for you, Tosser?'

'It was the hardest one of the lot, Aubrey. We didn't know whether to go on, and risk getting deeper and deeper, or call in the police from the word go. I thought of asking them in after the first gauge glasses were smashed, but Bob here was determined to catch the fellow on his own.'

'But you called in the police eventually?'

'Oh yes. Perhaps it wasn't necessary.' Tosser laughed ponderously. 'That fellow could probably feel Bob hard on his heels.'

'Yes, it's always difficult to decide whether to let the police and outsiders in.' Aubrey's complacent voice made Bob Markready want to get up and assault him: it was easy to be so damned judicious and collected after the event. 'The trouble is that when you *don't* let them in, it's likely to be all that much bigger an explosion when it does get out. The Admiralty tend to get the wrong end of the stick in these matters. They're so remote, you see.'

Tosser nodded. 'Perhaps we shouldn't have played it so close to our chests.'

Bob Markready felt the blood thudding in his ears, and the palms of his hands were wet. Unthinkable, that Tosser should actually be trying to betray him. But the alternative could only be that Tosser honestly believed that Aubrey was on a social visit. Or maybe Tosser was just too nice a man: there had been Captains who had betrayed their subordinates unwittingly, because they had been too innocent to realise that any defence was needed. Surely even Tosser must know by now that Aubrey was looking for a scapegoat.

Annabel had tried several times to show that the whole subject bored her. Aubrey allowed himself to be diverted temporarily, but returned again and again. 'Forgive me for keeping on with this, but I really am vastly interested. After all, it might happen to me some day.'

Bob Markready thought that unlikely: to be in the same predicament Aubrey must first go to sea, and he was as likely to do that as to grow gills. Nevertheless, he recognised that there was nothing to be gained by fobbing Aubrey off. He would merely reappear at Tosser's elbow somewhere else.

Aubrey persisted until the subject of the Well-wisher had been sucked dry. Bob Markready did not know, and would never know, whether his evidence had been accepted. Sometime in the future he might be received a little more cordially than usual when he visited the Director of Officers' Appointments, or he might find, on his last chance of promotion to Captain, that his name was not on the list. He had never received the attentions of someone like Aubrey in any of his previous appointments; but then, he remembered with humility, perhaps none of his previous appointments had been important enough.

Annabel was silent for most of the journey home, only speaking when they had nearly reached her house.

'Well. Do you think you passed your examination tonight?'

'You noticed.'

'Oh Bob, I could hardly not notice, could I? When you've been a naval wife for eleven years you get to know when people are clawing at each other's throats.'

'Did it look as bad as that?'

'It wasn't polite conversation, that much was obvious. It was frightening, Bob. You read about the night of the long knives. You never expect to see it actually happening.'

'Do you think the Captain noticed what was going on? He *must* have.'

'I don't think he did.'

'In a way, I hope he didn't. There was a time when I thought he was deliberately trying to do me down.'

'He wouldn't do that.'

'He wouldn't be the first Captain to sell his Commander or his First Lieutenant down the river.'

'But Tosser's not that kind!'

'That's what worries me most, Annabel. He's either much more naïve than I thought, or the hell of a lot more cunning.'

He winced, remembering Tosser's blunderings. The most damaging and lasting effect of Aubrey's visit would be the loss of confidence between himself and Tosser. Although he was sometimes puzzled by Tosser's insensitiveness, although he sometimes suspected that Tosser was more shrewd than he liked to appear, they had steadily built up their confidence in each other since the commission began. He had already begun to feel that in any circumstances connected with the ship, he could rely on the Captain. He could never be so sure of that again.

'Was that why we stayed there so long?'

'God, I hope I'm not as transparent as this to everyone!' Once more he was staggered by her intuitive overlooking of his own thoughts. 'But you're quite right. I wanted to make sure we left after Aubrey. I daren't leave him alone with Tosser. God knows what he would have told him.'

'But Aubrey can always see Tosser again somewhere else?'

'Yes, I thought of that at first. He could, but somehow I don't think he will. Whatever it was he came for, I think he's got. Tonight was the night, win or lose.'

He stopped the car in front of her house and switched off the engine. Annabel was content to sit quietly for a moment. Her heart had yearned over him that evening: he had looked so honest, and innocent, and had so plainly been trying to do his best, while that cunning little fox of a man stalked him.

'Bob, I felt really fond of you tonight, when that horrible little man was asking all those questions. I could have kissed you, you were so different to him.'

'I had an idea you were trying to help me. But he wasn't going to be side-tracked, was he? He was a creepy little man.'

He turned in his seat to look at her.

'You know, I'll have to decide what to do about you.'

'I'm not one of your problems!' Her quiet mood had changed swiftly to annoyance. The evening had shaken him and, she hoped, broken up his defence. But the old organisation man was still there, still searching for solutions where no solution was needed. 'Don't think you can solve me by putting up a notice about me in Daily Orders, or whatever you call them! I'm not a squad of sailors!'

'I'm sorry. I suppose I must have got into the habit of treating everything and everybody as problems to be solved. It's been a hell of an evening. I thought we were in for a quiet dinner and a chat with the Captain and his missis. And look what happened. Perhaps I'd better say good night now.'

'No, you will not! You'll come in and have a glass of whisky.'

Annabel had drawn the curtains and switched on a small electric fire before she went out. The room was warm and welcoming, reminding him of how cold and intimidating Laura's house had been. He was already tormented by the memories of Aubrey's questions. His mind ran like an ant over everything he and Tosser had said, wondering where they had made a mistake. The inquisition had been doubly terrifying because it had taken place in such ordinary surroundings, in such a common-place room. Torquemada had been wrong to arrange all those diabolical trappings. The dungeons, those pits and braziers and glowing branding irons, had been a waste of money. He could have achieved the same results in Laura McTigue's living-room.

Annabel watched his face, guessing at his thoughts. She knew, because she had lived with Tom and heard him talk about other officers, the extraordinary power these men had to hurt each other. Their loyalty was abnormally high, but when they did turn, they turned like vicious snakes.

'No, don't put any more lights on.' She took off her stole, and dropped it on a chair. 'It's cosier as it is.'

He cupped her face in his hands and then drew his fingers down the side of her throat and over her shoulders. He kissed her and buried his face in the hollow of her shoulder, in the rich scents of her skin. She caressed the nape of his neck with her finger-tips, pressing the shape and suppleness of her body against him.

He stepped back and held her at arm's length.

'Thank you.'

'*Thank you!*' She looked up, her eyebrows raised. 'Is that all? Just thank you?'

'Yes.'

She brushed him away and, gathering the skirts of her dress, knelt in an armchair and stretched one arm along its back.

'What a very complex man you are. Do you know what I thought when I saw you at that service in the hangar? You were different. Nobody else seemed to mind. It was their ship, too, but they didn't seem to care. But you cared. I liked that. I like somebody who commits himself. You looked such a simple uncomplicated person. Now I know you better I see that's not true. There's a whole side of life you seem to have cut away from yourself. Now why are you smiling?'

He shook his head. 'Just one of those disconnected thoughts.'

'Tell me.'

'You'll probably laugh at this, but I was just thinking of one ship I was in where I used to read the lesson on Sundays occasionally. Do you know the story of Uriah the Hittite?'

'Uriah the Hittite?' Annabel wrinkled her brow. 'I know the name, very vaguely. But tell me the story.'

'Well, Uriah had a very beautiful wife called Bathsheba, who slept with King David and became pregnant by him while her husband was away fighting the Philistines. When David heard that Bathsheba was going to have his child, he recalled Uriah from the battlefield and gave him some leave, expecting naturally enough that he would visit his wife while he was on leave and then David could blame the child on him.'

215

Annabel was deeply indignant. 'What a filthy thing to do.'

'But it didn't work, that's the point! Uriah wouldn't have it. He thought it quite wrong that he should go home and sleep with his wife while the rest of the army were still roughing it in the trenches, so to speak. The ark and Israel and Judah abide in tents, he said to David. My lord Joab and my lord's servants are encamped in the open fields. Shall I then go into my house, to eat and drink, and to lie with my wife? As thou livest, and as thy soul livest, I will not do this thing. It was rather a splendid thing to say, but it must have been damned frustrating for David. He extended Uriah's leave. He even got him drunk one night, but Uriah still wouldn't go and see Bathsheba. Myself, I've always thought Uriah the Hittite would have made a superb divisional officer. We could do with a few like him in *Leviathan* right now.'

'Bob, this ship means a lot to you, doesn't it?' Annabel swung round in her chair and clasped her knees up to her chin. 'You'd give anything to make a success of her, wouldn't you?'

He nodded.

'Is that all you want? Because you'll get it. I can see now you're going to make a success of that ship. I'm sure of it. What are you going to do when you wake up one morning and find you're successful? Where are you going from there?'

'I'll face that problem when it comes.'

'And in the meantime you're quite blind to everything else!' She thumped her fists on the arms of the chair. 'Hadn't you better get back then? Something terrible might have happened to your beloved ship while you're wasting time with me! I'd hate you to miss anything on my account!'

'Oh now, don't be annoyed with me, Annabel. What would you say if I told you I wasn't interested? Supposing I told you I was going to chuck it all in, because I didn't care any more? You'd be the first to tell me to get straight back to it, wouldn't you? You've got to understand you're something new to me, Annabel. It's a long time since anybody...' He gestured, groping for the word. '... *Attacked* me emotionally like this.'

'I don't think anyone could attack you. You've got this sort of chain-mail all over you. You're a cold fish, Bob. Have you *ever* had a girl-friend?'

216

'Oh yes, indeed I have. I've been engaged to be married. Twice, in fact.'

'*Have* you?' The news surprised her. She had not credited him with such a gallant background. So other women, too, must have had difficulties.

'What went wrong with the engagements?'

'It's a long story.' It was indeed a long story, and a long time ago; the experience now lay untouched in his memory, about as relevant to the present as some forgotten Victorian general's memoirs of an expedition against the Matabele.

'It was like something straight out of "The Importance of Being Earnest".' He struck an attitude, advancing one foot forward, and imitated a fruity contralto voice. 'To lose *one* fiancée, Mr Markready, may be regarded as a misfortune; to lose *both* looks like carelessness!'

Annabel's laughter burst from her before she could prevent it. 'I must say that's one way of putting it! I'm sorry I swore at you. But you can't blame a girl for being annoyed when she's treated like something pinned up on a notice-board, for action in due course.'

But Bob Markready was already regretting that he had put the matter so lightly. He doubted now whether he had succeeded in making the point he intended. Although his job exposed him, like an actor or a judge, to the public eye and he had developed a hard, unself-conscious carapace, he was still secretly a shy man. He admitted that he was preoccupied with *Leviathan*, but that was not the only consideration. He was forty-five, in the prime of life but, nevertheless, on the threshold of middle-age. He had been robbed twice. Annabel could be his last chance. It was important not to make a mistake now.

As he was going, Annabel took his arm. 'You didn't tell me how the story finished. Did Uriah acknowledge the child?'

He grinned. 'Ah well, that's the awkward bit, you see. When David finally realised that Uriah was too stupid or too honourable to do what he wanted, he sent him back to the army. And he told Joab his general to put Uriah in the forefront of the hottest battle, and retire from him, so he would be killed. And that's exactly what happened.'

Annabel stamped her foot. 'You really are the most incredible man. Here am I, standing on my front doorstep at one o'clock in the morning, talking about Uriah the Hittite.'

She watched him getting into his car. 'But I think I know why you told me that story. I believe I know what you're getting at. And I think you're wrong.'

14

The Commander had been so preoccupied by events below decks that he was not able to visit the flight deck until the flying training programme, that process of blending three or four dozen individual pilots into an integrated weapon, was well advanced. He had detected a growing feeling amongst the ship's officers that the Air Group were uninterested in the ship. They were satisfied to solve their perennial chess problems in the sky and on the flight deck, and remain indifferent to anything which happened below hangar deck level.

The root of the ship's officers' feeling, the Commander saw, lay in the nature of the island. The heart of the Air Group was in the island and it was separate from the rest of the ship. Although dwarfed by the ship's hull, the island was still a considerable structure, a small ship in its own right, with its own cabins, bathrooms, offices, workshops, galley and canteen. The island had six decks, containing the bridge and the ship's action information organisation, the aircraft direction and control rooms, the briefing and ready rooms, and many of the ship's communications and radar personnel. The ship was directed and fought from the island and it was a self-contained and self-sufficient world, with a private way of life and an atmosphere independent of the rest of the ship. Some officers, such as the Navigating Officer, the Operations Officer and the Captain himself, rarely left the island whilst the ship was at sea.

Externally, the island was studded with a score of small parapets, platforms, galleries and cat-walks from which spectators could watch the flying. All island vantage points were nicknamed by the Air Group 'goofing positions'. All spectators, whatever their rank or precedence in the ship, were 'goofers'.

Like every other goofer, the Commander quickly found his own favourite goofing position. He came across it by accident when he tried a door marked 'Private' and discovered that it opened on a small gallery, with room for two or three people, which looked out over the flight deck. The gallery was sometimes used by the ship's photographers when two cameras were required or when, for some reason, they tired of their normal post higher in the island by the gun direction position. On most days, the Commander had the tiny gallery to himself.

To the Commander, all things were new on the flight deck and from his first day he was captured by its marvellously various patterns and movements, by its alternate periods of uproar and quiet, by the climax and fulfilment of its launching and landing cycles. He wondered at his own child-like enjoyment as he watched the preparations for catapult launching. The shapes of the aircraft had a functional beauty in themselves but the concerted human activity around them lent dramatic additions of suspense and violence. A score of men shepherded an aircraft along its journey from the deck-park to the catapult, an extended line of aircraft directors in yellow jackets each receiving custody of the aircraft in turn and passing it on with neat, solicitous gestures. Forward, in the bows of the ship a single figure stood astride the catapult track, with his arms raised to guide the pilot on to the blocks, while the aircraft handlers, bodies and heads bent, clustered under the wings. Black-and-white helmeted men scuttled under the aircraft's belly to fit the catapult bridle and the hold-back which restrained the aircraft until it was at full power and ready for launching. The handlers ran from the aircraft and squatted between the catapults, holding their hands over their ears. One held up a board, to remind the pilot of brakes, flaps, and throttle. Another read off wind speeds from a hand anenometer and signalled them to the bridge. The Flight Deck Officer stood where he could catch the pilot's eye, and leaned against the wind, his trousers and jacket flapping. He held up a green flag and whirled it over his head, faster and faster, while the pilot opened his throttles until the aircraft was shuddering and straining to be released when, with a splendid pirouette and jack-knife, the flag whipped down. The aircraft was gone, already skimming out across the sea.

It seemed to the Commander that the flight deck contained all the proper ingredients of theatre: colour, and movement, and dialogue, suspense and tragedy and embarrassment. The play absorbed the spectator utterly because it combined the human fascination of watching other people at work with the unadmitted, subconscious wish that something would go wrong. Although there was grace and skill to see on the flight deck the spirit which compelled the spectators was that which urged the crowds in the Roman amphitheatres. They came because there was a chance of seeing another human being go close to death. There were always more goofers in the island on the day after an accident.

The Air Group suffered no serious accidents for some weeks after MacLauchlan's death. One of Roger Calvados' pilots and his observer were forced to eject after their tail-pipe temperature warning light burned, and were picked up by an RAF helicopter off Penzance, but there were no accidents on *Leviathan*'s flight deck until a fortnight after the Commander had discovered his gallery, when he had watched several days' faultless flying and had lost his first spellbound awe. He had almost decided that carrier flying, like any other evolution in the Navy, could be performed to a strict and predictable formula. The accident revived his initial admiration and impressed upon him the extent to which the Air Group depended for their lives on good fortune. Like the bull-dancers of ancient Crete, the aircrew practised their precarious art on sufferance: they were safe only while the beast ran true.

The Commander was watching two sections of Rupert Smith's Heavy Foot making rocket attacks on a splash target towed astern of the ship. Rocket firing was a chance for the fighter pilots to show off their expertise before their home crowd. For a spectator it was one of the most dramatic and satisfying of all flying demonstrations. The aircraft wheeled out of the sun in turn and hurtled towards the sea, to describe a thrilling flat curve in the air before releasing the fiery rocket tangents and pulling up and away. The rising and falling sounds of the jet engines, the smoke trails, the scattered shouts of the small crowd on the flight deck and their cheers at a hit, the significant splashes near the target, all reminded the Commander of the cheerful partisan atmosphere at a ship's football match.

After the serial, the target was winched on board, the ship turned into the wind and the crowd vanished from the flight deck. The first aircraft entered the landing circuit. The sun flashed on its wings as it banked far astern of the ship and, like a greyhound running always at the object in view, swept round to converge on the ship's course. Nose up, with wheels and flaps down and arrester hook trailing, in a curiously helpless questing attitude, the aircraft grew rapidly larger and flung itself over the round-down, landing heavily with an impact which shook the island.

The arrester hook engaged a wire and flailed the deck with it. While the pilot still had his throttles open to make sure of his recovery, the hook by a rare mischance took a second wire.

Under the combined decelerating force of two wires, the arrester hook broke out, leaving the aircraft free, but with much of its momentum destroyed.

The pilot seemed to realise his danger when he was level with the after end of the island and there was the boom and white-hot glare from the tail-pipes when he relit the after-burners. The jet screaming redoubled as the pilot opened his throttles wide to escape.

The cockpit canopy was drawn back and the Commander could see the pilot's face, calm and apparently untroubled, when the aircraft passed him. The pilot fought to regain height and speed down the length of the flight deck. His aircraft skidded towards the catapult tracks, lifted into the air, flew with its nose canted upwards at the point of stall, and sank below the forward edge of the flight deck. A broad feather of spray spouted up a cable length ahead of the ship.

Leviathan was already heeling sharply over, turning hard to starboard but the swing of the ship's advance and transfer through the water was carrying the propellers directly over the pilot's head. The Commander had barely seen the new danger when the ship came upright and began to turn back to port. *Leviathan* had swerved in her course, through a lateral distance of less than fifty feet, but enough to allow the sinking aircraft to pass clear down the port side.

Astern, the helicopter was hovering over the small shapes of the tailplane and the cockpit canopy which were being tumbled and washed by the turbulent water in the ship's wake. The ship turned again, obscuring the Commander's view, but before he had had time to move his position or to consider what was happening, the helicopter was thrashing the air in front of his gallery and landing on the flight deck where the doctor and the sick berth attendants were waiting. The pilot was sitting in the helicopter's rescue bay, bare-headed and grinning. When he stood up, the Commander saw that it was Stiggins, with his wet flying overalls clinging to his body.

Stiggins swung himself down to the flight deck and, becoming aware of his rapt audience in the island, mimed the motions of emptying water from his helmet, refilling it from a bottle, and drinking a toast. The goofers applauded, but the Commander felt a chill at his heart. He was not generally a superstitious man, but surely a fighter pilot was the last person who might mock the gods.

Less than a minute had elapsed between the arrester hook failure and the recovery of the pilot. The sequence had been a magnificent piece of co-ordination between the ship and the Air Group. The Commander made his way up to the bridge, curious to see who had handled the ship so well. When he reached the top step of the bridge access ladder he stopped, astounded. Julian Bird was bending over the wind speed indicator dial at the forward end of the compass platform, and was giving orders into the microphone to the steering position.

The Captain was sitting in Father's Chair, looking over his left shoulder at the flight deck. Hearing a footstep, he turned and followed the line of the Commander's astonished gaze. He got up from his chair and came aft.

The Captain kept his voice low, so that Bird could not hear. 'If you're wondering what I think you're wondering, Bob, the answer's yes.'

'He did that on his own?'

'Every bit. If I'd tried to take over, we'd have been on top of him before I could have said a word. As it happened, I couldn't have done it better myself.'

'Well, sir.' The Commander blew out a long, puzzled breath. 'That's a turn-up for the book.'

'I don't think I'm going to bother about any more of those quarterly reports. He may not be so hot on his sword-drill, but he's probably saved us one pilot.'

Commander (Air)'s head appeared round the door of Flyco. 'On again, sir, please?'

'What's the situation about those wires?'

'Joss Parkhurst says he's not sure about number four. He's leaving it down for this serial and then he's going to have a look at it.'

'Right.' The Captain climbed back into his chair. 'On we go again then, Bird. Courses and speeds as necessary for flying.'

'Aye aye, sir.' Bird looked up from the wind speed indicator. 'Wind still dropping and veering slightly, sir.'

'Never mind.' The Captain was as jovial as a man who had picked up an unexpected sixpence. 'You're in charge. You know what to do.'

The Commander could not see Bird's face, but every line of his back demonstrated his pleasure. He guessed that it was some time since Bird had been paid such a compliment. He remembered Stiggins, and went down to Flyco to enquire.

Flyco was the finest goofing position of all, a flying buttress of steel and toughened glass which soared out over the flight deck. From here, Commander (Air) and his assistant Lieutenant Commander (Flying), who was always known as Little F, directed *Leviathan*'s flying operations.

'Is your lad all right after his bath, Wings?'

'Yep. Fit as a flea. He says the water's lovely and warm, we ought to have hands to bathe. Cheeky little bugger.'

'Where is he now?'

'Sick bay. We'll keep him there for a bit.'

'Isn't there something about flying again immediately, to get your nerve back? Like falling off a horse?'

An unusual expression of uncertainty crossed Commander (Air)'s face. 'There's something in that. But in this case he's better off where he is. He might have a bit of delayed shock. He's as happy as Larry now, but in a few hour's time it may be a different story. When he realises that if the Officer of the Watch hadn't had his wits about him it might have been eight o'clock on the quarter-deck, rest on your arms reversed, and all that.'

The Commander was repelled by such callousness, until he appreciated that Commander (Air) was merely commenting upon a pilot's occupational risk, just as a diver might discuss another's attack of the bends.

Commander (Air) had been half-listening to the murmured voices from the Flyco broadcast speaker above his head. 'Excuse us now, Bob. We're landing on the rest. Can't keep 'em waiting for ever.'

Little F was speaking into a microphone and a booming echo

of his voice could be heard from outside on the flight deck. A buzzer sounded, and a square red light on the bulkhead changed to green. The Commander felt the deck throbbing underfoot again, as the ship picked up speed. Soon, he heard the thump of the next aircraft on the flight deck, the drop in noise level and the rising whine of the engine as the aircraft taxied, wings already half-folded, under Flyco and forward into Fly One.

On his way down through the island, the Commander stopped in the flat outside the Aircraft Control Room. The ACR was the hub round which the life of the flight deck revolved. It was the clearing house for flight deck information, the administrative authority for all aircraft movements inside the ship, a ready room for the helicopter pilots and deck landing control officers, the base depot for demands for fuel, high pressure air and flight deck vehicles, the rendezvous and briefing-room for any passengers travelling in the aircraft, and a general tea-house and waiting-room for anyone who had any occasion at all to be on the flight deck.

The quiet centre of the hub was the ACR Officer, Lieutenant Commander Roland Cartwright Dubonnet. Rowley Dubonnet was one of the ship's characters, known and beloved by the whole ship's company. In reminiscent moments he claimed to be descended from Charles II, through an ancestor born on the sinister side of the blanket. He was a tall, gangling man, loose-jointed, a creature of knobs and awkward stances. Like Sir Lancelot, he could have been described as an ill-made knight. His hair was dead white and stuck out from his head in a thatch. His face was red and craggy, and his voice low-pitched and musical, except on the telephone, where it became strident and imperative.

Rowley had developed the running of the ACR into an art which concealed art. While flying was in progress, the little compartment was a maelstrom of broadcasts, telephone calls, cross-checks, queries and complaints, with a constant flow of visitors, aircrew, onlookers and flight deck personnel. Rowley sat in the centre, making decisions imperturbably and tranquilly in surroundings where it did not seem possible for any man to make a rational comparison of events and arrive at a conclusion. He was courteous, when other men might have been carried foaming to their cabins. He worked at the end of the day at the same pace and in the same

225

manner as he had begun at the beginning. And when, once or twice in a ship's commission, Rowley Dubonnet lost his temper, the entire Air Group jumped at the double, knowing that a cataclysm had befallen them.

When the Commander looked through the ACR doorway, Rowley was on the telephone. He was leaning over the table, one foot resting on the seat of a chair, with the receiver wedged under his chin, and he was drinking a cup of coffee.

'I say again for the benefit of you ignorant sailors, I want four-three-seven struck down at the end of this serial and six-nine-four ranged for the next serial. No, it's US. Yes, that's why I want six-nine-four. Get it? Good. No hurry. Any time in the next three minutes will do.'

Rowley put down the hangar telephone, and the main exchange telephone rang at once.

'Death, where is thy sting?' Rowley seized the telephone, and tilted his head towards the deckhead. 'Yes, sir. No, I didn't know that, sir. Sir, I should explain . . .'

Rowley groaned quietly and laid the receiver on the table. He lit a cigarette and sipped his coffee contemplatively, while the voice still rattled thinly on the telephone. Outside, there was the crash and thunder of another landing. Rowley picked up the receiver again.

'I'll tell the Air Group Liaison Officer as soon as I see him, sir. Yes, sir, he took over the wardroom minerals account just before we commissioned. No, that's quite all right, sir.'

'Where grave, thy victory?' Rowley slammed down the receiver, stood up and stretched. 'Bloody Commander (S). The old robber. All pussers are robbers. *Barabbas* was a pusser. Wants to know what happened to the wardroom bloody mineral audit. I gave that up before the *last* audit.'

Something in the attitudes of the others sitting in the ACR warned Rowley that he had an audience. He swung round and saw the Commander.

'I'm most terribly sorry, sir, I didn't see you standing there.'

'That's all right, Rowley. This is purely a social call, though I can see it's a bad time for it . . .'

The Commander's voice was drowned by the sound of an aircraft flying low along the flight deck. Rowley cocked his head. 'Ho ho, what's this? Sounds like somebody bolting . . .'

The loudspeaker made a guttural announcement which the Commander missed, but Rowley reacted at once. 'Here you are, Enoch. The voice of the turtle. Got your ducky little flags?'

A tall pilot, as tall and gangling as Rowley himself, who had been sitting unobtrusively in the corner seat, took two glowing yellow and orange deck landing flags from a locker and went out.

Rowley noticed the Commander's interest. 'Deck landing mirror's on the blink, sir. We'll have to bat the last two on without it.'

He beckoned the Commander to a small angled window of armoured glass which jutted out from the line of the island and permitted a couple of watchers in the ACR a limited but adequate view of the flight deck forward and aft.

'Enoch's worth watching, sir, if he's on form.'

Enoch was running aft, hurdling over the outspread arrester wires with exaggerated care, until he reached his platform on the port after corner of the flight deck. Enoch was the ship's senior deck landing control officer, although his previous functions were taken over by the mirror and his duties were now advisory, when the squadrons were carrying out carrier-controlled approaches. Like Othello, his occupation was gone, except when the mirror was defective. Enoch was not one of those legendary batsmen who could bring an aircraft down to the deck on a wing and a prayer; he was not even particularly fond of the job, but he was competent and the pilots trusted him. In his tattered flying overalls and faded yellow jacket, he looked like a scarecrow warning crows off a stubble-field. The Commander had seen Enoch at work before and he knew that Enoch could mount a circus turn of his own, especially if he were controlling an inexperienced pilot who was intimidated by the raffish, spindly figure leering up at him from the batsman's platform.

Enoch nonchalantly batted the first of the remaining aircraft on to the deck. The second aircraft however, could not, or would not, lower its undercarriage. After the first wave-off, Enoch bounded from his platform and executed a very fair entrechât, while swinging his flags round in a great derisive circle.

Rowley was watching over the Commander's shoulder. 'What Enoch's trying to say, sir, is how the bloody hell can you expect me to bat you on if you don't bloody well bother to put your cart down?'

The loudspeaker crackled. *'Rig crash barrier. Stand-by for emergency landing. Aircraft without undercarriage.'*

Rowley sighed. 'This is obviously going to be one of those days.' He spoke over his shoulder. 'What's the firemain pressure, somebody?'

One of the ACR watch-keepers checked the gauge on the bulkhead.

'Coming up, sir.'

'Don't you normally divert them ashore when something like this happens, Rowley?'

'Normally we would, sir. But there may be some reason why not. There is a theory that provided you don't actually bounce over the side into the sea, you're safer landing on your belly on a flight deck than on an airfield. At least the boys are all round you here, right on the spot to give you a hand. How's that firemain pressure now?'

'O.K. sir, at thirty pounds.'

The pressure was important. In a few moments, the firefighting crews might need all the water they could get. The chatter and movement had stilled in the passageway outside the ACR. The flight deck had taken on a harder appearance of anticipation. Two men in steel helmets and fireproof suits had taken the axes from their belts and moved out clear of the parked flight deck vehicles aft of the island. The big crane was manned, and on the other side of the flight deck, the red skull-caps of the firefighting crews were gathering, ready to sprint. The crash barrier was already up, its long nylon threads swinging in the wind. The following helicopter edged closer to the ship. *Leviathan* was working up to full power, until the wind speed over the flight deck was nearly twice that required for a normal deck landing.

Down on the deck landing control platform, Enoch spat ostentatiously over the side and flicked his flags, to stream them clear in the wind. He stood, legs apart, crouching with his arms stretched out, his eyes following the aircraft as it flew round its final circuit. Then, like the taking of a fish on a line, Enoch established his communion with the pilot. He raised his flags and the aircraft responded, lowered them, and the aircraft sank. He knelt on one

228

knee and flapped his flags gently, languidly, coaxing the aircraft towards him with slow, downwards movements. He held the flags rigid for a moment, and then sharply cut them out of sight.

The aircraft glided whistling over the round-down, touched on its belly, skidded, took a wire and slewed over to the port side where it came to rest on the edge of the flight deck with its port wing in the air. The pilot climbed down into the arms of the men in the fire-proof suits. Enoch stuffed his flags under one arm and began to walk back to the ACR, while parties of aircraft handlers converged from both sides.

'*Cheers, Enoch! Top of the class and ten for neatness!*'

Enoch stopped in his stride, and sourly thrust two fingers up at Flyco.

The Commander envied the Air Group their opportunities for individual display and flair. By comparison, the duties of the rest of the ship's company, including those of the Commander himself, were made to look humdrum and unromantic. Flight deck personalities were larger than life. Their triumphs and disasters were public property. Their disappointments and their embarrassments were felt by the whole ship. To a man as new to aircraft carriers as the Commander, the Air Arm seemed to have outstripped the rest of the Navy in their standards of technique and equipment. Their working clothes were more colourful, and better suited to the wearer's duties. Their tools were lighter, better designed, and more plentiful. Their hours of work were more adaptable and their work itself seemed better planned and co-ordinated. Their mental approach was also more flexible; the squadron ratings cheerfully accepted irregular working hours and meal-times, to fit the flying programme. If the Commander had wished to change the times of the rest of the ship's company's dinner or rum issue, he could only have avoided widespread resentment and opposition by a long preliminary publicity campaign and consultations with other Heads of Departments, divisional officers, and the Welfare Committee.

The Commander's interest in the Air Group was not solely as a spectator. If the Captain were absent through sickness or accident then the Commander, and not Commander (Air), would become responsible for the ship and therefore for the flying programme. It was necessary for the Commander to be able to step into the Captain's place in an emergency, but the more closely he studied the Air Group the more certain he became that the squadrons would never allow themselves to be wholly integrated into the ship. The squadron ratings had a fierce loyalty to their squadrons, and only a nominal attachment to the ship. Certainly they joined in ship's activities: Roger Calvados' squadron cricket team was the best in the ship, while the aircraft handlers played deck hockey at a level approaching genius, but they played like guests on hotel tennis courts, as though they might literally fly away at any moment.

The Commander could never reconcile to himself the differences in the public and private behaviour of the aircrew officers. On the flight deck the pilots were surrounded in an aura of magic, like heroic figures from a medieval troubadour's tale, invested with a kind of romantic glamour. In the wardroom, they reverted to spotty, callow, boisterous young men, who picked their noses at meals, used their napkins as handkerchiefs, and surreptitiously tore the pin-up photographs from the mess magazines and took them away to their cabins. Some of them had monosyllabic but expressive nicknames, such as 'Freak', and 'Bones' and 'Horse', and they all spoke a special dialect with its own vocabulary in which, for instance, the word 'ace' meant anything superlative, desirable, well planned or well executed. 'Dank' was its antonym and 'fat' almost its synonym, meaning satisfied, ready, in a good or advantageous position. Every wardroom's conversation was always sprinkled with esoteric phrases and jokes but the aircrew added a further quality, feverish and anarchic, forming another private enclosure in what was already a closed society.

Relations between the aircrew and the rest of the wardroom were cordial enough on the surface but sometimes the pilots, obeying an occasional recurrence of mob instincts, ganged together to mock and insult one of the ship's officers. The Gunnery Officer was their favourite mark. He was an easy target, being too patently the regular professional naval officer, too obviously the artefact of Dartmouth and Whale Island, having absorbed too much of the vulnerable earnestness and naïveté which saturated the very atmosphere at both establishments. It was not the Commander's place to defend the Gunnery Officer but often, when he saw Guns' helpless baited face, he felt uneasy, as though he had half-heard a private and malicious joke told against himself.

The Air Group's irregular hours frequently left them off duty in ship's working hours, when many of the squadron officers gathered in the wardroom ante-rooms to play Uckers. The game was a coarsened form of Ludo. The aircrew were addicted to it, playing by the hour and sometimes, when there was little flying, by the day. A regular Uckers school gathered in the forward ante-room on every forenoon at sea.

The Commander himself rarely passed the ante-rooms in the middle of the forenoon and was normally too busy to take much notice, but one morning he was surprised by the cheering, laughter and applause from the forward ante-room.

A dozen pilots, in flying overalls, were gathered round a table in the middle of the room. A young steward called Dawson was manoeuvring a vacuum cleaner over the wardroom carpet, avoiding the outskirts of the group.

The sight of the steward attempting to get on with his work, while the officers were playing, fired the Commander's rage. He was through the door and had whirled down upon the group before they were aware of him.

'What's going on in here?'

The players stood up. The onlookers drew back. Dawson switched off his vacuum cleaner.

'What's going on in here?'

'We're playing uckers, sir.'

'*Uckers?*' The Commander's voice conveyed all his contempt that grown men should be discovered playing children's games in the middle of the working day. 'If you *have* to play kindergarten games, play them up in the island. You've got ready rooms to use as nurseries. Use them.'

The players stared at him in silence, while all the gossip, all the rumours they had heard, flooded back. They had been warned this Commander was anti-Air Group.

Stiggins, who happened to be holding the leather cup and had been about to throw, rattled the dice. It was no more than a nervous reflex gesture. The Commander interpreted it as a sign of impatience with his own presence and a signal to the others to continue with the game. Also, Stiggins was the only player whose name the Commander could readily remember.

'Stiggins, I don't know what you're like as a pilot, but if it's anything like your capacity as an officer I can tell you you've got a long way to go yet. Now clear out. All of you. Go and play your nursery games up in your nurseries. Not in the wardroom while the hands are working.'

The Commander did not expect the matter to end there. Nevertheless, he was disconcerted to find Rupert Smith, Roger Calvados and a third squadron CO, Jerry Malone, already waiting on him when he returned to his cabin. The squadron grapevine must have passed the news in the twinkling of an eye.

'All right gentlemen, come in. I imagine you're here to discuss the question of *uckers*.' A residue of contempt lingered in his voice.

'Yes, sir.' Roger Calvados had apparently been nominated as spokesman. 'We must apologise for what happened just now . . .'

'I accept your apology.'

'But in all fairness, sir . . .'

'Ah. I thought there would be something else.'

Roger Calvados flushed. 'In fairness, sir, we should point out that every one of those officers was up at six o'clock this morning. They've all flown one sortie today. Some of them have flown two.'

The Commander sat down at his desk. He had not intended to approach this so precipitately. However, now that three of the squadron commanders were actually here, he might as well take the opportunity.

'I'm well aware that the aircrew work awkward hours and they're often free when the rest of us are turned to. But that's no reason why they should make it so obvious they've nothing to do.'

Jerry Malone hitched his cap from under his right arm, across to his left. He was a pleasant, amiable man, the CO of the long-range, anti-submarine search squadron. He had served with a number of awkward senior officers in the past and he had generally managed to reach some sort of amicable compromise. But he had never encountered any man who looked as certain as this Commander that he was always in the right.

'The wardroom mess *is* the *aircrews'* mess, sir, just the same as anybody else.' Jerry Malone spoke apologetically, as though the Commander had missed an obvious point in mitigation.

'I'm aware of that, too. But the custom of the Service is for everyone, watch-keepers and those working special routines included, to turn to in the forenoons. It gives the messdeck sweepers a proper chance to clean up at least once in the day. It's the same for the wardroom, you'll find. The ship's watch-keeping officers all turn to in their departments during the forenoons, doing departmental or divisional work.'

'But most of the aircrew *have* no other duties, sir!'

'So I've noticed.' The Commander was grateful to Jerry Malone; he was acting as the perfect feed. 'In my opinion, every officer, I repeat *every* officer, has a duty to his department *and* a duty to the ship. Most of your officers contribute absolutely nothing to the ship. They fly on and off it, but they might just as well be flying from an air station ashore for all they know or care of what goes on under their feet. If you look at the list of officers on ship's and wardroom committees and societies, you won't find the name of a single junior aircrew officer amongst them. There are lots of things pilots can do when they're not actually flying. They could know a lot more about the ship, for a start. That's a duty laid down for all officers in Queen's Regulations and Admiralty Instructions. If you asked any of your sub-lieutenants a few simple questions on ship knowledge I doubt whether they could answer any of them. There are a number of training schemes you could do.'

'But they're not under training, sir! The permanent commission officers and the ex-Dartmouth fellows already do ship's duties, sir. But the short-service commission pilots are here as pilots, and nothing else.'

'I don't accept that. Chippy is here as a Shipwright Officer, but he's much more than that. He's also a member of the wardroom mess and a ship's officer.'

Although the Commander was broadening the issue from its original base, the squadron COs recognised that this was a question which was bound to have arisen sooner or later. Rupert Smith took up the argument.

'I think one or two of them would like to know more about the ship, sir, but I don't think they're confident enough to go wandering about the place on their own.'

The Commander acknowledged the point. A young pilot, knowing nothing of the ship, might well be chary of venturing into unfamiliar territory.

'That's something you as a squadron COs can fix up for them. I do know that the Heads of Departments and their ratings would be delighted and very flattered if some of the aircrew began to take an intelligent interest in what they were doing. I want to see a lot more participation in ship's affairs by the squadrons. It's just not good enough to treat the ship as a hotel. All right?'

'Yes, sir.'

Roger Calvados and Jerry Malone left, leaving Rupert Smith to linger in the doorway.

'Something else, Rupert?'

Rupert Smith looked embarrassed. 'Yes, there was something else, sir.' He carefully shut the door behind him. 'Sir, was there anything behind your remarks about Stiggins' ability as a pilot?'

'No? Should there have been?' The Commander shook his head, startled by the question. 'I haven't any idea what he's like as a pilot. To tell you the truth I only picked on him because he was the only one there whose name I could remember on the spur of the moment. Why?'

'Perhaps it was misreported to me, sir . . .'

'I only said . . .' The Commander shook his head again. 'Damned if I can remember what I said now, but whatever it was, it certainly wasn't intended to be a reflection on his *flying* ability. I was getting at him as an *uckers*-player, not as a pilot. Why do you ask?'

Rupert had been watching the Commander's face closely. Now, he believed him. 'It's difficult to put into words, sir. It's just that I've an idea young Stiggins is not going to make it. He's not improving as he should. He's edgy. But the last thing I want is for him to get the idea I think he's dodgy. That might put him off for good.'

'You mean, what they call "Lack of Moral Fibre"?'

'Oh, nothing as drastic as that. It's just . . .' Rupert hesitated. 'It's just that he's on edge. He might tip one way and be all right. But again, he might not. The omens are not good, though.'

'What omens?'

Rupert waved a hand vaguely; he was sorry now he had raised

234

the subject. 'Oh, just omens, sir. That's why I asked you whether you meant anything by your remark. I wondered if you'd noticed anything.'

'No. As I said, I didn't mean anything at all by it. Except that I was annoyed, of course. If it had been you standing there I'd probably have bawled you out instead. But these omens you talk about. What sort of thing do you mean?'

'It's very hard to define. You know it when you see it, or you think you do. It's a tone of voice, a look in the eye, or rather a look which should be there and isn't. Most pilots are a bit irresponsible, a bit happy-go-lucky. As the Americans say, they kick the tyre, light the fire, and smash off. It's when a fellow who used to be talkative suddenly goes all quiet, or when a chap who didn't drink much suddenly starts running up a mess-bill. Fellow starts going to the sickbay, hoping the quacks will find something wrong with him. He shows an enormous interest in his cab's defects. He hangs about the briefing-room at all hours, or else he forgets about briefing times altogether. Not because he intended to but because something in his subconscious wants him to miss them. Like a fellow who keeps on forgetting dentist's appointments. It's not *what* they do so much, it's the way they do it.'

'If you think all this about Stiggins, surely you ought to ground him, or whatever it is you do?'

'That's just it. I *don't* think it, not properly. It's just a kind of feeling I have that all's not well. If I tried to take any action now, everybody would think I'd gone off my chump.' Rupert scratched his head. 'I think he'll be all right in the end. I hope I'm right. If I'm not, he might kill himself, and someone else too.'

The Commander understood Rupert's dilemma. Any officer who was worth anything to the Navy had these times of doubt, when his own instincts conflicted with the evidence and with the routine laid down by the Service. The Commander decided, for his own part, to weight the scales against Stiggins.

'I'm not competent to judge Stiggins as a pilot, Rupert, but speaking purely of his qualities as an officer, I'd say he wasn't all that much of a bargain for the Queen. *But,* as your friend Malone took care to remind me just now, he's not here as an officer, he's here as a pilot!'

Rupert chuckled. 'I did think at the time, sir, that remark came under the heading of "Things Which Could Have Been Better Put".'

'Anyway, Rupert, let me know if there's anything I can do. Within my limited fish-head capacity, I'll be very happy to do what I can.'

'Thank you, sir.'

15

When Rupert Smith had gone, the Commander lit a cigarette and leaned back in his chair, savouring a most unaccustomed sensation of pleasure, mixed with relief. He knew that it was wrong, entirely reprehensible, and professionally unethical for any officer to derive the smallest pleasure from another officer's difficulties, but he could not wholly subdue a feeling of glee that the squadrons, too, had their problems. He was enormously reassured to know that all was not always what it seemed, even under those shining suits of flight deck armour.

'*Uckers* anyone?'

While the Commander had been enjoying his thoughts, the Captain's Secretary had poked his head round the cabin door.

'I hear you've been having an up-and-downer with our feathered friends, Bob?'

'Hardly that. I just objected to them advertising the fact they had nothing to do quite so blatantly.'

'Is this the end of a beautiful friendship?'

'What do you mean by that?'

'You seem to have been having a small love affair with the Air Group just recently. I wondered if this would make them return the ring.'

The Commander acknowledged that he could not spend so much time goofing without arousing comment, particularly from the Captain's Secretary. 'I will admit they fascinate me. I've never served in a carrier before, remember.'

'Don't let them blind you with glamour, Bob. Basically they're just a crowd of trogs, like the rest of us. It was high time somebody stamped on their blasted party games. They're using the place like a damned hotel.'

The Secretary's opinion was shared by most of the ship's officers, indeed the Commander was surprised by the strength of the ward-room feeling on the subject. He had believed that despite some frictions the wardroom in general had slowly been settling down together. The 'Uckers Affair' proved how brittle was their fellowship. To his consternation, the Commander found himself regarded as the ship's champion, who had put the squadrons in their place. His well-meaning efforts to integrate the squadrons by asking their CO's for more response from their junior officers had had exactly the opposite effect. Far from bringing the wardroom closer together, he had unwittingly disclosed a real rift between the ship and the Air Group. 'Uckers' became an emotive word, charged with double meanings. Even the most accepted and popular squadron officers began to enter the wardroom gingerly, looking defensive. The Gunnery Officer silenced a group of pilots by instructing them to run away and play uckers.

Leviathan's wardroom might quickly have split into two hostile camps, in the manner of the previous commission, but for the publication of the half-yearly promotion lists, on the last day of June. The lists provided a common grievance which effectively reunited the whole wardroom.

The majority of *Leviathan*'s lieutenant-commanders were in the seniority zones to be selected for promotion in their respective branches. Some of them, especially the Senior Engineer, Rowley Dubonnet and a few others who had served in the last commission, had already done enough, in the ship's opinion, to be promoted twice over. But although the promotion signal ran to three pages of foolscap paper, the lists did not contain the name of a single officer serving in *Leviathan*.

In spite of their disappointment, the wardroom took the news very well. The Commander had seen at least one name on the list which gave him personal satisfaction but, as he stood at the ante-room bar at lunch-time, he reflected that it would have done the Second Sea Lord and his preposterous hierarchy a power of good to stand where he was standing and to overhear the comments of the crowd mustered four-deep in front of the wardroom notice-board.

'... I must say, fellows, I look forward to these half-yearly lists. It means I'm guaranteed at least one good laugh every six months.'

'I don't see any familiar names anywhere?'

'There aren't any. Nobody in this ship's been promoted.'

'It's a bloody swindle. Those buggers up at the Admiralty need their heads looked at.'

'There are *other* officers, you know, George.'

'Are there? I thought we had so many on board there weren't any left for anywhere else?'

'. . . Never mind, Senior. I'm glad we're not going to lose you. Perhaps they just didn't want to change a winning combination.'

'Like hell they didn't.'

'. . . Look at this, men! *Charlie Doughty!* He finally made it! How about that. On the Wet List, too.'

'I thought he'd been passed over years ago. He's too bright to be promoted.'

'. . . What are all these horrible little sets of squalid initials after everybody's names?'

'Those are the Admiralty departments they're all working in.'

'Well, look at this then. Count them. There are twenty-six names on the Executive list and only five, *five* mind you, are serving in ships. And one of those I happen to know is in reserve. The rest are all ashore. And the four at sea are all promoted to the *Dry* list. What do you think of that?'

'Never go to sea if you want to get promoted. It's axiomatic these days.'

'*Axiomatic?* That's a big word for a little man, Tommy?'

'It means standard Admiralty practice.'

The First Lieutenant burst into the ante-room, waving a copy of the promotion signal and swinging a hand-bell.

'Unclean! Unclean! You untouchable lot, you!'

Beaky infiltrated through the crush and pinned a notice beside the promotion signal.

'Read it out, Beaky! We can't see it from here.'

Beaky adjusted his spectacles. 'It says, Owing to unforeseen circumstances, the Guest Night Dinner tonight, which was to have been a Feast of the Ascension, has now been renamed and re-classified as a Feast of the Passover.'

'Well said, *Beaky!*'

His duties as Mess Secretary temporarily fulfilled, Beaky made his way over to the bar.

'Anybody you know on that list, Beaky?' The Commander remembered that Beaky himself was eligible and might, theoretically, have been on the list.

'Most of the schoolies, sir. One fellow in particular. He joined

239

the Navy five years after me.'

Beaky sounded neither disappointed nor bitter. He had seen too many promotion signals for them to have any significance, other than that six more months had gone by.

'It just reminds me how time passes, sir. I can remember that fellow as a sprog schoolie two-striper. Now he's a Captain.'

'I know what you mean, Beaky. I feel a little older myself every time I see one of those infernal signals. I can remember waiting and hoping for my own brass-hat and wondering what the devil I was doing wrong while other people in my term were getting promoted. By the way, how many are coming to the Feast of the Passover tonight?'

'About ninety, sir. And about a dozen or so private guests.'

'About ninety.' The Commander had served long enough in *Leviathan* to have learned not to express his disappointment out loud.

'Is the Captain coming, sir? I heard he was going up to the Admiralty today.'

'He is. He won't be dining.'

Ninety officers were attending the Guest Night, out of a wardroom of nearly three hundred. It was a melancholy sign of change in the Service that two-thirds of a wardroom preferred to eat supper off their knees at home with their wives and watch television, rather than dine off five courses and drink wine with their fellow officers on board. The Commander could remember an Augustan Age when it would have been axiomatic – he smiled at his own use of the word – that every officer in the wardroom attended a Guest Night, unless he were physically prevented by duty or sickness.

A Guest Night Dinner had a special place in any wardroom's social calendar. Most wardrooms in large ships served two evening meals, a dinner at eight o'clock, and an earlier supper for officers who were on duty, or who wished to go ashore, or who were unwilling to change in the evenings. Ordinary mess dinners were held once a week, when the port was passed, and the Queen's health was drunk. Officers could invite guests for any meal at any time, but once a month, or when the ship's programme allowed, the wardroom gave a formal Guest Night Dinner to which Admirals and their staffs, or distinguished visitors, or the Captains

240

and officers of other ships and shore establishments were invited as guests of the mess.

No mess guests had been invited for dinner on promotion day, because the Mess Committee had been confident that in a wardroom with fifty commanders and lieutenant commanders, at least two or three would be promoted. The evening was to have been a private ship's celebration to 'wet the brass-hats'. Now, as Beaky's notice had so succinctly explained, *Leviathan*'s wardroom would not be celebrating success but drowning their disappointment.

The Commander himself had a guest and, when he had changed, he went up to meet him. While he walked the quarterdeck, he thought about his guest.

Charles Doughty had been promoted Commander on that day's list, but the dinner had not been arranged as a celebration, because neither the Commander nor Charles had expected the promotion. The Commander had been Charles' sea-father when he joined the Navy and, although an extra term's seniority was a great gulf at Dartmouth, they had become friends. They had served as midshipmen in the same gunroom and as lieutenants in the same cruiser. The Commander had been best man at Charles' wedding, and was god-father to his eldest son. Throughout their careers they had kept their friendship in unusually good repair for a Service notorious for its transient acquaintanceships. They corresponded regularly, and they gave each other dinner when the opportunity occurred.

The Commander valued Charles' friendship, and was still a little flattered by it. While he himself had plodded industriously, Charles had mounted like an eagle. He had the best brain of his term, he had won gold medals as a sub-lieutenant for essays on naval history, and his career had been marked by the number of original and radically revolutionary papers he had written on naval communications, his eventual choice of specialisation. Charles had a technical mind and had hankered to be an engineer officer but his father, himself a retired naval officer, would not hear of it; the old man would rather have seen his son become a waiter or a jockey than an engineer officer. So Charles had taken a B.Sc. degree in engineering by correspondence course. The growth of electronics in naval communications had found Charles eager, fascinated, and knowledgeable. At the same time, he was a cultured

241

and erudite man; the Commander still possessed the telegram Charles had sent him when he was promoted. The Commander was then serving as First Lieutenant of a frigate in Northern Ireland, running from Londonderry, and the telegram had read: 'Congratulations. Say Not The Struggle Naught Availeth. Psalm 75, verse 6, refers. Charles.' The Commander had turned up the verse and found: 'For promotion cometh neither from the east, nor from the west, nor from the south.'

Nothing in the Navy had ever seemed more certain than Charles' promotion: the Navy did not possess, nor was it attracting, enough talent to be able to dispense with officers of Charles' calibre. But during the critical period of his early years as a lieutenant commander Charles had served under a succession of Captains who had all enjoyed his company, made use of his abilities, picked his brains, and refused to recommend him for promotion.

At some time towards the end of this period Charles had taken fright. The Commander had noticed it at once. Although Charles was still gay, still as irreverent, still as brimming with ideas and arguments on the future salvation of the Navy, his voice held a note of desperation. Charles guessed, long before anyone else, that he was to be passed over. He had offered his resignation and expected to retire in the next few months. Today, by one of those ironies which sometimes convinced the Commander that the Admiralty had so far detached themselves from reality they were quite unfit to govern the Navy, Charles had at last been promoted – at his ultimate opportunity, and probably during his final year in the Service. Charles had been promoted to the Post List in time to increase his pension, while some other more junior officer, who still wished to make the Navy his career, had been deprived of his promotion.

The Commander turned at the end of the quarterdeck and saw Charles, wearing a boat-cloak and a brand-new commander's cap, mounting the gangway with long springing strides. As always, it warmed his heart to see the familiar features, those bushy-black eyebrows, the long, rather fleshy nose and the prominent blue-jowled chin with the dimple cleft. He hurried to join the quartermaster and the officer of the watch at the gangway and, as he saluted, was touched to see his old friend looking bashful under the unusual weight of the gold braid on his cap peak.

'Good evening, *Commander.*'

Charles jumped down to shake hands. 'Hello Bob! Isn't this the most incredible day!'

'I'm very glad for you, Charles. I can't say how glad I am. There's nobody I wanted to see promoted more. Very *very* many congratulations.'

'Ah thank you, Bob.'

'How's Julie?'

'Well, very well.'

'And the sprogs?'

'We're all absolutely on top-line, Bob! And I'm *still* absolutely stunned by it all!'

The Commander noticed that Charles was still wearing his lieutenant commander's mess jacket under his boat cloak.

'Still got your two-and-a-half stripes on, Charles?'

'I know! I was so taken aback by it all! I bought meself a new hat this afternoon and left a couple of uniforms to have the stripes changed but I forgot all about me mess undress until I came to put it on. I could have borrowed somebody's, I suppose, if I'd only thought.'

'Would you like to wear my spare jacket? It's a bit beer-stained, but at least it's got three stripes on it.'

'Bob, you've made my evening!'

Charles gave a light skip as he crossed the quarterdeck, and paused to wonder at himself.

'You know, this is really like having a new toy. The first time you play with it is always the best.'

In the Commander's cabin, wearing the Commander's spare mess jacket, Charles crooked an arm and stared at the three gold stripes.

'Just look at that.' He worked his shoulders inside the jacket. 'It's not a bad fit, either. They ought to tell you you're going to be promoted.'

'As from next time, they will. They're going to promulgate a provisional list six months in advance.'

'Next time would have been too late for me, Bob.'

'What are you going to do now, Charles? Are you still going to retire?'

'I don't know. I simply don't know. I haven't had time to think about it. I can't decide just like that. I've got the offer of a job

243

outside and we've just bought a house. There's the kids' schools to think about. There's a hell of a lot to it. Julie was delighted when I said I was going to pack it in. She may divorce me if I change my mind now! But don't let's dwell on that. How about *you*? Has success changed Robert Markready? I hear you're making this mighty vessel sit up and jump through hoops like a little spotty dog!'

'Oh, I wouldn't say that.'

As ever when Charles paid him a compliment, the Commander was embarrassed. Praise from Charles always made him duck away, with stupid and falsely modest disclaimers.

'Let's go down and start getting that splendid stripe of yours wet.'

Charles already knew some of *Leviathan*'s officers and others, when they saw him standing with the Commander, had heard of his promotion and came up to congratulate him. Those amongst them who might have been promoted themselves studied Charles with a certain envious curiosity. Charles was surprised to hear that nobody in *Leviathan* had been promoted.

'Is this true, Bob? No joy for anyone in this ship?'

'Strange but true, I'm afraid, Charles.'

'I bet it's a legacy from your last commission. It'll be all right once the word gets round that *Leviathan*'s fashionable again.'

The remark evoked a pleased rustle of response from Charles' audience. He had said exactly what many of them had been thinking privately but had hesitated to say out loud. They were grateful to him for saying what they could not say themselves. If Charles said or did nothing else that evening, he had already earned his dinner in *Leviathan*. Even Commander (S), standing on the outskirts of the circle, spoke low in the Commander's ear, 'Who's your genial friend, Bob?' Watching Charles talking to a group which included Jerry Malone, the Captain's Secretary, the Senior and the Padre, the thought occurred to the Commander that Charles would make an outstanding Commander of an aircraft carrier.

A string section of the Royal Marine Band were playing in a shallow cul-de-sac of the passageway opposite the wardroom main double doors. Inside the ante-room, the bar was only moderately crowded, although most of the officers dining were already present. The Commander saw that there were compensations for the low turn-out: the absentees gave those who were dining the opportunity to enjoy their dinner in an unusually civilised and leisurely manner, for *Leviathan*. Connolly, who was often disappointed by the officers' conservative drinking habits, had been encouraged to mix dry Martinis, a very rare drink in the wardroom. Officers who normally drank beer or gin before dinner were now drinking sherry or Martinis with a pleasant sense of anticipation. The faces, all scrubbed and shining above their clean stiff white shirts, were the faces the Commander could see on any night. But this was not just any night, this was a Guest Night.

The band was playing 'The Roast Beef of Old England', the traditional music to play the officers into dinner. The Chief Steward was at the Commander's elbow.

'Dinner is served, sir.'

'Thank you, Chief Steward. We're just coming. Shall we go in, Charles?'

While the officers were filing in and taking their places, the Chief Steward positioned himself in a particular corner of the wardroom from which he knew by experience he could supervise the whole dinner. The Chief Steward appeared to be looking rigidly to his front, but from the corner of one eye he could detect the smallest emergency at the serving hatches, and from the other he could discreetly watch the Commander and his guest, from whom he would take his cues during the dinner.

The Chief Steward dearly loved a Guest Night. Everyday meals, suppers, buffets and ordinary mess dinners could be arranged by an artisan. A Guest Night required the presence of an artist. The Chief Steward looked upon a Guest Night Dinner as the pinnacle of his art and as an opportunity to instruct and practise his stewards in the most complex and, he reminded them, the most rewarding exercise of their profession.

Leviathan's wardroom was a functional compartment, with a kind of utilitarian awkwardness which did not respond to ornament. The deckhead was too low and the line of the bulkheads too uneven for elegance but looking around him the Chief Steward felt that he and his department had done their best. The harsh fluorescent lighting units were switched off and the room lit by small shaded lamps placed at intervals along the main President's table and the three subsidiary tables which joined it at right angles.

The tables were decorated with trumpet-shaped silver vases filled with flowers and with a selection of the cups, trophies, tableaux of animals and palm trees, and other extravagant silver pieces which *Leviathan* and her predecessors of the name had acquired through the years. Each napkin had been folded into a tricorn hat by Steward Dawson, who had the knack of it, and the Chief Steward himself had checked the cutlery and the glasses at every place.

The Commander, as President, sat at the centre of the main table with Charles next to him. The First Lieutenant, who was Vice-President for the dinner, sat at the end of the long table opposite the Commander. The other officers and their guests sat according to the place cards written and set out by Beaky.

When everyone was ready, the Commander rapped once with his gavel and the Padre, who had the supreme clerical gift of brevity, said grace.

'God bless our dinners, and make us thankful. Amen.'

Amid the murmured amens, Steward Dawson's creations were torn apart, Connolly and the other bar stewards began serving sherry, and the Guest Night was under way.

The Commander, too, dearly loved a Guest Night. He loved every part of the ritual, from the Padre's grace to the Bandmaster's glass of port. For him, formal dinner in the wardroom was a significant, almost a mystical experience, as though he were taking part in a communion of the body and spirit of the Service. The Navy's great strength was that this communion was as portable as a Bedouin's tents and salt. The Commander had sat down to dine with four hundred other officers off walnut tables polished for a hundred years in a hall lined with funereal paintings of long-forgotten engagements under sail; he had eaten rijstaffel in the tropics, under the creaking punkahs, with geckos tut-tutting on the ceiling, when the Loyal Toast was raised above the insect-shrilling from the colonnades outside; and he had drunk to the Immortal Memory on Trafalgar Night at sea in a frigate in the North Atlantic, when the diners wore sea-boots and sweaters under their reefers, and cradled their plates in their arms to stop them pitching on the deck. The meaning was the same, wherever two or three officers were gathered together, to pass the port and drink to the health of the Queen.

Charles Doughty had known Bob Markready so long that he could guess his thoughts.

'There's something terribly reassuring about all this, isn't there, Bob?' Charles leaned forward and picked up the printed sheet of the band's programme, the 'music menu', as it was called. 'As long as the Royal Marine Band are playing excerpts from "The Yeomen of the Guard" and "Through The Shadows" by Friml, I know there's still hope for the world.'

'You're a romantic, Charles.'

'So are you, Bob. We wouldn't be here if we weren't romantics at heart.'

'Romantics are getting less and less fashionable, I'm afraid.'

Again, Charles read his thoughts with certainty. 'Don't let them get you down, Bob, whatever you do. Remember you're right, and they're wrong.'

'I suppose so.'

At previous dinners the Commander had noticed the tendency of officers of the same department to sit together in cliques and talk shop which they might just as well have exchanged in their offices. He had mentioned the point to Beaky, who had taken the hint and had distributed the place-cards with a fine disregard for rank or department. The Commander's own table included the Navigating Officer, the Air Ordnance Engineer Officer, Commander (L), Rupert Smith, two sub-lieutenants in Malone's squadron, Commander (S), Simmondson, the Senior Engineer, and the Gunner, who was sitting almost opposite the Commander.

At some time in the remote past, when he was a boy seaman, the Gunner had been given the nick-name of Poacher, but whatever gifts of stealth or agility which had once qualified him for the name had now vanished. Poacher was fat and balding, and slow and conservative. His single sub-lieutenant's stripe represented thirty years in the Service. He had served in the latter half of the previous commission, and he had tried to bring the old attitudes into the new commission. It was Poacher to whom the Commander had taken Dai Bach's complaint concerning the Gunnery Branch's monopoly of the Daily Orders. Poacher had refused to change, until the Commander was forced to give him a direct order. The Commander was often puzzled by the paradox of officers such as Poacher. They were Special Duties List officers and they were generally masters of their trade, entitled to the respect of younger General List officers. Their greater experience should have made them bold and confident. In practice, there were no officers more cautious. Poacher himself was a past-master in ensuring that he personally was fire-proof. Like the Master-at-Arms, he read the small print. Whatever happened in his department, Poacher's own yard-arm was always clear.

Poacher was looking pensively at the cutlery arrayed in front of him.

'You're looking very thoughtful, Poacher?'

'Just thinking of the time when I first put up me thin stripe, sir. The wife said to me, we'd better learn how to set the table for a four course meal, now that you're an awficer. I said, all you've got to remember is, the bottle-opener goes on the right. But she wouldn't have it. We've got to learn, she said, now that you're an awficer. So do you know what we did, sir? We travelled on restaurant cars in trains. That was in the days when they still had four course meals. We travelled up and down, eatin' that food, until the wife got the hang of it. And we've never once given a four course meal at our house, all the time we've been married!'

Charles and the Commander were charmed by the story. It presented Poacher as he used to be, when he was newly promoted and must have believed the world was at his feet. Special Duties officers with Poacher's background – Branch Officers as they were once called, Warrant Officers as they were known before that – were now in the majority in *Leviathan*'s wardroom and in every wardroom in the Fleet. Their arrival was the result of a revolutionised promotion system and was the symptom of a more democratic Navy, but the Commander could not welcome them unreservedly. Such men were almost always corrupted by security, as Poacher himself had been. They took more from a wardroom then they gave. Poacher, and men like him, were slowly draining some vital comic vitamin from wardroom life. They were taking all the fun out of it.

The Chief Steward was controlling the dinner in a sequence of tidal rhythms, rising and falling as each course began and ended. He believed that a proper meal should be served at a proper pace, neither too fast nor too slow, and from the clear soup to the angels

on horseback, by way of the grilled trout and the Aylesbury duck-
lings, the Chief Steward directed the dinner with nods, gestures
and *sotto voce* instructions, speeding up a supply here, restraining
an impetuous steward there. Meanwhile the wardroom had come
alive with conversation. It was small talk, the common currency
of dinner tables all over the country. Traditionally, officers did
not talk shop nor discuss women at dinner, on pain of a fine of a
round of port, but it would have been a poor dinner without either.
The talk was of ships and men, and weather and women, of
politics and pay, and leaves and leave-takings. Towards the end
of the meal, a few pilots began the ritual throwing of bread-
crumbs, and the lights flashed on and off several times at the table
furthest from the Commander. The tables were cleared, the port
glasses set out, the decanters placed, and the stoppers removed.
The decanters were sent circulating and when they had returned the
Commander replaced the stoppers and offered the Loyal Toast
to the First Lieutenant.

'Mr Vice, the Queen.'

'Gentlemen, the Queen!'

When the cigars were lit, when legs were stretched well under
the tables and when, in a few unobtrusive cases, top trouser buttons
had been undone, the Commander rapped his gavel on the pad
and stood up.

The wardroom realising that speech time was upon them,
responded with a mixture of cheers and protests.

'Honoured guests. Gentlemen. There are no speeches tonight...'
The Commander waited for the expected burst of wild and
exaggerated cheering. '... There are no speeches tonight, but I
know that none of us would feel our guests had been properly
dined if we did not express our pleasure in their company. Gentlemen, I ask you to rise with me and drink to our guests.'

Their glasses in their hands, the wardroom rose, leaving in their
ranks random gaps where guests remained seated, with sheepish
and pleased expressions on their faces.

'Our guests!'

In the hubbub of cheering and table-thumping which broke out
as the wardroom sat down, the Commander nudged Charles.

'Would you like to reply, Charles? Briefly?'

Charles looked startled. 'Oh no, I don't think so. Does one of

249

us have to . . . ? All right, I suppose so . . .'

The Commander wielded his gavel until he had pounded the wardroom into silence. 'Gentlemen, Commander Doughty would like to reply on behalf of our guests.'

Wardroom cheering was capable of many fine shades of meaning. The roar which greeted Charles conveyed polite welcome for a guest, dismay at yet another speech, and malicious amusement at his reluctant expression.

'Mr President. Gentlemen. Fellow guests. Mr President's introduction was not strictly accurate because I'd no idea I was to be called upon to reply . . .'

'Sit down then!'

'Never fear, I'll sit down soon. But now that I am replying, may I just make one very quick point? When I came on board tonight I was astonished to hear that by some incredible oversight of Their Lordships *nobody* in this ship was promoted today . . .'

Charles' voice was engulfed by boos, protests, cries of 'Shame', and one hollow voice proclaiming 'there'll be some changes when the revolution comes.'

'May I . . . May I, speaking as your guest tonight, *assure* you that it's only a matter of time? I don't honestly believe there's anybody, anywhere in the Navy, who hasn't heard by now that *Leviathan*'s a new ship these days. If the dinner you've just given us is any guide, I'm sure you'll *all* be promoted! On behalf of your guests, thank you for having us. We'd like to come again. Thank you.'

The subject of that day's promotion lists had been hanging in the air, aching to be mentioned, all evening. It might have remained, like Amfortas' wound, unspoken and unhealed, if Charles had not exorcised it. Charles had taken a frightening risk in speaking of promotion in *Leviathan*'s wardroom. He might have been hooted out of the mess. But such were his self-possession and clear sincerity that *Leviathan*'s officers warmed to him, as their guest who transparently wished them well.

'That was a generous thought, Charles.'

'I had to say something, Bob. You rather sprang that on me.'

After the speeches, the dinner began to break up. Groups of officers left the tables to go into the ante-rooms or to walk on the quarterdeck for a little while. Others turned their chairs inwards, to form small pockets of conversation. A nucleus remained at the top table, because they had begun to discuss that subject which could hold naval officers all night, which transcended sex, or politics, or the arts, or promotion, namely, the state of the Navy.

16

The Commander rarely permitted himself any criticism of the Service, and certainly not in public, in the wardroom. But a Guest Night allowed a kind of saturnalian licence. It was a night for confidences, when any officer could unburden himself. Only the meanest-spirited senior officer remembered and held against a junior anything said at a Guest Night. The Commander had dined and wined well, and as always, he was stimulated by Charles' company.

'... The trouble with the Navy now is that we simply are not preparing for *war*. I know this is an unfashionable view, but the Navy as a whole is just going through the motions of earning its pay. Nobody ever stops to think, is what we're doing now helping us to prepare ourselves for *war*? There are only a handful of places in the Service where you'll find people honestly thinking about what they're paid to do. A few operational frigates perhaps, a few operational submarines whose captains have got the right ideas. A few front-line squadrons whose CO's have stopped to consider *why* they're being paid flying pay. All the rest are having a damned good jolly at the taxpayer's expense.'

The Commander's eye lighted on the decanter which Connolly had just replaced. He removed the stopper and passed the decanter to Charles, who carefully refilled his glass.

'Do you know, I was thinking of something just like that the other day, Bob. A few months ago Julie and I took a furnished house out near Petersfield. We worked out it would be cheaper to make it into an official Admiralty hiring. That meant we had to submit to all the official rigmarole, including the little man from the Surveyor of Lands Department, who used to come out every so often and look at the place. God knows what he came for. Perhaps he was checking to see whether my wife and I were running the place as an impromptu brothel, or maybe he just wanted a day out in the country. He was civil enough, mind you. He used to pat the sprogs on the head, hob and nob with my wife about this and that, and he was very obliging about breakages and inventories and all that crap. He was obviously doing his job, and doing it quite well, according to his lights. But after he'd gone I used to think, now what the hell has *he* got to do with preparing the Navy for action against the enemy?'

The port had reached Rupert Smith, who stopped in the act of filling his glass. 'Ah, but you can't really count him. I mean, strictly speaking he's not in the Navy at all.'

'Oh, but he is. His salary comes out of the Navy Estimates. When Parliament sit down and vote so many millions a year for the defence of the country at sea, they mean him just as much as they mean you or me.'

Commander (L), sitting opposite Rupert, had also been vastly stimulated by Charles' company and conversation throughout dinner. After a time the conversation in any wardroom, however large, tended to lapse into well-worn ruts. Charles had introduced a refreshingly new and irreverent outlook.

'Now you're bringing in another subject altogether, Charles. Should we bother with married quarters, and welfare officers, and families, and all that? Should the Navy concern itself with everybody's private lives?'

'Definitely not.' Charles looked round the table. 'I think you've put your finger on the crucial thing. The basic trouble is that the Navy is trying to compete with civilian employers on their own ground, and it hasn't a hope of winning. All the recruiting in the last few years, all the soft soap handed out to parents and teachers, has been designed to convince them that if little Willy joins the Navy he'll be in a good safe job with a good safe chance of promotion and a good safe pension at the end of it. Well, it isn't like that and it never bloody well has been like that. The Admiralty have been making a rod for their own backs. Lately they've been attracting just the sort of boy they *don't* want. When the going gets a bit rough, what does he do? He says the hell with it and slaps in to retire. If the recruiting figures fall, what do the Admiralty do? They *lower* the standard, to get more bods.'

'But surely that's the logical thing to do, Charles?'

'Don't you see, it's a basic mistake in psychology! If you want to attract more people, you put the standard *up*. Not *down*. If you started a club and you wanted people to join it, you wouldn't make it a free-for-all. You make it as exclusive as you damned well can and in no time people are fighting each other to get in. If the recruiting figures fall, they should put the standard up, and up, and up again, until every boy and his parents and every school teacher in the land at last got it into his thick head that if a boy is taken on by the Navy he must, by *definition*, be a good kid!'

'Wouldn't you get a sort of élite then?' Charles was by now clearly in the chair. The questions were coming at him from all round the table.

'And why not an élite? The Prussian Army did it. An élite is *exactly* what we want. The great strength of this country, as I see it, is the tremendous talent everybody seems to have for going to sea. You get a war, they join the RNVR and before you can say "Jaggers Troup" they're all doing the job a damned sight better than the professionals could do it. What *we* must do, here, now, is to build up an efficient, fully-trained and knowledgeable nucleus.'

'In the next war, surely, there won't be time to build on a nucleus.'

Charles relaxed, slumping back in his chair. 'You don't *really* believe that, do you? That it'll all be over in the flight time it takes Big Brother to get here from somewhere behind the Urals? Look, the Great War and the last war were both going to be short. They were both supposed to be over by Christmas. One lasted more than four years and the other lasted nearly six.'

The Commander shook his head admiringly. It was good to hear Charles in full flow again. When Charles had his eye in, he was like a great batsman, dispatching anything bowled at him.

'Have some more port, Charles.'

'Thank you kindly.'

'To be effective, your nucleus must know what they're about, Charles. Ask any officer here what's the purpose of the Navy? He'll tell you quite correctly, it's the defence of the country at sea, in the politest manner possible. But then ask him, *how?* Using what? What ships, now and in the future. He won't tell you. Because he won't know. Because *nobody* knows. Is it nuclear submarines with missiles? Or is it brush-fire warfare using carriers with choppers and Commandos? Or do we concentrate on our anti-submarine commitment for NATO? Nobody knows. We've got a little of everything and damn-all of anything much. And this can only be our own fault. There's been a total breakdown of leadership from the top ever since the war ended. If the Sea Lords don't know their arses from their elbows you can hardly blame the odds and sods for being baffled. I agree with your point, Charles, but the way we're going we'll never get your nucleus. We'll just go on as we are, a sort of shapeless, aimless, pointless civil-servant-ridden amoeba thing.'

Charles licked his lips. 'I must remember that, Bob. A shapeless, aimless, pointless, civil-servant-ridden amoeba thing. That's jolly good. But it's not easy, Bob. Naval policy is never cut and dried.'

'Charles, I *know* it's not easy! That, I take it, is why we have gangs of senior and respected admirals to work it out for us, with their multitudinous staffs. To work it out and make sure that everyone from the politicians down to the last man in the rank and file knows all about it. The RAF have got it taped. There wouldn't *be* an RAF today if they hadn't known how to handle pressure groups. Our lads are not putting our case at all. All they're doing is turning us into a Navy of spectators. You know, the greatest single change in the Navy since the war has been the growth in the numbers of hangers-on, of sheer *passengers*. For every officer serving at sea there are *ten* ashore, advising him, working out new maintenance routines for him, telling him where he's gone wrong, *work-studying* him, and all the rest of the rubbish. Here we are, trying desperately hard to make this vessel into an efficient warship, and I use the words *war ship,* and all the time we're encompassed about by a great cloud of woolly-headed and well-meaning witnesses.'

The rest of the table listened, in a stunned silence. Unlike Charles, they had never heard the Commander in this form before. Most of the wardroom liked and respected the Commander, but they had tended to think of him as a dry, humourless old stick; some of them had even called him a pompous old virgin. Yet here he was, preaching fire, brimstone and sedition with the best of them. Poacher had intended to leave after the port was passed for the second time but he stayed on, transfixed, in his seat; he did not hear talk like this in a month of Sundays.

'. . . This ship's crawling with them, of course. It's a natural target for them. We had one fellow on board a fortnight ago. He called himself an Environmental Conditions Study Officer. He was a salt-horse two-and-a-half, with a wet little boffin with him as his winger. They had all sorts of instruments, wet and dry-bulb thermometers and things like football rattles for measuring temperature and humidity and so on. But all they could tell me at the end of their week was that according to their figures the atmosphere in most of the compartments in this ship was unfit to support human life!'

The whole table laughed like crazy men. It was an old joke but there had been such a man on board and they had all wondered what he and his assistant had been doing with their instruments.

The Senior Engineer was sitting quietly at one end of the table. For him, after dinner was a time for reflection, to admire his cigar and to hope that the telephone would never ring and the Engineer's Office messenger never hover round the ante-room door with bad news. The Senior had let the talk pass him by, but the mention of 'hangers-on' touched him on a raw wound. The Senior, more than any officer on board, had been plagued by outlandish and incomprehensible correspondence and by requests for absurd special facilities; it was the Senior who had had to take the Environmental Conditions Study Officer under his wing.

'I suppose all these jobs must give the dead-wood something to do, now that we missed our chance to get rid of them under the Golden Bowler scheme.'

The evocative words 'Golden Bowler' caused an immediate ripple of interest round the table. The Commander privately estimated that at least half the officers present that evening had probably applied for it.

'The trouble was, the offer was *too* good. A chance to get out of the Navy with a whacking great gratuity and a reasonable pension . . . anybody with the right sort of seniority would have been mad not to have gone in for it. I tried it myself, like every other engineer officer I know. But when I saw the list of those who'd got it, it wasn't the dead-wood at all, it was mostly fellows with a bit of go about them. The very people I should have thought the Navy couldn't afford to lose. The dead-wood is still with us. At least they had enough sense to stay where they were on a good thing. So much for the theory that naval officers should have a sense of vocation.'

'That's never been true, Senior.' Charles accepted the decanter which this time the Commander had passed without bothering to replace the stopper. 'That's just a fairy story cooked up at Dartmouth. You *might* get one or two who burn with a hard gemlike flame and are obviously going to be admirals. But the vast majority, certainly of our generation, have no sense of vocation at all, not in the proper sense. They joined the Navy and they work at it, and they're prepared to take the rough with the smooth, and they make the Navy good servants. Their Lordships will have had their money's worth from most of us by the time we retire. No, there's a far more serious point here which I think does more damage to the Navy than almost anything else. That's the whole question of retiring from the Service. At the moment, I think the system is absolutely monstrous. I've had personal experience of this. Anybody can change their minds about the Navy, especially if they joined it at thirteen, or even at seventeen. If you apply to resign they keep you waiting for years, literally two or three years, shilly-shallying, promising you this, promising you that, telling you "The appointing situation's a bit tricky at the moment, old boy, there's a shortage of people like you", and never saying when you can go. Meanwhile you may have a prospective employer, who may be willing to give you a job, if only you can *tell* him when you're going to be available. The whole thing's utterly scandalous. I can't think of another business, trade or profession where you can't leave if you want to, after giving a reasonable length of notice. My God, even a pongo can send in his papers without all this degrading chit-chat. I can't think of any employers except the Admiralty who would have the brass-bound gall to dare to impose it. And I can't think of any other set of employees except naval officers who would be weak-kneed enough to accept it.'

'What do you suggest then, Charles? Just let people go when they want to?'

'Why ever not? You've got to let them go some time, why not now instead of two years later? You might get a rush of people retiring to start with, but once it's all settled down you won't get any more people resigning than resign now. It won't make any difference to the system. It'll make a hell of a difference to the individual, though.'

'It's not always so easy to relieve people just like that, Charles.'

'Of course it is! Nobody's indispensable. You and your Captain both got pier-head jumps, didn't you? And you're making out all right?'

The Commander bowed his head to a riposte which was unanswerable, from any quarter. Charles went on to develop his theme and variations.

'There ought to be a system whereby any officer who applies to resign *knows* that he'll be on the beach six months later. As it is now, you get these old and bold two-and-a-halves, with no intention of resigning, propping up the bar lunch-time after lunch-time, just dripping about the Navy. They know they can go on griping about the Navy until they're forty-five and not a soul can touch them. They're quite safe. What effect they must have on junior officers in the same mess I just dare not think! There ought to be some way we can say to them "Look, if you feel like that about it, you know what you can do. You can be outside in six months' time if you want to. In the meantime, do us the kindness of shutting up." We don't want people like that.'

The others considered the proposition, discovering that it was fresh to them. They had all grown accustomed to a system of uncertainty about retirements. They no longer thought it peculiar that an officer should have to serve in a humiliating and degrading professional limbo, neither in the Service nor out of it, for years after he had applied to resign his commission.

'And it should work both ways, too. The Admiralty should use their powers to dispense with an officer far more often than they do at the moment. They should say "We're sorry. We still love you. But we don't want you." Let him have six months' notice, give him his cards, and send him on his way. I'm not saying naval officers should be hired and fired like hop-pickers. I *am* saying that there should be much more *needle* about it all.'

This was more like the old Charles. The Commander knew now that Charles had made up his mind to withdraw his resignation.

'. . . It all comes back to bad basic psychology again. Sometimes when you look at some of the asinine things the Board of Admiralty get up to, it's bloody hard to remember they're actually naval officers themselves, most of them. Take the famous Post and General Lists. The so-called Wet and Dry Lists. We all know we've got fewer ships than we used to have. We all know we have to go to sea to get promoted. But instead of leaving the few sea jobs open to all and letting us compete for them, what do they do? They split the list of newly-promoted executive Commanders right down the middle and say to them "All you from here to the left, you're all on the General List and you're never going to get another job at sea again." And this for a *naval officer!* A naval officer who can't go to sea. It's *incredible!* It's like saying to a doctor "You're doing jolly well, old boy, and we're going to put up your pay but we're afraid that from now on we shan't be able to let you practice on live patients!' And then the Admiralty are surprised, and rather hurt, when they find everybody on the Dry List is beginning to think of himself as a second-class citizen. What the hell did they *expect* to happen?'

Charles seized his glass and emptied it at one swallow. 'And that's quite apart from the legal aspect, of course.'

Commander (S) raised his head. 'What do you mean, the legal aspect?'

'Well, every officer promoted to the General List could bring a case against the Navy for breach of contract. When they joined the Navy, they did so presumably on the understanding that they were going to *sea* as a Captain, Commander or whatever rank Their Lordships saw fit to promote them. Now, the Admiralty have changed the most important term of reference of the whole job, without so much as a by-your-leave. A naval officer who can't go to sea, by command of Their Lordships. I can't get over it. It's like something out of Gilbert and Sullivan.'

'I don't think you'd have much success if you did bring an action.'

'I'm sure you wouldn't, Joe. But it's a thought, isn't it?'

'As a matter of interest, Charles, which List were you promoted on?'

Charles blushed. 'The Post List, actually. But that doesn't alter my main point, does it?'

'No, indeed it doesn't.' Commander (S) glanced at the Commander. 'You must invite this fellow more often, Bob. He's like a breath of cold fresh air.'

Charles looked down at the table. 'Hot air, more likely. Now I know I've been talking too much.'

Leading Steward Connolly had been following the decanter's progress up and down the table. The first glass of port at a Guest

Night was paid for by the mess, and subsequent glasses were an officer's own liability. Connolly noted each officer's consumption and later in the evening would present a chit for signature. Connolly had some experience of officers' post-prandial intake and this seemed to him to have all the signs of an all-night session. Seeing that the decanter was now empty again, Connolly smoothly replaced it with a full one.

When the Commander saw the fresh decanter he looked around the table. 'I think we've covered the ground pretty thoroughly, what do you think? Let's go and play party games.'

The Chief Steward had also remained in the wardroom, and was still standing at his post in the corner. The Commander paused in the doorway, when the other officers had gone out.

'Chief Steward, will you have a glass of port, and charge it to me? You too, Connolly.'

'Thank you, sir.' The Chief Steward deftly poured two glasses and gave one to Connolly.

'Your very good health, sir.'

'Thank you both. It was a very good meal, very well done by everyone concerned.'

'Thank you, sir.'

As they drank, the Chief Steward and Connolly were both aware that the port was not only a gesture of thanks, offered to them on behalf of all those who had served the food and the wine, but was also the sealing of an unspoken pact: the conversations they must both have overheard at table were just Guest Night talk.

While the Commander and his party had been talking, the rest of the wardroom had been working off the alcohol fumes with 'Field Gun's Crew', and 'Boat Race' and 'Moriarty, Where Art Thou?'

The ante-rooms looked as though they had been ransacked by the Goths and Visigoths. Chairs and tables were overturned. Carpets were crumpled back, and the bared deck was strewn with a litter of broken glass, pools of liquid, torn wing-collars, shirt studs, cuff-links, shredded bow-ties and discarded shoes. A small mountain of officers in the middle of the forward ante-room were playing 'High Cockalorum', Air Group against the rest, and as the Commander and Charles hopped around the edge, waiting their opportunity to dive into the foray, an observer in Jerry Malone's

260

squadron toppled from the pile and fell against the edge of the nearest table, tipping it over and sending the glasses on it cascading to the deck. He lay prone and still for a moment and then sat up, holding his jaw.

'Hey, Hamish! Hamish, you drunken clansman, you! Hamish, you've got a customer!'

Hamish McGeogh, the senior of the ship's surgeon lieutenants, struggled out of the mêlée. His eyes were fiery with battle and he had lost his jacket. His shirt gaped at the front, where the studs had been torn out, and one sleeve had been ripped off.

'What's up?'

'Customer. That fellow down there doesn't look too good.'

Hamish knelt by the observer, who was now mumbling through thickening lips.

'What's he done to himself, Hamish?'

'Might have fractured his jaw.' Hamish had changed already from a rollicking dinner guest to a doctor. His manner, in spite of his tattered appearance, was calm and objective. 'Give me a hand to help him up. I'll take him up to the sick-bay.'

The accident sobered the wardroom. The contestants separated, and began to repair their appearances, searching the deck for their studs and links. Geoffrey Goodall, Rupert's Senior Pilot, sat down at the piano and strummed the first bars of William Whiting's immortal naval hymn 'Eternal Father, Strong To Save'. Recognising the tune, a group quickly collected round the piano and began one of the traditional overtures to Guest Night singing 'It nearly broke her father's heart, When Lady Jane became a tart'. Two more pilots brought guitars, another a clarinet, and another a bongo drum. More pilots joined the group and the Commander saw that the squadrons were preparing to sing bawdy songs with the same unforgivable panache as they did everything else.

Wardroom singing was normally remarkable for its heartiness than for its harmonic accuracy, compensating in enthusiasm for a lack of tonal quality, but the squadrons sang in unusual concert, almost as though they had been trained as a choir. After 'Lady Jane', they had 'The Harlot of Jerusalem', and 'The Darkies' Sunday School', 'The Wild West Show' and 'They're Digging Up Father's Grave To Build A Sewer', and 'I Put My Finger In A

261

Woodpecker's Hole', and 'Poor little Angeline', and many, many more.

The Commander himself could never remember many of the words or even the chorus of a song until he had heard it sung over again. He was impressed, in spite of himself, by the range and depth of the squadrons' repertoire. Between them, the Air Group knew not just a few songs but every song, and not merely the first verse and the chorus but every verse.

The singing's inspiration was Rupert's guitarist, Chuck Beasley. A natural chorus leader with a light tenor voice admirably suited for folk songs in country and western style, he appeared to know the tune of every bawdy song ever composed and when one song flagged, he was always ready to lead another. Bawdy songs bawled loudly and untunefully merely disgusted the Commander, but the squadron's treatment of them was light and delicate and witty, giving them almost the proper nuances of folk-song. One song was a communal round in which the verses, each delivered by a fresh soloist designated by Chuck Beasley, were limericks of increasing lewdity concerning young women from the Cape, young men from Belgrave, and various young men and women from other, less probable, environments.

Jerry Malone himself contributed one of the first verses, singing in a hoarse, repressed baritone, as though unwilling to allow the words to escape.

> 'There was a Lesbian from Khartoum
> Who took a nancy-boy up to her room.
> She said "Now that we're here,
> Let's get it clear:
> Who's doing what, where, and to *whom?*"

The group took up the chorus. 'That was a filthy one, tell us another one, just like the other one, tell us another one, *do.*'

Chuck nodded to Rupert, who stood up and sang in a muted, ecclesiastical roar, intoning an original and startling litany.

> 'There was a young man from Bexhill,
> Whose penis was sharp as a pencil.
> He went through an actress,
> Nine feet of mattress,
> And buggered the bedroom utensil!'

'*That*, was a *feelthy* one, tell us another one, just like the other one, tell us another one, *do-oo!*'

When the limericks approached saturation, Chuck called upon a very young, baby-faced pilot whom the Commander could not remember ever having seen before.

'Come on, Bobby. Let's have "These Sordid Things".'

The song was evidently a well-known squadron party piece. The clarinet player ran up and down a scale soulfully several times. Chuck Beasley picked out several key notes, while Geoffrey Goodall struck up a thumping suggestive rhythm with his left hand. Between them, the three managed a surprising representation of a night-club trio. Meanwhile Bobby came forward and assumed a coy, shrinking attitude in front of an imaginary microphone, cupping his face in his hands and singing in an exact imitation of a throaty female torch-singer.

'A book on birth-control, with dog-eared pages.
That old french-letter, that we used for ages.
A bed without any springs!
These sordid things, remind me of you.'

Bobby fluttered his eyelashes plaintively, and shifted his stance on to the other foot, thrusting out his hip, while his audience whistled and stamped and shouted 'There's nothing queer about our Bobby!'

'Some blood-stained knickers, in a London taxi.
Your first abortion, that you got from Maxie.
And when you pee, Lord, how it stings!
These sordid things, remind me of you.'

Chuck Beasley noticed Charles standing on the outskirts of the group, laughing like a fool at the lyrics, and when Bobby had finished, he held up his hand.

'A guest! Let's have a song from one of the guests! We call on the guests to sing us a song!'

The cry was taken up. 'A song from the guests! Come on, Charles, let's have one from you!'

'But I don't know any filthy songs!'

'Well, let's have a clean one then!'

'All right. You asked for it.'

263

Charles stepped forward to the piano and placed one hand on his chest like a Victorian drawing-room baritone.

'Give me an A, somebody. La, la, la. Lalala. "Shenandoah". Ready?'

'Ready when you are.'

> 'Missouri, she's a mighty river.
>   Away, you rolling river!
> The Indian camp lies on her border:
> And away, I'm bound away, 'cross the wide Missouri.'

Charles' voice gained power and confidence.

> 'O Shenandoah, I love your daughter.
>   Away, you rolling river.
> I'll take you 'cross you rolling water.
> And away, we're bound away, 'cross the wide Moussouri.'

In spite of his protestations, Charles had a very good voice, strong and clear, and there was something in the song which touched the wardroom. One by one, they began to join in and by the end of the third verse every officer in the ante-room was singing the chorus. After Charles had led the line, he was answered by a great swelling bass response 'Away, you rolling river!' In all his experience of Guest Nights, the Commander had never heard singing like it. Most wardrooms acquired their own song, to act as a perpetual reminder of that commission; after tonight, *Leviathan*'s song could only be 'Shenandoah'.

The last verse was sung pianissimo, ending in a whisper, and a triumphant silence. In the clamouring of the applause afterwards, the Commander clapped Charles on the back.

'Come and have a glass of whisky, Charles! You deserve it after that.'

'I reckon I do, Bob.'

'I didn't know you could sing like that.'

'Well, I didn't know *you* could sing like that!'

'Neither did we.'

'Thank you, Connolly.' Charles accepted his glass of whisky, while the Commander noted that even as a one-night guest Charles had taken the trouble to learn the bar steward's name.

'You know, nobody's ever given the Navy credit for its singing.'

'*Singing?*'

'Yes, *singing*. It's always played a tremendous part in the Navy's life, ever since the days of the sea-shanties. The sailors love singing. If you have a ship's concert, there's nothing Jolly John likes better than a good sing-song to end up with. It's the sign of a happy ship. Your Secretary Bird was telling me something about your last commission.'

'Oh, was he? It's not a pretty story.'

'So I gather. He was telling me they had a concert towards the end of the commission and hardly anybody turned up. Those that did just refused to sing. They just sat on their hands and looked boot-faced.'

'I hadn't heard this one.' In spite of himself, the Commander was still morbidly interested in the debacles of the previous commission.

'Your Scratch said he went himself, because he thought he ought to support the ship's activities, but he and the other officers were the only ones singing. He said he's never been so embarrassed in his life.'

'It must have been bad, if it embarrassed Scratch.'

'However, I don't suppose that would happen if you had a concert now.'

'I hope to God not, Charles.'

'I'm sure it wouldn't. Who . . . Who on earth is this?'

Stiggins was staggering away from a group of pilots by the bar and was aiming for the Commander as though he had been waiting the chance to speak to him. He had half a pint of beer in his hand and he was plainly drunk. His features were smeared by alcohol and he had the mark of a bruise on one cheek-bone. His bow-tie was still around his neck but untied and the front of his shirt was splashed red with port or wine.

He blinked rapidly as he spoke, concentrating upon every word.

'I've got . . . I've got a bone to pick with you, sir. Sir?'

'You've *what?*'

'I said . . .' Stiggins swallowed, with his mouth open, making a liquid retching noise in the back of his throat. 'I've got a bone to pick with you. About uckers. With you, sir.'

'*You've* got a bone to pick with *me!* How dare you, you common little clod-hopper . . .'

'Sir . . . I said . . . I'm not a clod-hopper, sir . . .' Stiggins stopped, and belched, and pointed a finger at the Commander. 'I wasn't the only one playing uckers. It wasn't right to pick on me . . .'

'. . . Excuse us, sir. We'll take him to bed.' Rupert Smith and Geoffrey Goodall had moved around the Commander and swooped upon Stiggins, each taking one of his arms.

Charles stared after them, as they hustled Stiggins towards the door.

'What on *earth* was all that about, Bob? Who was that extraordinary tragic little man?'

The Commander was surprised by his own calmness. The incident should have horrified and disgusted him but it had left him, it seemed, entirely unmoved.

'Just one of the pilots, Charles. Too much to drink, I expect.'

'But what was all that about uckers?'

'It's a long story, Charles, and there's nothing to it.'

'But what is it?'

'I'm not going to bore you with it.'

The Commander knew that Charles would be far from bored: if he told him, Charles would analyse the incident and no doubt he would arrive at some professional solution which the Commander should have discovered for himself. The Commander could not bear, just at that moment, any more talk about Stiggins.

'Let's drop it, Charles, shall we?'

But the incident evidently remained in Charles' mind, because he referred to it again when the Commander went with him to the quarterdeck to see him off.

'That funny little man, Bob. He was rather tragic. He's not typical of the aircrew, is he?'

'Good heavens, no. Why?'

'I wondered why you used the word "common". Did you mean "common or garden" or "common or lower-class"?'

'I don't know what I meant. I was so hopping mad.'

'You didn't look it, Bob. You didn't even look surprised. Are the squadrons hard to get on with?'

The Commander winced. Charles had touched on the one part of his work in *Leviathan* which the Commander knew was not progressing; when he was honest with himself, he had to admit

266

that his relations with some of the aircrew officers were still secretly as uneasy and as unsatisfactory as they had been on the day the squadrons joined.

'We rub along. Sometimes we agree to differ. Charles, you still haven't told me whether you're going to retire or not.'

Charles paused on the gangway. 'Oh, I expect I shall. I'll do what most retired NO's do, be a mannequin in a french-letter factory, or something.'

'Let me know.'

'Of course I will, Bob. And thank you for a splendid evening. I mean that.'

As he watched Charles jauntily walking down the gangway, humming the tune of 'Shenandoah', the Commander knew that now Charles had achieved the most precarious advancement of all, he would no more retire from the Navy than cut off his arm.

17

When the Captain came on board on the morning after the Guest Night, the Commander was up on the quarterdeck to meet him. The Captain had his newspaper rolled up and was slapping it against his thigh as he walked up the gangway. He had the cheerfully possessive air of a man with coveted information.

'How did the Guest Night go, Bob?'

'Very well indeed, sir.'

'Sorry I wasn't there, but I thought I'd be better employed up in London.'

The Commander followed the Captain up to the cuddy.

'I know why you're following me about, Bob. You want to know what happened up at the front office yesterday?'

'There's been a certain amount of speculation, sir.'

'I bet there has! Well, there's nothing much to tell. I trotted round a few of the bazaars and kept my ear to the ground.'

The Captain's voice was uncommonly bland and casual. The Commander studied him closely. Could it be that the Captain was becoming an intriguer? Was Tosser, like high-reaching Buckingham, growing circumspect? The great ship seemed to have developed in him a keener awareness, a kind of peripheral vision, as far as his own career prospects were concerned. A few months ago, the idea of Tosser 'trotting round a few of the bazaars' and 'keeping his ear to the ground' would have been unimaginable.

'Nothing was said in so many words, but I understood that yesterday's promotion list was pure coincidence. As a matter of fact, I had a quiet hint a week or two ago that we were out in the cold this time. But it had nothing to do with last commission. The next list may well be *Leviathan*'s benefit day. I'd be grateful if you'd discreetly spread that around. I don't want officers to get the impression they'll never be promoted whilst they're serving in this ship. That would be quite wrong.'

The Commander was ready to accept the Captain's interpretation, though he privately doubted whether the wardroom as a whole would believe it. 'I'll certainly drop a word in the right ears, sir.'

'Good.' The Captain searched among the papers in the 'In' basket on his cabin desk, and passed one to the Commander. 'Then there's just this.'

The letter was hand-written, and phrased in official language, beginning formally 'Sir, I have the honour to request permission to resign my commission in Her Majesty's Service . . .' The Commander read quickly through the text, noting the words 'no longer any sense of fulfilment', 'dwindling prospects', and reached the signature. 'I have the honour to be, Sir, Your obedient servant, Julian Everest Bird, Lieutenant, Royal Navy.'

The Commander turned down his lower lip. 'Coo, that's a poke in the eye, if ever there was one. I thought he was doing quite well?'

'So did I. Could be his wife behind it. They often are.'

The Commander shook his head. 'I don't think so, sir, not in this case. I've met his wife and she definitely gave me the impression she wanted him to stay in the Service.'

'Anyway, you see him, find out what it's all about. See if you can shake him.'

The Commander thought it a curious custom of the Service that an officer who wished to resign should be interviewed officially by a senior before his letter of resignation was allowed to leave the ship. Surely every officer could be trusted to know the full implication of applying to resign his commission. If he made such an application frivolously or peevishly then he was not fit to hold a commission. His letter should be forwarded at once. If he were serious, then no interview was likely to dissuade him, indeed it might be wrong to try and dissuade him. Again, his application should be forwarded without delay. Therefore there seemed no justification for an interview. However, the Commander sent for Bird, and prepared himself for the classical form of interrogation in such circumstances.

'Why do you want to leave the Navy *now*, Bird?'

Bird had anticipated both the interview and the question. He was calm and determined, recognising that this was just the opening manoeuvre in a protracted struggle.

'It's as hard to say why I want to leave now, sir, as to say why

269

I joined it in the first place. I just don't think the Navy's what it's supposed to be, sir. I think we're all taking part in the biggest confidence trick played on the nation since the time of Charles the Second.'

The comparison was nice and in many ways apt. The Commander acknowledged it. But there was an obvious line of counterattack.

'Are you suggesting there's an element of criminal fraud in the Navy, today? Misappropriation of government funds and property, as there was in Charles the Second's reign?'

'Oh no, sir, I wasn't suggesting that.' Bird was taken aback that his analogy had been pursued further than he had intended. 'All I meant was that the Navy is not capable of doing what it's supposed to do and yet we're all drawing the pay for it. That's not our fault, I suppose. What's far worse is that the Navy's getting more and more like an ordinary job. If I'm going to do an ordinary job, then I'd rather do it outside.'

The Commander recalled Charles' words: in competing with pay and benefits with jobs ashore, the Navy had undoubtedly laid itself open to unfavourable comparisons. The Commander thought it ironical that duty should compel him to argue against this young man. In Bird he recognised a fellow-romantic.

'If you think the Navy's not doing its job, then surely it would be more logical to stay in it and make it work, make it into something worthwhile?'

The question was unanswerable, or rather it had no answer a lieutenant could give a commander. If they had been equals, Bird could have said to the Commander 'What about the two captains and four commanders who retired voluntarily last month? Why didn't someone say that to them? They would have had a damned sight more chance of succeeding than a lieutenant would.' It would have been the complete answer, but Bird knew that he could never give it.

'That's perfectly true, sir, but one person can't do much.'

'No, but a hundred like you can! What would happen if everybody retired?'

'But everybody is, sir! Half my term at Dartmouth have gone or are thinking of going. Most of the officers in this very wardroom are only waiting the right time to go, putting in enough time to qualify for a pension and still be young enough to get a job outside. Then they're off. They're all time-servers, *clock-watchers . . .*'

'That's enough, Bird. There's no need to be offensive.'

'I'm sorry, sir.'

'What particularly caused you to apply to resign just now?'

Bird shrugged helplessly. 'Oh it's any number of things, sir. For instance, my wife and I have been married four years and in that four years I've had six different appointments. Admittedly one change was my own fault, but the longest notice we've ever had of a new appointment was a month. The shortest was one day. I was told at lunch-time that I had to join a new ship by lunch-time the following day.'

'This is something we've always had to put up with in the Service. We've always had to move around a lot. It goes with the job.'

'I know that, sir. My wife and I both appreciate that. But it seems to have got much worse in the last year or so, particularly for two-stripers.'

This, the Commander had heard from other sources, was fair comment. There was a shortage of lieutenants in the Fleet. Their appointing had lately fallen into confusion and disrepute. The Director of Officers' Appointments' department had been drawn into the saddest of vicious circles. The shortage of officers had meant that they had had to juggle with the appointments of those that were available. Frequent changes of appointment had caused discontent, premature retirements, and thus a still greater shortage. It seemed a fair criticism of the Navy, that even when they received their young officers, who had cost so much to recruit and to train, they hardly knew how to deploy them efficiently. The Commander could understand the effect of uncertain appointing upon young officers and their families, but he did not believe that it was his family which weighed most with Bird.

'*Is* it because you have to keep moving your family?'

'No, sir, that's not the main thing, though it does come into it a bit. The main thing is that you never seem to get a proper go at a job. You never get a chance to make anything of it before you're on your way again. It's as if nobody really cared how the job was done. They're only concerned that there should be somebody on board, wearing that uniform and drawing the pay, so they can tick that job off on the watch and station bill. But whether it's you who's doing the job for three months, or another bloke who comes along for six months, or another fellow after him, nobody seems to care very much.'

The Commander had been trying to approach Bird by logic. He realised now that if there had ever been a time when Bird could be won by reason, that time had long passed.

'Do you . . . Look, I don't want to sound trite or pompous, but don't you feel you're running out on something? Don't you feel you're turning your back on something worthwhile?'

'I did feel it was worthwhile once, sir, but not any more.'

'You'll leave nothing of yourself behind?'

The Commander saw from Bird's face that he had reached him at last.

'Of course I'll leave something of myself behind, sir. Anyone who serves in the Navy and leaves it and just walks away saying it's cost him nothing is a fool. I'm cutting my losses, sir.'

Having won a small advantage, the Commander changed his advance again. 'Why were you under report, Bird?'

Bird's mouth tightened, and he clasped his hands behind his back, looking down at the deck like a sulky schoolboy.

'I was under report when I joined this ship, sir.'

'I *know* that. But why?'

'It was something that happened in my last ship, sir.'

'What ship was that?'

'It was a frigate, sir.'

'What happened? Come on, Bird, I don't see why I should have to drag it out of you. It's past and done with now.'

But it was not: the Commander could see Bird summoning himself to undergo it once more in the telling. 'I had an argument with the Chief, sir. He was an ex-tiffy, and I suppose he was a very good engineer officer, but he was one of those people who always think they've had a green rub. He was always dripping about something the Captain had said, or the ship's programme, or the Navy in general. It got on my nerves until one day I got fed up with it and told him to shut up or get out or retire or something. That was the start. And then the very same day I was officer of the watch on the bridge when we nearly hit a merchant ship.

272

I did everything wrong. I didn't tell the Captain early enough. They had the right of way and I didn't take the proper avoiding action. We had to go full astern together and they only missed us by about a hundred yards. That put the lid on it, sir. What with the atmosphere in the wardroom and then that, I was more or less hoofed off the ship and sent here.'

'Don't you feel that things have been going better for you here?'

'Yes they have, sir.'

'Well then?'

'Well, sir, I've just got a draft chit.'

'*No!*'

'Yes sir. My relief's joining on the first of next month.'

'I didn't know that!'

Bird was surprised by the Commander's consternation. 'It was in the CW List last week, sir.'

'I must have missed it.'

The lists of changes in officers' appointments were published daily by the Admiralty and when they arrived in the ship the Captain's Secretary underlined in red ink any changes which affected *Leviathan* and circulated the lists to all Heads of Departments and their offices. The Commander was one of the first to see them, but he remembered that lately he had been too busy to do more than glance at the commanders' appointments, initial the lists and pass them back. He would have conducted his interview with Bird quite differently if he had known.

'... So you see what I mean, sir? Where do we go from here?' It's all starting all over again.' Bird was speaking rapidly and angrily, now that the real source of his discontent was uncovered. 'There's just no point to it all, sir. I admit we were a bit cynical when we joined this ship, just as you said, but I myself very quickly realised that it *was* a tremendous challenge and more and more people are realising it now. If they can win in this ship it'll be the biggest victory they'll ever have. And just as I'm getting stuck into it, I get moved on. It makes me think that my job couldn't be all that important, because it obviously doesn't matter who does it.'

The Commander heard him out, bitterly acknowledging that he had grossly misconducted the interview. He might, just possibly, be able to get Bird's new appointment quashed, but it was not

273

likely and he would merely be setting up a fresh chain reaction of disturbance affecting several other lieutenants. Bird was obviously sorry to leave and that was a good omen, which the Commander hugged to himself. The great ship had changed so much that at least one of her officers was sorry to leave her. Meanwhile, the Commander was furiously angry with himself. Bird was now irrevocably committed to that dreary waste-land of uncertainty where officers who were about to retire dragged out their last months in the Service. He might be there for years, as Charles had said, negotiating with the Admiralty on the one hand and prospective employers on the other, hoping to agree on a common date for release. From now on, Bird would only have half his mind and energies for the Navy. They might just as well let him go now. Charles was quite right: there ought to be some definite time-scale for retirements.

'Then I take it you're not likely to change your mind?'

'No sir, definitely not.'

The Commander let Bird go, and went up on to the quarter-deck himself, to think over the interview. He had been too late and too clumsy to save that one, but he knew there would be others.

He could imagine the atmosphere in that wardroom in Bird's last ship. Such an argument between a senior and a junior member would have split the mess in half. Bird's disastrous watch on the bridge so soon afterwards would have appeared as a triumph for that Engineer Officer. Bird would have been discredited and the Engineer Officer vindicated: enthusiasm never paid in the Navy. But Bird was surely too stable a character to let one incident in one ship deflect him. New ships, new cap tallies, the Commander had said so himself at the start of the commission. There was a deeper cause of discontent. What was this general malaise which young officers seemed to catch just at the time when the Navy should have been opening out before them? Why did they falter, just when they were about to reap the first real rewards of their training? The Navy was shrinking, its prospects becoming more uncertain year by year, but it was still more than just another job. It was still a vocation, a Service unlike any other, carrying rewards which no other profession could match. Annabel said there would not be so many divorces if there were not so much talk of divorce;

perhaps there would not be so many resignations if so many officers did not talk of resigning. Charles had been quite right about that. People infected each other. Disloyalty was contagious. The disloyal elements should be cut out of the Navy before they could do harm to others.

The Commander had no doubt that Bird had talent, in spite of his unpromising start in the ship. He remembered Bird's sailors, on the first divisions of the commission. And no officer on board could have handled the ship better when he avoided running down Stiggins' aircraft that day. The Commander remembered that he had heard little recently of the ship's boats – a sure sign that Bird as Boats Officer was doing his job. He was sure that he had detected, behind the defiant echoes of Bird's voice, the trace of a plea for reassurance. Maybe Bird had wanted to be won over. Perhaps if he had been able to convey to him some spark of his own feeling for the Service, if only a pale reflection, he could have persuaded Bird to withdraw his letter. But where was the achievement in that? In another year, in another appointment, Bird might reapply. The whole tedious cycle would start up again.

The Commander halted by the gangway. The First Lieutenant was just coming on board, in plain clothes. The Commander looked at his wrist-watch. It was twenty minutes past nine. The hands had been working for more than an hour. Requestmen and Defaulters would be sounded off in a few minutes. The First Lieutenant, of all people, was adrift.

The First Lieutenant raised his hat, to salute the quarterdeck, and stepped down beside the Commander.

'I apologise for being late, sir.'

'That's all right, Number One. Bit hung-over this morning?'

'No, sir. I'm afraid I overslept a bit.' The First Lieutenant's voice was unrepentant, even defiant.

The First Lieutenant could have slipped on board unseen. It had been his luck to encounter the Commander. But the lateness and this truculence were so out of character that the Commander looked at him more intently. Number One did not look like a man who had overslept; he looked as though he had hardly slept at all.

'Are you all right, Number One?'

'Yes, sir.'

'You could have rung up and got Hamish or someone to come

and visit you if you weren't feeling well . . .'

'I'm quite all right, sir, I assure you.'

The Commander was not convinced, and the First Lieutenant read it in his face. He had been making his way towards the after screen door but he stopped, and turned back.

'If you must know, sir, the trouble with me this morning is that I'm only just getting used to the idea of being passed over.'

The Commander was amazed. 'That wasn't your . . . Was that your last chance yesterday?'

'Yes it was.'

'But I thought you . . .'

The Commander could not finish the remark. For some reason he and the rest of the wardroom had always assumed that the First Lieutenant was already passed over, although nobody had ever bothered to confirm it.

'Strange as it may seem, I still had a chance until yesterday. Not that I was very optimistic. Your chances get less and less as you get near the end of the zone. Mine must have been about a hundred to one against yesterday. But one does keep hoping . . .'

'Of course.'

The First Lieutenant put his hand inside the crown of his hat and spun the hat on the end of his forefinger. It was an absurdly carefree gesture. 'I knew the chances were against me but still, I always *knew* I was going to be promoted. I got quite excited about it five years ago. And I got excited again when I came to this ship. But when the previous Captain left, I knew that was it. The new Captain just wouldn't have time to recommend me. I *still* can't quite believe it.'

The First Lieutenant's promotion had been one of the subsidiary casualties of the last commission. It had been one small personal edifice which had gone down with the main structure. The Commander was silent, admiring the First Lieutenant's self-control. He had betrayed no sign at all yesterday that he had been hurt. His manner, his conversation, his performance with that idiotic hand-bell, even his behaviour at the Guest Night, had concealed his disappointment, although Beaky's notice about the Feast of the Passover and Charles' little speech must both have rubbed salt in it.

'It didn't really hit me until this morning. I got up this morning

276

and thought, oh *bugger* it all. If it hadn't been for my wife, I don't think I would have come on board at all today.'

'If you'd only said something to me . . .'

'Thank you, sir, but it's got to be faced sometime.'

'What are you going to do?'

'In the future, you mean. What can I do? I don't want to retire. I can't afford to retire. Besides, what the devil would I do if I did retire. I'll just go on in the Service, all passion spent, as they say. I think I'd better get below now, sir, if you don't mind. Hanging around here in plain clothes is only shouting out that I've been adrift.'

The Commander watched the First Lieutenant hurrying, with bent head, towards the screen door. There was nothing he could say to him. To be passed over was a form of professional bankruptcy, and sympathy was inappropriate. One could sympathise with a man who had been struck down by the irrational chance of an Act of God, but this was an act of man, the end result of bad luck, bad timing, and bad reports. It was said that incompetent men were sometimes promoted, but no really competent officer was ever passed over. Nevertheless, the Commander knew there had been exceptions to that rule and he believed it possible the First Lieutenant might be one. The Commander had come to rely on the First Lieutenant's common sense and his experience of the ship and the Service. He was an asset to the wardroom, and his sayings, whimsical and good-humoured, were often quoted by the rest of the officers.

While talking to the First Lieutenant, the Commander had subconsciously been noting the normal progress of a working forenoon going on all around him. In the last few minutes, he had been aware that the routine was being disturbed.

Rowley Dubonnet and two squadron officers had been manoeuvring a giant scroll of canvas out of the after screen door. They had spread it out, leaning it against the quarterdeck bulkhead. Light blue paint was still glistening wet in places on the canvas.

'What's that, Rowley? You building your own aircraft?'

Rowley straightened up, grinning. 'No sir, this is part of the décor for the Summer Ball next week. There are six lengths like this. That blue colour's just the background. We're putting them

277

here to dry and then we're going to paint on them.'

'What's it going to be?'

Rowley glanced conspiratorially at the other two. 'That's a secret, sir. You'll see on the night.'

The Commander remembered that Rowley was chairman of the Ball Committee. As the bugle notes of Requestmen and Defaulters rang out and he went up the ladder to the keyboard flat he remembered, too, with a sudden return of good humour, that Annabel had said she would be very pleased to come.

The Summer Ball was the largest and most elaborate of the year's wardroom social functions. No wife, however unsociable her husband, would permit him to miss it. As the First Lieutenant said, 'Now thrive the hairdressers, and every wife in Portsmouth is on fire.' For the Summer Ball was their night, the wives' night, when for one evening their husbands' ship was ready and anxious to receive them. If any girl, in her innocent and virginal days, had ever believed that marriage to a naval officer would give her the entrée to a glittering world of receptions and uniforms and decorations, then the Summer Ball was her annual reassurance; if she had ever harboured dreams of making a grand arrival, to music, wearing a ball dress, and with her husband in his best uniform beside her, then the Summer Ball was her chance to make them true. Summer Balls were the stuff of dreams. They were anachronisms, unnecessary and expensive. No wardroom needed a Summer Ball. Most wardrooms could not afford them. All wardrooms of any size held them.

The evening of *Leviathan*'s Summer Ball was calm and warm. Towards dusk the wind which earlier had hampered the sailors rigging canvas screens on the quarterdeck and the gangway dropped away to nothing. Overhead the sky was misty blue-grey, with puffs of pink-lined cloud and, to the west, layers of saffron yellow and deep blue and dark orange.

Feeling uncomfortably formal in his white waistcoat and miniature medals, the Commander stopped his car outside Annabel's house. Before he could reach her door, she opened it herself.

He took a pace back. 'By heaven just look at that!' He gasped, and chuckled, simultaneously. 'By golly, I've never seen anything like that!'

Annabel was wearing a dress for princesses, of flame-coloured brocade with narrow panels of black slashed in the skirt, decorated with patterns of fern fronds, and crescent moons and palm leaves picked out in thousands of sparkling black fragments sewn into the material. The bodice was stiffened satin, with a halter neck cut out above her breasts in the bold shape of a heart. She wore long black gloves which reached above her elbows and she had a fur stole over one arm. She was carrying a tiny glittering black evening bag. She wore her hair dressed high in the same style as when he had first met her.

'Well.'

She looked at him, holding his cap in front of him, with an expression on his face like a small boy going to the circus.

'I know what you're thinking, Bob. Everything but the kitchen sink.'

'No, by God, I wasn't thinking that! I was thinking I ought really to have called for you in a sedan chair.'

He clicked his heels together, and offered her his arm.

'Marm?'

'With pleasure, sir.'

Her dress made a delicious rustling sound and her shoes, which were sandals studded with iridescent glass squares, flashed and sparkled as she walked. He opened the car door, struggling to keep his face straight and solemn, while his heart thumped with the wild, giddy glee of a man who calls for a woman and finds her a thousand times more beautiful than he had ever hoped or re-membered.

'I went mad today, and bought you something.'

He leaned over and picked up a small package from the back seat, peeling off the cellophane wrapping.

'An orchid!'

The flower was a rich, creamy white, with fiery red drops stained on its petals. It was a sensuous flower, luxurious and dramatic. He had chosen it that afternoon in the florists', paying more for it than he would have believed any flower could cost.

Annabel held the orchid up. It was an extravagant and costly flower, the first gift he had ever given her.

'Thank you, Bob. I don't think anyone's ever given me an orchid before.'

279

'Does it go with the colour of your dress?'

She looked down. He saw at once that the colours clashed slightly.

'Of course it does.'

'You tell a beautiful untruth.'

'No, no, I am telling the truth. It's a *heavenly* flower.'

She searched in her bag for a pin.

'That reminds me. I've got something else for you.'

He took the jewel box from the glove compartment and snapped the lid open.

Annabel dropped the flower in her surprise. 'Bob, that's *beautiful!*'

The brooch was made of two overlapping beech leaves in gold. The metal had been beaten thin to the texture of natural leaves. The Commander himself had been impressed by the workmanship, by the way the leaves sprang from their stalks, by their veined surfaces and crinkled edges.

'It's a very long time since anyone gave me such presents, Bob. Thank you.' She pinned the flower to her dress then kissed him. 'What a wonderful way to start the evening.'

'What's that perfume you're wearing?'

'Damned if I'll tell you!'

'All right then, let us go to the Ball.'

The Commander had wanted Annabel to see *Leviathan* looking at her best, and he was a much better showman than the rest of the wardroom would ever have suspected. He had timed their arrival to reach the ship just after dusk.

Annabel stood by the car, and looked up at the great ship.

'Bob, what a lovely sight!'

18

The Electrical Department, supervised by Commander (L) and the Deputy Electrical Officer in person, had worked since early that morning to light *Leviathan* for the Ball. Dai Bach resented, and complained to the Commander, of the excessive man-hours expended on ship's illuminations, but he acknowledged the Commander's point that they were at least good advertisement for his Branch. *Leviathan*'s silhouette was too harsh and angular to be softened by even the most skilful lighting effects, but by dusk Commander (L) and his department had done what they could.

Batteries of yellow floodlights on the jetty and the flight deck threw a charitable warmth over the irregular masses and contours of the ship's side and the island. Looped strings of coloured lights pricked out the edges of the flight deck, the quarterdeck and the gangways; the great ship seemed to wear them submissively, as though knowing that their negligible light only accentuated the huge shadowy caverns in her flanks. When the lights were switched on, the great ship loomed up against the night sky, grudgingly *en fête,* and as massive and as intractable as ever, like a medieval border castle decorated for the wedding of the earl's eldest daughter.

The quarterdeck gangway had been enclosed with a canvas screen. Annabel looked up the dim, mysterious tunnel, which was lit by a line of red and white bulbs set in the ridge of the roof.

'This is like going to see Father Christmas.'

'Yes, it is rather. Can you manage?'

'Oh yes. I specially avoided very high heels.'

The Commander was aware that the quarterdeck watch-keepers actually competed to keep the watches on the night of the wardroom Summer Ball. He would not have cared to spend his own evening watching other men taking their women to a dance, but the gangway staff seemed to take a vicarious pleasure in it; for some unfathomable reason, the sailors derived a cynical relish from the spectacle of the officers and their ladies disporting themselves. He was aware, too, that of all the women who arrived on board during the evening, 'the Commander's bird' would arouse the keenest interest amongst the ship's company. Thus, at the top of the gangway, when Annabel bent forward and hitched up her skirts and her sandals described two flashing, jewelled arcs on the quarterdeck, the Commander was pleased and complacent and yet almost ashamed of his own vanity when he saw the looks on the assembled faces of the quartermaster, the sideboys, the Royal Marine bugler, and Poacher, who was officer of the watch.

'Good evening, Poacher. Is the Captain on board yet?'

Poacher dropped his arm from the salute. 'Not yet, sir.'

'What time's the Commander-in-Chief coming?'

'About eleven o'clock, sir. The Flag Lieutenant's just rung us up.'

'Good, good.'

If he had had no partner, the Commander would have remained on the quarterdeck to welcome guests on board, as President of the Wardroom Mess. Tonight, with Annabel beside him, it was every man for himself. He guided Annabel towards the ladder. 'Would you like to put your stole in my cabin, and do your face and all that?'

'Do you think my face needs doing?'

'Well, no, but you know what I mean.'

'Yes, of course, Bob.' She slipped her hand through his arm and sensed at once, by the way his body stiffened, that she had transgressed. Resignedly, Annabel recognised the familiar rejection of any public sign of affection; her sons were sometimes exactly the same, at school.

'Why's that man called Poacher?'

'God knows. Perhaps he used to be one.' He pulled back the curtain from his cabin doorway. 'Here we are. Du côte de chez Markready.'

Annabel had been very curious to see his cabin. This was like a privileged excursion into an exclusively masculine world. The cabin was much larger than any Tom had ever been given, and she was depressed by its neatness and organisation. His clothes were looked after and folded carefully. His shoes were polished and laid out in a line. No doubt his laundry was meticulously sorted and collected regularly. He obviously had an efficient and all-seeing steward. She looked at the titles of his books, the two telephones on the desk, the gramophone records in their battered travelling case, the papers piled in the trays, the squash racquet and the golf clubs in one corner. This was the home of a fully-occupied and self-sufficient man. He hardly needed a wife.

His cabin was even bigger than she had at first realised. There was a sleeping cabin next door, separated by a curtain. The curtain was drawn back and she could see a bunk, a chest of drawers and a wardrobe, with a gun-case lying on top of it. A clothes brush and a pair of silver-backed hair-brushes lay on the chest and, next to the wardrobe, a long leather sword-case.

He was taking a bottle of champagne from the basin by the bunk, and stripping the gold foil from the cork.

'We haven't got an ice-bucket, so I kept it in the basin.'

'Champagne?' For a moment, she had the idiotic thought that she was to be seduced at once. But surely not, not with the Commander-in-Chief coming on board at eleven o'clock? Annabel giggled, and put her hand in front of her mouth.

'What's the matter?'

'Nothing. I just had the stupid thought that perhaps you were going to make love to me now.'

He looked up: the thought had never crossed his mind. He cleared his throat. 'This is hardly the place.'

The cork popped and he hastily poured two glasses, so that the foam rose and creamed over the rims. He wiped the base of one glass with a handkerchief and gave it to her.

'Sorry about the mess. Here's to us.'

'Here's to *us*.' She laid a slight stress on the word, just as he had done.

They drank together, and looked up at the same time, and they both shared an instant of delighted communion. They were both delighted to be there, with each other.

He set his glass down. 'You know, I've got a kind of feeling I'm going to enjoy this evening. I don't know when I've looked forward to a Summer Ball more.'

'Thank you, Bob.'

She picked up the silver-framed photograph from his desk. It was of a middle-aged man in some form of admiral's uniform.

'Is this your father?'

'Yes, that's the old man.'

'There's a family resemblance, quite clearly.'

'So they say. But I'm afraid I'm not as bright as he was.'

She knew the question was unnecessary, but asked it. 'Did you go to Dartmouth?'

He looked astonished. 'Yes, of course I did.'

She put the photograph back. His background was just as she had expected: a naval family, Dartmouth at the age of thirteen, and a life given over to the Navy. He would have been conditioned to it, directly or indirectly, from his earliest years. She thought of Tom, who had joined the Navy when he was twenty-one and who had never quite given in to the pressures they had tried to exert on him. Tom had transferred to a permanent commission, but he had stayed an amateur at heart. Men like Tom, however brilliant, never really stood a chance against men like this. The game had not been bred into them. The difference was almost indefinable, but Annabel could recognise it when she saw it: a way of speaking, though not necessarily an accent, a way of upbringing, though not entirely of family background, a combination of many small differences, like the tiny brush-marks which distinguished the original from the reproductions. Annabel was suddenly angry that she might have something to offer one of these men only when the Navy had failed him. His self-control was so magnificent, she longed to pierce it.

'Did you wear a sailor's suit when you were small?'

He appeared not to notice the edge in her voice. 'Yes, I'm afraid I did. They were the rig of the day then.'

'Didn't old ladies come up and say what a dear little boy you were?'

'Indeed they did. I've always thought my parents took a horrible chance with that sailor's suit. It might have put me off the Navy for good.'

'Surely there was no chance of *that?*'

He looked at her, aware that her first mood of excitement had changed.

'No, there wasn't, really. It was always the thing I was going to do, as soon as I was old enough.'

All at once, Annabel was ashamed of her attack. If she had had a brother, she would not have blamed him for following their father into the family business. This was Bob's father's family business.

'I'm sorry I was so bitchy about it.'

'That's all right, I didn't realise you were being bitchy.' He was honestly surprised by her admission. 'There are certain things about the Navy which always bring out the worst in everyone. Including me. Let's go down and join the great ceilidh. I want to see the ante-room. Rowley and his boys have been hard at it all day.'

'What about our champagne?'

'I'll take the bottle with us.'

While the Electrical Department had been labouring to improve *Leviathan*'s exterior, Rowley Dubonnet and his committee had been at work below, converting the forward ante-room into that combination of dim lighting, low headroom and strident music so dear to the festive naval officer's heart.

'Golly.' The Commander stared about him. 'This looks pretty intimate.'

The ante-room had been transformed into a night-club, which was called The Bowels of *Leviathan*. The double doors were surround by a painted canvas screen representing the jaws and teeth of a gigantic sea monster whose grey-green canvas body extended down the passageway. The Bowels was lit by oil lanterns, hanging from the pipes and trunkings in the deckhead. The ante-room chairs had been removed and replaced by small barrels and packing cases. The tables were covered in rough sail-cloth and each had a bottle standing on it, with a candle in the neck. A shirt-sleeved band, with guitars and drums, were playing in the recess at the end of the room, and a small space in front of them had been left clear for dancing. Although it was still early for the Ball, the air was already frowsty with the smell of paraffin and tobacco smoke.

The Commander chose a table and put his champagne bottle on it.

'Which will you have, Annabel, a barrel or a packing case?'

'A barrel, thank you. I don't want to ladder my stockings straight off.'

Annabel sat down, put her handbag on the table and pulled off her gloves, while the Commander struck a match and lit the candle.

'Bob, this is *very* sexy. Have you noticed the walls?'

The squadrons all had their artists and the Commander had seen some of their line-books, in which cartoons, newspaper headlines, extracts from the Daily Orders, signals and squadron photographs were pasted to make a witty and informative history of the squadron's commission. The squadron artists had collaborated to paint the mural for The Bowels and between them they had created a surrealist but entirely credible marine world of cartoons. The Captain was represented as hoary Neptune, drawn in his chariot of conch-shells by a quarter of seahorses which were easily recognisable as the Operations, Direction, Navigating and Communications Officers. The Commander himself was there as Ulysses, in a coracle and accompanied by the fellow-argonauts Commander (E), Commander (L), Commander (S) and the PMO, all repelling the blandishments of a group of sirens in flying helmets. Commander (Air) was airborne as Daedalus, in close formation with Little F as Icarus, who had one wing heavily bandaged. A mournful, hangdog shark had the face of the Gunnery Officer, and the pilot fish swimming in front of him was clearly Poacher. Enoch was transmogrified into a lobster, the Captain's Secretary peered out of a giant clam shell, and Rupert Smith's face was superimposed on a crab wearing several pairs of heavy boots. Every square foot of the mural was populated by some species of natural or fabulous marine biology, a host of whales, tritons, mermaids, flying fish and dolphins, all recognisable as members of the wardroom.

Many of the officers and their wives were attending dinner parties before coming on to the Ball, and The Bowels was still only half full. The Commander had refused invitations to dinner because he had intended to keep Annabel to himself but this selfish ambition was quickly thwarted by the Air Group. The news had spread that Annabel Powell was present at the Ball, and with a non-flyer. Their table began to be visited by aircrew officers from *Leviathan* and their guests from other ships and air stations. Some of the visiting aviators asked Annabel to dance. All kissed her warmly, in a manner which suggested they were renewing an old acquaintanceship. The Commander watched them resentfully, remembering that he had only kissed her twice himself. From their conversation it appeared that every aircrew officer in the Navy over the age of thirty knew Annabel from way back. The Fleet

Air Arm evidently retained a proprietary interest in her. She was a good-looking woman who had once been married to one of them, and she was still their property. Few of the visiting pilots troubled to conceal from the Commander their surprise that Annabel should choose to come to *Leviathan*'s Summer Ball in the company of a fish-head.

During one of Annabel's absences on the dance floor, the Commander noticed Monica Bird sitting at a table behind him. She was sitting alone, looking about her as though taking a farewell. The Commander remembered that indeed this might well be her last Summer Ball. He swivelled round to face her.

'Good evening. How are you?'

'You didn't convince him then.'

She spoke as though she assumed he would take her meaning without preamble, as though there could be only one subject of conversation between them.

'No. I tried quite hard, believe me. I think your husband's mind was made up long before he came to see me.'

'Made up his mind!' He was stabbed by her flashing look and tone of contempt. 'He doesn't know what his mind is!'

He spread out his hands, palms upwards, trying to conciliate her. '*I* can't assume that. If an officer applies to ...'

'Julian's a very ordinary person, you know. Being in the Navy was the only thing special about him. Why did they take him and train him and then make him unhappy?'

He shook his head. The question was unanswerable. 'Have you got any ideas about jobs outside?'

'No, of course not!' She looked at him disgustedly, as though he were getting more and more wilfully stupid. 'He can't *do* anything except the Navy. We'll get something in PR or personnel or something eventually. It's going to take him years to find out how the civilian world even works.'

'I'm sorry. I did what I could.' He made the only reasonable point still open to him. 'But if *you* can't convince him, then I'm sure I couldn't.'

She turned her head away impatiently. He followed her glance. The rest of their party were arriving. Bird, with a bottle of champagne in each hand, was approaching the table with Fisher, and Simmondson and Ben Krieger and their partners. Bird was

287

laughing and indicating their table. He hardly looked like a man who had weighed up the full consequences of a letter of resignation which might, the Commander now realised, cost him not only his commission but also his marriage.

Annabel was being led back to the table by a short, fat pilot with ginger side-whiskers who kissed her lightly on the cheek before she sat down.

'Bye bye, 'Bel. Lovely to see you again.' The short fat pilot gave the Commander a look of total animosity, and left.

'I don't think your fly-boy friends like me very much, Annabel. Who was that stuffy little man?'

'Judd, you mean? He was an usher at our wedding.'

'Oh my goodness, I'm sorry, I didn't mean to insult him.'

'Judd wouldn't mind.'

The Captain's Secretary and Fanny were passing, on their way to a table nearer the band. The Secretary leaned over Annabel as he passed, and sniffed.

' "Je Reviens", still?'

Annabel good-humouredly warded him off with one hand. Fanny watched, with a sour smile.

While the Secretary was talking to Annabel, Fanny composed her face in a noticeably *déjà vu* expression, like a parson's wife who knew all the sermons by heart but whom duty compelled to sit in the front pew every Sunday. After intercepting one of his apologetic glances at her, the Commander wondered whether the Secretary, that invulnerable man, was actually vulnerable through Fanny.

That the Secretary should also be renewing his long-standing acquaintance with Annabel was too much for the Commander. He stood up again, abruptly.

'Let's go up and try the other band in the hangar, shall we, Annabel?'

Annabel took her cue at once. 'Oh good, is there dancing up there, too?'

The hangar fire curtain had been lowered and the after end of the lower hangar cleared as a main ballroom – The Bowels having been intended as a secondary diversion. Another, and much larger band in dinner jackets were playing on a platform in front of the liftwell; there had been a suggestion that the band should play on the after lift itself but the Commander, with memories of the commissioning service, had forbidden it.

Again, the dance committee had done their best with a wholly functional compartment. A fountain, with a small pool, ingeniously made from an inflatable rubber life-raft and supplied with water from the ship's firemain, had been rigged in the centre of the floor. The sides of the pool were banked with flowers and there were flowers around the edges of the dance floor: Laura McTigue and a working party of wives had come on board during the afternoon to arrange them. There was a bar in one corner of the hangar and several dozen tables had been set out round the floor.

Yet the hangar had the cold atmosphere of a party which had not begun. Most of the tables were empty and nobody was dancing. It seemed that the hangar was not popular and The Bowels would be the vortex of the Ball (for a reason, as the Commander later discovered, which the dance committee could not have foreseen: aviation fuel had been inadvertently pumped up to the flight deck earlier in the evening and there could be no smoking in the hangar while the pipe systems were venting).

The Commander was intimidated by the wide, empty floor, but Annabel walked on without hesitation. The band, reassured that the new couple intended to dance, began an ironical rendering of 'This Could Be The Start Of Something Big'.

The Commander had learned to dance at Dartmouth, but the crisp figures taught him there had been blurred and corrupted by time. However, the music played at wardroom Summer Balls had not altered materially since the 1930s and the Commander's one-paced, two-step shuffle was adequate enough for the waltzes, fox-trots, quicksteps and indeed for all the recognisable Summer Ball rhythms.

But dancing alone on the floor with Annabel and conscious of his own deficiencies, the Commander felt exposed and vulnerable.

'I'm sorry we've got to do this all by ourselves.'

'I'm not. It's not often we get a lovely floor all to ourselves and a band ready to play whatever we want. Ask them to play "As Time Goes By" next.'

'Does that have memories for you?'

'Good heavens, no. I just like it. The one with memories is "These Foolish Things". You should never ask for that one, because it's bound to remind a girl of her last boy-friend.'

'Is that so?' The Commander stored away the information, recognising it as tactical advice of the first importance.

A few more couples, perhaps encouraged by the Commander's well-meaning example, were taking the floor. The band were putting their weight into their work, now that they were being called upon seriously to earn their money.

'I hope you weren't too annoyed when I had to keep on leaving you while we were down in that night-club place?'

'Not at all. That's the penalty for taking a good-looking girl to a hop.'

'Thank you, Bob. They were all old friends of Tom's.'

'Even the Secretary?'

'Oh yes.' She leaned back, to gaze at him at arm's length. 'It was Tony who first introduced us.'

'Did he? I didn't know that. Was the Secretary an old flame of yours.'

'What a horrible way of putting it. He did propose to me once, yes.'

'Did he, by God! And after that, I suppose . . .'

'She's got lots of money.'

'Well, yes.' He was disconcerted by her directness. 'I *suppose* that was what I was going to ask.'

'Of course it was. I can hear your brain working, Bob.'

The Commander grinned. There was nobody quite like Annabel for slicing through inessentials and getting to the nub of the matter.

After 'As Time Goes By', the Commander asked for 'Slow Boat To China'. He was surprised by his own sentimentality: requesting numbers from the band was an affectation he associated with Ship's Company dances. It struck him that this was the first time he had ever had any influence, however fleeting, on the tunes played at a Summer Ball. The music was normally something one accepted, like the weather, or one's partner's dress.

Stiggins came on to the floor, with the blonde girl who had been his partner at the informal dance just after commissioning. They began to cut expertly in and out of the other couples, dipping and whirling together and, whenever there was a long enough clear space, linking sequences of rapid intricate steps. The Commander, jogging comfortably round the floor with Annabel, regarded

Stiggins with suspicion and a little contempt. Flashy steps were for the sailors. There was something peculiar about any officer who had reached Stiggins' standard.

As though they were themselves bored with Stiggins' display, the band broke off and played a long and exaggeratedly discordant chord. The band-leader announced the eightsome reel.

The Commander sighed. 'Oh Lord. Wherever two or three Englishmen are gathered together, they will have Scottish tribal dancing.'

But when the sets were formed, and when it was his turn to leap into the centre of the circle and to hooch and cavort like a wild Highland steer, Annabel confirmed a truth she had always suspected, that to Bob, as to almost all regular naval officers, so-called Scottish tribal dances were the only dances worth performing.

Their set included Hamish McGeogh and his partner, a young Scots nurse from the General Hospital. They were keen to see the dance properly performed but their Hibernian expertise was not required except, curiously, by Stiggins. The Commander watched with a certain triumphant satisfaction Stiggins' hesitations and blunderings, and Hamish's frenzied promptings and pushings. As John Bowler would certainly have pointed out, chassées and whisks were all very well for stoker mechanics, but it took an officer and a gentleman to do the eightsome reel.

The reel left the dancers hot and weary, and thinking of supper. The band put down their instruments, to indicate that surely there was now an interval.

Supper was the one part of a Summer Ball which Annabel disliked. She could shut her eyes and see the whole meal, from consomme to coffee. She knew that it would be a buffet supper of a peculiarly naval kind, laid out with a lavish, if heavy, hand.

When Annabel stepped into the wardroom and noted the tables, elevated for the occasion on special wooden blocks, she saw that *Leviathan*'s buffet supper was in the classic naval Summer Ball tradition. There was cold consomme, and ham, and a huge half-excavated turkey, and tongue and chicken and sliced sausage, and plates of cole-slaw and sauerkraut, halved boiled eggs in mayonnaise, bacon and egg pie, bowls of lettuce hearts and chives and tomatoes and beetroot, and jellies and trifles and ice cream. It was like a tea-party for Balshazzar's children. Annabel supposed that naval officers' palates were ruined at an early age by nicotine and alcohol: if the messman had attempted any variation from the prescriptive Summer Ball buffet menu, the officers would have felt as deprived and as outraged as though they had been offered hamburgers for their Christmas dinners.

But Annabel could see that Bob at least was happy. There were great territories of human emotional experience to which he seemed wholly insensitive, but here, for a traditional wardroom occasion, he was at home. This was his element. . . . This was his ship and his wardroom, and these were his friends. When the Commander-in-Chief and Lady Metcalf visited the wardroom during supper and she and Bob went to pay their respects, Annabel noticed that Bob talked to the Admiral with an unembarrassed, professional equality which Tom, for all his self-confidence, could never have assumed.

The Commander was much less confident than he appeared. The Commander-in-Chief puzzled him. The Navy liked their admirals extrovert and jolly. This man was introverted and solemn. He had too much hair for an admiral. He looked like a senior boffin, or a higher civil servant of the administrative grade; the Commander had heard that his staff sometimes called the Admiral 'Fruity', because the nick-name was so beautifully inappropriate. The Commander could not imagine this man imitating the actions of Cunningham in the Mediterranean, or of Fraser in the North Atlantic. He was one of a new race of post-war admirals, dedicated but glamourless (although paradoxically, the Commander would not have been surprised if he had been told that the Commander-in-Chief kept a book of press cuttings).

While talking to the Admiral, the Commander was conscious that he was being summed up, measured against some recent and unfamiliar formula. This man had information, friends, standards, interests, which admirals never used to have. He was a regular officer and had begun at Dartmouth but somewhere in his career he had absorbed, by some kind of bureaucratic osmosis, in Aubrey McConnell's phrase, attitudes and opinions entirely orientated on Whitehall.

These attitudes emerged most painfully in casual, unguarded

remarks, which hurt the Commander more than if they had been intended to wound.

The Admiral had dined already, and he waved his token cup of coffee as a baton, to gather attention.

'. . . Remarkable progress, considering it's a scratch wardroom. That's one of the unexpected joys of the Service. One can always be surprised by the results achieved by interim complements.'

The Commander was dumbfounded. *Scratch* wardroom? *Interim* complements? Were they, after all, a scratch collection of bodies, doing what they could for *Leviathan,* in their interim way, until the *real* wardroom were appointed? Either the Admiral was unaware of the insult to *Leviathan*'s present wardroom implied in his remarks, or he had completely misread the lesson of the last commission. *Leviathan*'s last wardroom had been hand-picked men and as hand-picked men they had failed, utterly and comprehensively. Furthermore, the Commander thought it was now obvious that *Leviathan*'s previous wardroom had never had a chance of succeeding, any more than a football team composed entirely of gifted centre-forwards. As someone had told the Commander when he first joined the ship, there had been too many chiefs in *Leviathan* and not enough Indians. The Commander knew that he was never likely to be asked to serve on such an admiral's staff. If he ever needed help, he could not look to this Commander-in-Chief.

Lady Metcalf, however, was cast from the original mould of admiral's ladies. She was a small woman, with a way of straightening her spine and thrusting out her bosom when she made a point in conversation. She used a lorgnette, although her eyesight was quite adequate. She had the mannerisms of a great political hostess, including a trick of offering a man one or more fingers on shaking hands; the number of fingers offered depended upon the reputation and future professional prospects of the officer being presented. A full handshake from Lady M. was reckoned in the Fleet to be equivalent to an early brass hat. When *Leviathan* commissioned, her Captain and her Commander had both been assessed at one finger only.

The Captain, accompanying the Admiral into the wardroom, was wearing an expression as though Lady Metcalf had embraced him with both hands. A Summer Ball was too formal an occasion to be judged by normal social standards; a Summer Ball could no more be called successful than an investiture at Buckingham Palace. But a Ball which was gay and crowded, which was brilliantly decorated, when there was laughter in the wardroom and the officers spoke up cheerfully when the Admiral addressed them, such a Ball naturally reflected the greatest credit on the Captain of the ship. Tosser was basking in the credit, and he stopped to pass on a due portion.

'The Admiral's enjoying himself very much, Bob.'

'I'm glad to hear that, sir.'

'He told me he went to this ship's last Summer Ball and he said it was an experience he's no wish to repeat.' The Admiral had told the Captain in confidence, knowing that he would certainly pass the information to his officers. 'By the way, how many fingers did you get from Lady M.?'

'Four, sir.'

'Same here. Good work, boy.' The Captain clapped the Commander heartily on the shoulder. Lady Metcalf's idiosyncrasies were absurd, but still significant. 'I'm on my way up to the hangar now. The Admiral wants to dance.'

The Commander nodded, and watched the Captain go, feeling like a helmsman watching a competitor catch a fluky gust of wind and draw ahead. Tosser had caught a new breeze and was leaving his Commander behind. As Tosser left the wardroom in the train of the Admiral's retinue, he looked more like an auxiliary of the Admiral's staff than the Captain of a private ship. The Commander recalled an odd remark made by the First Lieutenant: 'The bureaucrats are taking over the Navy, sir. But when they do, make sure you're on the committee.' Tosser was laying the foundations of his seat on the committee.

'They're a nice couple, aren't they?'

The Commander scowled. He had been thinking of a way to describe his encounter with the Admiral. Nice was not the adjective which would have occurred to him.

'Yes, they are. Lady M.'s a bit frightening.'

'Oh, but she's not really, Bob. She's been very kind to me. She's always ringing up to ask me to things. I think she was afraid I was going to fade away. You're *not* going to hide in a corner and *hug* your weeds, she told me.' Annabel laughed. 'As if I would.'

294

Annabel's imitation of Lady Metcalf's voice, and the sharp jerk of her body as she said the words were so exact that the Commander had a vivid picture of that fierce little lady herself. Admiral's wives were often accused of meddling in Service affairs. He thought it a pity that Lady M. did not interfere more often. The abstracts which so engrossed her husband would mean nothing to her. *People* were Lady Metcalf's concern.

Supper was nearly over, and the wardroom was emptying.

'Are we going back to dance now, Bob?'

'I hadn't really thought. Why, what would you like to do?'

'Well, it seems silly but I've never ever been on a flight deck. Would it be all right if we went up there and had a look?'

'Of course it would.'

They joined a straggling pilgrimage which was climbing the ladders leading up to the flight deck. Several of the wives were also taking the opportunity to see something of their husbands' ship while they were on board.

The aftermost access ladder to the flight deck on the starboard side rose from a short passageway which also formed a cabin flat. The cabins there were unpopular because they were tiny and awkwardly-shaped. The nearest bathroom was two decks below and, by some quirk of the ship's domestic water system, was always the first to run short of hot water. The thunder of landing aircraft and the rumble of arrester wires on the flight deck directly overhead made the cabins uninhabitable while flying was in progress. Beaky allocated them to the most junior aircrew officers on the principle. 'They make the noise, let them put up with it.'

The small cabin flat was deserted at that time of night, but as the Commander escorted Annabel along the passageway he heard a sound from one of the cabins.

'What the devil was that?'

'What?'

'That.' The sound was a muffled, groaning whisper. 'There it is again.'

The Commander started forward, and Annabel grasped his arm tightly.

'Don't go, Bob! There's nothing wrong! *Bob!*'

'How do you know there's nothing wrong? It sounded to me like someone in pain.'

'Bob, it *isn't!* Don't look!'

The Commander shook off her hand. 'It sounded like this one.' He seized the handle, and wrenched the cabin door open.

The scene in the cabin might have been a *tableau vivant* dedicated to Priapus. The blonde girl who had been dancing with Stiggins was naked and spread-eagled, face down on the end of the bunk. Her dress and her stockings were scattered over the cabin deck. Stiggins was naked only from the waist down. He had mounted the girl, and his head was buried in her hair, his arms clasped round her body. His half-clothed male figure and the nude body of the girl momentarily composed a picture of extraordinary and unnatural sexual activity, like a centaur covering a mare. They had been surprised at the moment of coition and, for a few seconds, they lay without movement on the bunk.

In his amazement, the Commander said the first words which occurred to him.

'Good God, you might at least have taken off your jacket!'

Stiggins lifted his head, becoming aware of the Commander and of the faces filling the doorway behind him. He withdrew from the girl and stood up, white-faced and shocked.

'Get dressed, both of you!'

Stiggins picked up his trousers and held them in front of him. The girl was slower, rising from the bunk as though from sleep.' Her movements were languorous and drowsy, and she rubbed her eyes with her fingers. She lowered her hands, and when she recognised the Commander and the audience behind him, began to scream in the high drowning note of hysteria.

'Get *dressed.*' The Commander's voice cut the girl off.

She covered her body with her arms. 'I will get dressed. *Please* go. I *will* get dressed. I *will.*'

'Then do it.' The Commander folded his arms, like a farmer waiting to see trespassers off his land.

Annabel pulled at his sleeve. 'Bob, you're *not* going to stay and watch them! For goodness sake, leave them *alone!*'

The Commander shrugged her arm away.

'I told you both to get dressed. Now *do* it!'

The girl turned her back and stepped into her dress, pulling it up her body and thrusting her arms through the shoulder straps.

Her skin was flushed to the shoulders. Annabel could hear her sobbing.

'I don't know what you two think this ship is, but obviously it's the wrong place for you. You'd better get ashore, both of you.'

The Commander hooked his foot round the edge of the door and contemptuously slammed it shut. He turned to face the dozen officers and their wives who had been standing in the passageway behind him. Two of the wives were blushing and avoiding his eye, but some of the officers were openly smirking and the faces of the others, though they were trying to control their expressions, presented the appearance of a great communal leer.

'Well. Now you can all carry on to wherever you're going. The *peep-show* is over.'

They all dropped their eyes, shamefacedly, and in single file moved towards the ladder to the flight deck.

Annabel clasped her hands together, and drew them up to her mouth. 'Oh Bob, that was *awful*. I did guess what was happening in there and I did try to warn you. Why did you . . .'

'Do you still want to walk up on the flight deck?'

'Oh no, I'd rather find somewhere to sit down. I'm feeling quite weak at the knees.'

'We'll go back to my cabin then.'

'It wasn't fair to call it a peep-show, Bob. After all, it was you who stopped and opened the door.'

'That's not the point. I'm not worried about the *sexual* side of it. That's the only thing everybody ever seems to think of. If a fellow wants to make love to his girl friend, I don't object to that. That's their business, certainly not mine. But I do object if they start doing it in this ship. That *is* my business.'

Annabel sighed. There was nobody quite like Bob for the really crushing, undefeatable answer. In his cabin, she stood by the sleeping cabin curtain, watching him pull out the armchair for her to sit in.

'You're a cruel man, Bob.'

'You mean, making them get dressed?'

'If it had been me, I think I would have died of shame. That poor girl. I did feel sorry for her.'

'You needn't feel sorry for her, or for that randy young goat. It was their own fault. What do they think this ship is, some cheap run-down back-street hotel where they hire a room at ten bob an hour? The whole thing was utterly disgraceful.'

'You're being very hard on them, Bob. I remember some of the air station balls Tom and I used to go to, it was the recognised thing. They even had a special row of empty cabins. The girls used to say it was a pretty dull Summer Ball if they didn't have their clothes taken off sometime during the evening.'

'Maybe.' He frowned. He wanted to ask her if she had ever stripped at a Summer Ball but he hesitated, knowing that she would tell the truth. 'That may be all right for an air station, but it's not all right for this ship.'

'She had a lovely figure.'

'Yes, she did.'

His flat non-committal voice goaded her. Infuriated, Annabel got up from his arm-chair and stood by the door of his sleeping cabin. She had been roused and erotically stimulated by the sight of the love play up in that cabin. She now longed to behave out of character and so to shake this impregnable man by confronting him with some wholly unexpected advance. She could provoke him, if she left her normal self and recaptured the bold and teasing girl she once had been, the girl Tony had proposed to, nearly fifteen years before.

'Weren't you shocked at all?'

'No. As I keep saying . . .'

'Does this shock you?'

While she was speaking she unhooked the back of her dress and shrugged off the bodice, pressing the folds of cloth down to her hips. She clasped her hands behind her neck and arched her body, in a deliberately provocative pose.

He ran his fingers through his hair. 'I don't know what the devil's got into everybody tonight.'

Annabel laughed, doubling up, and holding her breasts in her hands. She had intended to shock and provoke him, but his expression of alarm and bewilderment was the last reaction she had expected.

There were tears in Annabel's eyes. 'Oh Bob, you are the nicest man. How does the Navy get hold of people like you?'

'That's not very kind. You make it sound as though I'm some sort of rare animal.'

'But you *are* a rare animal! Do you ever think about women?'

'Why do you ask?'

'Well, you seem so complete, somehow. You're so wrapped up in all this and you obviously love doing it. What would you do if the Navy ever let you down?'

'It's not something that lets you down. That doesn't come into it.' At last, he felt himself on firmer ground.

'Tell me what does come into it then.' She was pulling her dress up to her shoulders.

'You join it and work at it and if you're any good and you're reasonably lucky you get promoted. And if you're not...' He remembered Charles' forecast of the average naval officer's resettlement occupation. 'And if you're not lucky, you retire and become a bursar at a boys' school.'

'Now, *that's* not very kind.' She took his hand. 'Bob, I hope you're never, never going to be disappointed. The Navy doesn't need people like you. You make everybody feel ashamed. You make *me* feel ashamed.'

'I'm sorry.'

She turned her shoulder towards him. 'You'd better zip me up then.'

'There was something I wanted to say ...'

'Yes?'

'Annabel, will you be my wife?'

'*What?*'

She was touched by the phrasing of his proposal. He had not asked her to marry him, but to be his wife. Was there for him some deeper degree of meaning? His proposal made her more than ever ashamed. She admitted that she had dressed to kill that night. She had watched the other women at the Ball looking from Bob to her, appraising her, and knowing that she was in full war-paint that night. She had succeeded so easily that the victory was tasteless. In many ways he was a man of gigantic moral strength and maturity, but in others he seemed scarcely pubescent. Making him propose to her had been, as Tom would have said, like shooting fish in a barrel.

'Oh go away, you make me feel cheap and nasty.'

'I don't know why.'

'No, you wouldn't know why.'

19

The story of the Commander's encounter with Stiggins passed around the ship with the traditional speed of scandal. Tales of sexual adventure were always well received on the messdecks, and a tale which concerned a Commander, a pilot, and a blonde, had just the right admixture of lewdity and wardroom seniority to have an especial appeal for the ship's company. The Commander's actual words quickly became one of the ship's favourite catch-phrases: sailors faced with any difficult or unusual task would advise each other to take their jackets off. Conversely, a sailor who had failed in any undertaking would attribute his failure to the fact that he had kept his jacket on.

The Commander was unaware of the wide currency given to his *mot* until the Monday morning, a week after the Ball, when the ship was preparing to go to sea for the last fortnight of the flying training programme before the summer leave period. The Commander was on deck an hour before sailing to make his customary tour of the ship. He could not claim many definite successes in *Leviathan,* but he believed that one at least was the manner in which the ship now put to sea. He had at last succeeded in preventing the seemingly aimless hurrying and scurrying which used to accompany *Leviathan*'s sailings. The unemployed bystanders who used to clutter the upper deck just before sailing had been routed out and sent below. The postman coming on board with the final mail, the electricians unrigging the telephone cables, the tankies disconnecting and rolling up the fresh-water hoses, the berthing parties in overalls and heavy gloves, singling up the wires – every man the Commander could see on the upper deck was now moving with an air of purpose.

The Commander walked round to the starboard side of the ship, which faced the river. Steady rain was sweeping in through the side openings and drenching the deck. The Commander wondered why Monday mornings were always wet. The meteorologists would probably be able to disprove it, they always experienced dissimilar weather to everyone else, but in the Commander's

300

experience Monday sailing mornings were always damp and miserable.

The Commander stopped to watch the starboard crane preparing to hoist a pinnace. The pinnaces were heavy, round-bottomed and slow, but one was normally lowered, even when the ship was alongside a jetty, because it was useful for the Mate of the Upper Deck to inspect the ship's side, or for taking sports parties to the other side of the river, and for the engineering and electrical departments to take defective parts directly into the dockyard.

The pinnace coxswain and his crew were hooking on the slings in the boat and the Commander was pleased that he could put a name to each member even under their oilskin hoods: in most ships such a feat would have been taken for granted, but in *Leviathan* it was worthy of remark. The coxswain's name was Leading Seaman Drover and the Commander had punished him several times at the defaulter's table for leave-breaking, indeed, the Commander remembered, Drover at one time had been in danger of losing his leading rate.

'All hooked on down there in the boat, Cox'n?'

It was Stiggins' voice, from the boat-deck above. The Commander involuntarily stiffened, and began to to pay attention.

'Yes, sir, all hooked on in the boat.'

'Up jib!'

The slings tightened, the crane jib wire went rigid, and the pinnace rose out of the water. As the boat swam up past his level the Commander noted the heavy oil-streak along its water-line and he hoped that Bird, who was Boats Officer, would also notice it.

'Cox'n, what's that water pissing out of the bottom of your boat?' Stiggins' voice was bantering and jocular.

The Commander saw the surprise on Drover's face.

'We're draining out, sir.'

'What?'

'Draining *out*, sir! Taken the bung out of the 'ole!'

'There's no need to be cheeky, Cox'n. Why can't you pump it out?'

Drover's expression changed to exasperation. 'Because the bilge pump won't take a suction *all* the way down, sir. Have to drain the rest out. Can we stop for a minute till we've finished, sir?'

'All right. I suppose so.'

The Commander could hear the pinnace crew grumbling amongst themselves as he made his way towards the nearest boat-deck ladder. Rupert Smith had obviously taken his words to heart and had arranged for his pilots to participate in ship's affairs. The Commander welcomed the thought: certainly, hoisting a boat was an evolution every officer should be able to carry out whatever his specialisation. But still, working a crane required practise, and supervision. The Commander was uneasy that Stiggins should be in charge of hoisting the pinnace and some premonition made him hasten his step. He found himself hurrying, taking the steps of the ladder two at a time.

At the top of the ladder the Commander paused, uncertain whether to intervene. The pinnace was suspended high above him, its swinging checked by two lines secured forward and aft and manned by two seamen on the boat-deck. Stiggins was standing inboard of the row of curved crutches laid out to take the boat's weight. The boats artificer and the boats shipwright were by the base of the crane, but the Commander could see no sign of Bird.

'Have you finished pissing yet, Cox'n?'

'Yes.' Leading Seaman Drover's voice showed that he had not appreciated the joke.

'Right then! Train right, crane-driver. Full speed!'

The crane-head jerked and began to train inboard. The wire slanted and came upright again. The pinnace, gathering speed, swung in over the waiting crutches.

Still accelerating, the boat passed over the crutches, but Stiggins would not, or could not, give the order to stop training. He remained still, watching the boat hurtling towards him.

The Commander ran under the looming shape of the pinnace to catch the crane-driver's eye.

'Stop training!'

The Commander's order was too late. The crane-jib stopped abruptly but the pinnace, impelled by its own massive momentum, swung on and crashed into the gun sponson railing above the boat-deck, driving a large dent in the steel coaming and ripping a long jagged tear in its own side. The boat rebounded, and swung against the sponson again, while the sailors on the guide-lines were dragged to and fro across the boat-deck as they struggled to subdue

302

the boat's tremendous pendulum.

Bird came running from the other side of the crane pedestal. His eye fell on the damage to the pinnace's side.

'*Christ,* Alfred! What the hell have you been doing?'

The Commander rounded on him. 'And what the hell have *you* been doing?'

Bird pointed desperately in the direction he had come. 'I was just the other side of the crane, sir, talking to the boats engineer officer in the workshop, sir.'

'Why weren't you *here?* You're supposed to be the Boats Officer. It's *your* business to be present whenever a boat's hoisted. You don't just leave the job to some other incompetent jackass who obviously hasn't the first idea what he's about!'

'No, sir.'

'Neither of you two officers will go ashore until that boat is repaired and in the water again. Is that understood?'

'Aye aye, sir.' Bird looked hopelessly at the Commander; useless to tell him now that he had expressly forbidden Stiggins to swing the pinnace inboard until he returned.

'Is that understood, Stiggins?'

'Yes, sir. Understood.'

The Commander searched Stiggins' face carefully. Lately, since the Ball, Stiggins had cultivated a way of looking at the Commander whenever they met; it was a look of knowing complicity, as though they had both shared a lurid run ashore the night before. If the Commander had seen the least sign of that familiarity in Stiggins' face he would have placed him under close arrest for insolence.

But when the Commander was descending the ladder, and was very nearly out of earshot, he overheard Stiggins addressing the boats shipwright.

'Sorry about that, Chippy. I'm afraid you'll have to take your jacket off for this one.'

Leading Seaman Drover gave a shout of laughter. The Commander stopped short, struck by the fierce lightning of his rage. It was some moments before he could collect himself sufficiently to continue down the ladder.

When the ship had cleared the harbour and special sea dutymen had fallen out, the Commander was able to return to the problem

303

of Stiggins. It was clear now that the problem must be quickly resolved. The Commander admitted that he disliked Stiggins, but nevertheless he had always tried to avoid giving the appearance of having either scapegoats or favourites in the wardroom; he knew that there was no more destructive influence in a ship than a common belief that certain officers could do nothing right in the Commander's eyes, while others could do not wrong. But wherever he turned, he seemed to encounter Stiggins, and each new encounter was more public and more humiliating than the last. After the latest incident on the boat-deck, nothing would convince the Air Group that Stiggins was not the Commander's *bête noire*.

The problem continued to oppress the Commander while he dealt with his correspondence and his visitors, and saw his request-men and defaulters. At stand-easy, the Commander made up his mind that he must see Rupert Smith at once.

Rowley Dubonnet was in the ACR, surrounded by the customary circle of clients for his attention. He had his feet up on the table and was speaking on the telephone.

'How can I convince you, you stupid sailors? I *have* convinced you? Well then, on with it, chop chop. No hurry, any time in the next thirty seconds will do.'

Seeing the Commander, Rowley put down the telephone and swung his legs off the table. 'Good morning, sir.'

'Morning, Rowley. Any chance of finding out where Rupert Smith is right now?'

Rowley looked up at the figures chalked on the blackboard above his head. 'Rupert's up at the moment with his Heavy Foot. They're doing a simulated rocket attack. They should be back on deck in . . .' Rowley glanced at his wrist-watch. '. . . Quarter of an hour, or so, sir? But the ADR can give it you exactly, sir.'

'Thank you, Rowley.'

The Air Direction Room, with the adjacent Operations Room and Radar Direction Room, was the lynch-pin of the ship's action information organisation. It was a dim, blue air-conditioned compartment, with a high cathedral-like roof and dark cloistral recesses in which a hundred tiny lights glowed yellow and ruby red and emerald green. The Direction Officer and his staff sat among a congregation of consoles and computers, calculating in seconds,

304

yards and fractions of a knot, weaving a continuous thread of solutions for an air traffic control problem which was, as the Direction Officer was fond of explaining to the wardroom, sometimes more complex than at London Airport. The Direction Officer himself sat before a lighted console on a raised dais. Beside him, a rating wearing headphones was methodically marking up coloured numbers and symbols on the silvery surface of a wide transparent screen, etched with a pattern of lines radiating from its centre. The assistant direction officers and the direction room crew sat in the centre of the room, in lines like an orchestra and surrounded by banks of radar displays on which the silver electronic beams swept ceaselessly round, imprinting on the orange faces ghostly silhouettes of the nearby coast-line. The room was quiet except for the humming of the air-conditioning fans and the muted crackle from the broadcast speaker tuned to the aircraft net.

A petulant voice from the speaker began to complain above the crackling static.

'Come closer to me, fellows, *please*. What's the matter, do I stink or something?'

Another voice answered grimly. '*Someone* isn't using it.'

Rupert Smith's voice burst into the chatter, using the flat, monotone delivery of R/T voice procedure.

'Foxtrot Three Foxtrot Three, this is Foxtrot Leader Foxtrot Leader. Our turn now. One run only. One . . . run . . . only. Standby. *Break!*'

The broadcast had the immediate clarity of an eye-witness description. Listening, the Commander was given a vivid mental picture of the jets wheeling over to stand on their wing-tips and drop down through the layers of the sky.

'. . . From where I'm sitting, Alfred, that was *not* good. Far too high. Yours would all have gone in the next county.'

'Sorry, sir.' Stiggins' voice was muffled and tearful. 'Cab feels a bit funny this morning.'

'Oh *balls* to that.' Rupert sounded irritable. 'It's not the cab, it's the fellow driving it.'

The Commander had come to convince Rupert that he did not think Stiggins such a bad officer in spite of appearances to the contrary. Perhaps Rupert himself might need some persuasion.

The assistant direction officer was giving Rupert a course to return to the ship. As Rupert acknowledged, the Direction Officer swivelled in his chair and raised his eyebrows at the Commander.

The Commander pointed at the broadcast speaker. 'That's what I wanted to know.'

The Direction Officer nodded, and held up his thumb. 'First one should be landing on eight and a half minutes from now.'

'Good. I'll hang around.'

Jerry Malone, wearing flying overalls and flight deck beret, was leaning on the rail of the Commander's favourite gallery. The whole Air Group knew of the Commander's fondness for the little gallery. For the sake of good public relations, they had tacitly agreed to reserve it for him. However, the Commander normally watched flying in the afternoons. Jerry Malone was taken aback to see him in the middle of the forenoon.

'I'm sorry, sir, I was just on my way.'

'Don't push off, for God's sake, Jerry.' The Commander was pleased and mildly flattered by the unspoken assumption that this was his special goofing position. 'You've got a damned sight more business up here than I have. I'm just a bloody fish-head, skulking when I should be working. What's happening?'

'Nothing much, sir. We're just waiting for Rupert and his Heavy Foot to come on.'

The Commander took off his cap and stepped out on to the gallery, feeling the steady flying wind blowing through his hair. The early morning rain had cleared. The cloud level was lifting and was beginning to break up into wide spaces of blue sky. A broad patch of sunlight gleamed on the sea a mile to port. The wind was slowly freshening; *Leviathan* had begun the day's flying at twenty knots but had now slowed down, the Commander estimated, to no more than twelve or thirteen.

He took a deep breath, and prepared to enjoy once more the spectacle of the flight deck, to watch its tiny, important figures, their dramatic gestures and their brightly-coloured toy vehicles. The flight deck markings and numerals had been repainted during the few days in harbour and now showed up startlingly white and yellow against their grey and olive-green field.

The sound of a jet engine travelled up the starboard side, Doppler effect changing its note as it passed behind the island.

The Command was always taken slightly off balance by the suddenness of the aircrafts' arrivals. In one moment, the sky was empty, and in the next, the first aircraft was already turning ahead of the ship, wheels and flaps down, into the landing circuit. It was very like shooting pigeon: no sooner had one looked carefully round and decided that it was safe to light a cigarette than the first pigeon was there, threshing and swooping over the decoys.

The leading aircraft passed through the patch of sunlight on the port beam and a bold flash sparkled along its fuselage. Soon the landing cycle was in progress, with its ebbing and flooding tide of movement and stillness, its crescendo and quiet, as the aircraft of Rupert's squadron darted in and came to rest, each one suddenly large and real and formidable, on the after end of the flight deck.

Jerry Malone watched Rupert's Heavy Foot's landings with a critical professional eye. He turned and shouted in the Commander's ear.

'Here's someone flying along, fat, dumb, and happy!'

'What's that?'

Jerry Malone jerked his head to port, where one of the last of Rupert's squadron was on the downwind leg.

'Look mum, no wheels!'

'Good God yes!'

The aircraft was flying steadily enough, flaps lowered, at a height and speed possible for landing, but its undercarriage was still retracted.

'What happens now?'

Jerry Malone measured the distance to the approaching aircraft by eye. 'Almost too late to do much now. He's balled up his cockpit check. The ADR will remind him. He'll go round again, I expect.'

The pilot seemed unconscious of his omission and maintained his final approach bearing, clearly intending to land on. Two red warning rockets flared up from the port side of the flight deck and the aircraft lifted, half-rolled, and climbed in an awkward, clumsy turn away from the ship. It was an ungainly piece of flying, carried out as though the highly-trained co-ordination of the pilot's hand and eye and foot had been unbalanced.

Jerry Malone stared up at the retreating aircraft, shielding his

307

eyes with one hand. 'Of all the stupid, switched-off, clumsy bastards! He's acting like a learner-driver.'

The Commander caught the note of apology in Jerry Malone's voice. Jerry was attempting to excuse this profanity of the mysteries of a pilot's art.

The two remaining aircraft of Rupert's squadron landed on, almost unnoticed; the attention of *Leviathan*'s flight deck was directed past them at the inexplicable behaviour of the maverick aircraft, which was approaching the ship for the second time.

On his second pass, the pilot evidently had no intention of making a landing. The aircraft flew high and slow over the flight deck and the puzzled upturned faces clustered on it, as though inspecting an unfamiliar and possibly hostile landing strip.

The Commander admitted his ignorance of the finer points of flying techniques, but this exhibition baffled him.

'What do you think's the matter, Jerry?'

'No idea, sir. It could be he's frozen up.'

'Frozen up?'

'Sometimes a bloke just seizes up with fright, sir.' Jerry Malone was tired of shouting and he leaned back into the gallery doorway, to shelter his voice from the wind. 'It doesn't often happen with a fellow who's got this far, but it can happen. He can't face the thought of another deck landing. But he can't think what else to do. So he just flies on and on, waiting for something to turn up. Sometimes he snaps out of it. Sometimes he gets so shit scared he just ejects. And sometimes he manages to drive himself on all right. It's like those rock climbers, sir. They get themselves into such a state they can't go up or down.'

'What can the ship do about it?'

'Nothing at all. You can't physically stop him landing on, that's the trouble. If he's gonna go, he's gonna go, and there ain't nothin' you can do to stop him.' Jerry Malone scratched his cheek. 'Though I'll bet the ADR are having a bloody good try, right now.'

The Commander could imagine it. A great jagged hole had been torn in the Direction Officer's careful web. His neat vectors and courses to fly were useless. By now, he would have abandoned his electronic orchestra. He would be trying to regain control of the pilot by voice.

'What would you do now, Jerry?'

'If I was the pilot, you mean, or if I was in the ADR?'

The Commander grinned briefly. 'If you were in the ADR.'

'Only thing now would be to tell him to divert ashore some-where. But he probably hasn't got enough juice left for that now. There's obviously something very wrong indeed. If he's really froze, you won't get a word of sense out of him. He won't even hear you. But we'll see this time. He may be all right.' Jerry Malone looked astern, judging the angle and rate of the air-craft's next approach. 'Though it don't look good to me. If he tries to land on at that speed, he's a dead duck.'

The third pass was lower, and almost twice as fast. The air-craft approached from dead astern, heading straight and true for the centre-line of the flight deck. Enoch climbed on to his platform and, while the aircraft was still more than a mile away, began to make slow overhead passes with his flags. His movements were unmistakable gestures of rejection; a newcomer to the flight deck could not have misunderstood their meaning.

The aircraft maintained its course as though the pilot had steeled himself to fly it and would not be diverted. Enoch continued to wave off until the aircraft was within a hundred yards. Two more rockets soared upwards. Enoch dived for his life into the safety net, while the aircraft drove low over him, sliced through the rocket trails, and fled screaming and rocking a few feet above the flight deck, the blast of its jet exhaust reverberating against the island.

'Jesus wept!'

Jerry Malone and the Commander had both flattened them-selves against the bulkhead when the aircraft passed them.

'He must have gone off his nut! That foot was hard down on the loud pedal the whole way! He couldn't have been far off his max at sea level! I'd watch out next time around, sir. He might do anything. I wonder who it is?'

Jerry Malone leaned over the rail and shouted to someone stand-ing outside the ACR door. The Commander could not hear the reply.

'It's your friend, sir. Alfred Stiggins.'

'What the devil do you mean, *my* friend?'

Jerry Malone dropped his eyes. 'I'm sorry, sir.'

'But what the devil did you mean, *my* friend? Sub-Lieutenant Stiggins is just the same to me as any other officer in this ship!'

'I'm very sorry, sir. I apologise.'

'I don't accept that . . .'

'Just a moment, sir.' Jerry Malone was looking over the Commander's shoulder. 'I don't think we can stay here much longer . . .'

Enoch had climbed back, and was standing on his platform, his hands on his hips. There was no evidence of his normal indignant acrobatics. He raised one hand towards Flyco, with the thumb turned down, and set off at a run towards the island.

'Stay there, Enoch!'

The Flyco broadcast boomed across the flight deck. Enoch returned, obviously reluctant, to his platform.

'Rig crash barrier! Clear the flight deck and all exposed island positions! Take cover! Take cover!'

The Commander gripped the gallery rail, his eyes following the flight of Stiggins' aircraft down the port side. He hardly noticed the fleeing men on the flight deck below him, or the crash barrier swinging up into place, or Jerry Malone's fingers tugging at his sleeve. He heard the repeated warning broadcasts from Flyco but he could not connect them with any action on his own part.

Once more, Enoch waved off and jumped for his life. Again the two red warning rockets soared when the aircraft crossed the round-down.

The aircraft jinked like a snipe, showed its pale underbelly for a moment and then, almost quicker than the eye could follow, banked and flashed into the island.

The impact knocked the Commander backwards and downwards, buckling his left leg under his body. The aircraft's port wing swung over his head and sliced down at the base of the small gallery, tearing half of it from its supports. The Commander's hands were wrung by the shock of the aircraft's impact, transmitted through the gallery rails. He felt a fine liquid mist settling on his face and he heard the rumbling explosion of the flame-ball expanding and overtaking the still fleeing sections of the disintegrating aircraft. The shattered wing dropped away and uncovered a billowing column of smoke which blotted out the island, enveloping the Commander and filling his nostrils with the very odour of death.

The ship turned, and the smoke rolled away waist-high across the flight-deck. The two men in steel helmets and fire-proof suits

310

were marching deliberately towards the cockpit, stiff-kneed, stepping over the debris. The fire-fighting parties had surrounded the aircraft in a ring, some of them kneeling, aiming their hoses at the fire. The foam jets gathered and converged and spattered down on the cockpit. Beyond, more men were running towards the fire, unreeling hoses as they came.

The axes flashed in the air. The sound of each blow was sharp and clear above the consuming roar of the fire. The helmeted men methodically smashed the cockpit canopy and together wrenched back the framework. They had their hands on the body, which was hunched forward with its head resting on the instrument panel, when Hamish McGeogh's shout held them back. Hamish's beret and blue battledress blouse were stained with gouts of foam. He and one of the helmeted men pulled the body upright.

The face under the flying helmet was blackened, except for light patches under the eye-sockets which had been shielded from the fire blast. The skin was heat-shrivelled, and drawn taut around the mouth and nostrils. The tongue was a bright purple where it protruded between the clenched teeth. As they lifted the body from the cockpit, supporting its head in their hands, pieces of charred parachute straps and fragments of the flying overalls were whisked away by the wind.

The Commander lay back and stared upwards at the sky. He could hear the shouts, hoses sluicing, flight-deck vehicles starting, the clanging of parts of the aircraft being kicked and trodden underfoot, and the sound of the wind in the signal halyards and radar aerials high above him. It was all far away, like the confusion of a distant battlefield.

'Commander, sir?'

The Commander sat up. He felt slime on his hand and looking down, saw that he had vomited into his lap.

'Commander, sir, are you all right?'

The gallery had been smashed downwards, so far that he had to lean back again before he could see Jerry Malone, standing in the doorway above. The guard-rails which had been to his right had gone. The gallery was canted at an angle and it gave way, slowly springing back again, whenever he moved.

'Are you all *right*, sir?'

The Commander turned over and crouched on all fours. Jerry

Malone grasped him around the waist and manhandled him up into the passageway.

'Sir, you look in a bit of a mess!'

The Commander shook his head and at once lost his balance, falling against the passage bulkhead. He levered himself upright again with one hand.

'No, I'm quite all right, Jerry. Not a scratch. My left leg's a bit numb . . .'

The passageway was unusually dark. Water was flowing along the deck and spilling out through the gallery doorway. There was still so much noise from outside on the flight deck. Figures were passing to and fro at the end where the passageway was brighter, flashing across the opening so quickly the Commander could not recognise them. He looked out of the doorway at the flight deck. Far below, one of the fire-fighting party was attacking the scummy lake of foam, breaking it up by playing his hose in criss-cross patterns in front of him as he advanced. On the other side of the aircraft they were brushing the foam away and hosing it down the flight deck scuppers. Jumbo, the largest flight deck crane, had been brought up and two men were rigging a wire strop under the aircraft's fuselage. Another small party were handling the severed port wing and, as the Commander watched them, it turned over and fell with a mild, tinny sound. The Commander felt his mouth flooding with saliva.

'Excuse me.'

The Commander swung away from Jerry Malone. He ran from the gallery door, stumbling down the ladders, staggering from side to side along the passageways, bullocking his way past the puzzled crowds of oncoming sailors, along the whole length of the upper deck, through the looming doorways one by one, to the quietness of his sleeping cabin where he leaned over the basin and was sick again.

The Commander stayed until he was sure he was not about to vomit yet again. He stripped off his uniform and sat on the bed. The numbness in his leg had spread to the rest of his body. His ears still rang with the thunder of the aircraft's impact. His nostrils were still full of the smell of the fire.

After some time, he heard a knock at the day-cabin door.

'Who's that? What do you want?'

'It's the PMO, Bob. I was told you were a bit too close to that one for comfort. I thought I'd come and have a look at you.'

'I'm as fit as a flea, Angus, really I am. My hands are still stinging a bit, and my leg was a bit numb, but I'm actually as fit as a flea. No doubt about that at all . . .'

The Commander stopped. In the silence, he knew that he had been babbling.

'Who told you about me being there?'

'Wings. They saw you from Flyco. You were up on some gallery. When they couldn't see you afterwards they began to look for you on the flight deck. Wings thought you'd been hit by that aircraft.'

'Oh Lord.'

'Let's see that leg. Can you move it?'

'Oh yes.' The Commander stretched out his left leg and swung it from the knee. 'What about Stiggins?'

'He's dead. He broke his neck. You don't feel any pain when you do that?' The PMO grasped the Commander's ankle and yanked it sideways. 'Does that hurt?'

'Not very much.'

'Good. You'll have a fine bruise on your leg tomorrow. Can you stand up?'

'Of course.' The Commander stood up, and his calves and thighs began to tremble uncontrollably. He looked down at himself helplessly, and sat back on the bed. The PMO noted the Commander's shivering, and the pallor of his face.

'Yes.' The PMO stroked his chin. He would have liked to have known more about the accident. The Commander's antipathy to the Air Group was well known; it was ironic they should be responsible for so nearly killing him.

'I want you to stay in your bunk for the rest of today, Bob, and keep yourself warm and well wrapped up . . .'

'But I can't do that! I'm perfectly well and there's a hell of a lot to be done after that thing just now . . .'

'There's nothing you need do personally. You may feel well enough now, or you say you do, but you might not in a couple of hours. There is such a thing as delayed shock . . .'

'But Angus, there is absolutely nothing *wrong* with me . . .'

'You take this.' The PMO filled a tooth-glass with water. 'It'll help you sleep.'

313

The Commander examined the long celluloid capsule in his palm. 'What a bloody enormous pill. It looks big enough to knock out an elephant.'

'It'll stop you thinking about the accident. People tend to do that, instead of going to sleep.'

The Commander swallowed the pill, drank some water, and lay back on his bunk. The PMO pulled the blankets over him and switched off the light.

The Commander remembered the appalling speed of that aircraft and its thunderous impact. It had not been one sound, but an organ range of successive sounds. He felt himself falling backwards and downwards again, into that abyss of apocalyptic smoke and flame. It was like the coming of doomsday. For a time, as he lay upon that gallery, the Commander had thought himself a dead man. He would not have believed that one of those beautiful machines could generate such violence.

When he awoke, his cabin was darker, but still smelled faintly of vomit and charred cloth. The ship was stopped. Small waves slapped against the ship's sides and sea-gulls cried, with sudden threshings of their wings, as they alighted on the water below his cabin scuttle. He heard a movement in the outer cabin.

'Mulligan? Is that Mulligan?'

'Yes, sir?' His steward stood in the doorway.

'What time is it?'

'Just after nine o'clock, sir.'

'In the evening?'

'Yes, sir.'

'Is it still the same day?'

Mulligan grinned. 'Yes, sir, it's still the same day.'

'Where are we then?'

'Spithead, sir. We're going up harbour tomorrow morning, sir.'

'Good God.' The Commander swung his legs out of the blankets, furious that decisions had been taken, the ship's programme altered, while he had been lying drugged in his bed. His head felt leaden, and his mouth tasted raw and bitter. He tried his left leg; it was stiff and sore, but could bear his weight. His uniform jacket, with a smeared stain down one side, was hanging by the wardrobe.

'Just seeing what I could do about your uniform, sir. It's in a

314

shocking state, sir.'

'Never mind about that now, Mulligan. Can you get me something to eat?'

'Dinner's over now, sir, but I can get some coffee and wedges, sir.'

'You do that, Mulligan. I'm ravenous.'

As Mulligan left the cabin, Commander (Air) came in, holding up the Commander's cap.

'Brought you back your tit-fer-tat, Bob. Somebody found it on the flight deck.'

The cap was battered and trodden. The peak was crumpled and the cover stained with oil and foam.

'How do you feel now?'

'I feel like that cap. Quite honestly, Wings, I feel a bloody fool.'

Commander (Air) was disarmed by such candour. Bob Markready was too strong, too confident, and had subordinated Air Group interests to the ship too often for Commander (Air) to like him; he had also jeopardised his own life and Commander (Air)'s career by carelessly involving himself in a flight deck accident. But still, he was mollified by the Commander's admission.

'Little F and I nearly had a heart attack when we saw you still up there on that catwalk.'

'I'd no business to be up there.'

'Why *were* you up there, Bob? Didn't you hear the pipes to clear all goofing positions? We actually addressed you personally, by *name!*'

'I know, I heard 'em all right. But I couldn't seem to connect them with me. I couldn't take my eyes off that damned aircraft. I just stood there, absolutely hypnotised. Even when I saw it heading right towards me I still couldn't move a muscle.'

'Well, there was hardly time to do much then.'

'No. But what a mess, Wings. That sight. That poor bloody pilot. I'll never forget it. It's going to haunt me.'

'I've seen worse than that, much worse.' Commander (Air)'s voice held an undertone of triumph: perhaps this would teach Bob Markready that flying from a carrier was not just a circus show to while away idle hours in the afternoons. 'You're lucky he hardly had any fuel left. If he'd been topped up, you'd have

315

been roasted up there, like a little chicken on a little spit.'

Mulligan came in with a plate of sandwiches and a pot of coffee.

'God, that was quick, Mulligan!'

'I had 'em ready in the captain's pantry, sir, in case you woke up.'

'That reminds me, Bob. I think the Boss wants to see you.'

'I'm sure he does. Mulligan, while I have a bath, get me out a clean shirt and my mess jacket, will you?'

'Will you be wearing mess undress *tonight*, sir?'

'Of course. What the devil else should I be wearing?'

'Aye aye, sir.'

'Can I try one of your wedges, Bob?'

'Only one. I'm starving.'

Commander (Air) picked up a sandwich, and opened it. 'Roast chicken. Very appropriate, Mulligan. By the way, if the Captain asks you about the island, tell him things are more or less back to normal now.'

'What about the island?'

'I keep forgetting, you missed it. Luckily, there's not as much structural damage as there might have been but the bulkhead where he hit had two fuse-boxes and a main junction box on it, plus the rising main pipe for the island firemain supply. So most of the lights went out, and half the island was flooded with water. It was quite a carnival for a time. When you've finished in the cuddy, Bob, come down to the ante-room. I reckon the Air Group owe you a drink.'

'I don't know about that. I reckon I should buy you one.'

The Commander approached the cuddy feeling like a man who has overslept and missed his ship. *Leviathan* had been damaged and signals had been sent, repairs organised, the ship's programme altered and a score of decisions taken, every one of them of concern to the Commander, while he had been sleeping in his cabin. He regretted that he had ever given in to the PMO; he should have abided by his original decision and stayed on his feet.

The Captain was sitting at his desk, wearing his dressing-gown over his uniform.

'Come in, Bob. I was just writing to that lad's parents. Are you fit now? Wings tells me we near as dammit lost our Commander this morning.'

316

'I must apologise for being in the wrong place at the wrong time, sir.'

'Not to worry.' Tosser's face reflected a somewhat malicious humour; it was not often he caught his very *parfait* Executive Officer at a disadvantage. 'How are you feeling now?'

'Quite all right, sir. There was never very much wrong with me. It was all the PMO's idea.'

'Well, now that you're back, do you know what's happening?'

'Only partly, sir.'

'The dockyard wizards came on board when we anchored this evening. They say they can repair the island in a fortnight. It won't be a hundred per cent job, but it'll do until our next refit. So we're going up harbour at six o'clock tomorrow morning. In a way, we're lucky it hit just where it did. A little higher and a little further forrard and he'd have gone straight into the ADR, . and then we *would* have been buggered. Quite apart, of course . . .' the Captain looked up '. . . from losing our Commander.'

The Commander reddened. 'Yes, sir.'

'Anyway, let's have a drink now, and forget all about it.'

'I wonder if you'd excuse me, sir? I haven't been back down to the wardroom yet. I want to get my finger back on the pulse.'

The Captain nodded. He knew from his own experience how important it was for a Commander constantly to gauge the temper of the wardroom. Bob had been out of circulation for nearly twelve hours. It was a long hiatus after a fatal accident on the flight deck.

On his way down to the ante-room, the Commander decided that he must now reconstruct his relationship with the Air Group. The accident that day had made all his previous attitudes obsolete. He had never dreamed they lived in the shadow of such violence. He had noticed, and rather resented, the special respect and consideration the ship's company paid to the aircrew; he now understood that this was the proper respect due from the men who were safe to the men who stood in danger.

The Commander was aware of the change in the atmosphere of the ante-room as soon as he set foot in it. Some current of opinion had swept through the wardroom in his absence, and he could detect its aftermath. On his way towards the bar, he felt as though he was trudging through the ashes of some recent conflagration and it was a sign of his estrangement from wardroom opinion that he could not guess what it was.

There was so little sound that at first he thought the ante-room was empty and wondered whether all-night leave had been granted: that, too, was one of his decisions, which must have been taken by someone else.

Commander (Air) and several other officers were standing by the bar. There was a large group of aircrew officers in the annex by the piano. The Commander was puzzled by their presence, until he remembered 'Cock Robin'. Perhaps they had only just finished singing.

But, as though the Commander's entrance had been their cue, the pilots began to sing.

'All the birds of the air fell a-sighing and a-sobbing
When they heard of the death of poor Cock Robin.
When they heard of the *death* of poor Cock *Robin*.'

Chuck Beasley, standing next to the piano, took up the first verse so strongly as to drown out any alternative words.

'*Who* killed Cock Robin?'
'I' said the Commander,
With my little *slander*,
I killed Cock Robin . . .'

20

The pilots' voices faltered, suddenly conscience-stricken, and died away, appalled by the enormity of the words. Only Chuck Beasley continued to sing a few bars of the chorus alone, before he too was silent.

The other officers present held their breath, as though waiting for a storm to break, for the Commander to burst in amongst the singers, and scatter them and dismiss them, ordering them to report to him, with their squadron commanding officers, in the morning.

The Commander would have done as they expected, if he had been himself. Instead, he chose the weakest and most uncharacteristic course. He turned his back on the singers and brushing past someone who had put out a hand to detain him, he left the ante-room and fled back to his cabin.

The Commander had always feared *Leviathan*'s special power to hurt him. The great ship reserved for every man on board that personal form of failure which would wound him most deeply. The Commander, and his little slander, had killed Cock Robin; for the Commander those words were the very libretto of failure. The after-effects of the accident and the sedation, the shock of those words, and the first awareness that success in *Leviathan* was not his to command after all, utterly crushed him. The Commander sat down at his desk, laid his head on his arms, and began to weep as he had not wept since he was a small boy.

'Bob! *Bob!*'

The Commander heard the Secretary's voice and felt his hand on his shoulder. He lifted his head, but he could not turn round and reveal his weakness.

'Were you there, Scratch?'

'Yes, I was.' The Secretary's voice was tight with rage. 'And I've never heard anything like it in all my life!'

'What a . . . What a terrible thing to say . . .'

'I've *never* heard anything like it! I could hardly believe my ears!'

'They must have meant it, Scratch.'

'Never you mind whether they meant it or not, Bob. I'm just going round now to get a few people together. We're going to find that young yobbo and then we're going to break his guitar over his head. By the time we've finished with him, it'll be many a long day before he sings funny songs again . . .'

'Scratch, I forbid you, do you hear me?'

The Commander braced his hands against the edge of his desk and forced himself upwards. His eyes were prickling, as his tears dried. He was once more in control of himself and despising his own weakness.

'I positively forbid you, do you understand? If you do that, we're heading for a repetition of last commission and I'm *not* having that! It's not that important.'

'But this *is* important, Bob. You cannot just leave it as it is. You've got to do something.'

But the Secretary was already having second thoughts. These wardroom scenes appealed to the social historian in him; he took an anthropologist's interest in the oddities of his fellow officers. Sometimes, at the end of *Leviathan*'s previous commission, he had whimsically compared himself to Macaulay's traveller from New Zealand, standing alone on the broken arch of the wardroom, surveying the ruined careers of its members. But he had taken a risk by staying in *Leviathan*. His own career might not survive another such sequence of events.

'All right, Bob. I won't do anything myself. But *you* certainly ought to. You can't let it drop. You can't let them get away with something like this, Bob. It's bloody nearly *anarchy*. My advice to you is to send for Rupert Smith and that young hoodlum of his right *now* . . .'

'There's no need for that.'

Commander (Air) was standing in the cabin doorway, with Rupert Smith behind him. They were both breathing hard, as though they had been running. Commander (Air) was looking at the Commander from under lowered eyebrows, with a curiously baffled hostility.

'We've just seen the Captain, Bob. There's a boat going ashore in half an hour. Beasley will be on it. He's packing his gear now.'

The Commander was bewildered by their sudden appearance.

'But how can you do that? Just send him ashore like that?'

'We can do anything we like. After what happened in the ante-room just now we don't want him in any of our squadrons and we'll make quite sure nobody else does either. We'll see to that. It's fixed. All I can do now is apologise on behalf of the...'

'*You* apologise!' The Secretary's voice was shrill and venomous. 'How *dare* you apologise! You knew what those louts of yours were going to do. You *must* have known, yet you didn't raise a finger to stop them. And now you come trying to crawl out of it...'

'*That,* is the most stupid and slanderous statement I've ever heard, even from you, Scratch.'

'Even from me?' The Secretary checked himself, drawing back like a man who sees an ugly piece of excrement in his way. He had known instinctively for a long time that he and Commander (Air) disliked each other, without ever putting their dislike to the proof; they had muffled their social contacts in a common daily round of politeness. Now, politeness would serve no longer.

'Are you honestly trying to tell me those ill-mannered louts down there would have done that if they hadn't thought you were at least half behind them? It's inconceivable! You talk as though sending one pilot ashore solved the whole thing. There were *dozens* of them there! The whole blasted Air Group have some-how got the idea in their heads that Bob Markready here was in some mysterious way responsible for that pilot's death today. That idea can only have come from you. Now the whole thing's blown up in your face and you're trying to squeeze out of it. Please sir, no sir, nothing to do with me sir, but I'll do what I can sir. It's a load of bloody rubbish and you know it! Well, you're not getting away with it. Packing his bags *indeed*. The only person who should be packing his bags is *you!*'

Commander (Air) was numbed by the assault. He too had known that the Captain's Secretary was not a friend. But he had never guessed he was such an enemy. The Secretary was junior to him in the Navy List, but he was the kind of officer who carried in-fluential wardroom opinion with him, and he had the ear of the Captain. He had friends outside the ship and he was not an enemy Commander (Air) could afford. The Secretary and the Commander had the benefit of the same background, a common strength Com-mander (Air) himself lacked. Commander (Air) had only reached his present position by avoiding such enemies. He stretched out his hands in an appealing, conciliatory gesture.

'I'm sorry you should think that way, Scratch, but I do assure you . . .'

'And don't call me *Scratch!*' Knowing he had Commander (Air) beat, the Secretary felt his anger changing to contempt; it only remained to press the victory home. 'That's a name my *friends* use.'

'I hardly think this is the way for officers to talk to each other . . .'

'I'm talking to you in the only way you and your sort understand. You and your aircrew have done nothing but behave like a herd of pigs at a feeding trough ever since you came on board. You're not officers, you don't even pretend to behave like officers. You're just a lot of jumped-up Secondary Modern schoolboys in second-hand sailor suits!'

It could only be a matter of moments before they came to blows. Awaking from his brief and unusual role of victim, the Commander sprang from his chair.

'That's enough! No more of that.' He brought his clenched fists down, chopping the air between the two contestants. 'I don't want to hear any more about this, *ever again*. I suggest you both go to bed and forget about it. I don't want *any* more discussion, do you hear me?'

The Captain's Secretary and Commander (Air) separated, and retreated from each other, the Secretary wearing the fulfilled expression of a man who had purged himself of a long-standing complaint, while Commander (Air) looked as though he had stumbled into a mine-field. The Commander was left alone, to shoulder the real burden of failure. The incident in the ante-room had been trivial compared with its aftermath, here in his cabin. The Secretary had been unjust: Wings could surely not be held accountable for all his pilots' actions. The Commander suspected that the Secretary had made use of the occasion to discharge a private ill-feeling. But the cause of the quarrel was unimportant: that they had quarrelled at all, and so bitterly, was enough. The Commander had truly believed that *Leviathan*'s officers were evolving a common interest in their ship which transcended departmental loyalties; he had seen the welcome signs in the be-

322

haviour of small wardroom committees, in conversations with individual officers, and in a wardroom atmosphere more cheerful and volatile than any the ship had ever known. But at the first pressure, all the Commander's small triumphs were demolished; *Leviathan*'s wardroom were apparently still as ready to split into incompatible factions as it had ever been.

The Captain did not know of the quarrel nor, when he went to see him, did the Commander consider telling him. To the Captain, Commander (Air)'s visit with Rupert Smith had come as a thunderclap from a clear sky.

'I wasn't aware there was this sort of feeling in the wardroom, Bob?'

'Neither was I, sir.' The Commander recognised the admission of his failure; it was his business to know what the wardroom were thinking. Again he despised himself for having given way to the PMO. 'I'm sure this is an isolated incident, sir. There was a lot of tension in the mess this evening. I suppose it's understandable after a fatal accident. Not that I'm condoning what happened for a minute, sir.'

'I have to ask you this, Bob.' Tosser looked uncomfortable. 'I suppose there *is* nothing in it? You didn't give the impression you were after that pilot, did you? Even unknowingly? I have to ask you this, you know.'

'Sir, I can assure you Stiggins was no more and no less to me than any other pilot.' The Commander was able to answer with sincerity. 'Though I will admit . . .'

'Yes? Admit what?'

'I did seem to come across this particular pilot always just when he seemed to be making an idiot of himself. But there was nothing personal in it. I barely knew him personally.'

'Well, I suppose there's bound to be frictions in a wardroom the size of yours.' Tosser spoke anxiously. He also had felt the shadow of implication pass over him. In his experience, incidents like this never happened out of the blue; the warning signs were always there beforehand. 'In all my time in the Service, I've never heard of anything like it. I hope everyone will learn the lesson.'

The swiftness and savagery of Chuck Beasley's punishment discouraged any wardroom gossip. Intriguing though the circumstances of his dismissal had been, the officers dared not discuss

323

them in public, for fear of attracting some of the lightning upon themselves. Beasley was a short-service commission officer who would in any case be leaving the Service in three years' time. The consequences were perhaps not as serious for him as for a General List officer. But if Beasley had ever had hopes of transferring to a permanent commission, or of leaving the Navy with a favourable recommendation to take with him into civilian life, he could now abandon them. The Fleet Air Arm grape-vine would see to it that his history followed him. The wardroom knew that Chuck Beasley would pay the penalty for that verse of Cock Robin for many years to come. Meanwhile, until the board of inquiry was convened, there was an unnatural friendliness between the ship and the Air Group. Both sides of the wardroom exerted themselves to be cordial. As the First Lieutenant said, 'There's nothing like an execution for encouraging the others.'

The Commander himself was occupied by his own guilt in the affair. Since that verse of Cock Robin, the Air Group had been behaving towards him with an unusual and irritating gentleness. He felt he should make some gesture of goodwill to the Air Group. He could, for instance, offer Commander (Air) his services as a witness.

'After all, you could hardly get a closer eye-witness than I was, could you?'

'We can't put you up as a witness, Bob.'

'Why not? I was bloody nearly *in* the accident!'

'Precisely. If you gave evidence we'd have to explain what the hell you were doing standing up there, wouldn't we?'

'Ah yes. I see.'

So there were to be even further consequences of Stiggins' death. Commander (Air) had been given a powerful lever to the Commander's discredit and he would not hesitate to use it. Wings had not, and never would, forgive him for having been a party to that disgraceful quarrel with the Captain's Secretary.

On the morning when the board of inquiry assembled in *Leviathan,* the Commander's first visitor after breakfast was Rupert Smith.

Rupert entered the Commander's cabin warily, like a man unsure of his welcome. He and the Commander had been good friends until the night after Stiggins' death. Since then, they had barely exchanged a word.

'If I could have your advice on something, please, sir?'

The Commander looked at him coldly. 'Yes?'

'I've been trying to decide what to do for days. I've reached the stage where I really must have somebody else's opinion.'

The Commander put down his pen, and relaxed. If he wanted to make some gesture to the Air Group, then here was his opportunity. Rupert was clearly perplexed and in trouble.

'Bring up a chair, Rupert. If I can help you, I'll be very glad to. But if it's anything to do with flying or the Air Group ...' He waved his hands in a general disclaimer. 'You've come to the wrong bloke.'

'Well, it is about my squadron, sir, but I don't think it's something we can decide all by ourselves.' Rupert pulled his wallet from his jacket pocket and took out a letter. 'It's this, sir. I'd like you to read it. I found it in Stiggins' effects the other day.'

'*Stiggins* again!' The Commander was unable to keep the exasperation from his voice; he was becoming neurotic about the name. 'Should *I* be reading this?'

'I think you ought to, sir.'

The letter was written on both sides of two sheets of blue writing paper. The first page had the ship's crest and a motto embossed at the head.

' "My Darling Charmian". Who's Charmian?'

Rupert sighed. 'The blonde bit you found him busy rodgering on the night of the Ball, sir.'

'Oh God. Do I really have to read this?'

'Yes please, sir.'

The Commander began to read, under protest, but soon sat up straight and read the letter with growing amazement. On paper, Stiggins revealed a fluency and a talent for self-expression which the Commander had never suspected in him. Nothing in his letter conformed to the image of himself which Stiggins had presented to the world. The phrases, written in a clear mature hand, illuminated a personality both tender and thoughtful. The letter was an outpouring of love and hope and doubt from a young man haunted, as the Commander himself was haunted, by the spectres of failure. The letter referred constantly to the night of the

325

Summer Ball and the Commander realised with shame that his intrusion had almost wrecked their love affair. There were two separate references to himself, and his shame deepened. He was mortified to learn that under that self-confident and cheeky exterior, Stiggins had been afraid of him.

'It's the next to last paragraph that's vital, sir.'

'I see. "Sometimes I seriously wonder if I can do it all. We're going to sea again tomorrow and I know it's going to be another terrible day. Have you ever had that feeling where you're trying as hard as you can, and you know everyone else is trying to help you, and it's still no good? I wake up very early on mornings before flying and I lie awake and I wonder whether just once it's going to be all right. But it never is. Things are really getting on top of me. I feel like that fellow Atlas, bending lower and lower and lower under a great weight which gets heavier all the time. Things are going a bit better in this ship, but not for me. Everybody else is leaping ahead, except me. I'm sure you would know what to do. It's a great comfort to me to be able to think, whatever happens, 'Never mind, there's always Charmian'. (I hope I *can* still say that, after what happened.) I wonder if it wouldn't be best just to make an end to it all. I sometimes do think like that, you know . . ." '

'*Now* then.' The Commander laid the letter on his desk, and carefully read the paragraph again. 'I see what you're getting at. You think he might have done it on purpose?'

'That letter doesn't prove anything, sir.'

'No, but it does suggest it.'

'Looking at it selfishly, sir, in a roundabout sort of way it wouldn't be a bad solution for the squadron and myself . . .'

'Why?'

'Because I'm damned certain this board of inquiry are going to ask us some pretty awkward questions about his previous flying performance. If we don't play our cards just right they may even suggest we were at fault for not sending him ashore long ago.'

'For incompetence?'

'He won't be much loss to the squadron and that's a fact, sir. He was making very little progress, in fact he was probably slipping back a bit. But I kept on hoping, you know how it is.'

'Yes, I know just what you mean.'

326

'In spite of that, he was quite a willing little fellow in his way, sir, and he was quite popular in the squadron, believe it or not. He was one of the few who actually volunteered to take more part in ship's activities and try and learn something about how the other half lives. But I wasn't thinking of the squadron, or of the ship generally. I was thinking of the effect on his parents. I don't know what sort of people they are, I've never met them, but some families regard suicide as almost worse than murder, sir. If this *was* suicide, of course.'

'Where do they live?'

'Oh, Staffordshire, somewhere. One of the pottery towns, I forget which one.'

The Commander caught Rupert's eye. They were both thinking of a grey West Midland town, a street of small terraced houses, and a man and his wife so proud of their son, who was a pilot in the Fleet Air Arm. The boy might well have been the first of their family to join the Navy as an officer. The suspicion that their son had so despaired of his life that he had ended it might crush them.

'On the other hand, sir, the letter is evidence and I suppose we ought to show it to the board because it does give some indication of his state of mind. Although he did say something while we were up, about his cab feeling funny. I didn't take much notice. He was always finding excuses. But that was much earlier. The board are going to be far more interested in those passes he made at the deck. I must say they were very, very strange indeed, as you know yourself, sir. And there's this girl. I suppose the letter is legally her property. It might mean a lot to her to get a last letter from him. You can see why I've been worried about this, sir.'

'How did you find the letter? Was it sealed?'

'No, it was in his writing case, with the envelope already addressed.'

'Has anyone else seen it?'

'I can't be sure, but I think not. I went up to his cabin almost immediately afterwards, to see if I could find his parents' address. Being Stiggins, of course his next-of-kin card wasn't properly filled in.'

'And now, what you really want to know is, what shall we do with this letter?'

327

Rupert nodded.

'Well, I can answer that one right away. Have you got the envelope with you?'

The Commander placed the large glass ashtray in the centre of his desk. He crumpled the letter and the envelope together, struck a match, and set light to the paper. He dropped the burning paper into the ashtray and poked the ashes with the matchstick, before tipping the pieces into his waste-paper basket.

'That's it.' He looked up, to catch an expression of mingled relief and guilt on Rupert Smith's face.

'I admit I'm very glad you did that, sir. I wouldn't have had the courage to do it myself.'

'We'll never know whether it was the right thing to do or not. All we can say is, it *seemed* the right thing to do *now*.'

Rupert Smith was both surprised and relieved that the Commander had burned the letter. Asking the Commander's advice had been an act of desperation and, knowing the Commander, Rupert had expected him to reinforce his own half-formed resolve to produce the letter as evidence. Ironically, he was not sure now whether burning the letter had increased or diminished the Commander's stature in his eyes.

'I know it's a bit late in the day, sir, but I really do apologise for what happened the other night. I honestly didn't know what they were going to do, and I'm sure Commander (Air) didn't either.'

'Never mind about that now, Rupert. I said I didn't want to hear any more about it and I meant what I said. The best of luck at the inquiry.'

The conversation of the wardroom at lunch-time was almost wholly on the subject of the board of inquiry. It was as though the presence of the official board had released private speculation. The Commander himself was anxious to know how the inquiry was progressing. Commander (Air) was standing alone at the bar, looking thoughtful and disgruntled.

'I take it from your expression the inquest is not going well, Wings?

Commander (Air) scowled. 'Not good. It'll be death by misadventure, or pilot error, or call it what you will. But there's a strong insinuation that we should have sacked Stiggins long ago.

They must think I'm psychic. How can we be expected to know when a madman is suddenly going to run amok on us?'

The Commander understood why Rupert had brought Stiggins' letter to him, instead of taking it to Commander (Air). Wings would have made no bones about it; he would have produced the letter as evidence. He might even have enlarged upon it, to absolve himself and his Air Group. It was now clear to the Commander how and why men like Aubrey McConnell operated. The board of inquiry were charged with the duty of investigating and reporting upon the circumstances of Stiggins' death but already two important pieces of evidence, his own presence at the scene of the accident, and Stiggins' letter, had been suppressed. He himself had connived at both omissions. It was no wonder that a man like Aubrey McConnell came round afterwards to establish the true facts. Looking at Wings' baffled and angry face, the Commander felt a twinge of remorse and having justified Rupert, he yearned for justification himself.

Annabel listened to the story, without interrupting. She was secretly delighted to hear of the letter: it showed that even Bob Markready was vulnerable to human impulses and misgivings.

'What a *good* thing to do, Bob. Of course it was dishonest, but it was just the right thing to do. Think of that poor boy's parents.'

He was disconcerted by her approval. 'I wouldn't say it was dishonest, Annabel. The letter didn't actually prove anything . . .'

'Bob, you know it was dishonest.'

'Yes, I suppose it was really. But I don't regret it.'

'And nor you should.'

Annabel was sitting on the long sofa, with her legs tucked underneath her. She was wearing a rig which he supposed could be termed '*après* ski': black trousers, an orange and black patterned sweater, sandals, and a bright orange band in her hair. He was sitting on the floor, with his legs stretched out towards the fire and his head resting against the arm of the sofa.

'If I was in that big ship, Bob, I think I'd be afraid of you.'

'Whatever for?'

'Anyone who annoys you seems to disappear into smoke. Just because they get in your way and won't do what you say.'

He straightened his back indignantly. 'Who's got in my way and won't do what I say?'

329

'This pilot, and that poor little sailor who jumped over the side...'

'That poor little sailor, as you call him, was a saboteur, a criminal. If I'd had my way with him he'd be locked up in jail right now. Jumping over the side was his own affair entirely.'

'Knowing that somebody like you was after him, stalking him, bound to catch him in the end? He must have been frightened to death.'

'Nonsense.'

'You're a frightening person, Bob. You don't see it yourself. You're always so right, and so upright. It's a pity Tom isn't in that ship with you. He'd have supported you, even if he didn't always agree with you. But some of those others I met.... You must tear through them like a great big tank covered in armour!'

He examined the analogy and supposed that, to an outsider, it must seem close to the truth. 'I only tear through them, as you put it, because they think of themselves all the time. I'm trying to make them see it's the Service and the ship that count, not the individual.'

'Nobody thinks that way nowadays.'

'I *know* it's not the way people think nowadays! But that's how they're damned well going to think as long as I'm in that ship!'

'There's no need to shout at me, Bob. I'm not on your quarter-deck.'

'I'm sorry, Annabel. But this is the one great point that's always cropping up. It may be my fault. I may have missed some vital turn in the Navy that's happened just recently. Something's happened in the last few years and I seem to be the only one who doesn't know what it is. I was brought up to believe that you got on with it and did what you were supposed to be doing without arguing and without second thoughts. Nowadays it seems to be more fashionable to keep looking over your shoulder to check whether your pay and allowances are still catching up with you. You say I'm a frightening person. That's not true. *They* frighten *me*.'

He paused, to consider what he had said. These introspective moods were new, and were becoming more frequent. The great ship was tempering him with melancholy. Six months ago, he had boarded the ship like young Lochinvar, but he had lost that first fine rapturous arrogance. Did nobody else feel the great ship pressing upon them, searching their hearts, probing their weaknesses? Did none of them realise that *Leviathan* was one test they must survive? Perhaps none of them did, and when there was no challenge, there could be no achievement.

'You're making it so hard for yourself, Bob. Why don't you just do your job, as you say, like everyone else?'

'I wish it was so cut and dried. I haven't told you what happened afterwards, after that boy was killed. They've got a stupid song they sing . . .'

'Cock Robin?'

'You know about it?'

'Of course I know about it.'

'Well, they waited. They waited, I'm telling you, until I got down into the wardroom and then they started to sing. I don't think I'll ever forget the words as long as I live. Who killed Cock Robin? I, said the Commander, with my little slander. I killed Cock Robin.'

'Bob, they didn't!' Annabel was horrified, by the words and by his anguished face. 'They couldn't have been so cruel!'

'They did. They could, and they did.'

She could see his face working, his teeth gritting, reliving the moment when he had heard them singing. It was grotesque. It was lawless. The naval officers she knew simply did not behave like that to each other. He must have hurt them, and they had struck back. They had stumbled on some flaw in him. He would run on in that ship, he might achieve the semblance of success, but she knew intuitively that the reward he looked for had already gone.

'Did you hate that pilot?'

'Did I hate that pilot.' As he repeated the words, he knew the truth. 'Yes, I think I did, and I think "hate" is the right word.'

He marvelled at his own candour. She could force him to hold up a mirror to himself. To dissemble in front of her was pointless, like cheating to capture a pawn, when he could honestly take the queen.

'And I think I hated that sailor who jumped over the side. They both . . . I don't know how to put it . . . They both threatened me. They were threatening something which meant a great deal to me.

331

In that way you could say that by hating him I was responsible for his death. But we were all responsible, every one of us. The ship was too much for him. And that's only half the story. It's all very well to say I killed him. He as near as dammit killed me.'

'How could he do that?'

'By hitting the island within a few feet of me! Another yard higher and I'd have been a dead duck. Ask for me tomorrow, as they say, and you'd have found me a grave man.'

She lightly ran her fingers down the side of his face. 'I'm glad he didn't hit you, Bob.'

'So am I, by God. But it gave me a good shaking up. And it also gave me a new outlook towards the aircrew. Funny they should sing that verse just when I was beginning to see their point of view.'

Annabel took her fingers away sharply. It was just impossible to divert his thoughts for long from that ship. She had been looking forward to the evening, after he telephoned, but he had come in with his nerves jangling, with all the stresses and tensions of that ship sparking and crackling from him like an electric current.

'Oh you and your silly arguments with each other! You're like a lot of schoolboys. You're not even as sensible as schoolboys. I don't know why you come here. You don't want sex, you don't even want someone to talk to. I think you just want someone to talk *at*. I thought you were lonely and I used to think at least I cheered you up a bit, but I don't even do that now. I'm always trying to make you see there's a whole world going on outside that damned ship and you never take any notice of me. You're all as selfish as each other. All you can think about it is yourself and that wretched ship . . .'

The telephone rang on the small table by the fireplace.

'Oh *blast* that thing!' She guessed that the call was for him, from that ship. 'You answer it. You're nearest.'

He picked up the receiver and recognised the First Lieutenant's voice.

'Commander, sir? Number One here, sorry to disturb you . . .'

'What do you mean, *disturb* me?'

'I'm sorry, sir, but we've just had a signal from the Admiralty asking us to reply with our earliest date for going to sea.'

'Does it mention the repairs to the island?'

332

'Yes, it says dockyard workmen must go to sea with us if necessary. The Captain's on board now, sir.'

'Right, I'll come back right away. By the way, how did you know I was here?'

The First Lieutenant's voice altered subtly. 'I just guessed, sir.'

'I see. Well, I'll be back in about ten minutes.'

He replaced the receiver, and assumed a passable Yorkshire accent.

'Ah'm sorry, lass, but there's trouble down at t'mill.'

'What sort of trouble?'

'It looks as if we've got to go to sea in a hurry.'

'But there's nothing very serious happening at the moment. Where will you go?'

'I don't know. Mediterranean, possibly.'

'But that means I may not see you again for *ages!*'

Her outburst surprised them both. He bent down and took her hands and drew her off the sofa. 'Judging by what you were saying just now, I didn't think that would bother you. Annabel, the other night I asked you to marry me and I didn't get a firm answer, yes or no. Can I ask you again, now?'

'I don't know, Bob.' She turned her head away. 'I can't decide.'

'All right. But I'll write to you while I'm away this time.'

'Thank you. I'll look forward to that.'

When he kissed her, Annabel sensed from the feel of his arms that he was already gone from her. He was already looking past her, at that ship, anticipating the sailing.

'You won't say anything to anybody about what I've told you tonight, will you?'

'Of course not!'

She was stung by his assumption that she conformed to one of his stock images of women: they had coffee mornings, and gossiped, and told All. But perhaps his power to irritate her was one of her minor symptoms of love.

21

On his way up from the quarterdeck to the cuddy, the Commander overtook Commander (L), also hurrying in the same direction and looking at his watch like the White Rabbit.

'I hear a dreadful rumour, Bob. We're going to sea, is that true?'

'Looks like it. Let's get inside and find out.'

It was an informal, almost domestic, scene in the Captain's cabin, reminding the Commander of a cadet captain's meeting at Dartmouth. The Heads of Departments were there, with a few other officers such as the Navigating Officer, the Operations Officer and the First Lieutenant. They were all in plain clothes, except the First Lieutenant, sitting perched on the dining table and the arms of chairs. The Captain himself, in corduroy trousers and sports jacket and looking as though he had come straight in from his garden, was dispensing whisky all round from a decanter.

'Come in, Bob. Get yourself a glass. Come in, Dai. Have you both seen the signal?'

'Number One read it out to me over the telephone, sir.'

'Good. Then you know as much as any of us. The thing is, men, when *can* we be ready for sea? You were saying, Chief?'

'Oil fuel, water, dieso, no problem, sir. We can top up tomorrow.'

'Avgas?'

'Plenty, sir.'

'What about the island?'

'Well, sir. Our main concern, apart from the actual plating, is that damaged firemain pipe. The dockyard are making us a new one and that won't be ready in time but we might get the old one back and try patching it. After all, it's only cracked. As for the plating, we haven't a hope of that inside another week but we could possibly rig up some form of wooden shield. At least keep the wind and rain out. I'll have to see what the constructors say tomorrow, sir.'

'What about taking the dockyard maties with us?'

Commander (E) shook his head. 'I doubt if they'll wear that, sir, in spite of that signal. Besides, I expect we'll be doing so much flying they won't get a proper chance to work on the island.'

'I see. How about you, Joe?'

Commander (S) shrugged. 'No obvious problems, sir. We stored for a month last time and we came back after the first day, so we're still pretty well topped up.'

'How about rum?'

'Plenty of rum, sir.'

'Dai, what about the electrical side?'

'We've got two new junction boxes for the island, but we can't fit 'em because there's no bulkhead to fit 'em on yet. Most of the island is on alternative supply. We can go to sea on it, but we'll have no stand-by supply if anything happens.'

'I hardly think somebody is going to drive into the island *again*. The main thing is, can we go to sea and fit the junction boxes on the way?'

'Certainly we can do that, sir.'

'Good. How about tides, Pilot?'

'High tide just before midnight tomorrow, sir. Failing that, just after midday the day after tomorrow.' In spite of her great draught, *Leviathan* could put to sea at any stage of the tide, but the Navigating Officer knew that the Captain preferred to move the ship at high water slack.

The Captain looked round the assembled faces.

'Can we say midnight tomorrow then?'

The Heads of Departments exchanged cautious glances. They knew from hard experience that *Leviathan* was not easily hurried. The great ship had her own tempo and if it were artificially accelerated things began to go wrong. Seeing the doubts on their faces, the Commander was afraid that the meeting was about to disintegrate into departmental evasiveness and face-saving, but to his great joy none of the officers present made any objection. It was an omen; it might even be the beginning of success.

'Right. If nobody has any objections, I'll send a signal saying we can be ready at midnight tomorrow. If there's any snag, we can always amend it.'

But the tone of the Captain's voice made it clear he would not readily agree to a postponement; if anyone had doubts, they should speak up now.

'Do we know where we're going, sir?'

The Captain laughed and slapped his knee. 'That's just it! What's the latest buzz, Ops?'

The Commander was gratified to see the Operations Officer's blank look. He had noticed, and deplored, a habit of the officers concerned with the ship's tactical deployment, with planning and logistics, of forming an aristocracy of their own. The Operations Officer, with the Navigating, Communications and Direction Officers had their own in-jokes and private confabulations which excluded other executive officers and indeed officers of all other specialisations except occasionally the Captain's Secretary. The Operations Officer was normally the fountain-head of all information on the ship's programme; it was pleasant to see him looking nonplussed for once.

'There isn't a latest buzz, sir.' The Operations Officer's expression delicately conveyed his combined annoyance at having to admit ignorance, and the Captain's use of the word 'buzz'. 'Somebody up in the front office has heard a rumour something's going to happen somewhere and they're taking precautions. But *where,* they're not saying. All I've been able to find out is that when we do sail we shall officially be on a communications exercise. That's our cover story. If you ask me, sir, I'd say that the most likely place is the Med.'

The Captain nodded. 'I'd put my money on that, too. Well, let's get to bed, men. Busy day tomorrow.'

The Commander held up his glass. 'I think we should wish ourselves luck, sir.'

Obeying a common impulse, the officers present rose to their feet and held up their glasses. It was not sentimentality, but a mutual awareness that their ship might be approaching a time of great trial, when they would need each other's help.

'Here's luck to us!'

Leaving the meeting, the Commander made a mental note to ask Mulligan to look out his white tropical uniforms in the morning. The Mediterranean was by far the most likely theatre: although most alarms came to nothing, it had been rare since the war for any large warship to complete a two-year commission without at least one emergency preparation to sail for the Mediterranean. When he returned to his cabin after breakfast the next

336

morning, the Commander was surprised to find Mulligan brushing his greatcoat.

'Heard a buzz we were going to the Arctic, sir.'

'The *Arctic!*'

'Yes, sir. Strong buzz right round the ship, sir. We're off to the Arctic for six weeks.'

'Six weeks in the Arctic, Mulligan, you must be mad! Who told you that?'

Mulligan looked puzzled. He could not remember who had told him. As the Commander knew, messdeck rumours were not passed by word of mouth. They were hatched in the air and propagated like mushroom spores throughout the ship so that two thousand men could turn out of their bunks in the morning, all possessing the same information. The Commander respected messdeck rumours. Many of them were unabashed fabrications or wishful thinking, but some were based on intelligent guesswork as accurate as any staff officer's appreciation. The sailors frequently arrived at the correct conclusions while the staff were still drafting the relevant signals.

'If you want my opinion, Mulligan, I'd say we were going to the Med and I'd be grateful if you'd have a look at my white uniforms some time today.'

'Aye aye, sir.'

The Commander was disgruntled to see that Mulligan continued to brush his greatcoat.

The Mystery Tour, as they were already calling it, seemed to have captured the ship's company's imagination. It was a day when nothing was too much trouble, when enough hands to do a job miraculously appeared at the right time and in the place they were needed. The Commander was astonished by his own inactivity. He had begun the day vigorously and enthusiastically to ensure that nothing would deflect *Leviathan* from her great opportunity, but he soon became aware that he was needlessly wasting his energies; the day was too short and there was too much to be done for supervision. The sailors were responding as though they had realised for the first time that they and their ship were needed. It struck the Commander that it was possible for a ship's company to know too much about the ship's programme; a little mystery acted as a tonic.

337

One personal anticipation remained in the Commander's mind all day and in the evening, before the ship-to-shore lines were disconnected, he telephoned her. Annabel answered at once, as though she had been standing by the telephone. He was warmed by the change in the timbre of her voice when she recognised the caller.

'Oh Bob, I'm so glad you called. I was just sitting here thinking of all those terrible things I said to you last night.'

'You needn't worry, Annabel. They weren't all that terrible and they were probably true. I have been selfish, I can see that.'

'I shouldn't have said it, all the same.'

'Don't *worry* about it. You know, I'm so pleased to have somebody to ring up when I go away. It's a new experience for me. How are you this evening?'

'A bit miserable. Just thinking I spoiled our last evening. It may be ages before you come back. Do you know where you're going yet?'

'No, it's still a Mystery Tour. Plenty of buzzes, but no hard news.'

'Perhaps you'll know soon.'

'Perhaps. I hope so.'

They were both silent. He yearned to hear her voice again. He wished she would go on speaking, so that he could just listen and then say good-bye.

'. . . Annabel, I made you an offer last night. It wasn't very well put but I wasn't just making polite conversation . . .'

'I know you weren't, Bob.'

'When I get back I'm going to make you the same offer again. That'll be the third time. I'm like the Bellman. What I say three times must be true . . .'

'Bob, I want you to know that . . .'

Her voice was swamped by a buzzing and a roaring and the exchange operator insisting that the shore lines must now be disconnected. The Commander swore, pleaded, gave the operator a direct order to keep one line open, but the receiver was dead. The Commander threw it back on its rest and stood up. The Master-at-Arms was standing in the cabin doorway, his fist poised to knock.

'What is it, Master?'

The Master-at-Arms was wearing a bewildered expression, like a man simultaneously triumphant and disappointed.

'No absentees, sir.'

'None at *all?*' It was sensational news.

'Not one, sir.'

'Well, there's a turn-up for the book!'

'We've got three ratings on compassionate leave, sir, and nine on sick leave. They're all accounted for, sir. The rest are all on board, sir. Mind you, sir . . .' The Master-at-Arms was determined not to give credit where it was due. 'We only gave leave from four o'clock this afternoon, sir. They haven't had time to go adrift, hardly.'

'Don't you believe it, Master. They could go over the wall in a quarter of an hour, if they put their minds to it. This must be a record for this ship surely?'

'I've never known it before, sir.' The Master's voice was grudging.

The Commander smiled at the Master's face. He could understand his mixed feelings: a clean defaulters' sheet was bad for business.

'It's the most splendid news I've heard for a long time, Master. I congratulate you!'

There was, as the Commander realised, no cause to congratulate the Master-at-Arms, but it was an ancient custom to reward the bearer of good tidings, and this news was like an unexpected and incredible bonus. The Commander himself had decided, against the advice of the First Lieutenant and the Senior Engineer, to grant short leave that evening, before the ship sailed. The sailors might have taken the opportunity to absent themselves in large numbers to avoid sailing with the ship, but the Commander had weighed up the ship's company's mood and had taken the risk; that they had all, every one of them, returned on board was his vindication. It was yet another portent, a magnificent omen.

Leviathan sailed as planned on the midnight tide and steamed at economical speed westwards down the English Channel. The westerly course was not yet significant, although it did confirm that their destination could still be the Mediterranean. The Commander noted that Mulligan had looked out all his heaviest sweaters and a pair of fur-lined boots.

339

The next morning, after breakfast, the Captain addressed the ship's company over the ship's broadcast. The Commander listened in the ante-room as he stirred his after breakfast cup of coffee.

'D'you hear there?'

The bosun's mate's traditional warning that a pipe of especial interest was about to be made stilled all movement in the ante-room and the passageways. Officers and stewards stood where they were to listen, like men waiting to hear the result of a valuable sweepstake.

'. . . This is the Captain speaking. I don't want to keep you in any more suspense about where we're going. We've just received a signal from the Admiralty directing us to go on patrol in a position well inside the Arctic Circle. So that is where we are now going.'

The Commander mentally tipped his hat to Mulligan's intelligence system; clearly, the stewards' messdeck had sources of information denied to the Operations Officer.

'I can't tell you why we're going up there. You know as much about it as I do. I understand there's a possibility of some trouble in the Middle East and we're being sent to sea as a precaution. If there is an international incident then it will be our job to do what we can and after it's all over we shall probably steam up and down interminably while the politicians talk about an agreement. I expect a lot of you have taken part in this sort of thing before.'

'It will be very cold where we're going, even at this time of year. I know it's summer here, but the Arctic summer is very short and very cold compared with ours. From tomorrow night, when we shall be well up the west coast of Scotland, dress regulations will be relaxed. Anyone can wear what they like, to keep warm.'

The Commander continued to drink his coffee imperturbably, betraying no sign that anything in the Captain's speech had affected him. Tosser was audibly nervous again; he was probably reading his points off a piece of paper. But he might at least have consulted his Commander before relaxing dress regulations.

'. . . I know our work-up's not officially finished yet and strictly speaking we're not yet fully operational but the Commander-in-Chief has told me he thinks *Leviathan* is fully capable now of doing whatever is required of her. I agree with him and I'm sure you will, too. It's our job now to prove he's right. We'll have an anti-submarine screen of three frigates with us but otherwise we shall be by ourselves and it'll all be up to us. That's all I want to say to you now. I'll let you know at once about our programme and the future as soon as I have any facts. We shall go to Flying Stations now, to land on replacement aircraft. That's all.'

In the hubbub of conversation which broke out in the ante-room, the First Lieutenant, sitting in the armchair next to the Commander, raised his coffee cup in a sardonic salute.

'Nay, my fair cousin, wish not a man from England! If we are marked to die, then three frigates and an aircraft carrier are enough to do our country loss. And if to live, the fewer men, the greater share of brass-hats!'

The First Lieutenant caught the Commander's eye, and they both smiled. They both knew what the Captain had been trying to say, but it had been a poor and a stilted speech; Tosser was not cast in the heroic mould, even for peace-time. The First Lieutenant had taken off his speech cruelly, but exactly. He also mocked another point, which had been puzzling the Commander.

'And another thing, sir. Why the devil are we going up there? Now thrive the armourers in the Middle East, so we're sending you lucky bastards up to the *Arctic*, well out of harm's way.'

'Perhaps the Middle East is a feint. This may be the real thing.'

'God, I hope not. I want to see my grandchildren.'

'Since this is Shakespeare week, Number One, how about stiffening the sinews and summoning up the blood to exercise your nuclear rounds and alarm routine? I'm told they're flying on the Big One today.'

'Aye aye, sir. We'll do it this forenoon.'

The replacement aircraft flown on that morning included four additional all-weather fighter-bombers for Roger Calvados' squadron. The Admiral might have expressed his complete faith in *Leviathan* but his staff were not so sanguine: Roger Calvados' squadron were not yet considered practised enough in low-flying and stand-off bombing techniques to deliver a nuclear warhead under operational conditions. The four extra pilots, who had just completed a full tour in another carrier, would fly the nuclear weapon, which was known on board as 'Big One', if it were ever required while *Leviathan* was on her patrol.

The presence of Big One on board generated a pleasurable tension throughout the ship. Big One was the ultimate item in storing for war. *Leviathan*'s armoury was now complete. If the ship's company had ever had reservations about *Leviathan*'s operational ability, Big One dispelled them. As the First Lieutenant said, 'Big One means business'.

The Commander met the Big One pilots in the wardroom at lunch-time and found them surprisingly cheerful, for men who had been deprived of their imminent summer leave and sent to sea at short notice. In a few days they would become indistinguishable from the rest of the aircrew, but in the meantime the Commander was amused to see the subtle respect paid to them by *Leviathan*'s pilots. *Leviathan*'s Air Group were pretty sure of themselves; the four newcomers, with their observers, reminded *Leviathan*'s pilots that they were still officially makee-learns.

At dusk, the three frigates came out from Londonderry to take up station on *Leviathan* in the North Channel. *Leviathan* exercised darken ship while the frigates wheeled around her, like bridesmaids, pointing out scuttles, doors and upper-deck openings which had been left uncovered. The four ships, now designated as a Task Force under the Captain's command cleared the Irish coast and followed in the wake of a south-westerly gale to seaward of the Hebrides, and northwards towards the Arctic Circle.

In the latitude of the Shetlands, the gale blew away to the east and the wind dropped to light airs. The sea subsided into a plain of milky-blue hummocks, heaving and shifting with no common direction, on which the mottled black-and-white dots of herring gulls and shearwaters rode in scattered groups, waiting for the wind, so that they could resume their majestic sail-planing. The gulls sat motionless until the passing wave of the ship's wake lifted them and gave them the impetus, one by one, to launch themselves into the air. Red-beaked puffins huddled tight like partridges, rising in covies as the ships approached them and flying a hundred yards before settling again, their feet and wingtips scoring lines on the water surface.

As the Task Force steamed northwards, there were sudden clinging mists, and spectacular sunsets, and freaks of visibility: a lookout reported, and confirmed, the blue and white marbled shape of the nearest Faeroes at seventy miles. The nights shortened until the officer of the watch could read a signal by daylight on the bridge at half past eleven at night. The weather grew colder and taking the Captain at his word the ship's company blossomed into a parade of heavy oiled-wool sweaters and wind-cheaters and lumber-jackets and duffle-coats, balaclava helmets and fur caps, mittens and fur-lined boots. The First Lieutenant wore a sheepskin-lined leather waistcoat and Rowley Dubonnet sat all day long in the ACR wearing a cossack hat and an overcoat with a high furry astrakhan collar.

The Commander's misgivings about the wearing of bizarre arctic rigs in the wardroom were inhibited by the Captain's expressed permission, but when Jerry Malone appeared for dinner one night in a shocking-pink sweater with 'Block That Kick' across the shoulders, a souvenir of his flying training course at Saker, the Commander sent for Beaky and instructed him to post a notice forbidding any but recognised Service dress in the mess. The Commander himself continued to change for dinner and to wear a bow-tie every night.

Fifty miles north of The Faeroes, the Task Force kept a rendezvous with a fleet tanker, to replenish with oil fuel. Replenishment at sea was one of the evolutions which had gone well throughout *Leviathan*'s work-up, but in the first operational replenishment of the ship's existence the fuelling parties were self-consciously aware that this was not an exercise. They tried too hard, and their over-eagerness accumulated a series of small but maddening delays.

The Chief GI, normally an immaculate shot, missed twice with the Coston gun line, the bolt and its thin captive thread falling each time into the plunging sea short of the tanker. The seamen in the forward fuelling space fumbled the handling of the telephone link, so that the telephone cable, complete with box and marker line were dragged over the side. The electrician's mate on the after winch, over-anxious to play his part, anticipated an order and blew the winch-motor fuses. The engine-room party, usually so deft with the hoses, were all thumbs in the haste to connect up and by a misunderstanding of the signals the tanker began to pump before they were ready. Oil fuel sprayed the after fuelling pocket bulkhead and spread down the ship's side in a heavy dark stain. *Leviathan*'s replenishment parties had the mortification of seeing a frigate come alongside the tanker's opposite beam, refuel, and draw away again before their own hoses were connected. All three frigates had completed fuelling and had resumed their stations in the screen two hours before *Leviathan*'s hoses were disconnected. When the last line had been slipped, and the tanker was receding towards the southern horizon, *Leviathan*'s oil-soaked fuelling parties stood in the fuelling spaces and looked at each other in bewilderment and despair.

But the Commander was not discouraged. Mistakes had been made, but they had been made for the right reasons. He would never reprove the ship's company for over-enthusiasm. It had been too rare a complaint in *Leviathan*. He was coming down from the after fuelling space, tired but very well satisfied, when he noticed that the ship was slowing down.

The bridge telephone was answered by the Captain himself.

'Bridge. Whatd'you want?' Tosser's voice was abrupt and snappy.

'Commander here, sir. I was just ringing up to find out why we were stopping?'

'We've got to stop, Bob.' The Commander guessed that the Captain was masking his irritation for the sake of politeness; any other caller would have received a short reception. 'We should have stopped before, but we couldn't while we were fuelling. Chief tells me we've got condenseritis. We're stopping to declutch the shaft.'

'Which unit is it, sir?'

' "B" Engine Room. Ironic, isn't it? Just as we're trying to be operational for the first time in our lives the main engines start falling over on us.'

Like many executive officers of his seniority, the Commander knew little of engineering except what he had gleaned from technical officers' talk in the mess. But there were several emotive engineering words and 'condenseritis' was one, with the same impact on the engine-room department as 'cancer' or 'cholera' on the medical profession. It meant that one or more of the tubes which circulated sea-water through the giant condensers under the main turbines were leaking salt into the boiler feed. Salt in the feed water would cripple the boilers and, if neglected, could bring the ship to a standstill.

344

The Commander could do nothing to assist the repairs. His presence in the engine-room might even hinder them. Yet he longed to go below, if only to demonstrate to Commander (E) that at least someone from the upper deck was interested. He waited until after dinner, to give Commander (E) and the Senior time to organise their department.

'B' Engine Room was unnaturally quiet and cool. The main turbines were still, their massive ahead and astern throttle wheels lashed shut with rope. A large section of the deck plating beside the turbines had been torn up. The Senior Engineer and Ben Krieger, the senior watch-keeper, were standing by the opening.

Although he was obviously bathed and shaved and wearing evening dress with a bow-tie, while they were in oily overalls, the Commander was at once reassured from their expressions that the men in the engine-room were delighted to see him there. It was one of the Engine-room Department's perennial complaints, that nobody knew nor cared about their difficulties.

'This is very bad luck, Senior.'

'It couldn't have happened at a worse time, sir.'

'What d'you think's gone wrong?'

'We think it's one tube which has gone *phut*, just like that. We got a hell of a cloud all at once. Let's have another test, Ben.'

Krieger picked up a test-tube from the watch-keeper's desk and rinsed it with clear water from a drain-tap under the main instrument panel. He filled the test-tube from the tap, held the bottle of silver nitrate over it, and tipped some drops into the water. The drops immediately dissolved in an opaque, milky cloud which swirled down to the bottom of the tube.

'That looks bad.'

'It is bad, sir. It's so bad we can't measure it on the salinometer. The reading's way over the top of the scale.'

The Commander sucked his teeth sympathetically. He looked down through the opening in the deck plates. There were three men working amongst the tangle of pipes which snaked across the engine-room bilges. One man, his overalls rolled down to his waist, his back and shoulders streaked with oil, was squatting on the huge pipe which carried sea-water to the condenser. As the Commander watched, the oily spanner slipped from his fingers and splashed into the water in the bilges. The others gave

345

a sarcastic cheer.

'Goodbyeeee! Don't cryeeee!' They seemed oblivious of their audience above. 'Joe, you'm going to have to take your jacket off, Joe!'

The artificer addressed as 'Joe' philosophically lay prone along the pipe and put his hand in the water, searching for the spanner.

'What are they doing down there, Senior?'

'Taking the condenser inspection door off, sir.'

'Are you only just taking the door off *now?*'

The Senior looked reproachfully at the Commander. His eyes said '*Et tu, Brute?*' 'We had to wait for the turbine and condenser to cool down, sir.'

'Of course you did! I'm sorry, I forgot. You'll have to excuse my upper deck ignorance, Senior. What are you going to do when you get the door off?'

'We'll do what's called a Canterbury Test, sir. That inspection door is on the sea-water side of the condenser. We've drained the water level to below the door so that we can take it off and have a look at the end of the tubes. Then we'll put a small air pressure of about five pounds on the turbine, that's the *steam* side of the condenser, sir. The bubbles coming up through the water will show us which tube is leaking.'

'But what happens if your leaking tube is *above* the water level?'

The Senior chuckled. 'We've actually thought of that one, sir. If we don't get any joy from the tubes below the water, we'll put soap solution on the ends of tubes above the water. Then they'll show us bubbles too, if they're leaking.'

'I see.' The Commander shook his head. 'Clever chaps, these Chinese stokers.'

Below them, Joe had taken off the last nuts and prised the door from its seating. The door-hole gaped like an open mouth in the pouched gargoyle cheeks of the condenser body. Water slopped over the edge. The Senior nodded to Krieger. There was a hissing sound of air pouring into the turbine. Krieger studied the small gauge fitted high up on the turbine casing.

'Sir!' Joe had withdrawn his head from the door-opening. 'Looks like a whole tube gone, sir! Bubbling up like nobody's business!' He bent his head inside again and again withdrew. 'Looks like more than one, sir. Three or four, maybe!'

'Oh Christ.' The Senior Engineer crouched on the deck plates and let himself down on to the pipes below. 'Let's have a look.'

The Commander recognised that it was time to go. As he left, they were dragging two portable ventilation fans into position, and a stoker came down the ladder with some mugs threaded on a string and a large fanny of hot cocoa. The Senior and his men were evidently making a night of it.

The Commander left the engine-room elated and optimistic. The last time he had visited that engine-room, on the night the gauge glasses were smashed, the Senior and Krieger had been close to defeat. Their faces had been hopeless. Their ratings had turned their backs on them. Now there was a new feeling. They knew what was wrong and they were setting about putting it right. Every man in that engine-room had been personally involved, and the Senior and Krieger had behaved like men who knew they had their department behind them.

After rounds on every night at sea, the Commander went up to the bridge to see the Captain. He valued the discussions; much of the day-to-day policy of the ship was decided during them. They were his opportunity to keep the Captain in touch and to give him, so to speak, the state of the nation. The Commander quickened his step towards the bridge. In spite of the clumsy replenishment that afternoon, he had good news of the ship. But as he mounted the final ladder to the bridge, he heard the Captain's voice.

'. . . I want that set working by the morning, Dai. I don't care what you have to do or how many hands you have to put on it. That set has *got* to be serviceable by six o'clock tomorrow morning. I'm not interested in progress reports. The only thing I want to hear is that that set is working again. Don't come and see me again until it is. And it had better be by six o'clock tomorrow.'

When they met at the top of the ladder, Commander (L) reached out a hand and roughly pulled the Commander out of his way, and went down without looking back.

The Captain was sitting in his chair. His silhouette against the pale light from the bridge windows was huge and brooding and angry. He turned on the Commander like a man discovering a heaven-sent scapegoat.

'Tomorrow morning, Commander, we're going to fly off the

first operational sorties this ship's ever done. And *now* he comes and tells me the nine-nine-seven's not working. Without that, we might just as well pack it in and all go home. Just as we're starting to earn our money, the whole damned ship starts falling to pieces round our ears. First condenseritis, now this. And as for that replenishment this afternoon, *that* was just about the most inept exhibition I've ever seen, even for this ship!'

The Commander caught his breath. Even for *this* ship?

'That's not fair, sir.'

'*What's* not fair, sir?'

While the Captain went on to exercise his sense of grievance, the Commander did not attempt to justify himself or the ship's company again. If the Captain wished to relieve his feelings, then it was his occasional privilege to use his Commander as a whipping-boy. Watching Tosser's face, the Commander knew that the great ship was testing him, too. An independent detached command under operational conditions was a very rare opportunity in peace-time. Tosser was bluff and open and generous, but he had showed that he could also be shrewd, even cunning. He had been given a golden chance of an admiral's flag, and he knew it. The Commander was no longer put out by Tosser's insensitiveness; he had come to accept it, as part of the Captain's personality. Once more, it appeared that the Captain had totally misunderstood the temper of the ship's company. He was afraid they were about to fail him. He simply was not sensitive enough to appreciate that, on the contrary, they were about to succeed for him. Because he was genuinely unaware, he blamed the Commander – the one man who had always promised him that *Leviathan* would succeed.

The sound-powered direct telephone from the controlling engine-room, on its bracket by the Captain's chair, gave a long, unbearable wail.

'Goddammit, just because they're all deaf down there.' The Captain grunted as he listened to the message. 'Thank you, Chief.'

The Captain's voice was grudging, reluctantly pleased. He looked at the Commander. 'That's one consolation. We should be back on four shafts by two o'clock tomorrow morning. Now, all we need is a few radar sets, and both catapults working, and perhaps we *may* be fit for flying.'

This sarcasm was both unnecessary and unworthy. The Commander left the bridge fervently hoping that the Air Group's performance would restore the Captain's good humour.

Flying began at six o'clock the next morning, with all radar sets, four shafts and both catapults, but the Commander's further hopes were disappointed. First night nerves had also affected the Air Group. Although the Commander did not personally watch any of the flying, nothing on the flight deck could be kept secret and soon the whole ship knew that the Air Group were going through a bad patch. The aircrew's conversation in the wardroom was all of elementary errors in flight deck drill. Commander (Air) and Little F appeared less and less frequently in the ante-room. For the first time in the commission, Rowley Dubonnet lost his temper.

On the fifth day, after the first fatal accident of the patrol, Commander (Air) appeared for dinner. He looked tired and subdued. The last week had obviously chastened him. He answered the Commander's enquiries with uncommon civility.

'It's all basic stuff, Bob. Silly little things, except for today. But you can't get annoyed with anybody. Because they're obviously trying their hardest. Perhaps that's the trouble. They're trying too hard.'

'I've only heard gossip, Wings. What sort of things have gone wrong?'

'Oh, the most stupid things. On the very first day, some parking chocks were blown over the side by a jet exhaust, all because nobody was looking after them. And then some lunatic started up his fuel bowser in the morning without making sure there was any lub. oil in the engine. And then that handler who didn't look where he was going, fell thirty feet down the after lift-well and broke his ankle. Damned lucky he didn't break his back. Only yesterday Geoff Goodall was actually on the booster ready to go off when somebody noticed one of his wing locking bolts wasn't properly in. If he'd gone off like that, that wing would have folded up on him before he'd gone a hundred yards. And of course we've had constant trouble with the catapults. I know it's not Joss Parkhurst's fault. He's doing his best, but I doubt if we've had both boosters going for more than half an hour at a time all this week. It's like a string of beads. Once you lose one, the whole lot tends to run off. Our problem is literally to try and tie a bloody knot in it.'

'How was that fellow killed today?'

'Again, just one of those stupid things. He just dropped into the oggin on the down-wind leg, without saying a dickey-bird to anyone. Just like MacLachlan, early on. But this time, I've got an idea what happened. I can't prove a thing, but from what I hear I'm bloody certain he took off with a faulty fuel gauge.'

'Is that serious?'

'Christ, it's vital.' The Commander flinched before Wings' look of contempt for his ignorance. 'Brother, if you've got duff fuel gauges you *don't* fly. For the very reason of what happened today. He thought he had enough to get back on, and he didn't. Just for the sake of doing *one* more sortie we're now shy of one aircraft and one pilot. It just shows it don't pay to cut corners. By the way, I haven't seen you up there recently, Bob? Are you missing your favourite little gallery?'

'Not really. Actually, I was thinking of coming up to have a goof sometime tomorrow.'

'Well, try and bring us some better luck, for God's sake.'

The site of the Commander's little gallery was now covered by temporary scaffolding and wooden shielding and he watched the flying from the passageway by Flyco. Three or four pilots were standing there when he arrived and he was dismayed to note the hush in their conversation when they saw him. It seemed that he was still a Jonah, associated with Stiggins and with disaster.

The pilots were in Roger Calvados' squadron and they were watching others of their squadron returning, with comments on each landing. The Commander leaned against the window-sill and settled to enjoy the performance which never failed to enthral him. He watched one aircraft as it flew downwind and began its beautiful, calculated swing in towards the ship. The turn, he had been told, was everything.

The aircraft was straightening on its finals when, amazingly and irrationally, the tail dipped, the aircraft twisted and began to climb, the blast from its after-burners pressing a ragged trough in the sea. There was a buzz of comment in the passageway and somebody saying, 'What's up with old George?' The Commander heard a mutter beside him of 'Aileron jammed'.

'Is that what it is?'

'Looks like it, sir.' The speaker was Dryburgh, one of the pair who had missed the ship on that Whitsun week-end, so long ago. His face was muffled in a balaclava helmet under his flight deck beret. He was evidently pleased to be able to offer expert information to an officer as senior as the Commander.

'He's climbing to get a bit of height before he ejects.'

'*Eject?* Surely not!'

'I bet he is. It's all you can do, sir. You certainly couldn't make a pass at the desk. You've only got to look at him, sir.'

Dryburgh pointed upwards. The climb was steeper now, and the Commander had to stoop to peer up through the window. The aircraft was rolling slowly, boring up into the sky in a gentle spiral.

A voice was whispering in the passageway.

'Come on George, now's your time. Let's have you, George, don't mess about. Come *on*, George.'

The aircraft was still climbing, a bright speck in the sky.

'Take your chance, George.'

The aircraft stalled, lost momentum and fell on its back. They waited for the explosive spurt of the capsules and the drifting dandelion tufts of the parachutes but the aircraft spun downwards intact and nothing had separated from it when the wing-blades turned over and flashed once like Excalibur before cutting into the sea. A brief curtain of spray hid the spot and itself vanished. The impact was soundless, but the island rang with the silent cry of agony from the watchers in *Leviathan*.

The helicopter was hovering over the faint line of turbulence in the sea. The nearest frigate was heading towards it, sea-boat already manned and lowered to the water. The helicopter gave up the search to the frigate and flew back to its position on the quarter; there was no question of a diversion airfield, which would have betrayed the Task Force's presence, and the remaining aircraft in the air had to be recovered.

The sound of the next aircraft to land on and the whistling of its jet engines cruising underneath the island windows masked the Captain's voice. He had evidently been shouting for some time before the Commander heard him.

The Captain was standing at the end of the passageway, at the top of the short flight of steps leading to the bridge. His gloved hands were pressed against the bulkheads, as if trying to force the island asunder. His rage included them all – the Commander, the pilots beside him, and the stricken figure of Commander (Air) in the Flyco door.

'What was that pilot's name?'

'Lieutenant George Barry, sir.'

'And what was his observer's name?'

Commander (Air) hesitated, and Little F spoke over his shoulder.

'Sub-Lieutenant Michael Barnes, sir.'

The Captain's lips parted to speak.

The Commander cringed, knowing that Tosser was about to say something so unforgivable, so unimaginably cruel and terrible, that he would wreck *Leviathan* as surely as though he had ripped the bottom out of her.

The Captain stood rigid, struggling with his rage, and then dropped his arms. He turned without speaking and went back to his chair on the bridge.

Dryburgh and the other pilots, alarmed and baffled by the Captain's anger, edged away and one by one slipped out of sight down the ladder. The Commander stopped in the door of Flyco. Little F was staring at the next aircraft approaching. Commander (Air) leaned against the bulkhead, his head bowed. When he looked up, the Commander read his face: beneath the bluster and the surface self-confidence, Wings was a weak man. He had not the resilience to take the Captain's assault and spring back again.

'I shouldn't worry too much, Wings. The Captain's got great hopes of the ship. He knows we're all doing our best.'

'I suppose so.' Commander (Air) bit his lip. 'But what was he going to say?'

'I think maybe it's just as well he didn't say it.'

'Maybe. Let's hope that's all for now.'

'Let's hope so.'

The Commander was still thinking of those words when he passed the ACR on his way down through the island and felt the tremor of the deck beneath his feet and heard the rising, clamouring note of the engine. The shadow of wings darkened the doorway to the flight deck and the voices around him were drowned in a drawn-out grinding rumble. Like a man impelled to rush to the scene of a road accident, the Commander joined the crowd tumbling out of the ACR door.

The bitter and forgotten flight deck wind flooded cold into his mouth and nostrils and forced tears into his eyes. In front of him, the flight deck was filled with running figures, crossing and jinking and converging on each other. A blow on the back almost knocked him to his knees. 'Get out of the *fucking* way!' A hose slithered past his feet and the two red-helmeted men pulling it were bent low, their legs pumping, driving onwards like horses in their traces. The long, curving scrape-mark in the flight deck paint led to the aircraft, one of the long range turbo-prop aircraft from Jerry Malone's anti-submarine search squadron, which was lying upside down beside the forward lift. The tailfin was buckled and the propeller blades crumpled. The two main wheels pointed at the sky, still spinning. The nose-wheel was bent and partly retracted.

One of the crew was already limping away, his arm round the shoulder of a deck handler. Another was standing by the tail, his flying helmet in his hand, and shouting inexplicably at the men beside him. A small group of men knelt by the cockpit. They had removed the access panel and were easing the pilot out of his straps.

When they carried the stretcher towards him, the Commander looked for the face. It was Jerry Malone.

'He's not dead?'

The stretcher bearers ignored the question.

'Hamish, he's not dead?'

Hamish, walking beside the stretcher, recognised the Commander.

'No. He's unconscious.'

The wind was carrying a heavy smell of fuel. The fire-fighting parties had their hoses playing on the fuselage and on the flight deck around the aircraft.

'Get *back*, blast you!' The Flight Deck Officer's face was an angry red above the yellow of his jacket. 'Get back, all of you!'

The circle round the aircraft opened out. The fire-fighting parties and the deck handlers withdrew, anticipating the explosion. The Flight Deck Officer squatted on one knee. He rested his chin on one hand, and studied the aircraft. The flight deck was quiet, waiting the word. The man nearest the Commander was crouched in the position of a sprinter in his blocks. The Commander would hear his hoarse breathing.

The Flight Deck Officer stood up, and waved his men on. *'Right!'*

The deck handlers swarmed forward, splashing through the water from the fire-hoses. Jumbo the big crane backed into position. Ropes and wire strops were passed round the fuselage and the aircraft was lifted and dragged, its wrecked cockpit canopy and tailfin grinding along the deck, until the propeller boss and part of the nose projected diagonally into a corner of the lift.

Several deck handlers leaped on to the lift, as it descended for a few feet, and stopped. Jumbo hoisted the aircraft until its fuselage was vertical and the aircraft's weight was taken on the wing leading edges which then stretched like a hypotenuse across the right-angled corner of the lift-well.

Jumbo's wheels were chocked. Wire strops were passed round the propeller boss and through a welded ring on Jumbo's chassis frame and connected by a heavy four-sheaved block and tackle. Six deck handlers manned the tackle downhaul. Meanwhile, a double line was looped over the tailplane and manned by the handlers on the lift.

While Jumbo lowered its purchase on the fuselage, the handlers on the flight deck and the lift hauled away together on the tail-line and the block and tackle. The aircraft pivoted on its wing leading edges, the fuselage swinging downwards, away from the crane, until it was once more horizontal and the cockpit upright. The lift was raised until it touched the main wheel tyres.

The Flight Deck Officer gestured with his thumb and a leading pilot's mate from Jerry Malone's squadron ran along the port wing, mounted into the cockpit, settled in the pilot's seat, and began to pump up the aircraft's hydraulic system by hand. The nose-wheel slowly swung down and locked. The handlers on the lift placed chocks on the wheels and the lift rose slightly, until it took the aircraft's weight.

'Now see if you can get the wings folded!'

The leading pilot's mate held up one thumb. In a moment, his head nodded vigorously as he began to pump again. The port wing jerked, kinked in two sections along its length and slowly, as though to avoid further damage, folded itself back over the fuselage behind the cockpit. The handlers gathered under the starboard wing and pressed upwards. The wing reluctantly rose to join the other.

The Flight Deck Chief stood on the edge of the lift-well, his hands on his hips and his great spade-beard jutting.

'Now strike that bastard down. I don't never want to see it again!'

With a faint ringing of bells the lift descended and the aircraft sank out of sight. Jumbo trundled back towards the island. The fire-parties collected their hoses. The deck-handlers ran and stooped and gathered up ropes and wire strops and the block and tackle before doubling back to the shelter and warmth of the ACR doorway.

The Commander hopped up and down, blowing through his chilled fingers. Like one of the ranks of Tuscany, he could scarce forbear to cheer. The method of righting the aircraft had been mechanically simple, but the Commander knew that it would never have occurred to him. The Flight Deck Officer and his team had rallied and carried out the evolution without consultations, without hesitations, and without pausing for congratulations afterwards. It had been a brilliant exhibition of ingenuity and timing and whole-hearted co-operation. The Commander looked up at the bridge windows, hoping that the Captain had been watching. Maybe this would convince him.

22

The last aircraft of the day was slanting in towards the ship. From the quarterdeck, the Commander and the First Lieutenant watched it approach and flash out of sight over their heads. They heard the muffled shock of the landing high on the flight deck above them.

'Number three wire, sir, would you say?'

The Commander grinned. 'Could be.'

Like regular commuters who could place their train exactly without looking from their newspapers, the ship's company below could now interpret flight deck sounds as accurately as though they were actually watching from the island.

The Commander and the First Lieutenant resumed their walk on the quarterdeck, adjusting their stride to match the pitching of the deck, exaggerated at this aftermost point in the ship. The settled weather of the last week had broken. *Leviathan* was steaming westwards into a mounting wind. The frigates in station on either beam were driving into the head sea, tossing cataracts of white foaming water along their upper decks. Far astern the fleet tanker, now a permanent member of the Task Force, was bobbing and dipping like a toy boat, now hidden in spray, now showing the pale mass of her bridge superstructure. Overhead the sky was chilled grey. Mackerel-scaled cloud streamers pointed their long scrolled fingers like wind-vanes to the east where a band of hard low cloud hid the mountains of northern Norway. It was just after eleven o'clock at night, but still broad daylight. The Commander always knew the direction of north instinctively, but he had not visited the Arctic since the war and he was still surprised by the peculiarity of seeing the late evening sun so close to the bearing of the Pole.

'We must stick out here like a sore prick, sir. All this excitement and secrecy about keeping radio silence, but they chatter all day long on the aircraft net.' The First Lieutenant jerked his head towards the north-east. '*They* know we're here. Did you see that so-called fishing trawler the other day, sir?'

'I did. Stiff with radar aerials and W/T antennae. Not a fishing net in sight.'

'I had the middle last night and he was on the radar screen the whole time, keeping station on us just over the horizon. He's even got sonar. You can hear him pinging away.'

'Perhaps he's fishing for fish?'

'One kind of fish maybe.'

'Still, it gives Ops something to do. He spends most of his day making tapes of him. It's mostly UHF stuff, I'm told. High speed morse and a few swear-words. The boffins in London will be as happy as sand-boys working them out.'

The First Lieutenant stopped at the rail, to watch a whitish sea bird with grey wings gliding smoothly towards the quarter-deck. He made a threatening fist at it and the horn-yellow beak gaped at him as the bird tipped its board-winged monoplane silhouette aside and planed away. The First Lieutenant stared after it.

'That's a funny looking shite-hawk.'

'That wasn't a sea-gull. That was a fulmar. They're supposed to be the reincarnations of drowned sailor-men, so they say. It's unlucky to kill them.'

'I thought that was the albatross?'

'It's unlucky to kill them, too. But you don't often see an albatross in the northern hemisphere.'

'You know about birds, sir?' The First Lieutenant's voice was respectful; like many naval officers and ratings, he himself was as ignorant as any landsman of the natural history above and below the surface of the sea. To the average sailor, all birds were shite-hawks and most fish were mackerel.

'I know a little about them. I always keep an eye out for them whenever I can. I seem to have had more time for bird-watching than usual, just lately.'

The Commander had never understood the Arctic's reputation for emptiness and bleakness. When *Leviathan* crossed the great submarine ridge which ran from the Shetlands to Greenland, the sky had erupted with sea birds and the sea itself had boiled over and split in tide-rips and currents as though shearing along planes of differing colours and densities. Even here, well above the Arctic Circle line, the last strength of the warm Gulf Stream flowed

357

north as far as Spitzbergen and the sea was a feeding ground for the beautiful birds of the high Arctic. The Commander had spent hours studying them from *Leviathan*'s quarterdeck, watching the silent preoccupied flights of the arctic terns, assembling as though meditating upon their coming migrations; the storm petrel, darting and flicking like a sea-swallow amongst the wave crests; and once, the breath-taking stoop of a great pirate skua to retrieve the fish disgorged by a discomfited kittiwake.

'I don't think I've ever had so much spare time on my hands. Didn't even get a defaulter this morning. Not even so much as a slack hammock. I suppose I shall have to buy the Master a pair of white gloves. I bet it's the first pair he's ever had in this ship.'

'I'll bet it is, sir. People seem to have lost the urge to get themselves into the rattle these days.'

The Task Force was turning to the north and they braced themselves to meet the swaying of the quarterdeck as the ship slithered across the beam sea. The Commander wondered why the Captain had chosen this course. Steaming into the wind would have made an easier night for the frigates.

'I went to see Jerry Malone this evening.'

'How is he, sir?'

'Merry as a cricket, apart from a stiff neck and two lovely black eyes. And he's got a long strip of sticking plaster down one side of his head. He only had concussion. The PMO's letting him out tomorrow.'

'Did you see his drama, sir?'

'I only heard the expensive noises as I was passing the ACR. Jerry can't remember a thing from the time he took off. He says he remembers going off on the booster and nothing more. I'm told he made the world's worst landing, bounced about thirty feet in the air, missed every wire, tipped a wing on the deck and so turned right over. He was lucky he didn't go over the side.' The Commander remembered the scene on the flight deck afterwards. 'I must say I took my hat off to the Flight Deck Officer and his team. The way they got that aircraft right side up again. No fuss, no messing about. I was very impressed, I can tell you.'

'I heard about it, sir. You know . . .'

The First Lieutenant appeared to be forming his thoughts in order. The Commander waited. The First Lieutenant's opinion

358

was always worth hearing; there was nobody in the wardroom better at summing up the ship's company, estimating what they would or would not tolerate.

'. . . On the surface things don't seem to have been going all that well so far, sir, but deep down, I'm convinced we're doing very well indeed. It could be the moment we're all waiting for is not far off. Except it won't be a moment. It'll be a general feeling. We'll all realise it at once.'

'Well if it's ever going to happen, it'll be on this trip. This is make or break.'

Leviathan's patrol had lengthened from the expected fortnight to three weeks, to a month, to six weeks, and finally to an indefinite period which even the stewards' messdeck could not forecast. REA Lethcombe, with his finger ever on the ship's company pulse, began to introduce the evening's broadcasts on Radio Leviathan with a few bars of Wagner's overture to 'The Flying Dutchman'. The ship's company heard of the *coup d'état* in the Middle East and the mobilisation of forces east of Suez, but the news seemed as irrelevant in *Leviathan* as the buzzing of flies far away. The *coup d'état* had failed and the political situation had been stabilised, but *Leviathan* remained in the Arctic, apparently forgotten, and gripped in an internal struggle which eclipsed anything in the ship's history.

During the long hours of daylight, the Air Group maintained continuous fighter cover overhead, with anti-submarine searches in front and to either side of the Task Force. On every fifth evening flying stopped while the Task Force refuelled from the tanker. The aircrew were flying four, five, and even six sorties a day. They came back from debriefing exhausted, and flung themselves down in the ready room, in the officers' bridge mess, or wherever they could sleep until their next briefing; there was always a line of sleeping pilots in the wardroom armchairs nearest the ante-room doors. Big One was kept at instant readiness in an aircraft on deck, armed, fuelled, and with a pilot in the cockpit at all times.

Meanwhile the rest of *Leviathan*'s complement had virtually split into two ship's companies. The flight deck party, the air maintenance and air ordnance departments and the fuelling groups broke into two watches, four hours on and four hours off, to range, fuel, arm, and strike down aircraft during the day, and to refit, refuel and rearm during the evening and the brief night. The flight deck engineering department were also in two watches on the catapult pumps and in the ram rooms, on the arrester gear control panels and the oxygen generating plant. The Aircraft Control Room, Air Direction Room and the Operations Room were manned by working complements day and night. Even the cooks in the galleys were in two watches, providing meals continuously for those who had been unable to reach the dining halls or the wardroom at the proper time.

The Captain isolated himself from the ship, withdrawing to a lonely pinnacle of command which no one could ascend except on duty. He left the compass platform only to wash and shave in his sea-cabin next to the bridge. Reports, signals, and meals were brought to his chair on the compass platform in which he sat for day after day, looking ahead of the ship, sometimes dozing between launches. Every hour, he roused himself and pressed the button beside his chair, which gave his permission for flying, and the launching and landing cycles would begin again.

The patrol had dislocated the forward planning of every department in the ship. None of the Heads of Departments had been prepared for so long a period away from base support. The aircraft from Jerry Malone's squadron which flew occasionally to the Shetlands could bring back only mail, more catapult bridles, and vital spare parts to keep defective aircraft in the air. The ship was thrown on her own resouces. The symptoms of *Leviathan*'s exhaustion were the staple of wardroom conversation.

The Commander could feel the great ship tiring but knew that this patrol was the ultimate test. No other trials would compare with it. If some part failed now, the failure would be permanent. No future success could compensate. The Commander could only jolly the wardroom along, listen to their complaints, make suggestions, and act, as he thought of himself, as a general wardroom damp shoulder. Commander (L) described his visits to the island every morning, to look at the radar aerials and to make his obeisance to them, willing them to continue turning. Joss Parkhurst counted the frayed strands on the catapult and arrester wires and told the Commander that every wire in the ship was nearing the end of its designed life. With vivid pantomime, the Senior Engineer illustrated how he had watched his steam leaks grow, from wisps to small jets, from small to larger jets, and from larger jets to raging torrents of steam; there could be no opportunity of repairing them until the main machinery was shut down in harbour. Chocolates and sweets, the Commander knew, were unobtainable in the canteen, with biscuits, soup, coffee, milk and fruit which the sailors liked to buy to supplement their official meals. Commander (S) held a conference of his department and informed the Commander afterwards that they would be breaking out emergency dry provisions in another week. To the Commander, this was disturbing news; green vegetables, sauces, and pickles had already disappeared from the wardroom and dining hall tables. However, once more there was nothing he could do but make light of the situation.

'I don't like the sound of that word "provisions", Joe. I'm like Winnie the Pooh. When they told him provisions would be taken to the North Pole, he said he would rather they took some food.'

Delicious Joe gave one short snort of laughter. The Commander's remark chimed perfectly with his own sense of humour. 'I'll tell the messman that, Bob.' He looked at the Commander with a new respect; it was a rare man who could so hold the wardroom together, encourage them, and crack jokes, when they were all tired, and near to breaking.

Imperceptibly, the sustained pressure of the patrol wore away *Leviathan*'s softer, corrupt parts and uncovered the ship's strong, basic nature. Each part was ground to a fine finish which fitted it indissolubly to its neighbour. Under the pressure ten thousand various parts of *Leviathan* melted, fused and set together. Sailors, naval airmen, stokers, cooks, artificers and electricians, their officers and their petty officers, became a true ship's company. *Leviathan*, for the first time, became a ship.

The Commander had almost expected such a miracle to be foreshadowed appropriately by ghostly horsemen riding the clouds, by comets blazing the sky and statues weeping blood. The moment came quite unheralded. He was first aware of it early one morning when he went up to the bridge to look at the weather and to clear his lungs.

The Captain was just stretching and getting up from his chair. His face was sagging with fatigue, his cheeks lined and bristly with stubble. His clothes hung baggily on him and the Commander guessed that Tosser had lost a good deal of weight in the previous weeks.

The Captain rubbed the bristles on his chin. 'I'm glad you're here, Bob. You can take over for a bit. I haven't left this damned place for about a month. I'm going back aft to my cabin and I'm going to have a proper bath and a proper breakfast. Will you take this next launch for me?'

'I'd be very glad to, sir.'

'Right.' The Captain described a wide gesture with his arm. His pointing finger traced the line of the horizon from port to starboard. 'The frigates are in position, as you can see. The tanker's five miles astern. Flag Fox is at the dip and young Bird here is just bringing us up on to a course for flying. The first aircraft is due to go off at seven o'clock.'

'Are we landing on after the launch?'

'Yes, four of Rupert's and one of Jerry Malone's, with some mail.'

'How about Big One, sir?'

'Big One's spotted aft at the moment. When the launch is over, they'll spot him forrard in Fly One in time for the landings.'

The Commander thought with sympathy of the Big One pilots, watch-keeping in that exposed and freezing cockpit, being trundled to and fro every hour to avoid the other aircraft launching and landing.

'As soon as you've finished flying and the chopper's back on board, turn to due east and go down wind at ten knots. Come back on to course and speed for flying in time for the next one at eight o'clock.'

'Do the frigates know the next course, sir?'

'Yes. They'll be waiting for you to say the word as soon as you've hauled down Flag Fox. O.K.?'

'Yes, sir.'

'Expect me back when you see me.'

When the Captain had gone down the ladder, the Commander checked the ship's position on the chart, the ship's heading on the gyro compass strip repeater, and the revolutions ordered on the counter. He turned to the hooded radar screen at the back of the bridge. The beam was sweeping round picking out the frigates and the tanker astern. He altered the range scale and in a few sweeps

362

the jagged coast of Norway painted on the right of the screen, at extreme range. The trawler, now nicknamed 'the Camp Follower', was still there on the port quarter. The Commander wound down the range strobe and measured the distance: twenty-five miles, out of sight over the horizon.

He walked out on to the small gallery which formed the port wing of the bridge. Immediately below on the flight deck, Hamish was chatting to two of the squadron engineer officers by the ACR door. The two men in fireproof suits and steel helmets were leaning against Jumbo's tyres. Their arms were folded, their heads bowed, nodding as though they were exchanging some ponderous repartee. A group of deck handlers were clustered in a circle. One of them jerked his head and they all laughed and separated, following the Flight Deck Chief forward to Fly One. Four of Roger Calvados' fighter-bomber aircraft were ranged in a line on the port side. The cockpit canopies were still open, and the pilots were talking to their leading pilot's mates who were standing on the wings by the pilots' shoulders. Far aft, on the lip of the flight deck, the helicopter was perched, its rotors already spinning. A yellow-jacketed figure stood beside it, holding up a green flag and looking over his shoulder at Flyco. The Commander stood for a moment, enjoying the scene and this sudden new vision of *Leviathan;* alive as he was to the invisible currents which flowed through a ship and revealed her spirit, he knew that the moment they had all worked for was at hand.

When the Commander returned to the bridge, Commander (Air)'s head appeared round the Flyco door. He, too, looked exhausted. Most of the Heads of Departments had come to a working arrangement to share the load with their seconds in command, but Wings was a soloist who allowed Little F, his *tenore comprimario,* a very limited role. The Commander could see that Wings had been trying to do too much himself.

Commander (Air) registered mock amazement at the Commander's solitary and elevated position. 'Now that you're in Father's Chair, Bob, I think you ought to know ...'

'Yes?' The Commander tensed. It would be his luck for something to go amiss just when the Captain had entrusted him with the ship.

'... We're all *ready!*'

363

'Oh. Thank you, Wings.'

Commander (Air) brandished an upturned thumb, and his head disappeared.

The Commander climbed up into the Captain's chair and at once felt himself being borne along by the great ship beneath him. This was the driving seat. This was where the lines of power converged. As John Bowler once said, 'The Can is carried here.'

Bird, bent over the compass ring, was also smiling, as though he were glad to see the Commander in Father's Chair. *Leviathan* had sailed before Bird's relief could arrive, and nobody knew when he would join now.

'Course and speed for flying, sir. Course two-seven-two, revolutions one-four-six. Wind's just about steady, force five, westerly, sir. One minute to go, sir.'

'Thank you, Bird.'

On an impulse, the Commander rang the controlling engine-room.

'We're flying in one minute's time.'

'Thank you, sir. We're all ready sir.'

'We're all ready.' The Commander repeated the words to himself as he took one last look round the horizon and leaned forward to press the flying button, knowing that the launch would be a good one.

'Flag Fox close up, sir.'

'Very good.' The white flag with the central red diamond, hauled close up to the yard-arm, indicated to ships in company that *Leviathan* was operating aircraft.

The green flag dropped and the helicopter aft lifted and wheeled away, like a grasshopper leaping in slow motion. Flyco broadcast counted down the seconds to the start. The smoke from the starting cartridges rose up in plumes like the helmet-feathers of a rank of knights. The aircraft swung out of line and moved forward, one by one, and the catapult *corps de ballet* dispatched them on their way. Behind them, an aircraft of Jerry Malone's squadron coughed smoke and its propeller blades turned slowly. The blades spun faster into shimmering discs, the stroboscopic shadings revolving anti-clockwise, as the pilot opened his throttles and coarsened his blade pitch. The chocks were slipped away and the aircraft waddled forward in the wake of the others, its fat bulbous body and tail-plane quivering in the buffeting of its own slip-stream.

The launch was perfect. The cycle progressed without delays or hesitations, just as the Commander had known it would, just as he had sometimes watched through glasses and known that a horse would come through the field and run on to win.

The Captain came back, shaved and refreshed, just before the next launch at eight o'clock.

'I didn't hear any frantic noises so I take it all's well. How did it go?'

'Very well, sir.' The Commander pointed down at the flight deck. 'I should buy this one if I were you, sir. It's a bargain at the money.'

The Captain laughed, the clear, free laughter of a man released from a long imprisonment. 'What's the position now?'

'It's all just as you left it, sir. Except we're now one more launch ahead.'

'One more, and one less. O.K., Bob, away you go and get some breakfast.'

There were two letters for the Commander in the mail which had arrived that morning. They were both from Annabel. She did not write at great length but, like a true naval wife, she wrote regularly; these were the eighth and ninth letters he had received from her since the ship sailed. She wrote of the minutiae of her life, of her news from the boys, the weather, and her neighbour's cat which had been run over by a car. Reading them, it seemed to him that her letters were shot through with loneliness; she wrote as though she were glad and relieved once more to have someone to write to. The point had not occurred to him before: for a naval officer's widow, the postman must be a daily reminder. He read the endings of her letters several times. 'With very much love, Annabel.'

Writing to a woman was a talent the Commander had left fallow for many years. Whenever he sat down to answer Annabel, he was conscious that he was not a good correspondent, that he had none of Stiggins' humble intensity. He began his letters stiffly, and too politely. It was never until the second page that he warmed to his subject.

'... We've talked a lot (probably far too much!) about this ship

365

and I know I've often bored you with all the things I've hoped for her. But I really am sure that something big has just happened recently. It's like being in a new ship. It's the most wonderful feeling in the world. This morning the Captain left me in charge of the ship while he went aft to have his breakfast there for a change. While I was up there I had this most marvellous feeling that everybody in the ship was backing me up.

'I told you that we had our own radio programme called Radio Leviathan. This is another thing that's been working well recently. Number One once said to me that a ship is always better when it's living off its own fat, and that's certainly true of Radio Leviathan. Nobody seems to want to listen to the BBC, except for the news, and even that seems to us here as if it was all happening somewhere on Mars. But everybody listens to Radio Leviathan. There are two programmes in particular. One is called "Down Your Hatch", where Simmondson (one of the junior electrical officers, I don't think you've met him) visits various messdecks and talks to the sailors and asks them to choose the records they particularly like. You know the sort of thing. The other is called "Between You And Me" and this time REA Lethcombe (he's the sailor who runs Radio Leviathan) interviews officers about their jobs in the ship and their experiences in the Service.

'You'd think that having an officer interview ratings and a rating interviewing officers would be the wrong way round, but in fact it isn't. Having an officer there for "Down Your Hatch" seems to make the sailors display themselves, sort of show off a bit. It puts a bit of what they would call "needle" into it. And "Between You And Me" is absolutely brilliant. I always listen to it when I'm changing for dinner in my cabin. You'd be amazed at the things Lethcombe finds out. Did you know that Beaky has four teen-aged daughters? (Perhaps you did, it's the sort of thing women always do seem to know.) But I certainly didn't. I didn't know that the Air Engineer Officer was once a prisoner in a Japanese POW camp in Malacca. Nor that the Master Gunner (that little fellow you met called Poacher) was once a clearance diver and a brilliant frogman. I didn't know these things and yet I've served in the same wardroom as these people for months! By the way, it's my turn to go on tomorrow night. I'll let you know how I get on.

366

'I was very grateful and very pleased to read the ending of your last letters. I think I have the right and I certainly have the wish to end mine the same way. With very much love, Bob.'

The Commander approached his Radio Leviathan broadcast with mixed feelings. He himself had suggested the interviews to Lethcombe long ago, just after the ship commissioned. Now, he was hoist with his own petard. He had intended the interviews as a subliminal aid to morale, to help the ship's company to understand and to make allowances for each other's difficulties. They had certainly had that effect: Dai Bach had said that since his interview on Radio Leviathan the daily slaughter of electric light bulbs and neon lighting fittings he had complained of had been cut by half. But Lethcombe had taken the interviews further than the Commander or anyone else had envisaged. They were no longer just polite propaganda. After early inhibitions, Lethcombe had matured into a perceptive and penetrating interviewer. Although his interviews made hypnotic listening, the Commander had heard that they were not always comfortable for the officer being interviewed.

Radio Leviathan's studio was a small and rather stuffy compartment in the base of the island. It had been fitted out with wireless receivers, two record turn-tables, a tape recorder, a control panel, and racks full of gramophone records on the bulkheads. There was a table in one corner, with two microphones on it, an ashtray, a decanter full of water and a glass. Lethcombe had an assistant at the control panel and he himself sat at the table opposite the Commander.

The Commander was impressed by the professional expertise of the programme. Lethcombe's assistant put a record on the turn-table and played the opening bars of the Scherzo from Mendelssohn's 'Italian' Symphony, which was the programme's signature tune. Lethcombe nodded in time to the music and when his assistant held up his thumb and the music faded, addressed himself to the microphone as though it were a fourth person in the studio.

'... *This* is Radio Leviathan, *your* most popular station north of the Arctic Circle. Good evening, and welcome to another programme in our series "Between You And Me". *Tonight* . . .' Lethcombe looked up, to warn the Commander to be ready. "Our

367

guest is the Commander. Good evening, sir, and thank you for coming along to the studio.'

The Commander cleared his throat. 'Good evening.'

'Sir, how did you feel when you heard you'd got a draft-chit to this ship? What were your first feelings?'

'Ah . . .' The Commander cleared his throat again. 'It's difficult to remember exactly at this distance. I had a feeling of pleasure, I recall. Certainly a feeling of a challenge . . .'

'Sir, when we first commissioned the Captain addressed us on the flight deck and said he admitted the previous commission had not been very successful but he was sure this would be a good one. *You* believed it could be done, sir. How?'

The Commander cleared his throat a third time. He must be giving the impression that he had some impediment in his throat, but in fact he was by now fighting for time to think. Lethcombe had launched a shrewd thunderbolt. The ship's company must have known all along of his secret dreams for the ship. They had read him like an open book. He cleared his throat for the last time and his voice suddenly found confidence.

'Yes, I did believe it could be done. You see, there are no bad ships, only bad ship's companies. I'm not saying that the last ship's company were necessarily bad, but what I felt we had to do this time was to get rid of that separate claustrophobic sort of existence which seemed to prevail. We seemed to be all in separate compartments, like cupboards, and we were each battling through a great mass of clothes hanging up in them. What we had to do was to get out, take a look at each other, and realise that we weren't all alone with things ganging up on us. There wasn't just *one* of us battling away all by himself, but two thousand of us, all working towards the same object. This, I think, was the main change in attitude we wanted.'

He picked up the decanter, poured himself a glass of water, and drank some of it. He expected another question, but Lethcombe was still looking at him.

'. . . I don't want to sound too much like a politician, but I do think we've achieved something in that direction. I think we're proving it every day of this patrol we're doing now. We're getting a little smoother, a little more confident, with every day that passes. After all, we've been up here about nine weeks now and nobody knows when we're going back. But we haven't shouted for help yet.'

'What would you say was the most difficult part of your job, sir? What gives you most furiously to think?'

'Being interviewed on Radio Leviathan, I think. No seriously, the most difficult part of the job is also the most difficult to describe. It's a question of planning, looking ahead and trying to forecast what will be required, where the ship will be then, how many hands will be needed, what time, how long it will take, and so on. It's like running a continuous almanack, working about a fortnight ahead. Take the Daily Orders, for instance. They appear on the notice boards for a particular day, but quite a lot of the information and routines on them were thrashed out and decided a week beforehand, sometimes months beforehand. You've got to keep on trying to forecast what's going to be happening a few weeks ahead.'

The Commander felt the table shiver beneath his fingers. In that tiny sound-proofed compartment he could not be sure he had heard the rumble of an explosion, but there had been some disturbance. He could hear its echoes and a perceptible change, a faltering in the ship's rhythm.

'What was that?'

Lethcombe looked bland and unconcerned, and pointed to the microphone to remind the Commander he was still on the air.

'Oh to hell with that!'

The smell of burning fuel from the ventilation louvres was now unmistakable. Its pungency filled the compartment and brought the Commander to his feet.

'There's something . . .'

His voice was drowned by the terrifying, high-pitched notes of the General Alarm, which overrode every other broadcast system in the ship.

'Fire! Fire! Fire! Fire in the upper hangar!' It was the urgent voice of the Petty Officer of the watch in Damage Control Headquarters. 'Hands to emergency stations! Assume damage control state one! Close all scuttles and X and Y openings! Fire! Fire! Fire in the upper hangar!'

The whole ship stood still, absorbing the news. While the broadcast continued with instructions to the firefighting and nuclear safeguard parties, the Commander hesitated at the studio door and then added himself to the stream of men who were doubling along the passageways and tumbling down the ladders with a gathering crescendo of stampeding feet and slamming hatches to their emergency stations. The Commander's own station was aft, in the secondary damage control headquarters, but he could make no progress against the men swarming up the first ladder to the island. He realised that he was struggling against the system of port and starboard side ladders he himself had devised to get the ship's company to their action stations quickly. He turned aside and joined the men descending the alternative ladder. At the bottom he cannoned into the Hangar Control Officer who was running aft along the passageway.

'Look where you're going, you stupid sod!' The Hangar Control Officer recognised the Commander. 'Jesus, this is a big one, sir!'

'Just a minute.' The Commander stared at him. 'What are you doing here? Why aren't you in Hangar Control?'

'Because I can't get into it for bloody smoke!' The Hangar Control Officer was still moving towards the next ladder. 'My lad in there just had time to lower the fire curtain and stop the ventilation and then beat it, but quick!'

'Where are you going now?'

'I'm going to try and have a look at it from the hangar access just down here, sir.'

The Commander followed him through the hatch. On their way he saw that the First Lieutenant's patient drills were having their reward. The damage control personnel were already at their posts. Four men, cowled in their long white anti-flash hoods and gloves, were hauling a portable pump from its stowage. In the next flat the lid of a magazine flooding cabinet was thrown open, exposing the row of valve handwheels; the artificer in charge of it was jingling his keys, jogging up and down on his toes and raising his knees like a runner warming up. They passed the open door of a damage control section base. The base was crowded and there were more men leaning against the bulkheads or squatting on their heels outside.

Their progress was growing steadily more difficult. More hatches and doors were being shut and clipped. The ship was sub-dividing into those separate sections for self-defence which had been

370

practised so often.

'Whereabouts in the hangar is the fire?'

'In the forrard section, sir. Looks as if one of the aircraft in there suddenly blew up and set them all off. I think there were about five in there, but I can't be sure. One of them may have fired its cannons into the next. That would set them off, and no mistake.'

'For God's sake, why were they armed?'

'They've always been armed, sir, ever since we left Pompey this time. We're operational now, sir.'

'Any men in there?'

'Bound to be. At least one hangar sentry and probably some others working in there when it happened.'

The door to the nearest hangar access airlock led from one of the seamen's messdecks. The half-drunk cups of tea on the tables, the towels looped over the lockers and the clothes left on the bunks showed how hastily the messdeck had been evacuated. The Commander made a mental note to mention them to the First Lieutenant; if this messdeck were ever flooded, those clothes and towels could clog the pump suctions and make it impossible to pump out the compartment.

There were four men on the messdeck, all wearing anti-flash clothing. One of them was standing by a sound-powered telephone. The others were clustered in front of the airlock door, peering through the glass observation panel.

'Stand back.'

Hot air gushed out of the airlock when the Commander opened the door, with the smell of steam, and burning paint and rubber. The Hangar Control Officer followed the Commander in and shut the outer door behind him. The bulkhead on the hangar side and the inner door were warm to the touch. The vibration of the fire and the cracks of explosions could be physically felt through the metal. The Commander put his eye to the inner observation panel and looked into the hangar.

Most of the hangar lighting had been extinguished and only one of the main lights showed as a pale yellow disc glowing through the smoke. To the Commander's left, the fire curtain was billowing and straining like a great grey sail. Just outside the airlock door the tail-plane of an aircraft was outlined in flame which had eaten away its tender parts and exposed its skeleton framework. On the

371

far side of the hangar a brilliant fresco of flames, like a row of dancing figures, described the silhouette of another aircraft which was burning along its entire length. The aircraft was unchocked and when the ship rolled it swung its black jet-snout at the airlock door and came forward a few feet clear of the smoke. The Commander recognised it as one of Roger Calvados' aircraft.

'Is Big One in there?'

'No, no, sir. Big One is either on the flight deck or down in the nuclear strong-room, sir. Hell's teeth, if Big One was in there we'd all be dead men by now!'

The Commander frowned. There was no need for such melo-dramatic talk. He understood that Big One was remarkably stable – more stable, it seemed, than the Hangar Control Officer.

A jet of fuel sprayed with an audible crackle across the centre of the hangar, igniting as it fell and forming a high blazing curtain. More fuel ran in a burning river, streaming smoke on its way to the hangar scuppers. A fiery current swept away the smoke and carried it spiralling upwards to the deckhead. The Commander saw the body of a man lying beyond the nearest aircraft. The burning fuel had flowed around him. His hands covered his face. His hair was burning in a halo of fire.

The airlock door shook and reverberated again, as under a stupendous hammer blow. The glass panel shattered and the noise of the fire entered the airlock, tearing through the jagged hole and cowing the men who stood there. The Commander's eardrums throbbed. The pressure was dropping as the fire sucked the oxygen out of the compartment.

The Hangar Control Officer had flung himself back against the outer door. 'That was a cannon-shell, sir!'

'*Spray!*'

The Hangar Control Officer's face clouded with indecision. The Commander thrust him aside and reached up to the lever in the corner. He pulled it and grasped the great red-painted hand-wheel set in the bulkhead. The wheel was stiff but began to spin more easily as he turned it.

The Commander placed both hands on the Hangar Control Officer's shoulders and shook him until he almost stumbled. 'Now keep on spraying! And in future when I give you an order you bloody well *do* it!'

372

The men outside scattered as the Commander burst open the outer door.

'Does that telephone go through to HQ One?'

The man nodded, gave the handle one swing, and handed the receiver to the Commander.

'This is the Commander. Put the First Lieutenant on.'

'He's not here, sir.'

'Not there?' His ears were still numbed and he could barely hear the reply. 'Where the devil is he?'

'I don't know, sir. Shipwright Officer here, sir.'

'Chippy, look. I'm spraying the upper hangar from this side, that's the starboard side, do you understand me?'

'Yes, sir.'

'Tell them to start spraying from the port side, the forrard section only. Tell the ACR to start hosing down the flight deck above the forrard section of the upper hangar. Tell them to spray the fire curtain from the after side. Get on to the engine-room and tell them to put on every pump they've got. We want all the fire-main pressure we can get. Have you got all that?'

'Yes, sir.'

'And when the First Lieutenant arrives, ask him to call me at this extension.' The Commander turned to the men in the mess-deck. 'Two of you get into breathing suits. Quickly.'

A cool wind was blowing through the shattered glass panel, carrying with it a mist of fine water particles. Larger drops of water were splashing outside the door. Clouds of smoke and steam obscured the hangar and blew against the observation panel. The metal of the inner door was now cool and moist. The explosions had stopped, the sound of the fire blanketed by the drumming water.

The Hangar Control Officer had regained his composure. 'I'm sorry about that just now, sir. It seemed such a drastic step to take. It's something you only read about in the manuals.'

The Commander could not imagine what the man was talking about. He was still preoccupied by the First Lieutenant's absence. It was not like Number One to be adrift, just when all his work was bearing fruit.

The Hangar Control Officer pointed at the forward bulkhead. 'I think we were just in time, sir. Just forrard here, there's the oxygen generating plant. It's tricky stuff at the best of times. If you heat it, it goes up like a torch. It could have blown the ship's side out.'

'Could it.' The Commander scowled. He must remember to talk to Commander (Air) about this man. In an emergency, such men spread the seeds of panic. 'Can the oxygen generating plant be sprayed from outside the hangar?'

'Yes sir, it's got its own separate spray system.'

'Well, go and *spray* it then! And stop *jabbering* about it!'

The Commander listened at the observation panel. He could hear nothing except the water drumming on the hangar deck. The fire was now sealed in a water-cooled box. By now they should be spraying on the flight deck above, and at one side, on the fire curtain. If necessary, they could cool down all sides, by hosing the bulkheads of the compartments and passageways adjacent to the hangar.

He opened the outer door and called into the messdeck. 'Tell HQ One to stop spraying port side.'

He shut off the spray valve and listened again. In a moment, the water slackened.

'They're shutting off port side, sir. And the First Lieutenant hasn't arrived yet.'

'Let's have this door open. Are those sets comfortable?'

The nearest man, masked in his breathing set, held up his thumb.

'You with the hose there. You go first. Make sure you've got your nozzle in the spray position and *not* the jet. Have you?'

The man nodded.

'In you go then.'

The man climbed awkwardly through the doorway, the water spurting and fanning out in a wide shield from his hose as he advanced into the hangar.

'You there. You follow him up. Make sure that hose doesn't get snagged up.'

Directed by the Commander, the fire-fighting parties entered the hangar from both sides, advancing behind protective walls of water from their hoses, to attack and subdue the fires in each aircraft in turn. Men with foam-making branch pipes followed them, the foam completing the work of the water. Some turned their attentions to the stores and equipment which were still smoking round the hangar bulkheads. The Commander ran to the body he had seen from the airlock door. It was, as he had guessed, the First Lieutenant.

He was lying on his back, his arms folded across his chest in the manner of a buried Crusader's effigy. His eyes were shut, his face composed. The hair on his head was frizzled black almost down to the scalp. Drops of water glistened on his forehead and water was leaking away on the deck from his sodden uniform. The Commander stood, looking down at him. The First Lieutenant had been a good friend. They had often wrangled, but their arguments had been between friends, between men who fundamentally believed in the same things. In a wardroom which contained much that seemed strange and hostile to the Commander, the First Lieutenant's had been a familiar face. He had been passed over for promotion and could have had no personal gain from *Leviathan*'s success but he had done his duty as well as any officer in the wardroom, because he had been trained for it and because, beneath his cynicism, he loved it.

The Commander discovered the PMO and Hamish standing beside him, with five or six sick-berth attendants carrying stretchers. The PMO knelt beside the body and pushed up one of the eyelids, gently disengaging his finger from the flesh which tried to stick to it.

'Was it the fire or the water, Angus?'

'Neither. Asphyxiation, most probably. What was he doing in here?'

'I don't know. He might have been passing through. Or he might have seen something and come in to lend a hand.'

The PMO stood up. 'Let's have a look at these others.'

There were two more charred and drenched bodies lying against the hangar bulkhead on the port side and a few yards forward of them, the legs and trunk of a man had collapsed across an aircraft mainwheel. The head and half the chest had been blown off; the boots and gaiters showed that the man had been a hangar sentry. The torn torso was still bleeding into the water and burnt debris on the hangar deck. One of the men in breathing sets tore off his mask and vomited into a hangar scupper.

The man's distress was contagious. The Commander felt his

mouth swimming with saliva. 'Look, if you've got nothing better to do than stand there puking, go and do it outside!'

A high pressure air connection had been blowing full bore further down the hangar. Someone traced the blackened valve and shut it off. In the quiet which followed, the hangar murmured with the hushed voices of the men gathered in it, looking and wondering at the devastation around them.

The forward lift descended with a jangling of bells, admitting a flood of daylight from the open flight deck above. Rowley Dubonnet stood on the edge of the lift as it stopped. His eyes travelled slowly round the hangar.

'Holy *Mother!*' His whisper carried to the ends of the hangar. 'What have we done to deserve this?'

Three aircraft in the section had been gutted to skeletons and the remaining two seriously burned. The green of the hangar deck was marked with great patches and contorted arabesques of scorched black where the fire had eddied to and fro across it. The paint had been stripped from the air bottles, tool-boxes, starting trolleys and nose-wheel forks which had been stowed along the sides of the hangar. Rubber had been burned out of watertight doors and ventilation flap seatings. Trunkings, battery charging connections and valve handwheels had all been twisted and warped by the fierce heat. Melted lead had dripped from electric cables and splashed on the hangar deck. Pipe joints had been burned out; water and hydraulic oil were spurting from the flanges, falling in tumbling waterfalls down the bulkheads, and mixing in spreading pools across the deck. Most of the stores and spare parts in the bulkhead and deckhead racks had been first burned and then drenched with foam and water.

More men were crowding into the hangar through the airlock doors. There was a flash from the Hangar Control Cabinet, and several more flashes down in the hangar; the Air Group photographers were recording the scene as evidence for the board of inquiry. The sick-berth attendants had taken away the stretchers. Joss Parkhurst emerged from the oxygen generating compartment door. He caught the Commander's eye.

'Good job someone had the wit to spray this place. A few more minutes and those oxygen bottles would have gone up like doomsday.'

376

'Mind your back please, sir.'

The Commander stood aside, to let the deck handlers manoeuvre the first of the burned-out aircraft up to the flight deck. He watched a messenger threading through the crowd, knowing that the man was coming to him.

'Captain's compliments, sir, he'd like to see all Heads of Departments on the bridge as soon as possible.'

When the rest of the Heads of Departments arrived, the Commander stood at the back of the bridge, taking no part in the discussion. He was appalled by their mood of suppressed exultation. They had all acted together to avert a mortal danger to the ship and their performance had certainly been worthy of praise. But the price had been too high. The Commander watched the faces around him mouthing irrelevancies. They were talking about damage to the electrical ring-main and to the leads to the island gyro-compass repeaters, about shattered hydraulic supply to 'A' turret and to the bomb lifts, and about fractured aviation fuel pipes and the loss of the oxygen generating plant. It was all idle chatter. The technical officers could argue the point whichever way they pleased. The main decision had already been taken for them. The Commander knew that *Leviathan*'s great patrol was over.

23

On *Leviathan*'s first evening in harbour, circumstances conspired to irritate the Commander. He could get no answer from Annabel's telephone. The wardroom was besieged throughout the day by casual visitors eager to hear first-hand accounts of the patrol and the hangar fire, but towards the evening the ante-rooms had emptied. The Commander foresaw that he would be left to dine, as he had so often done in the past, with the duty lieutenant commander and two or three bachelor duty officers. Aware that he was behaving out of character, the Commander changed into plain clothes, ate an early supper, and decided to go ashore.

He found the battery of his car flat. He had left the side-lights burning when he had returned to the ship so hurriedly two months before. He walked through the dockyard to the main gate and, again conscious that he was behaving oddly, turned off The Hard at random and began to walk aimlessly amongst back streets he could not remember ever having seen before.

If he was not a naval officer, the Commander decided, he would never visit Portsmouth again. It was a mean town, and he had always disliked it. It was a sailors' town, where sailors were unwelcome. Portsmouth had grown with the Navy but had sponged on it without gratitude; in Portsmouth the Navy was like a rich old relative, who paid the bills but was never introduced to visitors. He particularly disliked the Portsmouth accent; it was a kind of half-urban whine, neither true city nor true country. There was not a decent building in the place; even the Guildhall had only achieved a certain temporary dignity when it was wrecked by bombing. Portsmouth seemed to be populated by elderly men in naval raincoats who had served the Navy and were now serving themselves on pension. Everyone knew their rights in Portsmouth. Nothing memorable in his career had ever happened here. His memories were all far away. This was a town for commissioning and for fitting-out, for paying-off and for aftermaths.

The Commander stopped on a corner, opposite a large and ostentatious public house, with a hideous red neon sign. It was the kind of house the Commander would normally have shunned, but he made up his mind to continue an already surrealistic evening by going in for a drink.

In the Lounge Bar, which the Commander noted with disgust was sub-titled The Cuddy, the chairs, long bench seats and pillars were upholstered in red leather. The small tables round the room and the bar itself were topped with black glass. There was a long mirror behind the bar, polished and copper-coloured; some sort of electrical device was projecting coloured lights which played to and fro across the mirror, giving an unearthly miniature Aurora Borealis after-glow to the cupro-world reflected in it. The Commander advanced unwillingly towards the bar, once more having the sensation that his every movement that evening was being impelled by some personality outside himself. He looked gloomily at the labels on the pump-handles. Clearly this was a bar whose customers regarded draught beer as common. Here, they had a choice of fizzy beers, expelled from metal containers by compressed gas.

The landlord was obviously an ex-Chief Petty Officer. The Commander placed him almost automatically and knew, at the same time, that he had also been recognised as a naval officer.

The landlord offered cautious civilities. He had not only recognised the Commander as a naval officer but could make a guess at his rank and was surprised by his custom. There were other, longer-established and better known pubs for officers in Portsmouth; this was essentially a pub for the lads, and for their wives and girl-friends.

The Commander drank his beer, feeling its unwholesome prickle on his palate. His thoughts turned inevitably to *Leviathan*. She was now assured of a good commission. The whole ship re-echoed that assurance. Only he seemed to mourn the future lost in that fire. The great ship and her ship's company had been on the brink of a tremendous achievement. But now, the weeks of the patrol would be forgotten. People would only remember that *Leviathan* had been forced to return prematurely, because of a self-inflicted injury. He had set his heart on success in *Leviathan*, believing that the only alternative to success was failure; he had never suspected the possibility of a partial success. There was no doubt that in those last days in the Arctic the great ship had looked from

379

a distance at an immense prize. But she had not quite grasped it.

If only, by some miraculous transformation, *Leviathan* could go to sea again tomorrow. The longer she remained alongside, the further her spirit would be dissipated. The signs of deterioration were already there: on the passage home, every divisional officer in the ship had been swamped by requests for compassionate leave. Once it was known that the ship was going home, a hundred wives were facing difficult child-births, a score of close relatives appeared to be on their death-beds. The Commander prayed that the circumstances which had combined while *Leviathan* was at sea would still obtain when the repairs in the hangar were complete. *Leviathan* had just begun to live and move and function as a proper ship. She deserved another chance.

The Commander ordered again. Although he had been standing at the bar for some time and should have acquired the anonymity of his seniority there, he knew that he had not yet merged into the scenery. He was still unusual, even exotic, for that particular bar.

The room was now filling with Saturday night custom and the landlord had been reinforced by three barmen in white coats. From their nods, their laughter, and the witticisms they exchanged with the landlord, the Commander judged that most of the new customers were regulars. Amongst them were some of those middle-aged women with metallic laughs and down-trodden faces whose only habitat in any significant numbers were the public houses of Portsmouth; probably they were whores who had grown too old for the business but still gathered in their old haunts from force of habit.

Now that his house was doing business, the landlord wished the Commander gone. He so obviously did not fit in, staring about him like a visitor at a zoo. The Commander sensed the landlord's hostility and though he had been about to leave, now determined to remain. He rudely and purposely turned his back on the landlord and leaned his elbows on the bar. He tipped his hat back on his head, crossed his legs and surveyed the room with a botanist's detachment. None of *Leviathan*'s officers or ship's company would have recognised their Commander in such a posture.

He envied the rest of the clientele in the room. They looked such uncomplicated people. They came out on Saturday nights to drink, to see their friends and to stare at each other. Their cheeks

380

were red and round and they stretched out comfortably in their chairs and when they laughed they shut their eyes and showed their tongues and exposed their large polished teeth. Their glasses stood in battalions on the wet tables, their cigarette smoke rose in furious gusts, and their women laughed shrilly and competitively. These people never grappled with problems of morale and leadership. These happy drinkers never had to reconcile the self-interests of two thousand men bent on their own advancement. These people were concerned with birth and death and rent and taxes, realities which the Commander himself had almost forgotten.

He knocked the base of his empty glass heavily against the bar, to attract the landlord's attention. The landlord looked round at the insistent noise, and his eyes narrowed. With a small thrill of astonishment, the Commander realised that the landlord was now keeping an eye on him because he, the Commander, might just possibly make trouble. The Commander had not made trouble in a public house for twenty years but as he had jettisoned so much of his normal personality already he conceded that tonight might indeed be his night.

'The same again, sir?'

'No. Yes.' He grinned at the landlord, whose uneasiness was now plain. The Commander wondered whether he should have provoked the landlord by demanding some outlandish drink. With his fresh pint in his hand, he swung away from the bar and came face to face with two pilots from *Leviathan*.

'Good *evening*, sir!'

Their amazement showed in their voices and their faces. This was the last place they had expected to find the Commander, drinking by himself, on a Saturday night. The Commander read their faces and was at once defensively aggressive.

'Good evening to you.'

They were both in Rupert Smith's squadron, but he could not at first recall their names. There was a constant change-over of officers among the aircrew and he was not now quite so conscientious at remembering their names as he had been at the start of the commission.

'You're Padgett, aren't you?'

The taller and more self-possessed of the two smiled. 'Yes, sir. I joined just before we sailed on that last show.'

The Commander winced at the word. The young puppy was talking like a veteran Battle of Taranto pilot. He nodded at the other one.

'I can't remember your name, I'm afraid.'

'It's Disley, sir.'

'Ah yes, I've got it now.' He resented the surliness in the boy's tone. Disley, he remembered, had joined as Stiggins' replacement. He had short black hair cropped close to his scalp and there was something in his accent and his manners which revived uncomfortable memories.

The Commander belched loudly, and Padgett laughed. The solecism seemed to give him self-confidence.

'Can we buy you a drink, sir?'

'No thank you, I've got a glass of beer here.'

'Have a short then, sir?'

A short? To the Commander, the word had all the associations of commercial travellers' Christmas dinners, office parties, and car-loads of sales representatives disembarking at shoddily-smart fashionable hotels. But officers in the Service surely did not offer one another '*shorts*'?

'No thank you, Padgett. I'm quite happy.'

'Don't you drink with pilots then?'

Padgett thrust an arm across Disley's chest. 'Shut up, you stupid drongo.'

The Commander ignored them both. This public house was probably only one stop in their night's peregrinations. In a minute or two they would be on their way and he would be left in peace.

However, to the Commander's irritation, Padget obviously felt that it was up to him to make polite conversation in the meantime.

'Is this your normal local, sir?'

'No, it is *not*! And I don't have a *local*!'

'You don't normally come in here then, sir?'

'Good God. No I do *not*!' He was exasperated by this inane conversation. 'This is the first time I've been here and I'd say it will probably be the last. Now if you'll excuse me, I object to this conversation.'

But Padgett appeared unabashed. It seemed to be important to his self-esteem that he should not betray embarrassment before an officer as senior as the Commander. The Commander realised that he was once more confronted by a representative of the New Model Navy. Padgett represented another generation of naval officers who were indistinguishable from their ratings in either appearance, dress or manners. They were casual, agnostic and self-satisfied. It made him sick to look at them. He searched Padgett's face for consolation. If you are an officer, then reassure me that the Navy will survive. Stay me with the thought that the past has not been forgotten.

'Pity we had to come back like that, sir.'

'Like what?'

'Back from that last show, sir.'

He winced again. 'Well, I think we all did our best.'

Disley was glowering at him. 'It wasn't the Air Group's fault.'

'It wasn't anybody's fault.'

'What do you think of pilots then?'

'What do I think of *pilots?*' He was at first baffled, and then angry. 'What the devil do you mean by that?'

'Patrick, for God's sake . . .' Padgett tried to interpose himself between Disley and the Commander.

'You think we're the scum of the earth, don't you?' Disley's mouth was puckered, as though he were about to burst into tears.

The Commander gaped at him, astounded by the accusation and by the look of hatred on the boy's face. 'If you haven't anything more constructive to say than that, my boy, you can go . . .'

'I'm not your boy . . .'

'Patrick, *leave* it!'

'Give Lieutenant-Commander Smith my compliments and tell him I wish to see you in my cabin at nine o'clock to-morrow morning . . .'

'You do, don't you? It's the way you look at us, you think we're the dregs . . .'

The Commander turned to put his glass on the bar. The two of them were clearly not leaving, so he must leave, and at once, before there was an incident. But he felt Disley's hand on his shoulder, dragging him back.

'What the devil do you think you're doing . . .'

'You *do,* don't you?'

The Commander hardly felt the blow on his cheek and was not properly aware of what had happened until he felt the tingling

383

spreading from his cheek-bone down to his chin. He lifted his arm to ward off the second blow. His hat fell from his head and dropped behind him on the bar. A buzzing and murmuring filled the room and he heard the landlord's voice rising idiotically in his ear, saying, 'Oy, oy, I'm not having any of that in here . . .'

'Patrick, have you gone *mad!*'

The Commander braced himself against the bar. The unrealities of that evening fell away from him. He was once more the Commander, the Executive Officer of the ship, facing two terrified young officers.

Disley's hands were trembling, and his face was full of the terrible after-knowledge of what he had done.

'I'm sorry, sir, I'm really terribly sorry, sir . . .'

The Commander waved him down. 'Padgett, I charge you to take Lieutenant Disley back to the ship at once and place him under close arrest . . .'

'I'm really sorry, sir . . .'

'Keep silence. You will both return to the ship at once and report to the Officer of the Watch until I get there.'

The incident seemed to have dropped a curtain over events earlier in the evening. The Commander was now ice-cold sober, but he could not remember clearly what he had done before he arrived at the public house. He spent some time searching for his car before he remembered that he had walked from the ship. Nor could he remember the way he had come and the walk back to the ship took him half an hour of desperate half-walking, half-running through unfamiliar back streets.

Disley and Padgett were waiting on the quarterdeck. Rupert Smith was also there, in plain clothes and carrying a golf bag. The Commander was puzzled and enfuriated by Rupert's civilian suit and the golf clubs. 'Why aren't you in uniform?'

'I'm sorry, sir.' Rupert, too, was puzzled. 'I forgot my clubs and I just happened to be on board collecting them when my officers returned.'

The Commander's head whirled and he steadied himself against the watch-keeper's desk. 'I suppose you'll be the defending officer?'

'Well sir, I've only just heard the barest facts.' Rupert wore the dawning expression of a man realising that he has unwittingly walked into a hurricane. 'I really don't know what's happened, properly, sir. I hoped we could discuss it, sir.'

'Discuss it?' The Commander coughed and his mouth filled with stale-tasting saliva; the fresh air and the walk back to the ship had circulated the alcohol in his blood stream. 'There's nothing to discuss. I'm going to my cabin now, to change into uniform before . . . before . . .'

He paused. He could not remember what to do. An investigation should be started, evidence given, statements taken, at once, now, while the facts were fresh. But he could not remember the correct procedure. An investigation into a charge of striking a superior officer should be started immediately, in fairness to the accused man, but he felt powerless to set it in train.

The Commander put his hands over his face and drew them downwards until the tips of his fingers pressed against his chin. He could still feel the soreness of his cheek.

'I'm going to my cabin now.'

'May I come with you, sir?'

'Of course. If you want to. I can't see the point of it, but if you want to, certainly you can. Tell Lieutenant Disley to go to his cabin. He's not to leave it without an escort.'

In his cabin, the Commander's own possessions greeted him with their familiarity. He drew fresh strength from them. He had needed their reassurance. He sat in the chair at his desk and rested his head in his hands.

The shock of Disley's assault had not been physical. He had barely felt either blow strike him. The real hurt was in the knowledge that the attack had been on its way towards him for months, possibly since the day of his first meeting with Stiggins. Although his relations with the aircrew had improved since Stiggins' death, nobody in the wardroom would be really surprised to hear that an aircrew officer had struck the Commander. The irrationality of it, the sheer improbability of the circumstances, would be obscured; the wardroom would base their interpretation on a reputation rather than on the facts.

'Can you tell me what actually happened, sir?'

'I don't know what happened, really. I was standing in this pub . . .'

'Which pub, sir?'

'Do you know, I haven't any idea what the name of it was? I

385

doubt if I could even find it again. Isn't that incredible?'

'What happened in the pub, sir?'

'I was standing at the bar all by myself when your two pilots came in. Padgett was civil enough, according to his lights, but the other one, that was Disley, did nothing but stand and glare at me. He glared at me from the moment he came in. While I was talking, he suddenly seemed to take offence at something I said. I forget what it was now . . .'

The Commander bowed his head, recalling the scene in the bar. 'I remember, it was while we were saying what a pity it was we had to come back from the Arctic. And then he struck me. He struck me twice, actually. I'd no alternative but to tell him to return to the ship and consider himself under close arrest. I'm not sure I should have done that. Perhaps I should have called the patrol and let them do it. I don't know now. It all seems so bloody improbable I can hardly believe it happened.'

'I'm very glad you didn't call the patrol, sir.'

'Well, I'm *not!*' The remark touched off the Commander's latent indignation and his sense of outrage. 'I've served in the Navy ever since I was a boy of thirteen and I've never heard of another case of one officer striking another he barely knew! I tell you, I had to think hard to remember the fellow's name myself! But I can promise you this much, Rupert, I'm going to settle Disley's hash, once and for all. I'm going to raise such a whirlwind over this that will teach every damned pilot in the Fleet Air Arm to keep his fists in his pockets and a civil tongue in his head. If I do nothing else, I'll make certain of *that*. And *you* can say good-bye to your brasshat. By the time I've finished with you, neither you nor any of those little layabouts of yours will ever dare to raise your voices above a whisper again . . .'

'Sir, I realise you haven't a very high opinion of pilots . . .'

'Good *God* . . .' The Commander raised both fists and crashed them down on his desk in a spasm of pure rage. 'My opinion of pilots has nothing to do with it! How many times must I point out that I'm not against pilots on *principle!* I only object to their conduct when I'd have objected anyway, whoever they were. Whoever had been in that pub tonight, I'd see he was drummed out of the Service. Pilots are neither here nor there, can't you understand that? God blast you, why must you always be so

386

sensitive against discrimination? You're like a lot of bloody niggers, always on the lookout for insults. If I tell a ship's officer to go and do something he goes and does it and no back-chat. If you tell a pilot, he thinks he's being picked on!'

'I'm sorry, sir.'

'So you bloody well ought to be. Well, I suppose we'd better get the thing started.'

The investigation must start now, with the duty lieutenant commander as investigating officer. He must also telephone the Captain at his home, and consult the Captain's Secretary, if he was on board. The Commander placed both palms on his desk and half-rose from his chair. Then he sat down again, assailed by fears of the future. He was reluctant to set his hand to the instruments of naval justice. Short of actual mutiny, striking a superior officer was one of the most serious offences against the Naval Discipline Act. The indictment and the penalties had been framed in the days of sail. The Commander was about to summon up the dark vengeful furies of naval law and discipline. There would be the circumstantial letter, the eight o'clock gun, the assembly of the court. Disley would be publicly crucified. His own reputation would be damaged; in such cases, the injured officer was privately blamed as much as the offending officer. Meanwhile, the whispers would begin again that *Leviathan* had achieved nothing after all. The great ship was living up to her reputation still.

'There'll be a court martial, sir.'

The Commander nodded. 'Of course there will, d'you think I don't know that? It'll be a stinking one, too. These kind always are. They don't do anybody any good. They'll bring up all sorts of evidence about the effects of alcohol on the brain and loss of inhibitions and all that nonsense about locomotor ataxy. They'll end up by proving he's not only a hooligan but a lunatic as well. I remember when I was a two-striper I was the accused's friend for a sailor in my division. He thumped the Corporal of the Gangway when he was coming off drunk one night. It was the most trivial incident, basically. But by the time we'd finished the court martial you'd think the poor little bugger was a raving madman. I often wondered since whether that whole procedure wasn't making the thing much worse than it need be.'

'We could deal with this case internally, sir.'

'What do you mean, *internally?* You can't have an *internal* court martial.'

'No, sir. You needn't have a court martial at all.'

'Nonsense. We've got to have a court martial. He's had his little fun and games. Now he's got to wait for the hangman.'

'I wasn't thinking of Disley particularly, sir. I was thinking of us, of the ship generally. I was thinking of the effect on the ship right now of a court martial involving a ship's officer and one of the aircrew.'

'Do you think that hadn't already occurred to me?'

'I know it had, sir. I was about to suggest a way in which it could be avoided.'

The Commander swung round in his chair. 'Just what are you driving at?

Rupert Smith saw that he would not have a better opportunity of putting his suggestion. 'I was going to suggest, sir, that you leave Disley to Commander (Air) and me . . .'

'That's impossible, Rupert . . .'

'Please sir, let me finish. My squadron and I can make quite sure Disley won't profit by it, I can assure you, sir. I'm not asking this for Disley or even for the rest of my squadron. I'm asking for all of us. I'm certain that this ship very nearly achieved something really worthwhile the last time we were at sea. Everybody thinks that. And we could still do it, if we were given the chance. But if we have this court martial everything will be lost. Everything.' Rupert saw that the Commander was growing impatient. 'What I'm saying, sir, is that there are cases where the end justifies the means. There is absolutely no excuse whatever for what Disley did . . .'

'I'm glad you appreciate that, at least.'

'. . . And in normal circumstances I'd be the first to insist that we threw the book at him. But circumstances in this ship are not normal, sir. I think this ship is a special case and justifies a special solution. We've stretched a point before and I'm suggesting we stretch a point again. I'm asking you to do something dishonest, sir.'

'I'm *well* aware of that, thank you.' The Commander recognised the fine nuance of blackmail. Rupert was asking him to do once again, on a larger scale, and for the ship, what he had already done on a small scale for Stiggins. Dropping the charge against Disley would be fundamentally no more dishonest than burning Stiggins' letter. *La distance n'y fait rien; il n'y a que le premier pas qui coute.* The distance was nothing; it was the first step that counted. The Commander accepted that Rupert was sincere when he said he was looking beyond his own squadron, at the ship as a whole. If the request had been made by anyone else, it would have been unthinkable. But there was still the matter of Stiggins' letter. For the first time, the Commander regretted having burnt it.

'You're asking me to compound a serious offence against the Naval Discipline Act?'

'Yes, sir. That's exactly what I'm doing.'

'My God, Rupert, I have to give you credit, you're bloody bold enough! But it's not on, I'm afraid. I can't drop this, much as I'd like to. It's out of the question. We'd ...' In time, the Commander prevented himself adding 'We'd never get away with it'.

But Rupert had noted the Commander's hesitation. 'If you look at it, sir, you'll see that it's not out of the question, provided we do it tonight. We've stretched a point before ...'

'I know that, don't keep reminding me. The circumstances were quite different.'

'Basically, sir, they weren't all that different. At the moment, it's up to us. We've got a choice of two courses of action ...'

'No we haven't. There's only one thing we can possibly do.' The Commander felt himself being out-manoeuvred, herded in a direction he would like but dared not go. Rupert was like a sheepdog, ranging round him, nipping him, urging him towards an attractive but fatal path.

'If we assume just for the moment, sir, that we do have a choice, we can either go the whole hog, have a court martial, publicity, back to the bad old days, and work our weary way up again. Or, we can hush it up, to put it quite candidly, sir. But we'll never be able to keep it away from the rest of the wardroom. They'll all know what's happened, but they'll know you did what you did for the sake of the ship, sir.'

It was a subtle argument, and an appealing one. Whether or not there was ever a court martial, Disley would not escape punishment. His private forfeits, in the eyes of his fellow-officers, might well exceed any public penalty. The knowledge that he had been permitted to escape a court martial for the sake of the ship would be the final proof that there was now in *Leviathan* something worth preserving.

But the proposition was still fantastic. The case was indisputable, a clear-cut act prejudicial to good order and naval discipline. Furthermore, Disley had committed a breach of the peace, an offence against civil law. Nevertheless, the Commander was tempted.

Rupert watched the expressions cross the Commander's face and knew that he was tempted.

'The fact that a pilot is involved, sir, makes it all the more difficult. If you did this for a pilot, it would somehow show . . . I don't know how to describe it. It would show that we were all one wardroom.'

'I thought you said it should be done for the *ship?*' Against his will, the Commander found himself weakening. The advantages of Rupert's suggestion were so attractive. After the events of the evening, the Commander knew that he was not capable of making a balanced decision; whatever he decided now, he would probably regret after a night's sleep. He wished he could delay his decision until the morning but, as Rupert said, it should be done now.

'All right. I'll take no further action.' The Commander spoke slowly, with a sense of personal betrayal. 'I'm going to leave it to you.'

He was rending the veil of the ark of the temple with his own hands. His decision was wrong, but he hoped it would be shown that he had done the wrong, only for the sake of a greater right.

'Thank you very much indeed, sir! I'm sure that's the right thing to do!'

'I hope to God you're right, Rupert.'

Rupert was well aware of the implications of the Commander's decision. He also realised that, paradoxically, a less honourable man than the Commander would not have been capable of so large a dishonesty.

24

As the Commander ate his breakfast on Sunday morning he remembered his decision of the night before with a kind of defiant satisfaction. The decision was wrong, but he was prepared to stand by it. His conscience was not and never would be comforted but he was ready to live with his conscience for *Leviathan*'s sake.

The decision had been almost too easy. There had been no immediate thunder of retribution. The Commander secretly believed that the affair was not ended. It was not right that naval justice could be so readily diverted. The Commander expected repercussions, and when he saw the Secretary's face at his cabin door after breakfast, it was like the serving of a long-awaited summons.

The Secretary was in uniform, and the Commander remembered that he normally came on board on Sunday mornings in harbour before going to church in the barracks chapel. The Secretary was frowning at a sheet of paper in his hand.

'Bob, I've just intercepted something very odd from the Naval Provost Marshal's office. Were you by any chance involved in some sort of scuffle in a pub in town last night? It seems highly unlikely, but . . .'

'Yes, I was.' The Commander turned away his face, and dropped his head, nerving himself for the encounter to come. 'How did you know?'

The Secretary waved the sheet of paper. 'Patrol report just come on board.'

The Commander started. *'Patrol report!* What patrol report? There was no patrol.'

'The landlord called them. To protect himself, I suppose. There's a statement from him with the patrol report. Whoever it was had gone by the time the patrol arrived, but having been called they had to put in a report.'

'Let's have a look at that.' The Secretary passed him the report. There could be no doubt about it: there was the leading patrolman's name and official number, his report of how he had proceeded to the scene of the 'altercation'. The pub, the Commander noticed, was called 'The Admiral Of The Red'. There was the landlord's description of the incident.

'But how did they know who we were? How did they know what ship to send it to?'

The Secretary looked at the Commander curiously; he had caught an unexpected note of guilt in the Commander's voice.

'Your hat.'

His hat. It had fallen from his head during the scuffle and he had not given it another thought since. The hat had his name and initials stamped inside the band. That, and his description from the landlord, would have been more than enough.

'Where is my hat now?'

'In the Regulating Office, with a large patrolman standing over it. He wants a signature for it.'

'Right, I'll send Mulligan along to collect it. No. No, he's on week-end. I'll send . . . never mind, I'll send somebody.' The Commander's mind grappled with the problem of recovering the hat, while knowing and ignoring the far graver problem yawning like an abyss beyond. 'Thank you for telling me about this, Scratch. I'll go and see what I can do. You leave it with me.'

'Bob, what are we going to do about this patrol report? Or rather, what's *been* done about it?' The Secretary gazed steadily down at the Commander, who met his stare briefly and glanced away.

'Bob, I've got a horrible premonition you're going to need some advice. What's this all about? Perhaps I can help.'

'All right.'

The story was only twelve hours old, but it had already acquired the qualities of a legend, of a dream imperfectly remembered on wakening. Yet in telling it the Commander was surprised by the range and accuracy of the circumstantial detail he could remember. He obtained so great an emotional release from the telling that he told more than he had intended.

The Secretary listened with growing dismay. Everyone knew that Bob Markready was fanatical about *Leviathan*'s reputation, to the point of being unbalanced. He himself had saluted him for it; the ship had needed someone to believe in her. But he had never thought that Bob's enthusiasm would lead him to such an act of professional insanity.

'Let me get this straight, Bob. This pilot struck you, you say?'

'Yes. Twice.'

'So you put him under close arrest, told him to report back on board, is that right?'

'Yes.'

'And then his squadron CO came to see you, and as a result of what he said, you agreed to forget the whole thing?'

'Not to forget it, no. Rupert said he'd deal with it.'

'But as far as *you're* concerned, you reckon the thing's finished?'

'Yes. I fixed it with Rupert.'

'Hell's teeth!' The Secretary wheeled swiftly and made for the door. 'I'd better get the Captain on the blower quick. They've had twelve hours to cook up a story . . .'

'The Captain! There's no need to tell him anything. I tell you, I've dealt with it.'

'I'm sorry, Bob, but that's not good enough.'

Suddenly weary, the Commander took the Secretary's retreat as a betrayal.

'You hate me, don't you, Scratch?'

'Hate you?' The Secretary stopped in his stride, and turned round. 'Bob, you're either a very saintly man, or a very stupid one, I'm not sure which.'

'Why do you say that?'

The Secretary came back to the Commander's desk and put one forefinger on it, leaning on the finger until it bent under his weight.

'Bob, there is going to be *the* most Almighty row over this you ever saw in all your natural life. It's going to be a whopper, even for this ship.'

'Why should there be?'

The Secretary grimaced under the strain of trying to make his point. 'Striking a superior officer is just about the most lethal thing you can do to your career in peace-time, short of actually being party to a mutiny. It's rule one, line one, Bob. In big black letters, Thou shalt not strike thy superior *officer*. It wouldn't have made any difference if he hadn't known who you were, because that's no defence. You're still guilty of striking a superior officer even if you thought he was a dustman when you struck him. But this fellow *did* know who you were. It's because you *are* who you are that he struck you, and in front of a whole pub full of witnesses! And you blandly tell me it's all fixed: *Fixed!* It hasn't *started* yet! What's to prevent him saying in court in mitigation that you provoked him?'

'There was no question of that.'

'Ah. So *you* say. But you haven't got any evidence! By the time we get to a court martial they may be saying that it was you who thumped him first!'

'That's ridiculous.'

'But can you *prove* it? Far more ridiculous things have been accepted as evidence by courts martial, take my word for it. They're two to one against you and I bet you a dollar to a fiver they've spent half the night preparing their stories . . .'

'That's impossible. Rupert Smith and I agreed . . .'

'Bob, it doesn't *matter* what you and Rupert agreed. You may have believed it, but Rupert's no fool. He'd know that whatever you and he agreed last night wouldn't stand up in the light of day for more than two minutes. I'll lay you anything you like the first thing Rupert did when he left you was to go straight back to his two lads and start rehearsing them in their stories . . .'

'Scratch, that's a contemptible and despicable thing to say . . .'

'*Bob!*' For a mad second, the Secretary understood why the Commander had been assaulted. 'Can't you *understand?* You've put yourself in a very awkward position. You've not only failed in your duty to prosecute a very serious offence against the Naval Discipline Act but you've also laid yourself open to all sorts of counter-charges, simply because you haven't got the evidence to support your side of the case. Bob, why do you think *I* give a damn about this?'

'I've no idea, except that I imagine you enjoy stirring things up.'

The Secretary flushed a deep, angry red. 'That was not worthy of you, Bob.'

The Commander had already regretted it. 'I know it wasn't, and I'm sorry, Scratch. But you seem to be missing my purpose in all this. I had to make a choice between justice, pure and simple, and the effect of that justice on the ship's reputation.'

The Secretary had calmed himself, and had forced himself to remember that they all owed the Commander a great deal. He had led the wardroom to the brink of a great adventure. He must not be allowed to throw it all away by one lunatic decision.

'I know why you did it, Bob, and I know what you've done in this ship. That is exactly why I don't want to see you chuck it all away. When you first joined I admit I thought you were a bit of a nut-case. You acted as though *Leviathan* was no problem, as though you thought that anyone who cared deeply enough and tried hard enough was bound to succeed. Well, as things have turned out, you were right and the rest of us were all wrong. The whole wardroom acknowledges that. I know exactly why you did what you did. But don't you see that the consequences of letting Disley off are far worse for the ship than the consequences of court-martialling him? What happens now when a sailor comes up in front of you, charged with striking a leading hand? Are you going to press the charge? Because if you do, he'll say "But sir, it'll be bad publicity for the ship" and when you say "Nonsense, Captain's report" he'll say "Ah, but sir, you let that officer off for the very same thing. Why not me?" And *where* do we go from there?'

The Commander groaned as the Secretary's point sank in to the hilt. The argument was unanswerable. The Secretary was speaking with the voice of the Commander's own conscience, re-stating principles which the Commander himself believed in and from which he had allowed himself to be deflected. He had put the ship and himself before the Service. He had made a monstrous mistake. It remained now for him to try and put it right.

'Oh God. Of course you're right, Scratch. I should have known better. I *did* know better, but I allowed myself to be talked out of it. What do we do now?'

'Well, the most urgent thing is to get the investigation going at once. We've waited far too long as it is. We must get everybody concerned together in front of the DLC and try and get some evidence taken down. Disley's got to be charged and cautioned and put back under arrest. Open arrest I'd suggest, although I'm not sure of the exact routine. The whole thing's so damned irregular there probably isn't an exact routine. I'll have to go and look it up in the good book. Meanwhile, we must let the Boss know what's happening. The earlier we put him in the picture the better. Will you do that?'

'Yes, I'll telephone him now. When you get down to the quarter-deck, have a pipe made for the duty lieutenant commander and Rupert to come and see me here in my cabin.'

The Secretary thought over their conversation. They were probably too late now. The damage had been done. A whole new future for Bob Markready had been lost. 'You know what, Bob? I think you're too good to be true. The Navy isn't for the likes of you any more. You're like the last of the dinosaurs. You won't change, so you have to go. I can see what's going to happen. You're going to get chopped over this, simply because you're too nice a man.'

The full extent of how far his mistake had led him from normal Service practice was revealed to the Commander when he tried to explain matters to the Captain over the telephone. Tosser was almost comically baffled.

'I'm still not quite sure what the problem is, Bob. You say you're about to start the investigation. Fair enough. Though it might have been done last night. That was surely the best time, wasn't it, while everything was still fresh in everybody's minds?'

'I know, sir. But as I said, last night I decided not to have an investigation.'

'Well, you were there. I suppose you know best.' The Captain's voice was doubtful. 'Perhaps it was better to leave it until everybody had cooled off a bit. But I feel the officer concerned should at least have been charged and cautioned anyway, and the case stood over until the morning. He is still under arrest, I take it?'

'He's just about to be placed under open arrest, sir.'

'Just *about* to be? Bob, I'm obviously not going to get to the bottom of this over the telephone. We seem to be talking at cross purposes. Would you like me to come back on board?'

'If you wouldn't mind, sir, please.'

'I'll be with you as soon as I can.'

The duty lieutenant commander for the day was the Gunnery Officer. Of all the officers in *Leviathan*, the Gunnery Officer had changed the least. He remained, as he had been at the start of the commission, predictable, inflexible, and self-satisfied. He was the one officer the Commander would have preferred not to investigate Disley's case. But there was no help for it.

'What about the patrolmen and the landlord, sir? Do we have them up?'

'No, we've got the patrol report and the landlord's statement, we can do without them for the time being. Have you seen Rupert this morning?'

'He's ashore, sir. I heard Scratch checking with the quarter-deck.'

'Well, he'd better be told to come back then, and damned quick! I want to see him as soon as he gets back on board.'

There was no reason why Rupert should not have gone ashore, but the Commander was still surprised to hear that he had. There was nothing, he remembered, to prevent Disley going ashore and once ashore he might not return.

'What about Disley?'

'He's in his cabin, sir. One more point, sir. Where shall we have the investigation?'

'It had better be somewhere discreet. Try the wardroom guest-room.'

'Aye aye, sir. By the way, sir. I saw the Naval Provost Marshal's Land Rover coming along the jetty as I left the quarterdeck.'

'Thank you, Guns. I'll go and see what he wants.'

The appointment of Naval Provost Marshal was often a pro-fessional cul-de-sac, an appointment given to seaman lieutenant commanders who were passed over and were nearing retirement. Any breach of discipline within the port area was the Provost Marshal's concern and officially he was entitled to call upon the Commander to discuss any of *Leviathan*'s cases. But it was a rare and a conscientious Provost Marshal who personally pursued, on a Sunday morning, an insignificant and inconclusive report by one of his patrolmen. Any extra assistance required from the Naval Provost Marshal's department could have waited until Monday morning. Thus the Commander was well aware that the Provost Marshal's motive was not conscientiousness but scandal-mongering. That report had smelled of disgrace. To an eye as practised as the Provost Marshal's, there had been quite enough in it to arouse curiosity.

The Provost Marshal was talking to the officer of the watch when the Commander came down the quarterdeck ladder. He was wearing an expression of such complacent piety and tolerance for the misdeeds of a naughty world that the Commander itched to kick him over the side.

'Good morning, sir.' The Provost Marshal gave an unreasonably correct salute. 'I was just saying, for some reason or other this is the first time I've ever been in your magnificent vessel.'

'Good morning to you. It's good of you to call on us.'

'Ah well, sir.' The Provost Marshal's face sobered. 'This is not really a *social* call, sir.'

'Oh, isn't it?' The Commander composed his face in an expression of incomprehension.

The Provost Marshal looked disconcerted. 'It's about that report we sent on board this morning, sir. Some sort of disturbance ashore last night. Which I believe you yourself were concerned in, sir?' 'Yes, I was.'

'Well, sir, I wondered whether I could be of any assistance? Whether you wanted my patrolmen to attend at any time?'

'I don't think so, thank you. Not at the moment.' As he was speaking, the Commander noticed that unconsciously he had been shepherding the Provost Marshal back towards the gangway. He checked himself. He must not confirm the man's suspicions that the ship's officers might be hiding something.

'We'll certainly keep you informed, and let you know when we'll need your patrolmen. All right?'

'If there *is* anything we can do . . .' The Provost Marshal's voice betrayed his disappointed curiosity.

'Thank you very much. It was very kind of you to offer your help. We appreciate it.'

'Well, sir. I'll say good-bye, then sir?'

'Good, bye.'

The Captain drove up as the Provost Marshal was leaving. When he reached the quarterdeck, the Captain nodded in the direction of the departing Land Rover.

'What did the NPM want, Bob?'

'It was about this case, sir.'

'Oh dear. I didn't realise things had got so far.'

'Can we go up to the cuddy, sir? I ought really to explain to you just what's happened.'

At that moment, the Commander later decided, the Captain first became alarmed for his own future. Until then, what he had

398

heard had only been worrying and perplexing. Cases of striking a superior officer did sometimes occur even in the best-run ships. Provided they were handled properly they were routine professional problems, affecting nobody but the parties concerned. But now, Tosser was wary, alive to a possible threat to himself and his own career.

'If it's going to be as tricky as that, perhaps we ought to have the Secretary Bird there, what do you think?'

'I think that would be a good idea, sir.'

The Secretary had anticipated them, and was waiting outside the Captain's day-cabin. They had hardly settled, when the door burst open and Rupert Smith stood there, his face wild and his eyes accusing. One of his trouser bottoms was turned over and the Commander noticed, irrelevantly, that Rupert had put on his uniform in such haste he had forgotten to change his civilian socks.

'Sir, I wish to make a formal protest against the Commander!'

'What's all this?' The Captain looked from Rupert to the Commander. 'Why's he here?'

'Sir, last night a junior officer in my squadron was involved in an incident ashore with the Commander. When Commander Markready returned on board, sir, I agreed with him that no official action would be taken and he would leave me to settle it. But when I came on board just now, sir, I found my officer under open arrest and an official hearing of the case was just about to start, and I wish to make an official protest in the *strongest* terms, sir!'

The Commander closed his eyes. By mischance, he had not mentioned to the Captain on the telephone that the accused officer was in Rupert Smith's squadron. First the Naval Provost Marshal, and now Rupert, both appearing before he had had an opportunity to put the full facts to the Captain.

'You'd better tell me what this is all about, Bob. All the way, from the beginning.'

The story was still more of a fantasy in the re-telling. Even the Commander realised the improbabilities, the utter unlikeliness of the circumstances he was describing. It was unlikely that he should suddenly on a whim, decide to walk ashore by himself; that he should choose that particular public house and stay drinking there alone for an hour and a half; that two pilots should choose the same bar and pick an argument with him; and it was fantastic that one of them should eventually strike him. Only when he was describing the actual assault was the Commander interrupted, when Rupert sprang in with a correction.

'Disley disputes that, sir. He says somebody moved behind him and jogged his arm. He didn't meant to strike the Commander, sir.'

The Commander turned his head in time to catch the glitter of malicious triumph in the Secretary's eyes. They had both been right, after all. Rupert might have been sincere in believing that there would be no court martial, but he had not been above taking out some insurance with a little discreet coaching.

The Captain waved Rupert down. 'I don't want to hear all the legal arguments for the defence now. That can come later. Go on, Bob. It's the next part I want to hear.'

The Commander summoned himself to recapture his convictions of the night before, to rekindle some of the passionate appeals to which he had responded. It would have been difficult in any case, but Rupert's interruption had made it impossible; by attempting to mitigate Disley's action, Rupert had converted the suspicion of conspiracy into certainty. The considerations which had seemed so valid the night before, the arguments which had seemed so compelling at the time, now appeared not only meaningless but dishonest. The agreement the Commander had reached with Rupert emerged as nothing better than a disreputable attempt, hurriedly planned and clumsily executed, to cover up a scandal.

The Secretary listened with pity and foreboding. He could see what Bob meant. It should be obvious to anyone who knew him. But every word Bob was saying was hoisting the guillotine blade higher.

Just as the Commander was finishing, the Gunnery Officer knocked at the cabin door and came in. He apologised to the Captain, but addressed the Commander.

'We're all ready, when you are, sir. We're in the wardroom guest room.

'Just a minute, Guns.' The Captain held up his hand. 'I don't want anything started yet. Just leave it for the time being. Tell everyone concerned to carry on for the moment.'

'What about Lieutenant Disley, sir? Is he to remain under open arrest?'

'He's confined to his cabin.'

'Aye aye, sir.'

The Commander clenched his fists, willing the Captain to make the right decision. There could now be only one proper course of action: to begin the hearing of the case at once, and to carry it on as though nothing had delayed it. It could still be done, and Tosser was the man to do it. Six months ago, Tosser would not have hesitated. But lately, Tosser had become a political animal. *Leviathan* had made him devious. The Commander longed to press the point, but he, of all people was now least qualified to offer his advice.

'How exactly did *you* intend to punish Disley, Rupert?'

Rupert dropped his eyes. The question could not be answered, in public and at short notice. He could only give a lame and unconvincing reply. 'There are ways, sir, in a squadron.'

The Captain frowned. 'This seems to me more and more irregular. It's a lot more complicated than I thought. I think I'll have a word with the Chief of Staff.'

'Sir . . .' The Secretary's use of the title and the strained embarrassment on his face were both so uncharacteristic that the others looked at him in surprise. 'Sir, I think we ought to start the case right away, without any more delay. I really do, sir.'

'No, no. I want to take some advice. You come ashore with me, Scratch.'

The Commander let himself go, feeling the sweat flooding the palms of his hands. There was no more he could do. Nothing could now prevent the matter rising from the Chief of Staff up through the levels of the Navy. Each level would be a little further removed from the actual events, a little more reluctant to give a decision, and a little more ready to pass the matter even higher. Eventually it would rebound with a violence which might remove the Captain and the Commander from their appointments.

The Captain went ashore without any further discussion, taking the Secretary with him. The Commander stayed on board all day. He wrote letters after lunch, and walked on the flight deck for an hour after tea. Twice he telephoned Annabel's house, with no reply. Meanwhile the watches changed, the duty part fell in to sweep up the upper deck, the fire and emergency party mustered for exercise, the normal Sunday routine of the ship continued,

401

carrying on so imperturbably that it seemed to the Commander that he was the only man who still remembered the case or was still affected by it. As the hours passed, with no news, the Commander sensed the atmosphere subtly altering. It was not only Disley, but himself, who was now on trial.

The Secretary returned just before supper and joined the Commander where he was sitting on the ante-room club fender.

'Heard anything from Tosser, Bob?'

'No. I was hoping you might have some news.'

'Not me. I don't know where he is or what he's doing. I lost him when we left the Chief of Staff's house. Tosser's begun to move in mysterious ways, his wonders to perform, since he's been in this ship. I wasn't even allowed to be present when he talked to the Chief of Staff and I haven't any idea what he's been up to, then or since.'

The Secretary's voice was aggrieved and painfully surprised, like a puppet-master's after one of his creations has taken on a life and volition of its own. Every Secretary liked to feel that he was privy to his Captain's thoughts and no Secretary enjoyed losing his position as the Captain's *éminence grise*.

'This is all so bloody unnecessary, Bob. Talk about making a mountain out of a molehill. It's not what you'd call an original case, is it? Striking a superior officer is one of the oldest and dreariest charges in the book. There should be nothing to it. I don't know why Tosser's making all this fuss and bother about it. All he had to do this morning was to tell us to stop messing about and get on with it just as if nothing had happened. I don't know where he's got this idea that somehow he's affected.'

The Captain did not return to the ship until nearly noon on Monday morning. It was a sign of the change in the Commander's status over the week-end that he only heard of the Captain's arrival through the Secretary.

'Tosser's just come back from seeing the Commander-in-Chief, Bob. He asked me to tell you he'd like to see you now.'

'Thank you, Scratch. How is he this morning? What sort of mood is he in?'

'Not happy.' The Secretary's face was grim. 'But then, Judas Iscariot didn't exactly split himself with laughter, did he?'

402

The Commander gripped the Secretary's arm. 'What do you mean by that? '

'Just what I say.' The Secretary's voice was sneering. 'Tosser will tell you himself. Or that friend of his. One of them will tell you. I should get up there and get it over, Bob. And Bob . . . If I can give you some advice?'

'Please do.'

'I've been keeping my ear to the ground. If they offer you another job, *take it*. It'll be a good one. You won't get a better offer.'

Strangely, the chance that he might be leaving *Leviathan* did not surprise the Commander. The possibility had begun to loom over him all the week-end like a cloud, growing deeper and thicker and more imminent. Perhaps it was just the inevitable end-result of the train of events which had started when he walked ashore on Saturday evening.

'Thank you for the tip, Scratch. You've been a good friend.'

The Secretary turned his head away shamefacedly. 'No, I haven't.'

The other man whom the Secretary had mentioned as the Captain's friend was Aubrey McConnell. The Commander was not surprised to see him there; when there was blood in the water, one must expect the shark to follow.

He searched the Captain's face for any sign of uneasiness, but Tosser was at his most hearty and ebullient.

'Come in, Bob, come in. You'll be glad to hear we've at last got this whole thing sorted out.'

'I am glad to hear it, sir.'

'Yes, I've just been talking to C-in-C and he's decided it would be better if the whole matter was dropped. He feels there's been too much delay and too much uncertainty. The officer concerned has been kept in suspense for too long. The fairest thing would be to forget it.'

'Perhaps that would be best, sir.'

'As for us here . . .'

The Captain's voice faltered. The Commander looked hard at him. Come on, Tosser, that was the easy part. Now we come to the funeral drums and the sound of tumbrils. Tosser's face had lost its composure and had crumpled into the loose folds of shame.

403

'Perhaps I can explain it.' Aubrey McConnell put his finger-tips delicately together and fixed his gaze on them. 'In cases like this there is always a certain residual bitterness. It's better for everybody concerned if we make some changes. Let some fresh air in. Give people the chance to start off with a clean sheet again, somewhere else. Disley has been reappointed, and so has Padgett. They both left the ship this morning.' Aubrey looked up at the Commander. 'Now, there's just yourself.'

'*Me?*'

The Secretary had warned him. He had persuaded himself he was ready. But now that the moment had come he felt the full shock of it and the welling sense of outrage.

'I haven't any intention of leaving this ship.'

Aubrey smiled quickly. 'It's not a question of *your* intentions, Bob. It's felt that you'd be happier in some other appointment. It's been suggested that you join the staff in Washington, as Assistant Naval Attaché . . .'

'I *beg* your pardon! *What* did you say?'

Aubrey McConnell continued as though the Commander had not interrupted. 'If you agree, your appointment will be in the post tonight and it will appear in the CW List on Wednesday morning. You'll go to the States at the end of next month. After some leave, I imagine.'

'And if I don't agree?'

'But I'm sure you'll agree. This ship has a big programme ahead of her when the repairs to the hangar are complete and it's generally felt . . .'

'Who by?'

'. . . Let's just say it's generally felt that the ship would be better off with a Commander who had had no unfortunate experiences with the Air Group. I understand this was not the first incident between you and an aircrew officer.'

'That is a slanderous statement.'

Aubrey's lips pinched together. 'I don't think so, Commander.'

'I was appointed Executive Officer of this ship and I've done nothing to warrant my being dismissed from that appointment.' The Commander knew already that he had lost, but he was determined to make them fight. 'Everything I've done was done with the interests of the ship at heart. You'll find evidence of that

404

wherever you go in this ship. This new appointment you're suggesting is a breach of naval justice.'

Aubrey shrugged, as though the Commander had taken just the line he had expected. 'You can challenge the legality of your new appointment, if you wish. It's been tried before. I remember some years ago one fellow for reasons of his own didn't take up his appointment and he actually briefed a QC to defend him at his court martial. The silk came down to Portsmouth at so many guineas a day and tore the hide and guts out of Queen's Regulations and Admiralty Instructions. He found loop-holes in the Naval Discipline Act you could drive this ship through. But it didn't do the accused any good in the end. He went down the river just the same. The Service knows how to look after its own. If it's any consolation, your Commander (Air) is also being relieved, as soon as a suitable relief is available.'

The sly suggestion that he might be consoled by Commander (Air)'s downfall hurt and angered the Commander more than anything else Aubrey McConnell had said. 'I find that an incredible suggestion, sir. You must remember that not every officer in the Service has your outlook.'

The tinges of red high on Aubrey McConnell's cheekbones showed that he had been hit. Meanwhile, the Commander could spare a moment of remorse and pity for Commander (Air). This was the end for Wings. Beneath his bravado and his flippant cocksureness, Wings was a weak and an insecure man. He was a lightweight, lacking that indefinable quality which John Bowler would call 'bottom'. The Commander's own career might or might not survive this. But Wings was certainly finished.

'We're still waiting for your decision, Commander.'

The Commander knew that Aubrey expected him to appeal now to his Captain, but he refused to do so. Tosser must have been given an opportunity already that morning to defend his Commander, and clearly he had not taken it. Tosser's motive was plain enough; he saw in *Leviathan* his best chance of a rear-admiral's flag and if there was any choice between his promotion and his Commander, then his Commander must go. The Commander supposed that a man could not be blamed for trying to improve his own prospects, even at his subordinate's expense. He remembered telling Annabel, that night they had dined with Tosser and

Laura, that Tosser would not be the first Captain to sell his Executive Officer down the river. His own words had been prophetic.

Nevertheless, he could not resist inflicting some small discomfiture on Tosser.

'Do you agree with this, sir? Do *you* feel I've let you down?'

Tosser had put himself back in countenance whilst Aubrey had been speaking, but now he blushed again and looked ashamed.

'No, no, it's not that at all, Bob. There's no suggestion that you've let anyone down. I made that quite clear to the C-in-C this morning. I just feel that in the circumstances, as Aubrey has explained, it would be better for everybody if ... if ...'

'If I went. All right, then I agree.'

'Good man.' Aubrey slapped the arm of his chair. 'I was sure you would see this was the best solution. Your relief is on board. He's probably down in the wardroom now.'

'On *board?*' They had left him even less room for manoeuvre than he had realised. It had all been planned. The Commander wondered what might have happened if he had refused to take another appointment and had defied them to do their worst. But Aubrey had judged him rightly. If he had taken the issue to trial, the final result would have been the same, just as Aubrey said, but his own and *Leviathan*'s reputations would have been even further damaged.

The Captain's Secretary was standing outside and as the Commander shut the cabin door behind him, the Secretary made a gesture with his thumb, up or down?

The Commander put his thumb down. 'Are you waiting to go inside, Scratch?'

'Not me.' The Secretary gave a scornful laugh. 'I was just waiting for the cock to crow.'

'Do you know, I think you're taking this as much to heart as I am, Scratch.'

'I am. And the really humorous part of it hasn't struck Tosser yet. He's just messed up his best chance of promotion. He'll never get another Commander who'll do as much for him as you did. At least, he had the grace to offer you a decent job, I suppose?'

The news of the Commander's change of appointment had already percolated through the wardroom. Commander (S) was

406

reading the notices by the ante-room door when the Commander came in.

'Congratulations, Bob. Do I hear a buzz you're leaving this old crap-barge and going on to better things?'

The Commander glared at him. Could he be sincere, or was Delicious Joe exercising his notable talent for sarcasm? But it seemed that he was quite sincere.

'When are you going?'

'I don't know, Joe. It's all a bit vague at the moment. Excuse me a minute.' He had caught sight of Charles Doughty, making his way through the crowd at the bar towards him.

'Nice to see you, Charles.'

'And good to see you too, Bob. But I'm sorry it had to be me in this way.'

The Commander was looking over Charles' shoulder, searching for an unfamiliar face, and he missed the significance of Charles' words.

'Are you being looked after, Charles? Excuse me being a bit fraught but I'm looking for my relief.'

'It's me, Bob.'

'*You're* my relief?'

'Yes, I'm afraid so, Bob. I'm truly sorry it had to be me. I don't suppose they could find anyone else at such short notice.'

25

'I think that's about the lot, Charles. Can't tell you much more.'

'Well, I'm ready when you are.'

They were standing on the quarterdeck, watching the evening libertymen streaming along the jetty below them. A line of cars, with cyclists and pedestrians intermingling with them, was heading towards the caisson and the dockyard main gate.

'It's like watching the late shift packing up at a factory, isn't it, Bob?'

'That exact thought struck me when I first joined.' The Commander swung away from the quarterdeck rail. 'I think the best thing I can do now is to let you have the turn-over notes Tony Dempster left for me. They're only a few months out of date and you'll find quite a lot of it helpful.'

'I doubt it. A lot's happened since Tony left. He was talking about a completely different ship.'

'Maybe.' The Commander reddened. 'I'll leave them anyway.'

Their turn-over was almost complete. Charles was an experienced officer who had needed little more than an introduction to the ship's chief personalities and a warning of outstanding reports and urgent items of correspondence. It had not taken long. There was a Service saying that the more senior the officer, the less time he required to take over: a Captain could assume command in ten minutes, an Admiral in five. The organisation over which the Commander had laboured for so many months had passed out of his hands in an afternoon. There were still signals to be sent tomorrow, books to be mustered, forms to be counter-signed but these were only the visible seals of supercession. The main transfer of power and responsibility had already been accomplished.

Throughout the afternoon, the Commander had endured the uncomfortable pressures exerted upon a man who was about to be superseded. Charles had not been able to hide his eagerness to take over. The Commander hoped that he himself had been more tactful with Tony Dempster. As they toured the ship together,

Charles' questions had shown that he was already looking to the future, planning changes and innovations of his own, impressing his own personality upon the men they met, and generally feeling his way into the job, like a man trying on a new coat.

The Commander could see the coat already beginning to fit. Walking up and down the quarterdeck, he knew that the officer of the watch was now covertly keeping his eye on Charles, as well as himself. When the quartermaster approached them with a routine message, he seemed genuinely uncertain which of them to address as the Commander.

'The Commander's dead. Long live the Commander.'

'Amen, Bob. What are you planning to do with yourself this evening?'

'Don't know. Probably go ashore. I couldn't bear to stay on board.'

'I know how you feel, Bob. Look, there's a lot of points I want to get sorted out in my mind and I might as well start on them right away. D'you mind if I don't come with you?'

'Not at all.'

Bob Markready looked around the quarterdeck. It was not yet the moment of farewell, but its shadow was very close. This was not how he had expected to leave *Leviathan*. If there had been more time, he would have been dined out by the mess, just as Bird and the Senior and Beaky, who were all leaving, had been dined on the passage home. There would have been speeches, toasts, songs, reminiscences of the successes and failures of his term in office. On the night before he left the ship, the other Heads of Departments would have arranged a 'Sergeant's Run'. They would have taken him ashore, just as he had seen Bird being taken ashore by the ship's lieutenants, bought him beer, and told him for the first and the last time their real opinion of him. It would have been the send-off which was properly due to him; all officers, good or bad, competent or incompetent, were entitled to the traditional rites of leave-taking. They were his keepsakes, the only recognition the Service allowed that a man might be leaving behind a part of himself.

Charles sat in the cabin armchair while Bob Markready changed into plain clothes. Charles was torn between excitement and regret; *Leviathan* was a plum, which had dropped out of the sky,

409

but he wished he had not gained it at his old friend's expense. He still knew almost nothing definite about the circumstances which had brought him to *Leviathan*. He would have preferred to hear the facts from Bob himself, but the subject was too raw and sensitive. In any case, the story would by now have passed into the ship's mythology. He could hear an approximate version of it at any time in the next year. Meanwhile, Charles foresaw that no real harm had been done to Bob's career. In a month's time, when the cloud of controversy had cleared, Bob's achievements in *Leviathan* would be plain to all. He was going to join the staff in Washington, an appointment which many officers would have chosen before that of Commander of *Leviathan*. The only lasting harm might have been done to Bob himself. Charles knew that Bob Markready was only half-alive at a shore desk. To him, there was only one kind of worthwhile appointment: a sea-going job in a sea-going ship. It seemed to Charles ironical that Bob Markready should be going unwillingly and with a sense of disgrace to an appointment which many officers would have envied and looked upon as a happy omen for promotion.

'Ah well. Cheerio, Charles.' Bob Markready straightened his tie and patted his wallet pocket. 'I'm off ashore. I'll collect my gear in the morning. Then we'll both go and see the Captain and tell him you've got the weight.'

'I'll come down to the quarterdeck with you.'

Pausing on his way out of the cabin Bob Markready noticed, almost for the first time since his earliest days on board, the familiar pieces of ship's furniture which filled the cabin flat: the rifles chained in their racks, the line of ventilation valve hand-wheels on their polished spindles, the hot-water calorifier in its white lagging sheath, the fire extinguishers in their brackets, the drinking water-cooler, and, pushed up against the bulkhead in one corner, the tall desk behind which he had spent so many hours on his feet examining his requestmen and defaulters. On a small scale, this cabin flat was symbolic of all the changes there had been in *Leviathan*. When he joined, the fire extinguishers were missing, the water cooler out of order, the valve spindles green with verdigris, and the calorifier disconnected from its piping, with most of its lagging torn away He took his leave of all these familiar furnishings. There would be no time for nostalgia in the morning.

A warm roar of welcome, cheers, and hoots of laughter greeted Bob Markready when he appeared on the quarterdeck ladder. Charles guessed the significance of the uproar long before Bob Markready, and retired.

'I'll leave you to it, Bob. I don't think they want me this evening.'

'Come on, Bob! We're waiting for you! You're coming ashore with us! We're off to see the wizard!'

Leviathan's Heads of Departments were gathered in a merry group by the gangway. They all wore lounge suits and battered trilby hats, except Dai Bach, who was wearing a huge white stetson. Chief was waving a quart-sized pewter tankard, a relic of his engineering college days. The Air Engineer Officer, the Air Electrical Officer, Wings, Delicious Joe, the Schoolie and the PMO, they were all there in their drinking clothes and clearly in roaring fettle for the Commander's farewell party.

'What's this?'

'What d'you mean, what's this! We're taking you ashore, Bob!'

'Oh, I don't think I'm up to it.' His eyes prickled, and there was a hard lump in his throat.

'Come *on*, of course you are! This is a Sergeant's Run!'

The whole quarterdeck resounded with goodwill and friendliness. The officer of the watch and the gangway staff were all grinning widely. Everyone was delighted to see that the Commander was getting a proper run ashore to speed him on his way.

'No, please. Do excuse me. I couldn't bear it, honestly.' In the puzzled silence, he knew that his voice sounded sulky and ungracious.

The smiles dropped from the faces.

'Come on, Bob. If you're off tomorrow, we've got to pour you on your way tonight.'

'No, no, really I couldn't. Thank you.' The first blinding tears splashed his cheeks as he ran down the gangway to his car.

Again, he had forgotten that the battery was flat. He could not get out and try the starting handle in front of that wondering audience on the quarterdeck. Feeling the eyes on his back, he left the car and began to walk quickly, almost running, so that he could turn the corner and be out of sight. By the time he reached the main dockyard gate, he had succeeded in getting himself under

411

control. The demonstration on the quarterdeck had utterly un-
manned him. The unexpectedness of their affection had released
him from the state of numbed shock in which he had existed all
day. They had stripped off the self-deception with which he had
insulated himself. Now, he knew. He was really leaving *Leviathan*,
and the great ship had inflicted its final cruelty by spoiling his
leave-taking. The wardroom would never appreciate that he would
have been delighted to have accepted; only the unexpectedness of
the invitation had startled him into an ungenerous refusal. But the
wardroom would remember only that Bob Markready had refused.

If he had been driving, he might have gone anywhere. Walking,
there could be only one possible destination.

Annabel was standing in front of her house, watering the
geraniums which flowered in their small pots behind a railing.

'Hello, Bob! What's the matter with the car?'

'Flat battery.'

'Well, the walk's done you good. You're looking very fit.'

'I don't feel it.'

'Why not?'

He flung out an arm in a declamatory gesture. 'I could a tale
unfold, which would freeze the marrow of your bones.'

'Well, it can't be all that bad if you can joke about it.'

'It's so bad, I *can* only joke about it. I've got the sack from
Leviathan.'

'*Bob!* When?'

'Just now. Today. As from tomorrow morning, I'm on the dole.'

She could see it now. The bold confident ring of his footsteps
on the pavement had misled her. She could see defeat in the shape
of his face, in the line of his shoulders. He looked diminished and
shrunken.

'Come in and tell me, if you'd like to.'

'I tried to get you on the telephone over the week-end.'

'Oh Bob, if only I'd known! I took the boys back to school for
their autumn term last Friday and I stayed the week-end with
my parents. I've only just got back. You must have come back
early?'

'We did.'

She held her front door open with her arm. 'Come in. Get us
both a drink and tell me all about it.'

412

He had not intended to tell the story, ever again. He would leave that to the whisperers, the gossip-mongers. They would have a field day. But Annabel was entitled to know. He told her everything, from that first disastrous expedition to the 'Admiral of The Red', to his final and shameful flight from the ship. It was curious how the effect of a story altered with the character of the listener. His agreement with Rupert, which had seemed so discreditable in the Captain's cabin, now appeared honourable once more. Telling the story to Annabel, he recaptured some of his first convictions.

'The only important thing is, Bob, do *you* think you did right?'

'I thought so at the time. Now, I don't know. I made a mistake, there's no doubt about that. A bad one. I did it for the best, or at least I thought I was doing it for the best, but it was still a bad mistake. I'm not sure now why I did it. You could say that I was doing exactly what I've been telling everybody else not to do, to put oneself before the Service. Because, to be quite honest, it *was* better for me if there was no court martial. I tried not to think of that, but it may have been in the back of my mind. And I suppose I must have provoked that pilot in that pub. You can do that without saying a word. There's even a name for it in the Service. Dumb insolence. And yet, I don't know. Looking back on it all, if the circumstances were the same again, I'd probably go right ahead and do exactly the same again. I just don't know.'

He rubbed his eyelids with his fingers. The path which had once been so clear was now tangled over. He was no longer sure of his own motives. It was as well there would be no court martial. The most inexperienced prisoner's friend could have cut him up in cross-examination.

'All my thinking seems to be out of date, that's the trouble. I'm an obsolete model.'

'Bob, you're being self-pitying.'

'No, I'm not. On board they all think I'm some sort of dinosaur, the last of the species. When I first joined that ship somebody said to me "Don't take it all to heart. Don't get yourself personally involved." That attitude of mind is just incomprehensible to me. I don't know what they're talking about. I don't see how you can turn up to a ship from nine till five and then just go home in the evening as if nothing had happened. And yet that's what people

413

do nowadays, more and more of them. It's me that's odd, not them.'

He thought of all the men in *Leviathan* whom he had encouraged and urged and rebuked. He had tried to make them look beyond themselves. Some of them, he had even despised for their selfishness. Now he was dismissed, and they were still there.

'There are too many compromisers in the Navy. They've all come to terms. They won't *push*. They've set their sights too low. They won't go for the big prizes. They don't even think about them. They just go like hell for the tiny prizes.'

They had defeated him, just as they had defeated Tony Dempster. Next year it might be Charles Doughty's turn to show his successor round the ship and to appear courteous while he silently screamed at the injustice. On second thoughts, Charles would be a match for them. He would never engage *Leviathan* head on. He was more subtle. He would use the great ship's own strengths to overthrow and tame her. It was only idiots like Bob Markready who made a direct frontal attack, crying 'God for Harry, England and St George', and were knocked on the head just as they thought they were breaking through.

'I'm thinking of applying to retire, you know.'

'Oh Bob, don't be absurd. You're not the sort that resigns.'

'Certainly I didn't used to be. But I am now. I'm the sort they want to get rid of.'

'Now you *are* being self-pitying! They wouldn't send somebody they wanted to get rid of to Washington, would they?'

'No, that's probably right and if I'm really the sort of person they want to keep then I'm not sure any longer that I want to stay. Besides, I'm looking further than just my next appointment. Anyone who's got the intelligence to look around him can see the Service has been getting steadily smaller for a long time. It'll never get bigger, unless there's another war and nobody except a madman would want that. The opportunities are just getting less and less. There seems to be no purpose behind what we're doing. That patrol of ours in the Arctic was the most splendid thing, whatever anyone may say. It was one of the best performances put up by any ship. It's not enemy action, you see, but sheer grinding hard work and routine, *that's* what really separates the men from the boys. But when you think about it, what were we achieving? Nothing much, in the strategic sense. All that flying we did was to protect ourselves. If we hadn't been there the flying wouldn't have been necessary. The anti-submarine patrols might have done some good. They didn't find anything, but they might have done. Big One, I suppose, was some sort of deterrent.'

'What's Big One?'

'The Bomb. The nuclear weapon.'

'Golly, did you have that on board?'

'Yes, but we didn't have to drop it. We didn't actually have to *do* anything. If we hadn't been there, something might have happened. We didn't think about that at the time. It's only now we can look back and ask ourselves, what the devil were we *doing* up there?'

Annabel watched the expressions changing on his face. They were like pictures on a clear screen. He was as open as the sky. No wonder those clever little men had read him. He was a unicorn pursued by hunters. But the hunters had not caught him. He was the saddest sight of all, a unicorn who had trapped himself.

'I'm old as Commanders go nowadays, Annabel. The end of next year will be my last chance for Captain. It would have coincided with the end of *Leviathan*'s commission. The timing would have been just right. Now, God knows what will happen.'

'Won't this new job be any good?'

'Theoretically, yes. In practice, not so good. No Captain is going to recommend someone he doesn't know very well. My last chance will have come and gone before this new Captain feels he knows enough about me to recommend me. Up to this year, I was beginning to get a little desperate about becoming a Captain. But I really thought I had a chance in that ship. All my time as a Commander I seem to have been like a man going up a train and trying to choose a compartment, saying "Not this one, not that one". When I came to *Leviathan* I thought "This is it." I was going to take it to the end of the line and it was going to take me. Now, I feel as if I'd been dumped off half-way and nowhere to go.'

'Perhaps Tosser's already recommended you?'

He blew out his cheeks. 'Nothing would surprise me about that man. But d'you think it's likely?'

'No.'

'Nor do I. Damnation.' He started up, looking at his watch. 'Too late now. One thing I *must* do tomorrow. I should have done

415

it over the week-end but I forgot. I must go and see Number One's wife.'

'Poor Lucy. She's a friend of mine.'

'Have you seen her?'

'I called last week. Laura McTigue's been to see her, and Angie and a few of the others. I believe Lady Metcalf has called as well.'

'How is she?'

Annabel gave him a look of surprised contempt. 'Lucy, do you mean? How do you think she is?'

'I'm sorry. Didn't they have some children?'

'Three small boys, all at school.'

She heard him draw in a quick breath. 'That makes it worst of all. Honestly, I'd rather *Leviathan* was back as she was and he was still alive. It just wasn't worth it.'

The ship passed through a squall during the funeral. It was their coldest day in the Arctic. The rain hissed down on the sea and a polar wind whipped through the quarterdeck openings. The Padre wore mittens, and the lines of great-coated men drawn up on the quarterdeck shuffled their feet surreptitiously and puffed out their cheeks. The *coup de feu* had rattled over the heads of the bearers. They had committed to the deep the bodies of the First Lieutenant and the naval airmen who had died in the fire, sliding them down a wooden shute while the Gunner prudently caught hold of the Union flag. To be turned into corruption, looking to the resurrection of the body, when the Sea shall give up her dead. Funerals at sea were always more chilling. There was no wake, no lifting of the spirit, no belief in resurrection nor any reassurance that the dead had received its dead and those who were still alive could begin again. The bare-headed mourners on that quarterdeck had replaced their caps, fallen out, and filed away, each one knowing himself a little nearer to death.

Annabel knew that she would have to wait until this black mood had passed over, until he had sloughed off the very skin of that damnable ship. He had not yet remembered her as the woman he had asked to be his wife. He had not even mentioned the future. He was preoccupied with the past, sitting there with that abject, defeated expression on his face.

'Thank you for your letters, Bob. They were very good.'

'Were they?' He was genuinely surprised. 'I didn't think I was any good at writing letters.'

'You underestimate yourself. They gave a wonderful picture of what you were doing and how you were all getting on.'

'Did they really?' He was pleased, as a man complimented on an unsuspected talent.

'I liked the endings particularly. Perhaps you didn't know me well enough to write me a boring letter.'

He nodded admiringly. 'That's a very shrewd comment. Do you remember that letter I told you about, the one I burnt when I shouldn't have done?'

'Yes, of course I remember it.'

'He was writing to his girl-friend. She may even have been his fiancée, I don't know. There was something in that letter which struck me at the time and I've often thought about it since. He was saying that no matter what went wrong, he could always think of her and that would cheer him up a bit. Do you know, that's absolutely true. We had some hideous times in that ship and at the very height of it all I used to find myself saying more and more often, never mind, there's always Annabel. It was like finding another dimension to yourself, a part of yourself somewhere outside, away from it all, which you could refer to. It's a curious experience for me, because I've never looked outside myself for help before.'

He was a man of tremendous resilience. Already, the shadows were lifting. The man she had been waiting for was emerging. Soon, Annabel was sure, he would be in full view.

'There's another extraordinary thing. I've been all these years in the Service and never bothered very much about mail before. When the mail came on board, either there was something for me or there wasn't, but it didn't matter very much. This time while we were at sea I was an absolute addict for mail. I couldn't wait for it to come on board.'

His face had cleared and now his eyes were bright and attentive.

'And how are you, now that I am here? I've been so preoccupied with my own troubles and myself, I haven't even asked you how you are.'

'I'm very well.'

She had longed for his attention. Now that she was given it she turned her face away from him, as though his gaze burned her.

417

She had guessed long ago that *Leviathan* might fail him. She remembered she had even asked him what he would do when the moment of failure came. She had been afraid that if he returned to her he would be drained, only half a man. That ship would have had the best of him. She had been wrong. It was the ship which had possessed only half of him. The whole man was here, with her, now. He had not talked of love but his presence and his voice stimulated her as though he had used the very language of passion. A man's voice, tender and consoling, was the most erotic instrument of all. She yearned, she admitted it to herself, she yearned to go to bed with him. Why could he not walk over and take his winnings?

'You're not a romantic man, are you, Bob?'

'I've been accused of being a romantic.'

'But not where women are concerned.'

'No.' It was a fair description. 'At least, not lately.'

Once upon a time, he had been romantic enough. He had just been promoted lieutenant-commander and her father, a captain, had approved of the match. They had met at the Barracks cocktail party and had progressed smoothly towards their engagement, he accepting the inevitable approach of matrimony, she being gradually assimilated into the society of the wardroom wives, as a provisional member, soon to achieve full status. They might have married, and they might have lived happily ever after, except that he had left for the West Indies just as a particular Captain of Royal Marines returned from Hong Kong. He had been confident that to such a girl from such a family an engagement formally announced in *The Times* would have been as binding as a nun's vows. Her letter, enclosing his ring, had reminded him of the first and principal law of naval *affaires,* that proximity is the greater part of affection. He had admired his own stoical resignation when he read her letter, just as now he was surprised to recall his own celibacy in *Leviathan.* For *Leviathan,* he had bound himself in a monastic continence. Unaware of his own self-discipline, he had directed all his thoughts and energies towards the ship. Now he was freed. He could lift his head and open his ears to the magic pipes and timbrels. Annabel was awakening an old awareness in him, appealing to him in a language he had once known but had forgotten.

He sat clasping his hands together, and pulled at them in his embarrassment. How do I love thee? Let me count the ways. But he had misplaced the words he wanted to say. A knuckle cracked audibly, adding to his embarrassment.

'How can I tell you I love you? I've lost the knack of it.'

'Just saying it is good enough.'

'Then I do love you. I asked you to marry me. Will you?'

'Yes, of course. Provided one thing.'

'What's that?' He was taken aback by her reservation.

'Provided you've forgotten that ship.'

'Is *that* all?' He laughed with relief, and dismissed the ship with one wave of his hand. 'That's all gone, truly. It's in the past now. Tomorrow morning I'm going back there and wish them all the best of British luck. Then I'm going on leave. I've got some due from my last appointment and I've got a fortnight due now. I'm going to take the lot. I don't see why I shouldn't. If you can't beat 'em, join 'em.'

'When do you have to go to America?'

'When do *we* have to go to America. We'll go as soon as we get back from leave, and no sooner. We'll get married just as soon as I can fix the licence. And then we'll go to Amalfi, or Bermuda, or *Bognor*, wherever you like. I'm a rich man. At least, I feel rich.'

'Why can't we go before we get married?'

'Don't you mind?'

'Why should I mind?' She smiled at the hesitation on his face. 'There's a streak of the old Puritan in you, Bob.'

'Is there.'

His first kiss was questioning and inexperienced, like the first sweet half-remembered kisses of her girlhood, but then he became rough and hard, demanding more of her, until her strength drained away from her.

He felt her resist and then grow supple and compliant, and turn her hips to force her thigh between his. After his quick imperative movement she slackened her body and dropped her arms to her waist, to let her blouse slide from her shoulders. Her urgent and appealing whisper inflamed him.

'Not down here.'

He followed her up the dark staircase. A pale light from the street lamps shone through the window on her bared back as she

419

mounted the stairs, holding her blouse in front of her breasts.

Her bedroom was dark, and warm, and the curtains were drawn. She stood submissively, a woman willingly being stripped for the act of love, holding her arms above her head and looking down at his hands.

His was an act of love and rage and revenge and expiation. On her body he expunged the memories of the past. When he embraced her, he was embracing the future and her cries and murmurings hailed it. His weight dominated her, imposed his will on her, met and subdued her every thrust and twist. The tight heart-bands were bursting, the past was slipping away. This was where his success lay. This was his true reward.

Lying in his arms, Annabel felt once more cherished and safe. After an age when her heart had been frozen, the future could begin again. Her perceptions heightened by the sexual act, she knew that he was smiling in the darkness.

'You're a great bear, Bob. That wasn't love. That was rape. Now what are you grinning at?'

'I just had a stupid thought of the First Lieutenant. He used to make these profoundly vulgar remarks from time to time. He said there are two kinds of sound sleep. The sleep of the just, and the sleep of the just after.'

She lifted herself above him, so that her nipples brushed his chest.

'Are you telling me you want to go to sleep?'

'Never!'

He awoke early, from force of habit. The room was just light. There was a silk dressing-gown hanging behind the door. He got up and put it on, tying the three absurd tapes into bows.

He parted the curtain and looked out into the street. The nearest street lamp was still burning in the flat light of dawn, the house opposite still shuttered and blind. The cars parked in lines on both sides of the street were coated with a heavy dew. Over the roof-tops, a mile away, the great ship would be stirring now, humming like an enclosed city, making ready for another day. The great ship would be changing in minute ways, pushing out fresh shoots, and dying, and growing, and withering, building and solidifying, piece upon piece, like a vast coral structure. He felt no sense of loss; the night past had taken away the sting of failure. He had done what he could and surely no man could do more than that. He was separated from *Leviathan* by the layer of one day. Other days would bring more layers to insulate him. Soon he would be able to revisit *Leviathan* as a stranger and gape at her monstrous size as though for the first time. The great ship had not left him unchanged. Someone had once told him he was the last of his Dartmouth term to lose his innocence. Now he was one of the great majority. He had not beaten them, so he had joined them. The great ship had longed to be subdued; she had wanted a champion. He might have been the man, but he had failed. He had become one more of those who hurried about inside her, and left her unmarked. The great ship would even now be feeling out his successor, probing him, searching his strengths and weaknesses.

'That dressing-gown suits you.' Annabel was awake, with the blankets drawn circumspectly up to her chin. 'You're looking very gloomy.'

'I don't feel gloomy.' He let the curtain fall back. 'I was just thinking. If I had my time all over again, do you know, I'd do exactly the same?'